D1561536

Seal Up the Vision vividly portrays the an
the miraculous intervention of God in his life. This wonderful
book is sure to inspire people of all walks of life.

—WES ARNOLD
PASTOR, PROPHETIC MINISTRIES TABERNACLE
GAINSVILLE, TEXAS

From the edge of your seat this fictional novel will take you on a
roller coaster of prophetic events. Jennie Hassett cleverly parallels
the life of Daniel with a modern day event. Her book will challenge you to keep up as you journey through its mind-bending
shifts from the biblical past to futuristic events.

—KENT SIMPSON
FOUNDER, PROPHETIC MINISTRIES TABERNACLE

Jennie Hassett skillfully moves between present-day events and
those surrounding the exile of the Jews during the time of the
prophet Daniel. I greatly enjoyed her use of the story depicting
the lives of these familiar Old Testament figures. She masterfully
interweaves their stories with those of a group of present-day
individuals literally living out what Daniel prophesied concerning the end of the age. This book is fun for both the serious student and the casual reader looking for a great story.

—JOHN THOMPSON, DO

Does time travel really exist? It does when you read this book!
I marvel at this author's ability to tell two stories at the same
time. Her imagery paints a vivid picture of the reality of the life
of Daniel, then and now. The persecution faced by many Christians is accurately illustrated in this book, and the reality of God's
gracious provisions is evident on every page. I challenge anyone
who is having a hard time believing in the goodness of God to
dive into the adventures in this book and experience His love
firsthand!

—ALICIA L. WOODARD, LSW
EXECUTIVE DIRECTOR
COOKE CO. FRIENDS OF THE FAMILY
CRIME VICTIMS' ADVOCATE

Seal up the Vision

Jennie Hassett

CREATION HOUSE

A STRANG COMPANY

SEAL UP THE VISION by Jennie Hassett
Published by Creation House
A Strang Company
600 Rinehart Road
Lake Mary, Florida 32746
www.creationhouse.com

Scripture quotations are from the following:

+ King James Version of the Bible

+ Amplified Bible; Old Testament copyright © 1965, 1987 by the Zondervan Corporation. The Amplified New Testament copyright © 1954, 1958, 1987 by the Lockman Foundation. Used by permission.

+ New American Standard Bible. Copyright © 1960, 1962, 1963, 1968, 1971, 1972, 1973, 1975, 1977 by the Lockman Foundation. Used by permission. (www.Lockman.org)

Cover design by Terry Clifton

Library of Congress Control Number: 2005930409
International Standard Book Number: 1-59185-889-5

First Edition

05 06 07 08—87654321
Printed in the United States of America

CONTENTS

AUTHOR'S NOTE

MY PURPOSE IN writing this story is to demonstrate to this generation that it is possible for a young person to live a life of uncompromising godly integrity in the midst of a pagan society. I am convinced that in these last days God is raising up a vast multitude of young Daniels, Esthers, and Josephs to high positions of great honor. These young lives will, as did Daniel's, exert a powerful influence that will affect the destiny of nations, and prepare the way of the Lord.

Historians are divided on the interpretation of Esther 2:5–6. Was it Mordecai who was taken captive in 597 BC, or was it his great-grandfather Kish?

Some years ago I made the fascinating discovery that the footnotes of my Dake's Annotated Reference Bible hold the former position. Dake places the events surrounding Esther much earlier than most commentaries and, unlike other sources, makes her contemporary with Daniel. (See pages 488, 490, 492, 515, 516, 521of his reference Bible.) I found this to be quite intriguing and have incorporated it into this book.

As I tell the story of Daniel, I complement various scenes with "The Chronicles of Nebuchadnezzar." These are brief accounts that I have composed to reflect what the records of his day may have said.

I am including a brief timeline of events that form the historical basis for this book:

605 BC—First deportation (including Daniel and friends).

597 BC—Second deportation (Jehoiachin, Ezekiel, Mordecai).

586 BC—Third deportation; Jerusalem is burned; the temple is destroyed.

538 BC—Cyrus's decree; fifty thousand return with Zerubbabel.

536 BC—Rebuilding of the temple begins.

516 BC—Rebuilding of the temple is completed.

515 BC—Ezra returns to Jerusalem. According to Dake, the Artaxerxes of Ezra 7:1 is actually Darius I, who reigned from 522–483 BC. In the seventh year of his reign—515 BC, the same year of the temple dedication (Ezra 7:7)—Ezra returns.

PROLOGUE

T HE STORM HAD long since passed. The far distant rumbling of thunder receded gradually into silence. A small breeze coaxed the night-
blooming jasmine to release its intoxicating fragrance into the garden,
and a lark warbled its grateful welcome to the coming day. With this
official announcement, the first pale pink rays of dawn reached past the
clouds, illuminating the far bank of the great river below.

The man in the shadows smiled. He was a very old man, and the birdsong had evoked some long-forgotten memory that, judging from the
ever-increasing smile, only grew sweeter with the savoring. A habitual
early riser, he considered each new rising of the sun to be his own personal, treasured event. Indeed, it was.

He glanced back down the long corridor formed by the graceful stone
arches of his palatial home. The outer court was deserted at this early
morning hour, the only sound that of the stone eaves on the slate roof
emptying their rivulets of rainwater into the fishponds far below.

Emerging from the darkened pavilion and dodging the curtain of
dripping water, he carefully opened the ancient garden gate so as not to
awaken the sleeping household. With long, purposeful strides, he moved
quickly down the long series of terraced steps to the river. Pausing for
a long moment, head thrown back and eyes closed, he savored the cool
fragrance of the freshly washed earth.

Standing on a small rock jetty between two immense willows, the man
was an arresting sight. A commanding presence, his strong, erect bearing
bespoke a man of some great authority, perhaps even nobility. Taller than
most, he stood with feet apart, surveying the rain-swollen river.

Suddenly, he dropped to his knees. Clasping his hands in front of him, he bowed his head and began to pray fervently. For a long time he remained completely immobile, oblivious of the roaring current swirling around him. Finally he arose, a slight stiffness the only indication of his age. Apparently reluctant to leave, he lingered a bit longer, pacing slowly back and forth beneath the green canopy of willows.

Soon, however, the rays of the sun burst through the gilt-edged clouds with the energetic promise of a fresh new day. The man turned and strode back the way he had come, stopping along the way to inspect the new spring growth in his well-tended garden. The silence was shattered by cries of delight as three small children came tumbling down the path.

"Good morning, Great-Grandfather! Mama said the servants will bring us the morning meal outside on the upper terrace. Will you come and eat with us? Will you go to see the king today? Would you take us with you to the palace? Please, Great-Grandfather?"

The old man's deep hearty laugh echoed down the stone corridors as the children pulled him up the steps, disappearing into the cool depths of the house.

The Watchers waited patiently, staying at a respectful distance. After a long period of companionable silence, one spoke softly.

"He stayed longer than usual this time. I wonder if he knows."

"Quite possibly," replied the other. "This man Daniel is a mortal of very great integrity. He can be trusted." He lifted his gaze to the western horizon far beyond the river. "He has been carefully chosen, carefully prepared…and it will happen soon enough."

CHAPTER 1

TERROR

THE WET PAVEMENT barely touched the girl's feet as she ran for her life. Down the darkened street, into the alley, behind a garage, out through the gate and down the sidewalk she flew. Like a frightened deer, she never paused to look back. Her relentless pursuers were not far behind.

"O God, please help me!" She sobbed out the prayer from the depths of her terrified being and, as she rounded the corner, almost collided with a door standing ajar. Instinctively, without conscious thought, she ducked inside and pulled it shut. The blessed darkness closed in on her, and she sank, exhausted and grateful, to the floor.

As the pounding of her heart subsided, she whispered, "Thank You, oh, thank You...!" but then realized the terror was not yet passed.

Outside the fragile, broken door were eight members of the "Grave-diggers"—a vicious inner city gang who regularly preyed on the hapless victims of circumstance. Decades into the twenty-first century, lawlessness was now increasing at an alarming rate, and gangs like these were becoming much bolder. Since the police were woefully undermanned and overworked, the Gravediggers were able to operate with little fear of detection. Drug dealers, thugs, and cold-blooded murderers, they were part of a much larger gang that roamed the city streets at will.

Their bloodlust was running high this rainy night, and they exulted with unearthly howls as they closed in for the kill. Suddenly deprived of their quarry, an unreasoning rage was loosed in them as they searched up one street and down the next. Finally frustrated, they returned to the place where they had lost her. By now, their wrath knew no bounds. Screaming in fury, they prowled with heads lowered like unreasoning wild beasts, searching every crevice and corner.

Seal up the Vision

The girl was paralyzed, numb with fear, as she watched through the cracks in the slats nailed loosely onto the door. Unexpectedly, she glimpsed for just an instant their gruesome faces illuminated by a brilliant flash of lightning, closely followed by an unearthly roar of thunder.

Heavy raindrops that soon became torrents poured down on the unhappy predators, who turned and fled the wrath of the storm. Nearly unconscious from the strain, she leaned against the wall and waited. At some point, she drifted off into a fitful sleep.

A little while later, she awoke, still in her cramped position. As her sleep-drugged brain began to clear, she realized her precarious position and felt a twinge of alarm.

How long have I been out? she wondered. She pushed the lighted dial of her watch. *Nearly two hours! It's almost midnight! O God...,* and then she groaned. Remembering how this had begun only a few short hours before when she had to get off the freeway and look for an open gas station—her Firebird was nearly out of gas—she began to feel the terror closing in on her again.

Struggling to her feet, she nearly collapsed from stiff, sore joints, but she made her way carefully around the door frame and into the deserted street. Flattened against the shadows of the old warehouse, she waited. After a short time she realized that she was looking at an old phone booth under a dim street lamp nearly half a block away. The glass was shattered by bullet holes, and she had no idea if it would even be in working order.

No way, she thought. *It's too exposed under that streetlight. But I can't just stay here...*

Summoning her courage, she darted down the street, staying in the shadows until she was opposite the phone booth. *I'd better check my pocket for change,* she thought. *Good, a quarter. My purse and wallet are long gone. Oh, well, here goes—it's either now or never!*

She stepped out of the shadows and swiftly crossed to the phone booth. Stepping inside, she carefully closed the door, not wanting the sound of broken glass to betray her position. Quickly, she checked for a dial tone— *It works! Thank God!*—and dialed her parents' home. Sinking to the floor, she drew her knees up to her chin and waited. The phone rang several times, and she began to grow anxious. "This is the Mannheim residence; please leave your message at the sound of the beep."

Oh, no! Her head spinning, she tried to choke down the panic. *No! No...please, Mom and Dad, be there! I need you—NOW!* Then, gathering her wits, she stammered a message between sobs: "I'm stranded off the freeway between Industrial and Main—near an old warehouse—I'm in trouble—please come and get me. My car's gone; I have no money— they've been chasing me, and I'm so scared…"

Her head dropped onto her crossed arms. She stayed there for a few minutes longer, overcome with fatigue and despair. The phone dangled, unheeded, beside her.

"Get up, Sarah."

Her head jerked back, her eyes opened wide with alarm; she saw no one.

"GET UP, SARAH."

This time, the command from a deep male voice was unmistakable. She stood up, her mind whirling in confusion. "Daddy…?" Her voice quivered. She opened the door and scanned her surroundings. The street was still deserted, yet she stood completely still, waiting and listening with every fiber of her being.

A small red Mustang hurtled down the off-ramp of the freeway to her right. It disappeared from view, then turned sharply toward her, stopping only a few yards from the phone booth. An impossibly tall young man unfolded himself from the driver's side and walked around to check his rear tires. Obviously puzzled, he started forward to check under the hood when he saw her.

"Oh, please, help me," she pleaded. "Would you take me out of here? I've been robbed and nearly killed! You—you're in danger, too!"

"Well," he replied, "I just can't understand it—I kept hearing a loud flapping sound like my tire had gone flat, but…everything seems all right. Sure, I'll be glad to give you a lift. Hop in." He held open the door for her as she got in, but she was not looking at him. Her face was a frozen mask of terror as she pointed behind him.

He whirled around to see that the shadows had literally come alive and were moving toward them. One of the shadows was swinging a chain with something very heavy on the end of it; others were armed with various death-dealing implements. The girl's scream pierced the night air. The young driver vaulted the hood and was already gunning the accelerator before the scream subsided.

"Seat belts!" he ordered tersely. "Hang on—things may get a little wild!" He glanced at the girl on his right; her lips were tightly shut, but she was belted in.

The shadows were closing in much faster now, but the little Mustang plowed a furrow on the rain-drenched street. Streams of water and bodies diving for cover issued from both sides of the car. Street lamps flashed like strobe lights as they raced on. Finally, after many twists and turns, an entrance ramp appeared, and they were safely on the freeway heading west.

Only then did he release his death grip on the steering wheel and give a sidelong glance at his companion. She issued a long, shuddering sigh, closed her eyes, and seemed to be saying something that sounded like, "You did it again—how can I ever thank You..."

"You're welcome!" he said. She looked up, startled, then smiled. "Oh, yes—thank you so much. I don't know what I would have done if you hadn't come along. You saved my life!"

"Well," he replied, "now that I have achieved the enviable status of Sir Champion Knight, where can I take you, Lady Fair?"

She looked down at her hands. "Huntington Heights. Know where it is?"

He whistled softly, then glanced at her again, appraisingly. "No problem," he murmured.

Huntington Heights was the epitome of luxurious living, the habitat of the very elite. Those who made their homes there peopled the rarified air of high finance with long practiced and well-insulated ease.

The girl was casually dressed in jeans, blazer, and athletic running shoes, the standard, unassuming attire of the very wealthy. *Good thing she had those shoes on,* he thought. *She must have had a terrifying race against those cold-blooded thugs.* He glanced at her again; her eyes were half-closed: large liquid green eyes shadowed by long, thick lashes; red-gold hair pulled back from a small heart-shaped face. *Altogether appealing,* he thought.

At that moment, she twisted around, looking earnestly at him and said, "Please forgive my manners! You certainly deserve an explanation for all of this. I'm Sarah Mannheim. I'm a student at Brandeis University in Boston and was driving home for spring break when this happened. Oh, I could just kick myself for being so careless!" She turned away. "If I had only filled up at the university before I started..."

Her voice trailed off, and she looked at him beseechingly. "I guess you must think I'm one of those rich little airheads."

He grinned down at her. "No, I'm not prone to make those kind of snap judgments. Actually, you seem pretty self-reliant; escaping that murderous gang was no small feat!"

She lowered her eyes and murmured, "If you only knew—I was absolutely terrified, and to be perfectly truthful, I...well, I truly believe that I was not completely alone."

"What do you mean, not alone?" he inquired. "I'm sure you were surrounded by most unpleasant company."

"No, I don't mean them," she insisted rather breathlessly. "It was something else...a sense of a presence. Oh, I can't explain it rationally! All I know for sure is that...I was...protected." Her large green eyes filled with tears as she turned her head toward the window.

They were both silent for awhile. Then he spoke. "Well, I guess it's my turn. I'm Dan—Dan Shepherd. I am a sort-of engineer and was on my way home from a work seminar when this happened." He grew serious. "You know, I still cannot explain the sounds I heard that caused me to turn off the freeway, believing I had at least one flat tire, maybe two. I've never been so sure of anything in my life, so...maybe you were right, after all!"

She gave him a sidelong view of her dimples as she smiled mischievously. "You know, Dan, maybe if I had looked up sooner, I would have seen a huge, powerful angel running alongside your car and banging away at it!" The car erupted with raucous laughter, and all the pent-up tension dissolved as they chatted amiably.

"Oh, there's my turn," she said. The little red Mustang turned into a curving driveway bordered by tall poplar trees. The house was an old English Tudor with gabled roofs, leaded windows, and to the side, what appeared to be a carriage house connected by a breezeway. The only light was a post lantern beside the front door.

"My parents are out of town at a wedding; they probably won't be back until quite late. I completely forgot their plans and foolishly used my last quarter to dial their number at that phone booth back there," she explained sheepishly.

"How will you get in? You have no keys, right?"

"Oh, we always keep an extra key under the flowerpot on the back porch. I'll be fine," she assured him.

He got out and opened the door for her. "You're sure you'll be OK?"

"Absolutely." She shook his hand solemnly, looked down for a moment, and then met his eyes. "I know that you were *sent* to rescue me, that it was no accident. I want you to know that I will never, ever forget you, Dan Shepherd. Good night."

She disappeared around the back of the house. In a few minutes he saw the lights go on, and she waved to him from the window. "Well," he sighed as he drove away, "this has been some night, Lady Fair. You can be sure I won't forget you either."

———⊗⊗⊗———

Ruth Mannheim frowned as she stood at the kitchen sink. "Jack, would you come look at this? Our water filtration system just is not working right." Her husband put down his morning paper and came to take a closer look. "I'll call the repair people, honey. Use bottled water until then, and be careful. Better use those test kits we got last week. Even the bottled water isn't too safe any more."

Seeing his wife's distress, Jack stood quietly holding her awhile. "Honey, I know there's been a lot to worry you. That awful attack on Sarah last month, the fires and lootings just a few blocks away, Matt nearly conscripted into the U.N. forces…thank God I had enough connections to pull some strings there!"

They looked out the large bay window over the sink. The sky was gunmetal gray streaked with angry red clouds. Gone were the days of lovely pale pastel sunrises, and lately there wasn't much birdsong either. Ruth missed that most of all. She had always loved the cool, early morning hours spent in her flower garden, accompanied by the merry chirping and chattering of her little feathered friends.

She sighed and hugged her husband close, then turned to finish preparing breakfast. "Jack, I almost forgot to tell you. Deidre and I went to the supermarket yesterday and had to stand in line for nearly an hour. So little food is available now because of the terrible droughts, hurricanes, and floods destroying crops. They explained all of this over the P. A. system to us as we waited. Jack, you would not believe the terrible things we saw—people snarling and growling, fighting over the basic things we used to take for granted.

"Deidre didn't bring her supercharge card, and they nearly wouldn't take her personal check. I had to vouch for her—they took my fingerprint and retinal scan. It was horribly humiliating—I felt almost like a criminal!"

She filled their plates with pancakes and poured hot tea. "I'm sorry there is no coffee, orange juice, or milk. They were out of eggs, too…" Her voice faltered, and Jack reached over to take her hand.

"Ruth, I know things are becoming more and more difficult, and yet just think: we are so much better off than millions of others. This used to be a land of overflowing abundance. Now, all our resources are used up. We have been swallowed up by the U.N. We are literally a bankrupt nation—bankrupt financially, morally, and…and spiritually."

Ruth glanced at him, surprised. Her husband was not, by any stretch of the imagination, a religious man. Neither of them had been to the synagogue since their wedding nearly twenty-four years ago, when two extraordinary handsome young people had earnestly pledged their lifetime devotion to each other. Through bad times and good, it had proven to be an enduring, healthy, satisfying relationship. Of all their married friends, they alone had weathered the pitfalls that had destroyed so many other seemingly solid marriages.

The two were as different as day and night: she was small and fair; he was large-boned, olive- skinned; she was quiet and practical; he was outgoing, gregarious, and adventurous. Together they had achieved the classic American dream: two children, a beautiful home in the suburbs, and all the enviable perks that had accompanied their ascent to affluence. Now, she was trying hard not to give way to the uncertain terror of watching her carefully constructed world crumble around her.

Jack glanced at his watch, then leaned over and kissed his wife. "Honey, I have an eight o'clock meeting of the Builders' Association. It wouldn't look good for the chairman to be late! I'll call you later. Maybe Sarah could get away this weekend, and she and Matt could go out to dinner with us."

Ruth smiled as she waved to him from the French doors, and then turned to clean up the breakfast dishes. *Such a dreamer he is; Sarah can't afford the price of gas,* she thought with a sigh of resignation, *and we can no longer afford the $400.00 for a restaurant dinner. Our lives are changing fast, and I'm so afraid for my children. I'm constantly grieving over their lost hopes and crushed dreams. What a bleak future for them; no college for Matt unless he joins the military, and Jack adamantly opposes that. He—bless his conscientious heart—will not allow our children to sell their souls to a world government that has swallowed up our nation and robbed us of our freedom.*

"Shame on you, Ruth," she scolded herself aloud. "Lighten up. You'd think it was the end of the world, for heaven's sake."

CHAPTER 2

THE INVASION

THE OLD MAN was dreaming again. A soft spring breeze set the silken curtains of his luxuriant bed chamber to swaying. The only other movement in the room was the almost imperceptible twitching of the cat's tail as she perched on the thick, cool stone of the window sill waiting for an unwary bird to invade her domain. Her long and patient wait unrewarded, the huge ball of golden fur gracefully unwound, dropped to the floor, and padded soundlessly to the bed, where she leaped upward, disappearing into the mysterious folds and hollows of many large, colorful cushions. Soon, there issued from their depths the deep rumble of purring; the old man sighed and turned, his dreams undisturbed.

"Mishael! Daniel!" The two boys were startled as the woman's call reverberated over the darkening Judean hillside. "Your friends are looking for you. Come on home, boys."

They looked down to the foot of the hill; the evening lanterns were lit, and several figures were gathering around the gate. "Something's going on," said Daniel. "We'd better get home." The boys scrambled down the hill and ran the short distance to the house.

"Hananiah! Is Azariah here, too?" called Mishael as they entered the front gate.

"Yes, he's inside with his father. Your father is here too, Mishael, as is mine. Wait," he interposed excitedly. "Just wait until you hear; Uncle Elihu has brought news from the north. The invasion has begun!"

The two boys stopped in their tracks and stared in disbelief as their friend told them what he had heard. Daniel dropped his bow and arrows as he sat down heavily on a stone bench. He stared unseeing into the flickering shadows, his mind racing. Reality seemed to be receding, and as the voices droned on, he was instantly transported to another place where even the sounds and smells were strange and unfamiliar to him. He felt the shackles and the pain of the whip, the blackness of despair, and the choking loneliness envelop him as he strained to break the leather thongs that bound his wrists…

"Daniel?" The strange vision evaporated, and reality burst upon him once more as he looked up to see his two friends gazing anxiously at him. "Are you all right?"

He took a deep breath and stood to his feet. "I'm fine. Let's go inside— I want to hear what they are saying."

A large group of men gathered in the courtyard, listening intently to Elihu, a tall, muscular, sun-bronzed man standing in the center. The women and servants were standing in the shadows, listening also. Daniel went instinctively to his mother and put his arm around her. She was trembling, and her eyes were bright with unshed tears as she whispered, "I fear the worst for us, my son. This is what we have dreaded for so long…" Her voice broke. He held her closely to him as he listened to the speaker.

"Of course there is resistance. But the major battle will be for Jerusalem. The invading armies are like locusts that cover the land. Our brave soldiers cannot hold out against such a terrifying onslaught, so King Jehoiakim has recalled them all to defend Jerusalem.

"Even now, as we are gathered in this room, the forces of destruction are gathering like black storm clouds to break forth in a furious assault on our beloved city. The council in Jerusalem is advising all who can to flee into the wilderness or to Egypt and take as many provisions as they can. It may be a long siege, and the invader is ruthless."

The speaker paused for breath, and an excited murmur of voices went around the courtyard. Holding up his hand for silence, he resumed.

"I have said that the enemy is ruthless. Dear friends and neighbors, you and I have lived gentle, protected lives of relative ease. We have long enjoyed the blessings of Jehovah God and—yes, it's true—we have for too long taken them for granted.

"We all know the dire warnings the prophet Jeremiah cried out in the streets of Jerusalem, and most of us have dismissed him, and all the other prophetic warnings, as the ravings of lunatics. Now the truth is all too painfully clear. God is finally allowing judgment to fall on His own, unrepentant people."

Except for a few choked sobs from the shadows, there was a shocked silence as Elihu paused to look around at the gathering.

"The reports from those fleeing the invaders are terrifying. Nebuchadnezzar's armies have already swept through Damascus, Tyre, and Sidon and are now pressing south through the cities and towns of Galilee. They will be upon us in only a matter of weeks, and, my brothers—unless we find a way of escape—they will loot and burn our homes, put us to the sword, rape our wives and daughters, slaughter our infants, and take our cattle and horses to supply their army as they lay siege to Jerusalem.

"I cannot make any decisions for you, my brothers. I have decided that, since I have no wife or children, I will stay in Jerusalem and fight with our armies there. Any provisions you can donate for my warring friends will be most welcome.

"I will leave for Jerusalem by tomorrow at midday and must have everything assembled by then. My dear friends, we will most probably not meet again in this life. To those of you who will travel south or west in search of refuge, I commend you to the mercies of our God—the God of Abraham, Isaac, and Jacob. Remember, whether we live or whether we die, we are His and His alone."

A hush fell over the group as the men, one by one, stood and covered their heads in reverence. A small, elderly man stepped forth and, lifting his wrinkled, old tear-stained face to the moonlight, intoned the ancient anthem of his people: "*Shema, Yisrael! Adonai eluhenu, Adonai echad.* Hear, O Israel! The LORD is our God, the LORD is One."

"Amen," murmured the deep voices in unison, and the group moved closer together as if for comfort. Daniel's mother gave him a quick hug and disappeared into the kitchen. The four boys wandered into the garden and sat cross-legged in a circle around the fire pit.

Poking the dying embers, Mishael spoke first. "I wonder how long we really have before—before..." He could not bring himself to speak aloud the awful possibilities. The four boys sat in silence, each immersed in his own tortured thoughts, and then Daniel spoke.

"Of course our parents will try to get us to safety, but..."

"But what, Daniel?" queried Azariah, peering into his friend's face.

"Well, I wish I knew for certain what will happen. But," he exhaled a deep, shuddering breath, "I'm very much afraid that we will not escape but will be taken captive."

Mishael sprang to his feet, brandishing his bow. "Never!" he cried. "I will die before yielding to the infidel!"

"Me, too!" echoed Azariah, but Hananiah reached out to touch his friend's arm. "Why, Daniel? What is it that gives you this…this fatalistic attitude? You and I—all of us—have run together and roamed these hills around Jerusalem all our lives. We were born into the Judean nobility, and the future hope of Judah—of all Israel—rests with us. We have been trained from our earliest childhood by our parents to accept this responsibility. When we passed into manhood, we knew it and welcomed it as our inheritance when we were just twelve years old.

"You heard Hananiah's uncle Elihu—surely Jehovah would not allow us to suffer the humiliation of being taken as slaves to a strange country where they worship the god Baal! Now is not the time to give in to despair." The anguish rose in his voice as he looked around the circle of friends. "We have pledged our devotion to Jehovah and our loyalty to each other!"

Daniel rose to his feet and extended a hand to pull up his friend. "You are right, Hananiah. This is no time to talk of defeat. The enemy may be overwhelming, but God's mercy is to all generations. I think that means us, my friends."

The next Sabbath was a solemn one. Daniel's family had spent two nights inside Jerusalem, staying with his mother's brother, Uncle Saul, who was a very important temple official. His aunt Deborah was extraordinarily fond of young Daniel since she had no sons of her own, and she always made his favorite Sabbath dessert—baklava, a sweet, sticky concoction made with almonds and honey.

Since the terrible news of the invasion had spread through Jerusalem, the shops in the marketplace were packed with throngs of desperate people trying to stock up on provisions. Many were already streaming out of the gates with their poor, heavily laden donkeys stumbling beneath their impossible burdens.

SEAL UP THE VISION

Daniel watched, fascinated, from the tile-covered turrets of the house-top as thousands of people milled about in the city streets below. *They are like sheep without a shepherd*, he was thinking. *Where will they all go? How many will survive?*

He caught sight of a young, obviously pregnant girl struggling to push a small cart piled high with her precious household possessions. Behind her trailed two small children who were tied with a rope secured around her middle. They were dusty and tired, and Daniel guessed that they must have made the long journey into Jerusalem to find safety behind the massive walls of the city.

Where is your husband? wondered Daniel, as he watched her disappear into the dusty crowd. *Perhaps he was a soldier killed in the northern resistance, or more hopefully, perhaps he is stationed here in Jerusalem to defend the city.*

At that moment, a man on horseback blew a horn, and the crowd parted respectfully to admit a small contingent of soldiers. They were not marching in unison, but were walking rapidly, their armor clanking noisily. As they rounded the corner, some in the crowd shouted, "God keep you, brave warriors!"

"They are looking at their last hope of defense," said Uncle Saul grimly, as he joined Daniel on the parapet. "I am urging your father to proceed with all haste to a place of refuge in the southern wilderness. It is a very ancient city called Petra. I have seen it, Daniel," he said, his eyes shining. "It is a city actually carved out of the rock itself, and when the rays of the setting sun hit the pink stone, it turns red. Fiery red! You can't imagine: one thousand temples all cut from the stone, with a huge amphitheatre that would seat six thousand. There are natural springs and aquifers that supply water through aqueducts. This is a thriving city, the center of a widespread caravan trade that extends all the way from the fabled land of India in the East through Arabia to Africa in the West!"

His hand rested on Daniel's shoulder, and he gazed out over the roof-tops as he continued. "I will remain here, and your aunt Deborah has insisted that she will not leave me." He glanced over at the silent boy. "You are nearly a grown man now, Daniel. Your parents have raised you well; you do them great credit."

"Thank you, sir," murmured Daniel.

"Your father is not well, and the journey south into the wilderness may be hard on him. Therefore, I am entrusting the welfare of my sister—your mother—and the rest of the family to you."

Daniel bowed his head in deference as the older man invoked a blessing on him and then leaned out over the roof for one last look at the ancient holy city of Jerusalem.

"Look well, my son," said his uncle. "You and I will most probably never see this sight again. The temple is full of treasure, and it is rumored that Nebuchadnezzar has vowed to reduce it to rubble and take away all the gold and silver to his palace in Babylon."

He laughed grimly at Daniel's shocked expression. "Oh, yes, this is always the true objective of a tyrant conqueror—greed is the only over-ruling passion that would pull a spoiled Babylonian prince away from his life of indolent luxury and into a long, arduous, and expensive siege of a strange and faraway city. He will, no doubt, be as successful in this as he has been in his other ventures. The only difference," he continued thoughtfully, "is that now he is threatening to defile and destroy that which belongs to the living God."

He shuddered and turned away. "I would not like to be in his royal sandals on that day of reckoning when he comes face to face with... with...Him!"

The journey into the wilderness of Edom was finally under way. The caravan had stopped for the second night's rest, and everyone had retired to their tents when a commotion on the road stirred them awake. Three men on horseback galloped into the camp and dismounted, shouting for the caravan chieftain. When he appeared, sleepy and disheveled, they disappeared into his tent. After a few moments, he reappeared and raced to the top of the hill, pointing excitedly to the north.

Daniel and his father were close behind, and reaching the hilltop first, Daniel stopped in dismay as he saw the northern sky alight with orange flames. "Father, Hebron is burning! That is where Mishael's family is staying tonight; Hananiah and Azariah have not yet left Jerusalem!" His eyes filled with tears as he surveyed the alarming horizon.

His father, still puffing from the exertion, gasped. "Their parents were still making preparations when we left. Oh, how I wish they had left everything behind and departed with our caravan. They thought there would be more time. Nebuchadnezzar truly moves on his prey with lightning swiftness!" he muttered with uncharacteristic bitterness.

Daniel was quiet. His father looked at him in alarm. "Son, are you thinking of...surely you're not contemplating anything as foolish as going back there? Oh, son, we are only three days journey from our destination. We will most certainly be packing up and leaving this very night. We cannot wait for the morning light, for the enemy apparently did not stop at Jerusalem as we thought he would. No, it is moving relentlessly south."

His voice was pleading now as his son's continued silence unnerved him. Daniel's gaze was still fixed on the flickering orange clouds as he quietly replied, "Father, please understand. I must go north. I alone know the route you are taking, and if God grants, I alone can guide them to the wilderness refuge."

He turned and looked directly at his father, taking both of his hands. "Whatever happens, I can be happy knowing my mother and sisters are safe with you. Please, Father, give me your blessing." He knelt on the hill as his father, blinded and choked by tears, prayed Jehovah's blessing over his only son.

The sky was beginning to pale as Daniel rode his lathered horse into a small village near Hebron. He stopped and dismounted by a watering trough. It had been a harrowing night's journey, and Regina, his father's fastest Arabian mare, was snorting foam from her flaring nostrils, her sides heaving from the strenuous effort.

"Good girl." He patted her lovely, arching neck and stroked her soft, velvety nose as she nuzzled him affectionately.

Several women were coming to the well. Their usual early morning chatter was subdued as they moved swiftly to fill their jars.

"Please, can you tell me where the Ben Joseph family lives?" he inquired of one young matron. She pointed to a large white-walled compound at the end of the street. "If they are still there," she said tersely. "Many left in the middle of the night. They travel west, east, and south, but many of us must stay, not having the means to travel," she added bitterly, having noted his expensive saddle and rich, hued garments.

"Thank you kindly," he replied gratefully. When his horse had finished drinking, he led her down the street to the walled compound. Knocking on the gate brought no response, so he walked around back where he tethered his horse. "Is anyone home?" he shouted.

"Who is asking?" came a deep voice from the other side.

"It is Daniel, the son of Ephraim. I am looking for Mishael." There was a small commotion, and then the gate opened. There in the courtyard were dozens of horses and donkeys, heavily loaded for travel. People were running to and fro, frantically preparing for a journey.

"Daniel!" cried Mishael, as he descended on his friend with a massive bear hug. "I was so afraid I would never see you again!"

Daniel grinned as he held his friend at arm's length. "Don't you remember our vow of loyalty?" he remonstrated. "Besides, life in the wilderness would not be any fun without you. I'm going to guide your caravan to the ancient rock fortress of Petra. My uncle Saul gave me a detailed map, which I have left with my father after I committed it to memory. His caravan is well on their way and should arrive in three or four more days. We can catch up to them if we hurry!"

Mishael and his father conferred briefly with the other men, who agreed to follow Daniel. After calling together the entire household, Ari Ben Joseph pronounced a hurried blessing on them and, without a backward glance, led the procession out of town, turning south at the highway.

The road was already packed with early morning refugees fleeing the carnage in the north. Daniel reined back his mare in frustration. *It will be a slow-moving caravan,* he thought grimly, *and who knows what is pursuing us from the north?* He and Mishael rode on ahead and took a little path to the top of a hill. Resting their horses, they gasped with dismay as they surveyed the valley below. The line of refugees stretched out for two or three miles to the south.

"I passed quite a few during the night on my way back here," said Daniel, "but this is much worse than I thought. I wonder if there are any other side roads we might take to bypass the crowd." His voice took on a different tone as he twisted in the saddle. "Mishael, look. No, the other way—to the north. Do you see what I see?"

Mishael froze in disbelief as he gazed northward. "That cloud of dust on the highway—it is coming closer—moving so fast. Daniel, there must be over a hundred Chaldean horsemen, and they are closing in on our people. We've got to warn them!"

Both boys urged their horses down the hill at breakneck speed. "Hurry—the enemy is coming! Scatter to the hills!" they shouted as they rode. Reaching their caravan, they passed the alarming news to Ari Ben Joseph, who immediately deployed his people into two groups.

"Mishael, you and your father will lead one group westward over the hills. Try to reach Sharohen by the Brook Besor. I will lead the other group eastward to the caves around the Dead Sea. Hurry!"

There were tearful good-byes as the family separated in two directions, perhaps for the last time. They moved up the hills with as much speed as they could, but some of the small, heavily laden donkeys were straggling behind. "Take off their loads and lead them over to the other side of the hill!" shouted Ari. "You can come back after the troops have passed by and retrieve your baggage. We haven't much time!"

One young woman with an infant strapped to her back was desperately trying to unload her donkey. Her husband put down his cart to help her. Daniel dismounted and ran to help them.

"Here, take my horse," he shouted to the man. "Your wife and baby can ride in front, but hold them tightly. My horse is fast, and it's going to be a long ride!" As they disappeared over the top of the hill, Daniel freed the donkey from its load, and it suddenly seemed to develop wings as it also disappeared.

"Mishael—over here!' he called, and his friend leaned over and pulled him up behind the saddle as he galloped by. Then they turned southwest to follow their group. A strong wind from the north was carrying the soot and ashes that once were the city of Hebron, and it served to spur them onward.

The sun was fully up by now, and the invading army from the north was making its final push through the Judean hills south to Beersheba and west to Egypt. The lust for power and acquisition of new territory had fueled the conqueror's greedy appetite for more and yet more as he relentlessly drove on to envelop all of Israel and Egypt as far as the Nile River. Then he would turn again and go back to lay siege to Jerusalem, the golden city, the tantalizing prize.

The captain of the cavalry unit received word from his scouts that hundreds of terrified refugees were clogging the roads ahead of them and would impede their progress.

"Sound the battle trumpets," he growled. "That should clear the way. If we slaughter them on the roads it will only slow us down. Spread out," he ordered, "and ride four abreast on the highway. They will move!"

Thanks to the two young riders' early warning, which was quickly passed southward to all the refugees, the road emptied quickly; the hills were already swarming with hundreds of terrified travelers. The swift horses of the Chaldeans found unhindered progress as they thundered southward. Stopping only twice to water their horses, the captain was in a sour mood by the time the hot Judean sun had long passed its zenith and was lowering toward the western horizon. It had already been a long, grueling ride with the merciless sun beating down on their helmets, the endless, swirling dust stinging their eyes, and a brutal, sleepless night behind them. Butchering, slaughtering, and burning out the local populace were never a pleasant job, and the captain still felt the familiar nausea that never failed to accompany such a distasteful task.

"A pox on this cursed country," he mumbled, "and a double pox on our power-mad king who sent us here!"

Coming upon a good-sized oasis with plenty of well-watered trees was a welcome relief, and he quickly made his decision.

"We'll camp here," he announced.

"But, sir," replied his surprised lieutenant, "there is still an hour of good riding until sunset."

"By the time we have all the tents set up and my surveillance teams return from scouting the area, it will be well past sunset," replied the captain, dismounting. Later, in his tent, he managed to down quite a few draughts of good wine before drifting off to sleep. He dreamed of his home in Babylon and his wife and children waiting for him under the cool shade of the willows by the river. Soon, however, his dreams were rudely interrupted by a commotion outside the door of his tent.

"Sir, we beg to ask your permission to enter," his sergeant inquired tentatively.

"Come in," said the drowsy captain as he reluctantly abandoned his slumbers and struggled to a sitting position. "Well, what is it? I asked not to be disturbed!"

"Sir, the patrol came upon these prisoners, and we thought we should check with you before executing them as spies."

The sergeant bent to enter the tent, followed by two young boys who were manacled to a soldier.

"Well, well, well," laughed the captain. "What have we here? These two ruffians certainly do look like dangerous spies indeed. Do you think we ought to behead them on the spot?"

The soldiers glanced at each other uneasily. This appeared to be one of the captain's more mellow moments. Or perhaps the overabundance of wine consumed since their arrival may have contributed to his apparent sense of well-being. The simple truth was just that he had no more stomach for killing, especially mere children so near the age of his own.

Gesturing to the boys, he once again reclined on his couch, offering them a seat as well. *There is a limit to what one man can take*, he was thinking, as he watched the two stand proudly at attention, trying vainly to appear brave. *The tearstains streaking those dirty cheeks have given you away*, he thought languidly. *Still and all, you are just scared children, wanting desperately to live.*

"Well, young men—yes, I speak your language fluently—what have you two to say for yourselves? Are you spies like my sergeant said? What were you doing outside our camp? And more important—where are your parents?"

The boys lowered their heads. "They are gone, sir," said the taller one. "Our homes are gone, all our family; we were riding double on horseback trying to escape the invading armies when our horse pulled up lame. We walked as far as we could, then stopped here for water when your troops arrived."

The captain lapsed into a gloomy silence; he leaned back on one elbow and eyed the boys thoughtfully through half-closed eyes. He was very tired. He had seen enough brutality for an entire lifetime since he had come to this unfamiliar place, so far from his boyhood home and so far from the source of his stability and contentment—his beloved wife. *Besides*, he thought, *these two youths have the unmistakable demeanor of well-bred nobility, despite their bedraggled appearance.*

"Put them in fetters; Nebuchadnezzar has given orders that all high-born nobility be taken back with us as captives. We must have our trophies to parade down the streets of Babylon when we return," he added with thinly veiled sarcasm.

He raised his chalice and filled it unsteadily. "To the victors go the spoils! Off with you, now," and he dismissed them with a wave of the hand.

Later that night, the two exhausted prisoners, bound hand and feet, awoke from a deep sleep to the sound of distant thunder. Soon the rain was pelting down the sides of their tent, and Daniel whispered, "Mishael—are you awake?"

"I think so," came the muffled reply, "unless this is some ghastly nightmare!"

"Sorry, but it looks like we are going on a long, long journey…and it's no dream. Mishael," he continued breathlessly, "Do you realize that our families have escaped—at least for now!"

"Jehovah has kept us safe, while so many others have been slaughtered, or taken captive…"

Both boys fell silent, choking back the tears as they thought about their friends, hopelessly trapped in Jerusalem. Daniel remembered his promise to his uncle to bring his family to safety.

"I have failed; Jehovah will not," he murmured as he once again drifted into a dreamless sleep.

CHAPTER 3

A REFUGE

MATT MANNHEIM FELT his throat constrict as he watched the two flags ascend the flagpole, billowing out to full sail in the stiff early morning breeze.

"Guess I'll just never get used to the sight of Ol' Glory flying underneath the U.N. flag," he muttered tersely. He and his fellow JROTC officers saluted, turned smartly, and marched in unison up the steps of the high school auditorium.

Thank God, today's the last time; after graduation, I'm out of here—for good! he thought as the group headed backstage.

Matt had truly distinguished himself as an honor student, having been captain of the debate team three years in a row. He, much like his father, was an affable, gregarious young man who had many friends. However, some of those he had always considered his closest buddies had, inexplicably, begun to back off. Some were avoiding him entirely. There was even a recent ugly incident in which a small mob of unruly neighborhood kids had thrown rocks at him as he was riding home on his motorcycle, shouting "filthy Jew" and other unprintable obscenities.

This was the very first time in Matt's tender, sheltered, and privileged young life that he had encountered the mindless hatred of anti-Semitism, and it left a deep and indelible wound. To be the victim of random violence was bad enough, but to be actually singled out as a target of vicious hatred was a shattering experience.

Lately, Matt had begun to experience some vague uneasiness, something akin to—but not quite—loneliness or isolation. He wanted desperately to talk to his father but felt that it would be too awkward to explain something so nebulous. *Anyway,* he reasoned, *Dad seems to be pretty distracted himself, and Mom's been crying a lot lately. Maybe I can talk to Sis when she comes home from Boston next week. She barely escaped with her life when she was chased by those murderous thugs. So frightening! If they'd killed her...*

Deep in troubled thought, Matt almost missed his cue; as salutatorian of his graduating class, he was expected to give a short speech, and now, during rehearsal, he decided to deliver a few lines.

"Oh, no..." groaned his best friend, Rusty. "Here goes nothin'!"

"Don't worry—I'll keep it good and short for you!" grinned Matt, as he launched into the opening remarks of his well-planned speech. Gifted with a keen intellect combined with a considerable gift of gab, he never seemed to be at a loss for words. Nearly six feet tall and well-muscled from workouts with both the swim and track teams, he was blessed with the dark good looks of his father.

Matt's parents had high aspirations for their only son. They had always encouraged him to excel without exerting undue pressure to conform to their own expectations. Unlike so many other absentee parents of the twenty-first century, they had given both of their children that rarest and most priceless commodity of all: their time. This, more than anything else, had contributed to the unusual strength of the Mannheim family bond.

That afternoon, the bond was further strengthened by the enthusiastic hugs and congratulations from all the friends and family who gathered at the house for the postgraduation party. Ruth came outside, bearing a tray of hor d'oeuvres and waving a telegram from Sarah, who was in the process of taking her premed finals at Brandeis.

"Matt, your sister is so proud of you," she beamed as she handed him an envelope. Matt hugged his mother quickly and took the telegraph inside to find a quiet place to read it. A little while later, his father went to look for him and found him in the study, looking out the window.

"Are you OK, Matt?"

"Yes, Dad," he replied, somewhat subdued. "You know, I just...well, I've been thinking about next year." The muscles in his jaw were working as he continued looking out the window. "I haven't been offered the scholarships that some of the other guys—who scored much lower on the pre-college exams—have been given. My counselor finally told me why when I pressed him for an answer. He said he was sorry, but the growing anti-Jewish sentiment in this country was infiltrating every area of our society, and, quite frankly, I probably just don't have a chance."

Jack Mannheim went to stand by his son, his arm around his strong, young shoulders. They stood in silence for a few moments, watching their dancing guests in the backyard.

"Son, if anyone had told me five years ago that this would be happening, I would have laughed." He sighed heavily and sank down into the luxurious leather of the sofa.

"Your mother and I have seen this coming for a good long time, but somehow we hoped that it would bypass us. We are so much a part of the American fabric that it has been difficult to suddenly perceive ourselves as outcasts—isolated from all that we have held dear and familiar."

His brow furrowed as he continued. "Sarah has already told us that her applications to med school have been turned down, and she has worked so hard, done so well…" His voice broke, and Matt, worried, sat down opposite his father. Leaning forward, he spoke gently, "Oh, Dad, I didn't mean to worry you. Sarah and I are young—we'll find a way."

"But what about you and Mom? You haven't said much, but I've wondered if this is affecting your business."

"Yes, son, it has. Things are pretty bad; we have been forced to under-bid, considerably lower than we should, to secure any contracts at all. Some of the larger firms I've been dealing with for years now won't even return my calls. Your mother and I have come to realize that the odds are stacked against us, and we must make some decisive decisions—soon. Very soon."

Jack glanced at his worried son, and then, taking a deep breath, resumed. "We—your mother and I—want to involve you and Sarah in the decision-making process. We need to talk this over as a family, so we called Sarah and asked her to come home immediately after her last final exam tomorrow instead of waiting until next week."

Father and son sat quietly for a few moments as Matt digested this information, somewhat surprised at the urgency in his father's voice. Presently, Jack stood up and laid his hand on his troubled son's shoulder.

"Well, Matt, the party will be breaking up soon, and you're the guest of honor. We'd better go back outside."

As they left the study, Matt was thinking, *I wonder if I'll be seeing much more of my "friends" after today ... one thing I can be sure of, though—my family will always stick together, no matter what comes.*

The next day was relatively quiet. Jack came home from the office a little early and secluded himself in the study until dinnertime. Matt was upstairs in his room, packing away some of his huge collection of high school trophies when he spied Sarah's blue Firebird turning into the driveway. Bounding down the steps and out the front door, he smothered his sister in a bear hug as she emerged from the car. Laughing and talking animatedly, they entered the house, unaware of the storm clouds gathered overhead.

Their mother watched from an upstairs window until they had gone inside, then turned back to her desk where she had been writing some letters to her family. She straightened the desk, wiped the tears from her eyes, and then, putting the letters in her pocket for posting, went downstairs to greet her daughter.

"Sarah! Darling Sarah," she exclaimed with delight as the two embraced. "You're just in time for dinner. I've prepared your favorite: chicken Parmesan with fettuccine Alfredo."

As the family gathered around the table, there was an uncharacteristic silence as Jack looked at his family, then bowed his head. The unfamiliar words came slowly, hesitantly: "Almighty God, King of the universe, who brings forth food from the earth and bread for the eater—we give You thanks. Amen."

"Amen," echoed the family as they looked furtively at each other. Ruth briskly passed the food around as she asked Sarah about her exams. Matt was pensive, and not a little apprehensive, as he wondered if his father had suddenly "got religion."

They were busy devouring the last crumbs of Ruth's famous French silk chocolate pie when Jack cleared his throat and pushed back from the table.

"Ruth, thanks for a great meal. It was terrific—I couldn't eat another bite! Now, you know, Sarah, why we called you home early, don't you?"

She nodded mutely, somewhat apprehensive as she leaned forward, her eyes fixed on her father.

"Your mother and I want you to know that we will not make any decisions without you. That goes without saying. The conditions around us are worsening by the hour, and I want to fill you in on our tentative plans. I say *tentative* because they won't be considered in any way final until you two agree."

"About seven years ago, I became somewhat alarmed at the suicidal financial policies this country was pursuing. At that point, I quietly began selling off my stock options and liquidating certain assets. I have been systematically depositing the funds into an anonymous numbered Swiss bank account in Geneva. The fund is now in excess of twenty million dollars."

Matt let out a soft whistle, and Sarah gasped in astonishment.

"I have for some time now been in touch with certain Israeli authorities, looking for the safest migration route to Israel. You see," he took a deep breath, "I have it on the strictest authority from a friend in the State Department that no one who is a known evangelical Christian or Jew will be issued a passport or visa. This is an order from the top echelon of the government—and I don't mean the president!" he added tersely.

Matt and Sarah were too stunned to respond. They glanced at each other and looked at their mother, who was watching her children with a heavy heart.

"That isn't the worst of it. There have been several unconfirmed reports of Jewish homes and businesses being seized by the IRS for 'back taxes' and the owners imprisoned. Of course, we all know by now that these things will never be reported by the media."

He paused for a moment, then resumed in a subdued voice, "We have all stood by and watched this happen to the Christians in this country. A few have raised their voices against it, but most of us simply did nothing. Don't you see," he leaned forward earnestly, "it's been just like the Nazi holocaust, only in reverse order. And we said it couldn't happen here.

"This is soon going to erupt into a worldwide holocaust. Other nations are going in the same direction, first on the Christians, and then on the Jews. Consequently, there has been a steady stream of emigration from all parts of the world to Israel. This is the question before us now: do we stay and try to hang on to what we have left, or do we leave?"

The atmosphere in the room was electrified, and as if on cue, a flash of lightning followed by a heavy roll of thunder rattled the panes of the dining room windows. No one moved as the rain pelted the glass, running like tears down the windowpanes.

"We need to remember one very important thing: more than six million of our people died in Europe. Many of them had the means to escape, but they waited just a little too long, hoping somehow that the political situation would change in their favor. Whatever we do, we need to decide quickly—tonight, if possible."

The two young people looked at each other. An unspoken message passed between them; Sarah nodded slightly, and there was a trace of a smile on her lips as Matt spoke.

"We have to leave. There can be no possibility of staying; we are agreed on that, but the only question I have is this: is there still time to get our passports and visas?"

Jack reached for Ruth's hand as they simultaneously breathed a sigh of relief.

"My friend in the State Department has already taken care of that," he answered with a smile. "I have them in the safe in the study. Your grand-parents, God rest their souls, always longed to see Jerusalem. Now they will see it through your eyes."

There were a few minutes of silence, each lost in their own thoughts, and then Sarah finally spoke.

"I must confess, Mom and Dad, that I do have some regrets about leaving my life here behind—we all do—but at the same time, I'm more than ready. After so many rejections, I have finally realized and, I think, accepted the truth. I will never be allowed to practice medicine in this country. There's no turning back, now, is there?" Her eyes were swimming with tears as she stood. The family hugged each other and then cleared the dinner dishes away. They lingered longer than usual in the kitchen, discussing at length all the possibilities before them. Reluctantly, they each retired to their respective bedrooms, and soon the Mannheim resi-dence settled into darkness.

There was no moon that night; the storm had abated somewhat and the only sound was the steady dripping of a soft rain from the eaves. The Watchers assigned to the Mannheim household held silent vigil around the home. Aware of the forces of darkness closing in on God's chosen ones, they were stationed to provide protection and comfort for the besieged family and bring them safely to their appointed destination. Unaware of their privileged status, the occupants of the house were deep in dreamless sleep.

"The Spirit has spoken of this long ago," said one powerful angel to the others. "For I will take you, Israel, from among the nations where I have

scattered you, and gather you out of all the countries, and bring you into your own land…and you will be My people and I will be your God.'"

"Amen." As they considered the awesome task before them, the Watchers waited in silence.

Three days later, the arrangements finalized and all packages shipped overseas, the family converged one final time for last minute instructions. To avoid suspicion, each one would fly on a different airline to a different destination in Europe; then they would meet in Israel. The house had been placed on the market through a trusted real estate agent. It was deeded over to an uncle in Miami, who promised to use the proceeds to get other Jewish families out of the country.

The cars had been sold; only Matt's beloved custom-fitted motorcycle was being shipped with the family's belongings. Actually, to Ruth's surprise, her greatest regret was saying good-bye to the family's faithful old mongrel the children had named Gidget. She remembered with great fondness all the years she had fussed about the dirty footprints all over her clean kitchen floor and the dozens of prized tulips and geraniums he had dug up to bury a bone. Yet his slavish devotion to the children earned the big awkward dog his mistress' undying affection. Wherever they would call home in the years ahead, father and son would miss their early morning jogging companion. *He'll be happy*, thought Ruth, *out on Uncle Al's farm.*

They all met for breakfast at a small restaurant near the airport hotel where they were staying. Unrecognized, they painstakingly went over every detail of the plan. Hopefully, if all went well, they would post their good-bye letters to friends just before boarding the plane. Jack would fly to Geneva, where he would withdraw his funds. Ruth's flight would depart just before Jack's, going to London, where she planned to stay with a cousin. Mark and Sarah would fly to Rome and Athens respectively, each with a group of young tourists. After spending a few days there, they planned to board a cruise ship that had Tel Aviv among its many ports of call.

They checked their watches and, after paying for the meal, boarded the shuttle for the airport. Arriving at the entrance, there was only time for a quick hug before the four separated to their different terminals.

Ruth was keenly aware of her isolation as she stood in line to check her baggage. In a few minutes, her flight was announced, and she met her husband's eyes across the terminal as he watched her go. *God keep you, darling,* she thought, as she handed her boarding pass to the flight attendant.

Soon, safely buckled into her window seat, she tried to catch sight of him through the terminal windows. "There he is!" she muttered excitedly, but her heart leaped in alarm as she saw the uniformed security force moving swiftly through the crowd. Jack saw her distressed expression, looked behind him, then turned long enough to give her the thumbs-up signal, and disappeared into the crowd.

At the other end of the airport, Matt and Sarah were both waiting in line when they also caught sight of the security police, who were relentlessly moving through the crowd, asking for a show of ID.

They casually picked up their on-flight bags and sauntered into the baggage claim area. "OK, now what?" Sarah whispered.

"Don't panic," breathed Matt, who was sweating profusely. "Remember what Dad said: in case of an emergency, we meet at the shuttle bus area and go back to the hotel."

As they emerged into the brilliant morning sunlight, they looked in vain for their father. After a few minutes of nerve-wracking suspense, they boarded the bus, which was about to leave. Only a few yards away, a security officer was stopping outgoing passengers, who seemed annoyed as they had to put down their baggage and search for ID.

The bus slowly moved out into traffic, and the two young escapees were heartsick with worry. *I wonder if they made it,* both were thinking. As they arrived at their hotel, they disembarked and were helplessly wondering what to do when they heard a familiar voice behind them.

"Well, if it isn't the world travelers, stranded back on square one," said their father as he herded them unceremoniously into the hotel lobby. Sarah fought back tears of relief as she watched her father obtain another room. Safely upstairs, she erupted with questions. "Where's Mom? Are you sure she is OK? What do you think went wrong—how could they have known so soon?"

"Your mother is safely on her way to London, so don't worry. I'll cable her cousin as soon as she arrives so she'll know we survived. In the meantime, we need to lie low until the heat is off. And in answer to your question—I can only make an educated guess as to how the authorities were on to us so quickly. I have some suspicions, but right now there is no real answer."

Jack pulled out his address book and dialed a number. He made several phone calls, while Matt and Sarah talked quietly in the corner.

"Nobody home on a weekday," muttered Jack after hanging up from the last call, "And it's not really safe to leave a message."

Sarah stood up. "Dad, I'm going to call Dan." Jack registered his surprise.

"You remember Dan Shepherd. We've been seeing each other quite often since 'the rescue.' He drives down to Boston, and we go out to dinner or a movie. He's different from any other guy I've met. He's a complete gentleman, and…well, Dad, I trust him completely."

Jack regarded his daughter fondly. *She looks so frail and vulnerable,* he was thinking, *but she's a tough, resilient little cookie. I trust her judgment.*

"OK, Toots. Make the call," and he handed her the phone.

Later, as they ate lunch in the hotel grill, Sarah gave further explanation of her impulsive decision to call her friend as they waited for him.

"Dan is a quiet sort of guy, not really the kind I'm used to dating. He doesn't talk a lot about himself; he usually asks questions about me: how I'm feeling, what I'm doing, and why I'm doing it. He is extremely intelligent; his questions are incisive and probing, yet without being intrusive. I get the feeling that he is definitely not a self-centered person, but genuinely interested in others.

"The really strange part is, after our last date he hung around a lot longer than usual. He just kept holding my hand and looking at me. Just before he left, he said something odd. He said that if we ever needed help—he meant my family—he knew someone who could offer us sanctuary. That's the exact word he used: *sanctuary.* It was almost as if he knew what was coming."

They finished their meal and had no sooner closed the door to their hotel room when there was a knock.

Sudden tension filled the room. "Who is it?" inquired Sarah, her voice quavering.

"It's Dan. I got here as soon as I could."

The door opened, and Sarah was immediately enveloped in a hug. Matt and Jack stepped forward to greet Dan, and he moved inside self-consciously.

"Dad, Matt—I'd like you to meet Dan Shepherd." Her eyes shining,

Sarah made the introductions, and they pulled some chairs up to the round table by the window, where Jack gave Dan a somewhat terse synopsis of their predicament.

"So…the authorities are searching for you and could come bursting in here any moment." Dan leaned back and looked around the table, his eyes lingering on Sarah.

Then he rose decisively to his feet. "We need to leave immediately. We'll sort out the details later, once we're safely on our way." The room exploded into action as they grabbed their luggage and followed him out the door.

Descending in the elevator, Dan explained that he had already called a close friend, his former basketball coach. He had made it absolutely clear that any time Dan needed a private place to stay, his mountain cabin in the Poconos was available, no questions asked.

They all piled into the little red Mustang and before long were winding through the lovely hill country—cool, green, and far away from the terrors of the city.

The cabin was set far back from the road—almost inaccessible. "Good thing I've been here before," drawled the driver with a grin. "The coach brought our team up here several times. That was, oh, I guess about ten years ago, but it seems like yesterday. See those pines along the driveway? We carved our initials on them. Here's the cabin, so—everybody out. I'll go open up."

As Dan emerged from the car, stretching his tall frame, Matt was thinking, *I can sure see him playing basketball, but how in the world does he ever drive this tin can?* They unloaded their gear, took a short hike, and ate dinner. Jack and Matt retired early.

That night was unforgettable for Sarah. She and Dan walked out to the lake and sat on the pier, watching the moonlight dance on the water. A soft breeze gently riffled the surface of the lake, and the cry of a lonely night bird echoed from the far distant shore.

"How I wish we could hold on to this time forever," she sighed. "It almost seems unreal, after all we've been through."

Dan was silent, then drew his knees up under his chin, staring pensively at the lake.

"If wishes were horses, beggars would ride," he murmured. Noting Sarah's puzzled gaze, he grinned. "Don't worry, Lady Fair, you're still in good hands. Seriously, though, these people that own this cabin are pretty special. They'll be coming up tomorrow to meet you and to bring us some provisions."

Sarah gazed out over the lake, leaned back to look up at the stars, and murmured, "You knew, didn't you? Before anyone else, you sensed the danger," She looked up at him quizzically. "Tell me, Dan—just how did you know?"

Dan looked away, then stood up, offering her his hand. "C'mon, Sarah—let's walk for a while. It's a long story."

As they strolled down the moonlit beach, Sarah learned that six months ago, Dan's former university professor had placed an urgent call in the middle of the night and asked if they could meet. Dan had suggested an all-night diner near the university.

When he had arrived, he had found the older man hunched down in one of the corner booths, his eyes darting nervously around the nearly empty room. Dan, shocked to see his formerly immaculate professor's haggard, terror-stricken face, had taken a seat across from him and ordered coffee. The professor, a brilliant Jewish physicist who was working on a top-secret government project, had then unraveled a story so bizarre that Dan could hardly believe it.

A highly placed U.N. official had exerted enormous influence on the U.S. government to give him unlimited control over the Jewish population. Unfortunately, this official was a Neo-Nazi, a member of a revived S.S. brotherhood. Vicious and unrelenting in its pursuit of Hitler's long dormant dream of the systematic extermination of all Jews, thereby "purifying" the Aryan race, it had remained a covert organization for many decades, carefully maneuvering its people into places of authority and influence.

Now, the professor had continued, as he nervously sipped his coffee, the Neo-Nazis were removing the camouflage; whole families had disappeared, simply dropping out of sight. Jewish homes and businesses were being quietly, efficiently swallowed up, and the media never uttered a word of inquiry or protest. "My wife went out to walk the dog tonight," the professor had explained brokenly, "and she never came back. I received a call only three hours ago from our housekeeper; the

Neo-Nazis were on their way to the university to pick me up!"

Dan stopped for a moment, looking down at her. "He stayed here for a couple of weeks, Sarah; then we got him out of the country."

She slowly shook her head. "How sad for him."

The young couple talked well into the night and then reluctantly parted—Dan to the bunkhouse with the other men and Sarah to the main bedroom.

The next morning dawned bright and clear, a perfect late spring day in the mountains. Sarah was awakened by the sound of car doors slamming and children's voices, running feet, and screen doors thrown open. Alarmed, she bounced out of bed, washed quickly, and dressed in record time.

In the living room, she found Dan surrounded by several children and talking to a nice-looking young couple in their early thirties.

"Oh, here she is. Sarah, I'd like you to meet Randy and Paula Endicott. They own this wonderful place and insisted that I bring you here." The couple greeted her warmly, then set about putting away groceries and preparing breakfast. Presently, the screen door slammed again as Matt and Jack came in from their morning run. They shook hands with their genial host, thanking him profusely for his generosity, and went to take cold showers and then dress.

After breakfast, the children pulled Dan and Matt down to the pier, Sarah and Paula chatted happily in the kitchen, and Jack and Randy wandered out to the back porch.

"I sure could get used to this," grinned Jack. "Man! What a place. Randy, I hope you know we're technically fugitives from the law. We narrowly missed being caught in a dragnet at the airport, and I don't want to put you and your family in any jeopardy. We stopped on the way up here, and I cabled my wife's cousin in London a code letting her know we are all right. Other than that, I plan to remain incommunicado until we decide what to do."

He sat down on the porch swing, and his host leaned back against the railing.

"Jack, you'll be in no danger here, and there's something you should know about us. We are Christians, Paula and I. It was during the massive worldwide revivals in the first decade of this millennium that we both, as rebellious teenagers, heard God's call and yielded our lives to the Master.

Millions in the U.S. and abroad were swept into the kingdom of God, and our nation underwent an enormous transformation."

Randy paused, gazing down at his feet. "However," he resumed soberly, "we were so euphoric in those days that we began to take His great blessings for granted. We failed to discern and steward this great move of God as we should have, and we relaxed our vigilance in prayer. The backlash came with great fury. It now *seems* as if our country has fallen to the enemy, BUT..."

He took a deep breath and raised his head to look directly at Jack, "BUT the Lord has ordained this nation ultimately to fulfill her destiny."

Randy began to pace the deck, speaking earnestly. "Did you know that George Washington saw the entire future of this nation in a vision? An angel appeared to him, repeatedly calling him 'Son of the Republic,' and showed him three great 'perils' that would come upon this nation. God showed him *victory* each time! Jack, I believe we are now going through that last 'peril' right now. Paula and I are no strangers to harassment and persecution. We are only too glad to help you and your family."

He smiled at Jack's surprised reaction. "Oh, I know what you're thinking—why would a Christian help a Jew? Well, in the first place the Master I serve is Jewish: Yeshua Meshiach, Jesus Christ. He's forgiven me, claimed me as His own, and filled me with His Spirit. He's kept us safe through the most dangerous and harrowing circumstances. He is my Lord, my God, my hero, and my closest friend. I would gladly give my life for Him if I was called to do so—but I believe He has a purpose for me and for many others like myself."

Randy looked directly at the man in the swing. "Jack, you don't know Him yet. Not like that, you don't, but you will. Paula and I have been praying fervently for you and your family ever since Dan told us about you. We both are in complete agreement. God intends to use us to help you get to Israel."

Jack seemed to be, uncharacteristically, at a complete loss for words.

Randy sat on the porch railing and, as gently and clearly as possible, explained to his new friend Old Testament scriptures that clearly prophesied the regathering of Israel from the nations just prior to the Second Coming of the Messiah.

The two men were deeply engrossed in conversation for over an hour. Jack's earnest, probing questions elicited some comprehensive and illuminating answers from Randy, who warmed to his favorite subject with a passionate enthusiasm that intrigued his hearer. Although he was Jewish by birth, Jack's parents were remarkably nonreligious. Their infrequent trips to the synagogue were made only when his uncle Saul from Newark came to visit.

To his childish mind, God had seemed to be personified by the ancient, bearded rabbi who held the scrolls and read from the Torah, chanting incomprehensible phrases in a quavering, high-pitched monotone. The question of his Jewish origin, which had been pushed into the background as he grew older, now had been recurring with insistent frequency as he became the bewildered target of anti-Semitism.

Only now, surrounded by the cool, green freshness of the pine forest, did it begin to occur to him that he was, somehow, special to a God he had neither acknowledged nor recognized. As the wind softly stirred the tops of the trees, the men fell silent. Jack leaned back and closed his eyes, only a slight frown betraying his inner turmoil.

Randy smiled as he turned to look out over the shimmering water. *Poor guy,* he thought, *his world has been turned upside down. I would guess that he's been given enough light today to shatter a lifetime of illusions. Well, one thing I know for sure: the Spirit of the Lord will continue to water the seed of truth that's been sown, until it breaks through that old dead seed pod down there in the darkness, and pushes up into the light!*

CHAPTER 4

THE CAPTIVES

THE CARAVAN STRETCHED out for miles along the winding road from Damascus. The Syrian desert enveloped them on all sides, stretching endlessly as far as the eye could see. The merciless ball of fire overhead pulled every drop of moisture from the parched bodies chained together as they stumbled along in the dusty wake of the camels. The prisoners gazed with longing at the oxcarts shaded with colorful tarpaulins; what a relief it would be to ride in the comfort for a while, to wash their aching, burning feet and escape the relentless, suffocating heat.

Everyone knew, however, that the contents of the oxcarts, as well as the overloaded camels, were the great abundance of the temple treasure looted from Jerusalem by Nebuchadnezzar's legions. The gold, silver, and precious gems of Solomon's fabled temple were now en route to a pagan kingdom where the God of Israel was unknown.

Three hundred fifty Chaldean horsemen, well-seasoned, hardened, sun-bronzed warriors had been assigned to guard the treasure and escort the Hebrew captives to Babylon. It was an ironclad certainty that no group of bandits in their right minds would be insane enough to challenge Nebuchadnezzar's best men. The lure of such an unprecedented amount of riches, however, could possibly be hard to resist, so the soldiers kept a watchful eye on the surrounding hills as they rode.

Late afternoon brought some relief as scudding clouds began to cover the sun. The wind picked up considerably, and the pace of the animals quickened as they caught sight of the large green oasis still some miles ahead. For such a large caravan, it took a remarkably short time to unload and water the animals, set up tents, and prepare the evening meal.

Several groups of captives were cordoned off together, guards were posted, and the exhausted prisoners fell asleep almost immediately. In the blessed oblivion of slumber, cooled by the soft night winds, they found escape, however temporary, from their abject misery. Far beyond the release of tears, far beyond the borders of their homeland, all were keenly aware that they most probably would never see it again.

What unknown struggles lay ahead, no one could venture to guess. Their lives had been uprooted with such ruthless violence that the resulting grief, terror, and fear threatened to overload their broken hearts. Mercifully, however, a drugless stupor, an insulating layer of dullness covered the deep wound of grief, allowing it time to eventually, hopefully, heal.

The days passed, unmarked and unnoticed, and the remnant of a whole race of people stumbled forward toward an unknown destination. The nights passed all too quickly, for the coolness of the starlit desert provided the only respite from the relentless torment of each day's journey. All hope gradually died as their captors led them onward, removing them ever farther from their beloved homeland.

Nebuchadnezzar had issued strict edicts against any unnecessary abuse or torture of his captives. This seemingly humanitarian gesture was not prompted by kindness, but rather by a need to display his conquered subjects alive and in reasonably presentable condition to the citizens of his city. A ruler who took great pride in his accomplishments, Nebuchadnezzar would tolerate no interference with the fulfillment of his ambitious plan to ascend the throne as absolute, undisputed sovereign of the world.

On the fifteenth day of the seventh month, the ruler of the world awoke early, nursing a massive hangover. He groaned, and with a heroic effort, managed to sit on the edge of his bed. Holding his aching head gingerly with both hands, he groaned again, and immediately a servant appeared with a pitcher of cool water, a towel, and a small vial of powdered willow bark to assuage his master's pain. With great solicitude, he ministered to the king in what had recently become a morning ritual.

Since his army's triumphant return from Israel and Egypt the previous week, the palace had been filled to capacity with revelers who had come from all parts of the kingdom to celebrate the recent victories and to view the newest acquisitions from the conquered territories. Every night for a week, wine flowed like water; there was an abundance of exotic food, and even more exotic entertainment as each banquet master tried to outdo the others in opulence and luxury.

This morning, his royal highness stood by his window and surveyed the gardens below; he silently cursed himself for a fool. Drunkenness and carousing were not his usual indulgences, so the cumulative effect of a week's debauchery had severely depleted the young king's reserves. With firm resolve, he decided then and there on a strict course of abstinence.

This is the day, he was thinking. *They will be coming in the southern gate and parade down the main thoroughfare. When they reach the palace, I want the treasure opened and each piece carried up the steps. Let the crowds roar and howl as they see the glory of Solomon's temple laid before my feet.*

Yes! Solomon was nothing, he thought sourly. *Nothing compared to me. All of my life, I have heard of Solomon, Solomon, Solomon! As if the glory of his kingdom would never be surpassed—well, Solomon, everything that was yours is now mine! Your people, your vast treasures, your glory. Your land is devastated, your cities burned, and your God is defeated!*

As he was thinking these words, he was startled by what sounded like distant laughter. Peering through the early predawn mist, he saw no one.

"Your God is defeated, Solomon!" he spoke aloud with defiant arrogance. "You're long dead in the dust, and your God no longer cares for your people…" He felt a bit strange as he heard the echo of his own voice resounding in the empty chamber.

Shivering in the early morning chill, he returned to his bed and pulled the silken coverlet over his head. He finally drifted into a troubled sleep. As the sky began to lighten, the servant quickly entered the room and drew together the heavy draperies, throwing the vast bed chamber into darkness. As he was softly closing the door, he heard an unmistakable sound—one he had not heard since Nebuchadnezzar was a small boy. The king of Babylon was moaning in his sleep.

As the thousands of captives were led in chains into the Plain of Shinar, their first glimpse of the fabled city of Babylon was astonishing. The city was two hundred square miles of dazzling beauty surrounded by a water-filled moat. The city walls were eight hundred feet high and eighty-seven feet thick. Each of the four walls had twenty-five gates of iron and bronze, which at sunset reflected the brilliance of a thousand jewels.

The mighty Euphrates River divided the city, the eastern and western halves being connected by a bridge nearly eleven hundred feet long and thirty feet wide. At each end of the bridge was a royal palace defended by three concentric walls, the outer one being seven miles in circumference and three hundred feet high.

Nebuchadnezzar's private quarters were the most luxurious of any ruler in all of history. He had spared neither expense nor effort in bringing to his exquisite city the world's very best artisans, builders, musicians, and craftsmen to bring Babylon to the absolute zenith of her splendor.

The weary and footsore remnant of Judah entered their bondage through the Ishtar gate, magnificently decorated with blue-enameled bricks inset with red and white bulls and dragons. A breathtaking view met their astonished eyes as they entered: a broad avenue paved with red and white stones stretched before them, bordered by two thick walls decorated with sixty large blue ceramic lions. The magnificent royal palace stood near the gate, and to the south, in a large open area, was a towering ziggurat, the temple of the city god Marduk, which had been built by Hammurabi, the king of Babylon one thousand years before.

Their minds numbed with misery, their senses whirling in reaction to the strange mixture of sights, sounds, and smells of the city, the captives were paraded down this avenue to the cheers and howls of the local populace. Submitting to the strange sting of indignity, four young nobles—Daniel, Mishael, Hananiah, and Azariah—crowded closer together for comfort as they stood in the midst of the group.

Their heads held high, they ignored the pain of humiliation as best they could and strained to see if they could catch a glimpse of the fabled king of Babylon, whose magnificent palace at the end of the avenue seemed to soar to the sky. The four boys stiffened as the ear-shattering blare of the trumpets mingled with the deafening roar of the assembly.

Emerging from the elaborate carved doors appeared an imposing figure. Resplendent in blue and purple robes, his head encased in a towering, jeweled crown, he raised both fists, the universal sign of triumph.

"Nebuchadnezzar!" Daniel breathed. The roar of the crowd reached its crescendo, then finally died away.

Daniel was mesmerized as he watched the glorious treasure that had been

Solomon's disappear into the palace of a pagan king. Mishael and Hananiah, however, averted their eyes from the despairing scene before them.

Azariah laid his hand on Daniel's shoulder and spoke words of comfort to his devastated friends: "Well, at least we've come to the end of our journey. Tonight they have promised us food, water, and beds to sleep on. But the best part is—we're still alive, and we're together!"

∞

THREE MONTHS LATER

The four boys sat on the parapet of the palace wall, gazing off to the western horizon as the last rays of the sun cast long shadows across the valley. The river curved and undulated through the verdant plain like a shining ribbon of molten gold as it reflected the colorful sunset.

"Sometimes I think I can see it," sighed Mishael. "If I squint my eyes just so, I can see the turrets and spires of the temple, the Damascus gate in the wall, and the hills where we used to run and play."

"Yes, I know," said Azariah gravely. "But for Hananiah and me, the memories of Jerusalem are not so happy. It all seems like a terrible dream now, but I wake up sweating in the night sometimes, remembering…remembering…the screams, the terror, the separation from our parents. That was the worst," he continued, eyes closed and breathing hard, "to be alone in that crowd of people, all trampling each other trying to escape the enemy. My little sister held on to my hand, and somehow we found our way down into an aqueduct. We hid there for hours until some soldiers found us."

Hananiah nodded in mute agreement. He had not been able to speak of his experience since his reunion with his friends three months before, upon their arrival at Babylon. Outwardly he seemed the same cheerful, quiet, thoughtful boy they had always known, but inside he carried a deep and unapproachable sorrow. His friends closed ranks around him, forming a solid, silent phalanx of support, and their faithful comradeship was proving to be the very best medicine. By unspoken agreement, they had arranged to meet every evening on the roof of the palace outbuilding that served as a center of higher learning, originally established by one of Nebuchadnezzar's predecessors as a means of educating the royal family.

Upon their arrival in Babylon, the four Hebrew youths, exhausted and bewildered, had been taken immediately into the royal enclosure, fitted with new clothing, given new names, and plunged into the strange and alien customs of their captors. Education was considered of paramount importance in Babylon. It was not enough just to record a military victory and subjugate an entire nation. The victory could never be complete until the last vestiges of that nation's uniqueness had been completely eradicated and its people had totally assimilated into the new culture.

It was especially important that their leaders not be allowed to retain the old ways. Nebuchadnezzar knew full well the value of selecting only the very cream of the crop, the youngest and the best, to mold and reform their malleable young minds in his own image. These, he reasoned, would be the Judas goats who would eventually lead their people into a submissive acceptance of Babylonian culture.

Now, on the rooftop, their youthful countenances illuminated by the soft golden glow of the setting sun, the four Hebrew children were remembering their vow of faithfulness to Jehovah.

"We must never forget," said Daniel softly, "that He brought us here. We cannot allow ourselves to become bitter or angry as so many others have. He brought us here for a purpose, and He will keep us if we trust Him. The real danger is not that we might lose our lives, but that by compromising we might lose our integrity, and therefore lose our uniqueness as a nation belonging to the one true God. That is our very identity, our inheritance."

For a few minutes, no one spoke as they watched the glowing luminescence of the clouds fade into the lavender-blue of the evening. A huge pale apricot moon hung like a sentinel's lantern in the eastern sky, and Mishael spoke longingly. "How many times have we watched that same friendly face in the sky when we spent the night in our tree house on the hill? Remember how the night sounds used to frighten you, Daniel?"

"Me? Never!" laughed Daniel. "Well, maybe just a little, especially when we heard the wolves howling on nights when the moon was full. I never ran away, though, Mishael…not like someone else I know!"

"Yes, but I came back! I guess it was better to be scared together than to be scared alone." Mishael smiled at his friends, and they rose to go back to their quarters, descending the cool stone steps to the labyrinth of rooms below the great library.

———— ⌘ ————

Ashpenaz looked up from his accounting tablets. His eyes were smarting from the drifting smoke of the flickering oil lamps, and he was wearied from the day's work. Painstakingly accurate in every detail, the tablets recorded each item of treasure, where it had come from, and where it would repose in the temple of Baal at Babylon.

Nebuchadnezzar had chosen his chief of the eunuchs well: Ashpenaz had served him faithfully when his father, Nabopolassar, was ruler of Babylon. Now Ashpenaz had been entrusted with the most important burdens of royal concern to his master. One of his many assignments was to supervise the education of a group of young nobles recently brought from Jerusalem. Not only was he responsible for their education, but also the establishment of their general health and well-being, both mental and physical, came under his considerable jurisdiction.

To their surprise, the young men found their new schoolmaster a quietly authoritative, compassionate, and understanding father figure. Having himself experienced the great loss of his virility and manhood, he truly sympathized with the crushed and brokenhearted boys who had been so cruelly torn from all they held dear. With no children of his own, Ashpenaz's unfulfilled longings for a family found some measure of fulfillment in mentoring his young charges.

Ashpenaz stood, turned, and stretched, running his fingers wearily through an abundant mane of slightly graying hair. He had planned to retire early tonight, but the king's business had occupied the entire evening.

He turned back abruptly as the curtain over the door parted, and a servant entered, bowing respectfully. "Sir, there is a young gentleman from the Hebrew scholars who is asking to see you. I told him to go away, but he said it was important."

Ashpenaz was faintly irritated but replied without condescension, "What is his name?"

"Daniel, sir. He is waiting in the outer hall for your answer."

"Daniel, eh? I have been wanting to speak with this young man, so by all means, send him in." His mood brightened considerably as he returned to his chair, and, as Daniel entered, he motioned for him to be seated.

"Well, young man," Ashpenaz beamed, "what can I do for you? How is it that our star pupil is out and about at this late hour?"

He regarded his young charge affectionately, and Daniel's somewhat anxious countenance relaxed visibly as he sat down.

"Sir, I was afraid you might be angry, I mean…well, the hour is late, and I shouldn't be disturbing you. However," he rushed on, "I need to ask you something about the food."

"The food?" echoed Ashpenaz, obviously puzzled. "Is there something wrong with the food? You know, young man" he continued somewhat severely, "all the food you eat—every luxurious morsel—comes from the king's very own table and is carefully prepared by his own personal cooks and bakers. No expense is spared in providing you and your friends the very richest and most desirable food in the entire kingdom, possibly the entire world. Are you saying that you do not care for our food? Such an affront to the king's generosity could prove disastrous!"

Daniel's face fell as he listened to the chief eunuch, but he responded gamely. "Oh, sir, please understand: the food you provide for us is wonderful, varied, and abundant beyond imagining. What I am trying so poorly to say is that, while we are so grateful for the king's generosity, our poor bodies are used to more simple fare. Our God has given us certain foods that are listed in our Book of the Law as unclean. We have determined in our hearts not to defile ourselves by eating them. My friends and I would like to propose a trial period of only ten days: during that time we will eat only vegetables and water. At the end of ten days, we will allow you to decide which is best for us by comparing our appearance with that of the others who eat from the king's table."

Ashpenaz was privately horrified, but he gave no indication of his misgivings as he arose and paced the floor. Finally he spoke. "I must secure the king's permission to launch this strange project, but I promise you one thing, young Daniel." He smiled affectionately at the young captive and laid his hand reassuringly on Daniel's head. "I will do everything in my power to try to convince the king that this is a good and beneficial thing. Fair enough?"

"Fair enough, sir. May Jehovah repay you a thousandfold for your kindness." Daniel bowed low in respect as he backed out of the room.

Hurrying through the darkened quarters, he returned to his bed, where he knelt to give thanks. "And Lord, You know how I miss my own father; thank You for providing one for me here in this place."

SEAL UP THE VISION

The ten days passed quickly, and the four young friends were brought before Ashpenaz. He could hardly believe his eyes as he regarded their grinning faces and circled them several times before he could bring himself to speak.

"Remarkable. No, it's truly astounding. Now, tell me—what have you fellows been eating? Some kind of miracle food you brought from your country?"

"No, sir," replied Mishael. "The food we ate is grown right here in your own gardens and available in all your markets."

Ashpenaz was intrigued but remained expectantly silent as Azariah resumed the explanation.

"You see, sir, we were raised on a diet of mostly vegetables: beans, lentils, carrots, cabbages, leeks, onions, and peppers. There was an abundance of fresh and dried fruit: figs and raisins, kumquats, pears, dates, and wild blackberries we found down by the creek beds. Sometimes we found honey in an old hollow tree, but it was saved for special occasions."

"We had lamb on special holy days," chimed in Hananiah, "but except for the chickens and salted and dried fish we bought from the markets in Jerusalem, we seldom ate meat."

It was Daniel's turn to speak. "At first, when we came here and ate the king's food, it was like a fantasy come true. I ate all the baklava I could find, plus those little almond cakes, the poached trout in butter sauce and the date-filled pastries...but after the first month we began to notice a difference. Fatigue and a strange, sickening lassitude began to rob us of our natural energy. It became an effort just to climb the stairs to our classroom. I had no appetite and just picked at my meals. For no reason, I would go to sleep during the day and awaken depressed. We finally realized what the cause was and what we had to do to reverse it."

Ashpenaz was truly amazed at their wisdom and even more at their dedicated, disciplined response. *The king would do well to pay attention to their counsel,* he thought grimly. *He has been looking peaked and more than a little haggard as of late. I need to talk with him soon.*

They remained with the chief eunuch for a while longer, laughing and talking animatedly, then were ushered out.

"No more of that rich garbage: only the good stuff from now on, right?" called Ashpenaz as they disappeared into the courtyard.

He shook his head, still smiling, as he returned to the pile of clay tablets on his work table. Trying to return to his monotonous task was proving difficult, however, and he finally abandoned it. He walked out in the garden, taking in great, deep breaths of the fresh, cool autumn air. Suddenly, he felt an urge to run, to be free from the cares of his palace duties.

Glancing around to see if anyone was looking, he gathered up his tunic and, securing it in his belt, sprinted along the shaded path that led to the outer gate. Once free of the restraints of the walled garden, he ran. Through the pastures, past a stand of ancient terebinth oaks, out into a vast sloping meadow leading down to the river, he ran. His lungs bursting from the long unaccustomed exercise, he stood panting by the river's edge, watching the whirls and eddies as the crystal clear water flowed over the ancient, time-worn stones. Dropping to one knee, he drank, and when his thirst was satisfied, he sat back on his heels.

Ashpenaz had often found solace from his loneliness in the quiet after a rainstorm by walking in the vast hanging gardens at night or by climbing up to the lookout tower at sunrise. But he never, never came to the river. That brought painful memories, which all at once came flowing back as he sat quietly by the rippling water. The old familiar pain began to invade the long-concealed, well-camouflaged depths of his tortured soul.

Ashpenaz had long ago said the final good-bye to his lost love here at the river. She was even lovelier in the protected recesses of his memory than she ever could have been in the light of reality. Her dark eyes swimming with unshed tears, she had looked up to him longingly as he pulled her to him in one desperate, last embrace.

They had been so young, those two, and full of plans for the future, when Ashpenaz was taken from his family and placed in the service of King Nabopolassar, Nebuchadnezzar's father. She had received no word of him for many long months and had finally learned the worst: he had, at the tender age of seventeen, been castrated and placed in servitude as a eunuch.

The shame and humiliation had nearly killed him; only the memory of his beloved bride-to-be had kept him from killing himself. Desperate to see her, and yet consumed with shame and helpless rage at his condition, Ashpenaz had lived that first miserable year in a numbing whirlpool of indecision.

Finally, one night he had gotten word to her to meet him at the river. There had been moments of pure agony as he waited in the shadows.

Would she come, or would she despise him for being only half of a man? His heart had stuck in his throat as he heard her footsteps, and the moon had emerged from the clouds as she ran to him.

Breathlessly, they had clung to each other and cried, as they whispered their undying love. But they could spend only a few moments together; he had to leave before his absence was discovered.

"Good-bye, my love," she had whispered, and then the light of his life was gone. Stricken dumb with misery, he had returned to the palace. Ashpenaz never saw her again.

Now, nearly forty years had passed, and the bittersweet memory was as crystal clear as the water he had just tasted.

"Oh, my sweet Lilah," he groaned as he absently picked up a pebble to throw. He threw several more, then rose to his full height and threw several larger rocks as far as he could across the river. Finally, his anger spent, he walked slowly back to the palace. Curiously enough, he felt some measure of peaceful well-being that night; he resolved to go back to the river each day until his own private ghost was exorcized.

Several days later, he was again by the river's edge, enjoying the clear day and breathing deeply of the scented breeze from the hanging gardens. He bent down to pick up some pebbles and noticed a small package wrapped in red silk, weighted down by a large river stone. He unrolled the length of silk with growing wonder as he began to recognize a faintly familiar fragrance of jasmine flowers. A small brown parchment was rolled inside a tiny gold ring set with a topaz stone.

He stared at the ring and, feeling faint, sat down abruptly on a large rock. He rested his head back against a tree, eyes tightly shut, until his equilibrium returned. As he opened his eyes, a movement on the far side of the river caught his eye. Slowly, deliberately, a woman stepped out from among the trees to stand at the river's edge. She stopped, perfectly still, and watched him from behind her veil.

"No...it cannot be! Lilah?" he whispered incredulously, then remembered the parchment. With trembling fingers, he unrolled it and began to read:

> Ashpenaz, my love—
> My brother told me you have been seen down by the river. He is writing this for me. I am married and have four children and

six grandchildren. My husband is a kind man and is good to me.

Oh, my Ashpenaz, please know that I have never ceased loving you. I will always love you until the day I die.

Your Lilah

Stunned, he stood and looked across the water, filling his eyes with her form. Then as suddenly as she had come, she was gone. He knew it was for the last time.

Something rushed in to fill the aching, empty void of his poor, unloved heart, and in that exquisite moment—healing came to Ashpenaz. Instinctively, he raised his hands toward heaven and gave exuberant thanks to an unseen, unknown God.

CHAPTER 5

THE FLIGHT

THE TRAFFIC IN the Holland Tunnel was bumper to bumper. As Randy's ancient Toyota inched along toward the airport, Jack glanced anxiously at his watch in the illumination of the dashboard lights.

"Don't worry," grinned Randy, who had been noting Jack's growing apprehension. "Once we get to JFK, we should have plenty of time before the last flight to London. I think the traffic is unusually heavy because of the hurricane warnings: everyone wants to leave town!"

Matt leaned forward in the back seat. "Dad, I didn't know hurricanes ever got this far north."

"The weather patterns are changing drastically, son. I'd sure hate to see a category five hurricane hit the Big Apple, though. New York City wasn't built to withstand 200 mph winds."

As they emerged from the tunnel, Randy switched on the windshield wipers full speed, but the rain was coming in massive horizontal sheets as the wind picked up. Even Randy began to look a bit worried as he peered through the streams of water on the windshield.

Just as he was about to pull off the road, a large diesel truck hauling an oversized trailer pulled in front of Randy, and suddenly he could see; that is, he could see the taillights of the truck just ahead. Nothing else was visible, so he quietly made a decision to follow the truck.

Somehow, he was not surprised when, after a series of twists and turns, he saw several airport limos draw alongside and pass them. "We're headed the right way!" he exclaimed triumphantly. Immediately, however, he regretted his outburst when he glimpsed the surprised faces of his passengers, who obviously were unaware of their predicament.

Sarah leaned forward anxiously. "Are we nearly there? I can't see much of anything but a blur of lights through the rain. I was wondering, too, if planes can actually take off in weather like this."

Jack reached back for his daughter's hand. "There's only one way to find out, Toots. We may have to stick around for a while, but we'll make it out of here, I'm sure." *Wish I could believe that one myself,* he thought grimly as he watched the airport signs bending dangerously in the howling wind.

Randy's deep voice was quietly reassuring. "Yes, you will, and I'm believing for a quiet, uneventful flight once you leave. You may think this is a lousy time to travel—now, Matt, you were thinking that very thing, weren't you?"

Matt grinned self-consciously.

"However, much prayer and planning has paved the way for you to leave at the absolutely most perfect time. Think about it: the authorities are going to be up to their collective necks in crisis after crisis on a night like this. The computers will probably go on overload as last-minute passengers try to buy tickets, but all you have to do is hand your boarding pass to the flight attendant and walk on board.

"One thing I know for sure: God is never taken by surprise, son," he said, glancing back at Matt. "He always makes provision ahead of time for His people. All we have to do is follow meekly along behind Him. Those know-it-all eager beavers who are constantly running on ahead of Him, insisting on their own way, are the ones who get in such deep trouble."

Matt digested this timely bit of advice while he gazed at the rivulets of water streaming along his window. *I'm sure going to miss him,* he thought. *It's been so much fun playing one-on-one basketball with him and Dad and Dan this past week.*

He glanced over at his sister and felt a rush of protective affection for her as he realized that she was having to leave much more behind than he was: Dan had given her his solemn promise that he would do everything in his power to join them in Israel, hopefully some time in the next year.

Sarah was smiling as she absently fingered the small gold locket around her throat. Dan had given it to her on their last night together, explaining that it had belonged to his grandmother, and since it carried a tiny picture of the two of them inside, they really would not be apart.

Randy's car continued to follow the big diesel's taillights through the airport until it finally rolled to a stop—right in front of the British Airways terminal. Ten minutes later, the little group was huddled together in a corner of the terminal, shaking out their rain-soaked clothing in a vain attempt to get dry.

"I have a hair dryer in my overnight bag." Sarah pulled out what appeared to be a large shocking pink blowtorch and plugged it into the wall.

"If only the guys could see me now," laughed Matt as his sister riffled through his wet hair with a large purple comb.

"How much longer before our flight, Dad?" she asked over her shoulder.

"I don't know; Randy, can you see that display screen under 'Departures'?"

Randy wiped his glasses, walked out into the milling crowd, and in a few minutes returned, slightly out of breath.

"Good heavens, Jack, they're leaving early. Gate 37—you'll just make it if you hurry!"

Sarah paled and slapped the dryer back in her case. "Oh, Dad… Matt…this is it!" She led the way, running down the concourse. As they reached the entry ramp, she turned to give Randy a quick hug. As the men shook hands, Randy handed Jack a parcel.

"Care package from Paula," he said with a broad grin. "There's a note inside—it'll explain."

"Thanks for everything. You've been great!" said Matt, and disappeared after Sarah. Jack hesitated for only a moment, then said in a voice husky with emotion, "How can I ever thank you? We'll never forget you and Paula."

"God bless you," said Randy warmly. He watched his new friend board the plane.

"Last call for Global Airlines Flight 270 for London," the loudspeaker blared as Randy stood by the giant bank of windows, his head bowed in silent prayer for the travelers.

Across the concourse, the voice of a truck driver could be heard over the noise of the crowd as he leaned against the wall of the phone booth, gesticulating wildly with both hands as he shouted into the phone cradled against his shoulder: "I tell you, I don't know how I got to the airport. Yes,

I know I'm overdue, but…No, I'm draggin' this great big oversize load, y'know, and somehow I got stuck in the wrong lane…Oh, just forget it!" He slammed down the phone in frustration.

"Just ain't my day," he muttered as he stalked away.

The Watchers behind him smiled and quietly moved through the crowd. "I believe we have escort duty on Flight 270 for London. Shall we go?"

Jack stood in the balcony of their hotel room in Geneva and surveyed the breathtaking view. The cool, clear, brisk air was a tonic to his fatigued body, and he decided impulsively to spend a couple of extra days here.

"Ruth, come here and look at this magnificent view," he called. She stopped unpacking and stood beside him, slipping her hand under his arm.

"What a lovely city, Jack. Couldn't we stay just a little longer? It seems a shame to leave just as we got here."

"Great minds, same channels," he chuckled affectionately, looking down at her gleaming blonde hair.

It had been a unanimous decision to scrap their original plan of splitting up and traveling separately. "It's all of us together or not at all," Ruth had insisted on their last transatlantic phone call, and the others agreed, greatly relieved. Their arrival at Heathrow in London had been relatively uneventful; as planned, Ruth had met them there, and they had flown immediately to Geneva.

"Tomorrow, I'll take care of business at the bank, then we'll go sightseeing," Jack promised. Later that evening, they returned to their hotel suite after dinner; Ruth went to soak in the tub, while Jack removed his jacket and tie, flopped down on the bed, and flipped on the TV. There was an English-speaking news broadcast on the station he was watching; he lay back, relaxed, and listened. Almost immediately, he sat bolt upright, turning up the volume.

"And that is the latest on Hurricane Judith, a massive category five storm that has brought about the worst devastation in history on the East Coast, particularly to New York City, Newark, New Jersey, and Providence, Rhode Island. More on this later. Now, on a lighter note, William Serrano, an official in the State Department, has been arrested and charged with aiding and abetting a fugitive."

Seal up the Vision

The announcer paused and glanced off-camera with a slightly suppressed smile. "We say 'a' fugitive. Actually, it was a few more. Mr. Serrano was involved for several years, it has been alleged, in a massive plot to help smuggle nearly twenty thousand Jews out of the country. So far, no names have yet been revealed. The director of Mr. Serrano's agency was quoted as saying: 'Hey, we don't have any problems with Jews leaving the country. We just don't want them taking their nice, fat bank accounts with them.'"

Jack stared, incredulous, as the announcer went on.

"An effort is being made to secure all the necessary records. U.N. officials raided Mr. Serrano's office today; they found nothing but several large trash bags full of shredded paper. Mr. Serrano is being held without bail and could not be reached for comment."

At that moment, the phone rang. Switching off the TV, Jack picked up the phone and listened, his face grave with concern. He spoke briefly with the caller, then slowly replaced the receiver, sitting immobile in the darkness for a long time. Finally Ruth walked in, towel-drying her hair.

"Sarah and Matt should be back soon," she murmured, "and I want to hear their reaction to Geneva night life."

Jack sat on the edge of the bed and reached in his jacket pocket for a cigarette before he remembered. "Well, old habits die hard, don't they? I haven't smoked in over a year."

His wife stared at him. "What's wrong, Jack?"

"We may be in for some trouble." He related the news story and then the subsequent phone call from a Swiss banker who had warned them that Interpol had picked up their trail. "We need to close out our account in the morning and leave Geneva immediately."

Ruth came and sat down beside Jack. Surprisingly, she showed no reaction, but only smiled reassuringly.

"Let's just look at it this way, honey. We've been two or three steps ahead of them all the way. They didn't stop us there, and they won't stop us here."

She stood and stretched luxuriously. "I'm getting in the tub for a nice, long hot soak. Call me when they get in." And she disappeared into the mysterious steamy depths of the bathroom.

"What a woman!" Jack shook his head with an admiring grin for the wife he adored.

—∞∞∞—

"Herr Mannheim, would you follow me please?" The strident, clipped voice echoed through the ornate marble walls of the vast bank lobby. Jack rose and followed the pale, bespectacled, nattily dressed clerk down the hall and into a plush, paneled elevator.

Nazi type, Jack thought grimly. *I wonder what rank he holds in the firing squad.* The tight-lipped official hardly glanced at him as they traversed another marble hallway and entered a grey-carpeted office.

"You will wait here, please," he hissed, and disappeared into his inner sanctum. After what seemed like an interminable wait, the apparition once again made an appearance, standing stiffly at attention beside the door.

"You may now enter," he sneered. Jack surreptitiously wiped his sweaty palms on the velvet chair seat, rose, and, as he passed his guide, barely suppressed the urge to click his heels and salute. "Nice threads, Fred," he muttered and, receiving no reply, closed the door behind him. An elegant, silver-haired man seated in a large leather chair rose and came around the desk to shake his hand.

"Herr Mannheim, it is a great pleasure to meet you. I am Karl Morgenthal," he said with a great deal of warmth. "Won't you be seated, please?" He gestured toward another soft grey leather chair, and Jack felt the tension drain away as he sank into its soft depths. The frail old man offered him a cigar, which Jack politely declined, and then leaned back and surveyed his visitor curiously.

"I'll come right to the point, Jack—may I call you Jack?"

"Certainly."

"Well, I'm sure you're wondering about the delay in retrieving the money from your account. Be assured, there will be no problems. I asked to see you for a reason: have you by any chance been watching the news from your country?"

Jack swallowed hard. "Mr. Morgenthal, as I told you last night, we only arrived yesterday, but—yes. Late last night we did. Why do you ask?"

"I think it would be better if I just explain from the beginning. In the first place, if you have not guessed, I am Jewish, as I know you also are, Jack." There was a tense silence; Jack watched the bank officer warily.

"Your friend, Serrano, has been in touch with me through contacts in London and Brussels. He informed me of your plans and asked for my help. For the last several years he has helped thousands of Jews funnel their funds to Israel via Swiss accounts, therefore enabling many families to immigrate to Israel. The process has been accelerated recently and had been going quite well until a member of our organization made an innocent little slip of the tongue at a diplomatic cocktail party."

"As you know, Mr. Serrano is being detained by the authorities, but a plan is already set in motion to get him out of the country."

Jack, surprised, shifted in his chair. "How can that be possible? He's being held without bail in a federal prison. And another thing: how do you know they're not unraveling your whole organization? Is it possible that you could be next?"

Mr. Morgenthal leaned back and shrugged eloquently. *Very continental,* thought Jack, wryly.

"Jack, I can't guarantee anyone's safety; these are uncertain days, especially for Jews. But I will tell you one thing: those of us who went through the Holocaust once will never, never sit back and allow it to happen again." Slowly, deliberately, he rolled up his sleeve and held out his arm with the faintly inscribed numbers tattooed above the wrist.

"Bergen-Belsen." His deep, richly modulated voice was shaking. "All my family except one little boy—me—died at Dachau. A neighbor hid me, along with some other orphaned children, for nearly three years when we were finally discovered. She, even though she was not Jewish, was sent to Auschwitz, and all of us orphans sent to Bergen-Belsen, then to Theresienstadt in Czechoslovakia. How we survived that last year is best forgotten," he concluded wearily, as he buttoned his shirt sleeve.

"Now," he resumed somewhat briskly. "We have reason to believe you and your family are in danger. The authorities have already made inquiries about several dozen Jewish families who are missing. They have distributed your pictures to Interpol and are carefully watching the airports. Frankly, we are quite puzzled that you were able to escape detection in New York and again in London."

Jack smiled and shook his head. "I'll never know the answer to that, sir. Actually, I think if you had not warned us, we would have walked into a trap right here. My wife and I had decided last night to stay several days sightseeing in Geneva."

Mr. Morgenthal was silently assessing his visitor. *He seems fairly perceptive,* he thought, *but perhaps a bit naive when it comes to playing dangerous international games.*

"I think you may have already guessed that the bank employee stationed outside my door is an informer. But, please, do not worry yourself about that. He is small potatoes, and I have many powerful friends. Now," he added, taking some documents from a file in the drawer, "we will proceed to the vault and withdraw your funds."

Jack followed him meekly down the hall and through a labyrinth of corridors. The Nazi stooge was nowhere in sight; still he could not keep from glancing nervously over his shoulder from time to time.

He waited in the alcove, and soon Mr. Morgenthal reappeared, carrying a small black leather briefcase. "You will need cash to travel," he explained flatly. "It will give you anonymity. With that in mind, you might as well spare no expense; use it all—if you know what I mean." He peered at his guest significantly, waiting for a reply.

"Are you telling me that I might find myself in a position of having to bribe some officials somewhere along this journey?"

"Exactly," beamed his approving benefactor. "In this briefcase is $800,000 in U.S. dollars, Swiss francs, German marks, and several other currencies. The remainder of your account has been transferred electronically to the Nations Bank in Jerusalem. You will need to sign some papers, which I have with me."

After Jack signed the documents, they entered a small, windowless room, and Mr. Morgenthal carefully closed and locked the door.

"This is completely private and soundproof. It is where our customers open their safety deposit boxes. I need to give you some advice: leave as quickly and as quietly as you can; take your family out as if you are on a holiday, sightseeing, shopping, whatever, until you are sure you are not being followed. Just to be on the safe side, I will have a friend who is an experienced operative in our organization follow discreetly. Then you must go to the railway station and purchase tickets for Rome. However, you will not be going to Rome."

He pulled an envelope from his inside jacket pocket and handed it to Jack, who looked extremely puzzled.

"You will be going to Marseille, a very busy seaport in the south of France, where you will board a tramp steamer bound for Haifa. All your directions are inside the envelope. The reason for all this cloak-and-dagger business must be obvious to you by now," he concluded.

"You're telling me that it's not safe to fly, and they'll be watching the airports, therefore travel by rail or ship is the safer alternative, right?"

"Precisely. There is not enough manpower to cover every possible avenue of travel, so they will concentrate on the most likely. Any more questions?"

Jack glanced at his watch, picked up the briefcase, and rose to his feet, extending his hand. "We're greatly indebted to you, Mr. Morgenthal. If you are ever in Israel, look us up."

The two men shook hands, and, as he watched Jack walk out through the massive carved oak doors into the sunshine, Karl Morgenthal breathed a prayer: *Next year, in Jerusalem . . .*

The Buena Suerte was riding low in the water of the Marseille harbor. Her cargo hatches were loaded to capacity, so during the early hours of the night watch, an indeterminate amount of money was slipped to the captain, and several very large crates were hauled aboard and lashed to the deck.

The crew was already stirring, and the officers were finishing their coffee when the passengers began to trickle on board. A pea-souper of an early morning fog cast a surreal aura over the wharf. As Matt led the way up the creaking gangplank, he remarked, "This is awesome, you guys, just like *Casablanca*. Remember that old Bergman/Bogart film?"

Somewhat subdued by the eerie atmosphere, Matt was not aware of the muffled footsteps approaching them until the captain suddenly appeared out of the swirling fog, along with a short, stocky man in a navy pea-coat and seaman's cap.

"I'm Captain Montoya; I understand you folks are traveling as far as Haifa, along with about thirty other passengers. We will be making some stops in ports along the way to deliver cargo, so you're welcome to go ashore or stay aboard, whichever you wish. We should arrive at Haifa in four days. Carlo here will show you to your quarters and answer any questions."

He tipped his hat to the ladies and disappeared into the mist. Their guide led them up the steps and down through narrow corridors to their room.

"I know it ain't much," he laughed good-naturedly, "but, it'll be home for the next few days. The meals on board this ship will more than make up for the tight accommodations. Breakfast will be served in the ship's dinning room at exactly 0800. That'll give you time to unpack. Any questions? No? Then I'll see you at breakfast." And he also disappeared into the dingy depths of the ship's interior.

The Mannheim family of Huntington Heights, U.S.A., surveyed their "room" with some measure of dismay, for it was really nothing more than a small cubicle with a narrow passage between two sets of bunk beds. There was barely room under the lower bunks to store their suitcases, and Sarah noted the tiny bathroom forlornly.

"At least it does have a shower, although I wonder if we'll be allowed any hot water," she mourned.

"Lighten up, sis," called Matt as he vaulted into the top bunk. "This is an adventure we can tell our grandchildren someday!"

Jack and Ruth set about putting away their things, and soon it was time for breakfast. The dining room was already filling up with the other passengers, and in a few minutes the captain entered with his officers. When everyone was seated, Jack said under his breath, "I am beginning to wonder just how many of these people are in the same predicament that we are."

"You know, I had not even thought of that possibility, I've been so preoccupied with my own worries," replied Ruth. "Of course, the captain did tell us there were others going to Haifa." Lowering her voice, she continued. "Jack, do you think maybe the captain is part of the 'organization' that Mr. Morgenthal was referring to?"

"I don't think we're meant to know that, and in fact, the less we do know, the better it is for everyone all around. You know—'ask no questions, I'll tell you no lies.'" He smiled reassuringly, and just then the food arrived. And what food it was! Matt gasped in delight as the serving trays full of fresh fruit, Belgian waffles, French pastries, omelets, and aromatic platters of bacon and sausage were brought before them.

"I haven't seen food like this for—a long, long time," groaned Jack, as he helped himself liberally. "You know," he whispered, "this pretty much confirms what I've begun to suspect—this ship is dealing in black market goods. Where else could anyone find delicacies like this these days? Certainly not in any supermarket, right, Ruth?"

She nodded her head mutely, and the conversation came to an abrupt halt as everyone devoted themselves to the business at hand.

After breakfast, Sarah sought some privacy in her bunk as she curled up to write a long letter to Dan. Jack and Ruth sauntered up on deck and walked along the rail, savoring the brisk sea air. Matt decided to jog along the afterdeck to work off some of the Belgian waffles he had consumed.

Slaloming in and out of the many wooden crates lashed to the deck, he turned a corner and nearly collided with a burly seaman who was repairing a hawser.

"Hey there," he growled, "aren't you a little far from your territory?"

"Sorry," grinned Matt apologetically. "I didn't know this was off limits to passengers."

"Just passed a sign posted back there, about fifty feet behind you," he mumbled, returning to his task. "This area could be dangerous in high seas if one of these crates comes loose," he explained, a little less ungraciously.

"Well, thanks for the warning," and Matt turned back the way he had come. As he passed between two crates, he looked back. The seaman was not in sight, and he needed to satisfy his curiosity, so he ducked into a gap between the boxes. Pulling a small flashlight from his jacket pocket, he directed a beam of light between the wooden slats of the crate.

"Uzis!" he muttered in surprise. All automatic weapons had been banned in an international treaty agreement signed two years ago in a futile effort to stem the alarming rise in terrorist and criminal activities. To be caught manufacturing, transporting, selling, or owning one was a capital offense.

Matt was suddenly very uneasy, wanting at that moment nothing more than to escape the area undetected. As he started to ease out of his narrow crevice, however, he heard voices and froze. There was nowhere to go: no room to crouch down and no time to exit without being seen. Backing silently into the shadows, he flattened himself against the tiny alcove and waited, hardly daring to breathe.

I can't believe I was so stupid, he thought grimly. *If they catch me, they'll probably throw me overboard after they slit my throat.*

He stiffened as he heard the footsteps approach; the voices now louder, more distinct, seemed inches away as they volleyed back and forth in an angry, excitable, and rapid exchange of unintelligible gibberish.

Wish I had paid more attention in Spanish class, Matt thought despairingly. *Maybe I could figure out what kind of fate they're cooking up for me. O God, don't let them look this way!*

Just then he recognized the distinctive guttural voice of the captain as he and several others were approaching. Pandemonium broke loose, with several voices talking at once: then a sharp, staccato blast on a boat whistle was followed by a short silence, and the sound of running feet faded into the distance.

Matt stayed immobile a few minutes longer, then cautiously peered around the corner. The deck was now deserted. Like a flash, he fled the upper deck to the living quarters below, where he closed and locked the door. Panting from exertion and fright, he quickly changed, showered, and dressed in khaki shorts and polo shirt, then quietly closed the door as he left so not to awaken his sleeping sister.

Once more he climbed the steep metal stairs to the deck, where he strolled casually to a deck chair. Picking up a dog-eared *Rolling Stones* magazine, he pretended to read while observing the commotion on the foredeck.

Apparently the boat whistle he had heard belonged to a large glistening white patrol boat that had drawn alongside the *Buena Suerte.* A swarthy official in a spotlessly creased white uniform was shouting into a megaphone across the water; the captain shouted back, and one of the seamen standing on the gunwale tossed a package out into the air, which landed with a dull thud on the deck of the patrol boat. After inspecting its contents, the official flashed a brilliant toothy smile, then barked some orders to his men. The powerful engines roared to life, and they moved off, leaving a curving white wake behind them.

Most of the passengers were on the port side or down below, and the few who were relaxing on the starboard deck appeared oblivious to the activities of the crew. Matt concluded that this was a clear-cut case of bribery, something he had never actually seen but which was becoming increasingly common in the dog-eat-dog world eco-system.

Well, can you beat that—right out in front of God and everybody! Wonder where I am on the food chain? he philosophized darkly. *Shark food, I guess, if they had found me.* He shivered in spite of the warmth of the Mediterranean sun, which by midmorning had driven away the last vestiges of the earlier fog.

Seal up the Vision

Matt leaned back, closed his eyes, and, shading his face with the outdated magazine, began to drift off, when his reverie was interrupted.

"Is anyone sitting here?" a softly accented feminine voice inquired.

He slowly pulled down the magazine and squinted up into the sun. Shading his eyes with one hand, his blurred vision focused into reality, and he stifled a gasp as he sat up abruptly, nearly upsetting his chair.

There she was, the goddess of his dreams. *I knew I'd find you some day,* he thought, as he gazed heavenward at the object of his adoration. *This is one of those rare moments that will stand out for the rest of my natural life in an eternal freeze frame of bliss,* he decided dramatically as he slowly rose to his feet.

The girl was indeed extraordinarily beautiful. Her pale complexion was shaded by a large straw hat pulled down over a luxuriant wealth of blue-back hair. She was nearly as tall as Matt, slender and delicate, and wearing something pink and flowing, but it was her luminous blue eyes that held him mesmerized.

Stricken dumb with awe, he desperately tried to regain control of his senses, and finally managed to find his tongue. "Sure. I mean, uh, no. No, that is, the seat isn't taken."

The girl regarded him with a quixotic mixture of amusement and apprehension as she gingerly lowered herself onto the chair. Crossing her ankles delicately, she waited for a long moment, then suggested gently, "Perhaps you would like to sit down, too?"

Obeying meekly, the captain of the debate team was unable to formulate anything resembling intelligible speech, so he remained silent. The girl spoke first.

"My parents told me that we—your family and mine—are traveling to the same destination. My name is Heather," and she leaned forward with a dazzling smile to hold out her hand in greeting. "We are from England—a little town near Coventry called Linwood."

He shook her hand and replied, "My name is Matt, and we've come from America. We lived in a small suburb near Philadelphia. I guess your family, like ours, must have been through a lot to leave everything behind and move to a strange country. Was it hard to say good-bye to all your friends?"

She sighed wistfully, "Oh, I suppose it could have been much worse. Linwood is a very small village, and my parents and grandparents were born there. Most of the young people had fled to the larger cities, but I loved the peace and quiet of the country. I wonder sometimes if we'll ever see it again." Her long, dark lashes shadowed her cheeks as she gazed pensively out over the rippling water.

Matt nodded mutely, feeling a lump in his throat as he remembered the last letters he had written, the good-byes that could never be said, the last look at his boyhood home as they drove away.

"I think there's a song that says something about a chapter in our life is through," he sighed, "but…we're starting a new life, and there's a kind of excitement in not knowing what's ahead just around the corner."

The two continued their conversation uninterrupted until the steward rang the brass bell announcing the noon meal.

Both families sat at the same table; introductions were accomplished and the food consumed. Almost immediately afterward, Matt and Heather excused themselves to go up on deck.

Later, Sarah and her parents stretched out on their bunks to while away the afternoon hours by reading books taken from the small but amazingly well-stocked ship's library. For normally active people, it could be a long four days cooped up within the cramped confines of a tramp steamer.

An interesting family, Jack was thinking. *I'd like to get better acquainted— we ought to have plenty of opportunity on this voyage.*

Ruth was already immersed in her novel—a Gothic romance somewhere in the wild moors of Scotland.

Sarah was propped up on one elbow, wondering idly if Matt had finally fallen in love. *Yup, he's smitten!* she thought with a certain amount of smug satisfaction. *After all my thwarted attempts at matchmaking for my brother, Snow White shows up on board, and he's dead meat! Poor guy, he'll never know what hit him. She'll reel him in ever so gently, and he'll spend the rest of his life bragging about how he pursued and won the hand of the Unattainable Princess. Well, more power to him—may he live happily ever after!*

CHAPTER 6

THE DREAM

THE CHRONICLES OF NEBUCHADNEZZAR

In the seventh year, the month of Kislev, the King of Babylon encamped against the city of Judah. On the second day of the month of Adar, he seized the city. King Jehoiachin and ten thousand scribes, soldiers, artisans, prophets, priests and nobles were bound in fetters and brought to Babylon. Zedekiah, the uncle of Jehoiachin, was left to rule Judah as vassal king to Babylon.

In the sixteenth year, King Zedekiah rebelled, entering into an alliance with Psammetichus, pharaoh of Egypt. Once again the king of Babylon encamped against Jerusalem. The walls could not be breached all during the winter, so when the Egyptian army came up against the Chaldeans from the south, Nebuchadnezzar withdrew and fought them. With Egypt defeated, the pharaoh dead, the siege of Jerusalem resumed until the defenders were fatally weakened by the plague and famine. The king of Judah was captured near Jericho and given the punishment prescribed by the vassal treaty: his children were slaughtered before him, and he was blinded and led in chains to Babylon, where he died.

On the ninth day of the month of Abu, General Nebuzaradan removed the temple treasures and carried out the orders of the king of Babylon. Jerusalem was put to torch, the city walls were torn down, the surrounding towns were destroyed, and all but the very poorest of the peasants were carried away into captivity.

⎯⎯⎯⎯⎯⎯

Nebuchadnezzar brought all of the gold and silver from the temple of Jehovah into the temple of Baal in Babylon. The humiliation of defeat was further underscored for the grieving Hebrew nation by the latest undercurrent of information that was sweeping their clandestine gatherings like a tidal wave: the sacred ark of the covenant—which had for centuries been the holiest of all holy artifacts—was missing! For those few captives who had been most severely traumatized, this was the final blow, and they gradually lapsed into an embittered despair and eventually were completely swallowed up by the alien culture.

Most of the Jews in captivity, however, did not completely lose hope. Their desolation led them to close ranks against the inroads of the pagan civilization surrounding them, and they settled together in compacted groups. Some lived in the city of Babylon; some moved further away to settle on the Chebar, a canal leading from the Euphrates River, not far from Ur—the ancestral home of their nation's original patriarch, Abraham.

It was a curious anomaly that the victorious king of Babylon, once having completely conquered the nation of Judah and having secured the loyalty of their nobility, now allowed the captives to roam about freely. They were able to settle their homes and establish businesses wherever they wished.

Most importantly, however, those who had been meeting together secretly were now granted open access to their gatherings, which were very crucial to the retention and maintenance of their unique national heritage. They were finally allowed the heady freedom their fettered souls so craved: the freedom to suffer in silence together; to rejoice at a wedding or a new birth—together; or, more characteristically, to plunge into heated discussions and arguments—together.

In these gatherings, large and small, their homeland was kept alive in their collective memories as they shared their rich and colorful heritage, unique among all the nations, with each other and the children of the next generation. When a father passed his name on to his son, he also passed along a wealth accumulated by a long and unbroken ancestry: the never-ending fascination of the stories of long-dead heroes who had left the legacy of an undying faith in the God of Abraham, Isaac, Jacob, and Moses.

Seal up the Vision

The unbroken thread of this faith had continued through the most harrowing of circumstances—wars, famines, plagues, invasions, slavery—and now was being woven into the lives of these captives. As they sat around their evening hearth fires, they spoke aloud, reciting the old familiar stories of King David and of Solomon, who had built the magnificent temple, yet died an old, embittered man who had sold his birthright for a few thousand heathen wives.

They knew that their God could not be confined to temple enclosures of stone, no matter how magnificent. He had led them in their wanderings through strange desert lands long ago. He would not forsake them now, even in this alien, faraway place.

———⊗⊗⊗———

True to His nature, God did indeed raise up voices by the rivers of Babylon: the voice of the prophet was a continual reminder of the closeness, the faithfulness, and the forgiveness of their "El Gibbor"— the Mighty One.

Among the captives by the river Chebar dwelled a young man, called by his God to be a "watchman" to the house of Israel. He had been taken captive in his twenty-fifth year, and at the age of thirty, on the fifth day of the fourth month, Ezekiel's eyes were opened, and he saw the glory of God and the restoration of Israel.

Six years before the final destruction of Jerusalem, the prophetic warnings came. Over and over, the destruction of the Holy City was graphically illustrated to those Jews living in Babylon. However, along with the severe warnings of disaster came the clear promise of restoration and rebuilding. These prophecies came time and time again, always holding forth hope to combat despair.

At the very time of Jerusalem's total destruction, the Word of the Lord came to young Ezekiel in a most peculiar way:

> Your beautiful young bride, Sarah—the desire of your eyes—will succumb to an aneurysm of the brain this very day. Her sudden, tragic death will leave you, Ezekiel, numb and prostrate with grief, but you must not cry or grieve for her. This is to be as a sign to your people: their temple in Jerusalem—the desire of their eyes—will be taken and reduced to a heap of rubble.

The fulfillment of this prophecy came all too suddenly, and the people were—as the Lord had said—indeed far too stunned to perform the traditional acts of mourning. Truly, the fear of the Lord was evident upon the entire exiled nation.

The prophetic voice of Habakkuk was read from the scrolls, written nearly one hundred years before, in hushed and reverent awe by the priests:

> Behold ye among the heathen, and regard…for lo, I raise up the Chaldeans, that swift and terrible nation, which shall march through the breadth of your land, to possess the dwelling places that are not theirs. Their horsemen shall come from afar, fierce and dreadful; violent and relentless as the east wind, they shall gather up the captivity as the sand. They shall scoff at kings and scorn the princes. The stronghold shall fall as they build ramps, lay siege, and take it. Their king shall pass over the land, imputing his power to his pagan god!

So, slowly and surely, understanding of the ancient scrolls came to the enlightened readers. Even more incredible, two hundred years before, when Babylon had been just an insignificant third-rate power, the prophet Isaiah had been given foreknowledge by the Spirit of the Lord: the Jews would some day be returned from captivity to their homeland, the mighty, impregnable fortress of Babylon would fall to the Medes and eventually be given into the hands of a Persian king named Cyrus!

When the ancient scrolls of Isaiah were painstakingly copied by the scribes and read in the gatherings, people would shake their heads in wonder. No one could conceive of the far distant, relatively powerless group of tribes called the "Medes" overpowering mighty Babylon, the undisputed queen of earthly empires!

For the first three years of their captivity, Daniel and his friends were living in the palace in unaccustomed luxury as they were given an intensive education in the Chaldean language, literature, history, and culture. Under the tutelage of the great Ashpenaz himself, who had decided to personally take on the care of these four, they learned at a greatly accelerated rate those things that would be invaluable in their future service to the king.

However, something else was taking place as this new friendship progressed and deepened: Ashpenaz was learning much more from these four young Hebrews. There had been many times when, their daily studies finished, Daniel would take out the precious manuscripts given to them by a dying scribe along their long, arduous journey to Babylon. Because the poor man had no family, he exacted from the boys a promise to carefully guard the fragile treasure with their very lives.

Since Ashpenaz could not read the Hebrew characters, each one of the boys would patiently read to him portions of the manuscripts. In this way, over a period of time, he gradually came to know the source of their amazing strength—the God of Abraham, Isaac, and Jacob. He even took some of the more melodious psalms and had his court musicians set them to music. He often found solace from listening to the unfamiliar words and phrases.

So it came to pass that Ashpenaz called for the musicians to play the Hebrew psalms one night when the king of Babylon could not sleep. Nebuchadnezzar had seemed troubled of late, and Ashpenaz, always sensitive to even the slightest change in his master's moods, approached him one evening as he was walking on the terrace.

"Your Majesty, what is troubling you?" he inquired solicitously. Ashpenaz had been in charge of the king's affairs for many years—indeed, he had watched him grow from a chubby little toddler, through his boyhood years, and into a young man. He was inordinately fond of his master, although not unaware of his faults, not the least of which was his prodigious temper, vented in terrible fury on whomever had the misfortune to be anywhere near him at the time.

The young king was pacing the paving stones of the wisteria-shaded terrace, his brow furrowed in anxiety. "Ashpenaz, they have returned—the night terrors," he replied, his voice husky with emotion. "Last night, I was seized with a terrible agony of fear, and…there was a dream."

He stopped pacing and looked out at Ashpenaz under lowered brows. "I know that the dream was sent to me from the gods. This morning when I awoke, I immediately called for the court scribe to record its every detail, but when the scribe entered my chamber, all my memory of the dream had fled. I have been trying all day to recall the details, but Ashpenaz, I cannot."

Nebuchadnezzar looked out through the soft evening haze to the immense towers silhouetted against the southern horizon. "What are our priests, our temples, and our gods for, if they cannot resolve a problem such as this? I am the king of all earthly empires, and they exist to serve me."

His voice deepened in anger. "Have all the astrologers, the wise men, the scholars, the sorcerers, and the magicians be brought before me tomorrow. They will tell me the dream and its interpretation, and this matter will be put to rest."

He dismissed Ashpenaz with a wave of his hand, but as his faithful official was departing, he called out, "Send me your musicians—I would like to sleep tonight undisturbed by any dreams. And," he added softly, "Ashpenaz, send for the queen. I have need of her compliant warmth tonight."

Ashpenaz turned away with a smile. His steps echoed down the long stone corridor of the palace, and, descending the series of elaborate mosaic steps, he emerged into the darkness of a moonless night. Pausing to gaze upward to the starry heavens, he was suddenly enveloped in a wordless longing, and a deep sense of his aloneness pierced him through to the heart.

He stood there quietly for a little longer, then sighed deeply and whispered, "I, like you, O King, am loved…if only from afar."

———∞———

Twenty-four hours later, Arioch, the captain of the king's guard, hurried through the darkening corridors of the palace and rapped insistently on Ashpenaz's door. The servant who answered it was brushed aside as Arioch muttered harshly, "I need to see your master; be quick about it, man!"

When Ashpenaz appeared, the old soldier beamed with pleasure, grasping his hand in affectionate greeting. "It is good to see you again, my old friend. I wish we had time to sit and talk as we used to, but I have brought urgent news."

Ashpenaz called for some wine, and the servant who brought it retreated, bowing as the two men walked out to the garden beyond the range of listening ears. "The king called me to his chamber not an hour ago, with an order to execute all the wise men in the kingdom," explained Arioch as they reached the outer perimeter of the garden.

Ashpenaz groaned, paled visibly, and sat down unsteadily on a stone bench. Arioch tipped his head back and emptied his silver goblet.

"This is work for a butcher in the marketplace, not an old soldier like me. This means that all of the young scholars you have been teaching will be condemned. I don't mind telling you that I have grown quite fond of the four young Hebrews who climb up to the top of the palace wall every night. My sentinels tell me they are unfailingly kind and courteous, not like the arrogant young bucks that run loose in our city. It would be a shame to execute such fine young men."

Ashpenaz groaned again, "But why? What could have angered him to this extreme degree? I know the king better than any living person and have seen him very angry, even furious, but never condemning anyone to death without reason."

Arioch poured himself another goblet full of wine. "There was a gathering this morning in the great throne room. The king met with all his astrologers and prognosticators and wanted them to tell him what he had dreamed last night. No one could tell him, so he flew into a rage and ordered them out.

"His anger is now uncontrollable; they say he is breaking anything that can be broken. One of the servants brought him a tray of food since he had not eaten all day. He threw the tray, food and all, against the wall, knocking down a torch, which set the bedclothes on fire. He picked up the poor servant and bodily threw him out, screaming for someone to saddle his horse.

"The last we heard, he was riding like a madman through the streets of Babylon and out through the gate along the outer wall. I sent some of my men to follow him at a distance. I need your wise counsel, my friend. I cannot go through with this demented plan."

"Come," said Ashpenaz resolutely, as he rose and strode rapidly back to his house. "We must act quickly. Nebuchadnezzar is often subject to fits of anger, but he always returns to normality and will listen to reason if he is approached properly. My advice to you, my friend, is to do nothing tonight. I will handle the matter."

Arioch drained his goblet a second time and departed. Ashpenaz sent for Daniel immediately. When his young charge appeared, he was given a short summary of the situation.

"Arioch is a good man," said Daniel thoughtfully. "So the wise men could not tell the king the dream or its interpretation? That is not surprising; their source of knowledge is indeed supernatural, but necessarily limited, since it comes from the spirits of darkness. They do not know the true and living God. My friends and I will fast and pray, and our God will give us the answer."

Ashpenaz stared at his young friend, astounded. *Such amazing confidence,* he thought, *and that in the face of certain death if he fails.*

That night, the four young friends spent the evening in fasting and prayer, seeking earnestly the wisdom and discernment of the Spirit of the living God. Sometime in the early hours before dawn, Daniel fell into a deep sleep, and the answer came: the dream and its full meaning were revealed to him in its entirety during the night vision.

As the sky began to lighten with the first pink glow of dawn, Daniel awoke, curiously refreshed in spite of such a small amount of sleep. The events of the dream were vividly impressed on his mind, and he joyfully awoke his sleeping friends with the good news of God's intervention.

The four raced to the quarters of Ashpenaz, who was already awake and pacing the floor, his anxiety evident as the servants brought the boys before him. They bowed respectfully to their schoolmaster, then broke out into an excited explanation of the eventful night.

As everyone was talking at once, Ashpenaz held up his hand and asked, "I just want to know one thing, Daniel. Are you absolutely sure this dream came from your God?"

"Yes, sir," he replied, smiling broadly, "and I am ready this very moment for Arioch to take me before the king."

Ashpenaz rang for his servants to inform Arioch of their impending arrival, as Daniel and his friends bathed and dressed carefully in preparation for their appearance before Nebuchadnezzar.

When the king of Babylon had been informed that Arioch had found among the captives of Judah a man who would make his dream known to him, he demanded to have him brought before him immediately. He summoned the court, and a hastily assembled entourage followed the king in solemn procession as he mounted the steps to his magnificent throne.

Flanked by the famous golden lions and arrayed in his royal garments, he was an intimidating, threatening figure as his cloudy visage regarded the clear-eyed young Hebrew who now stood so quietly before him. Apparently, his rampage during the previous day had not assuaged his black mood, and Arioch felt pangs of dismay as he bowed low. *Young Daniel, this had better be good,* he thought as he gave the boy a sidelong glance and backed away.

"Your Majesty, this is the young Hebrew. He wishes to speak with you concerning the dream."

There was a tense silence, then Nebuchadnezzar held out his royal scepter and motioned Daniel to come closer. Daniel approached the throne and bowed low and waited.

Finally, the king leaned forward and spoke imperiously: "Are you able, young man, to make known to me the dream and its proper interpretation?"

Daniel's answer rang clearly throughout the whole room.

> O King, may you live forever, Your astrologers, sorcerers, and magicians could not discern this secret, but let it be known to you, O King, that there is a God in heaven that reveals secrets, and has chosen to make known to the King Nebuchadnezzar the events that are to occur in the last days.
>
> As for me, this secret is not revealed because I possess any greater wisdom and intelligence than anyone else, but for the sake of all the wise men in your kingdom, and for the sake of the king to know that God rules the affairs of nations and would give you understanding of the thoughts of your heart. This is the dream:
>
> In the visions of the night, you saw a great image, both bright and terrible, whose head was gold, his breast and arms of silver, his belly and thighs of brass, his legs of iron, and his feet of mixed iron and clay. Then, O King, you saw a great and massive stone which was cut without hands. This stone was cast at the feet of the image, and broke it in pieces. Then the rest of the image was shattered completely, becoming as the dust or chaff carried away by the wind. Then the stone became a great mountain and filled the whole earth.
>
> Now, this is the interpretation: God has given over to you a kingdom of great power and glory, rulership over the greater part of the earth. You, O King, are the head of gold. After you shall arise an inferior kingdom—the silver. Then another kingdom of brass shall rule the earth. After this will come the kingdom of

iron: a strong kingdom that will bruise and break those nations it rules. Then the last and final empire, the ten toes of mixed iron and clay, is the final empire ruled by ten kings divided from one another, as iron does not mix with clay.

Then, the God of Heaven, in the days of those ten kings, shall set up a kingdom that shall never be destroyed; it shall break into pieces and consume all these kingdoms, and it shall stand forever!

The great God has made known to the king what shall come to pass hereafter; the dream is certain, and the interpretation sure."

There was a stunned silence in Nebuchadnezzar's court. Arioch hardly dared to breathe, as all eyes were fixed on the king. Slowly, he arose, and the noise of his scepter echoed sharply through the hall as it fell, unheeded, from his fingers. They watched, gasping in shocked amazement as their ruler deliberately removed his crown and lowered himself prostrate in front of the young Hebrew, his head touching the cool marble.

Then rising, he took Daniel's hand and, standing beside him, spoke resoundingly. "Young Daniel, your God is a God of all gods, and Lord of kings, and a revealer of secrets. I hereby issue this royal decree, that sacrifices and oblations of sweet incense be offered to you in honor of your God!"

The king then called the scribes and ordered that it be recorded that on this day Daniel, called Belteshazzar, be given the position of highest authority in his kingdom, second only to the king.

In the weeks and months following this crucial event, Daniel found himself in unbelievably luxurious surroundings. He was given a large villa that was next to the river and included servants, a vast garden, stables, and—in an exuberant burst of royal generosity—several of the king's own harem girls.

It was with some difficulty that Daniel was able to gracefully decline the latter gift. He finally persuaded the somewhat astonished Nebuchadnezzar that the great God would not look kindly on Daniel breaking his vow of unmarried chastity. "When I am ready, O King," he explained gently to his sovereign, "God will give me a wife from among my own people, just as my ancestor Abraham sent his servant on a long journey back here to his own people in Ur to find a bride for his son Isaac."

Nebuchadnezzar was intrigued and wanted to hear more of the story, so Daniel spent the greater part of an afternoon recounting the history of his people. The king possessed a keen and inquisitive intelligence; furthermore, he exhibited a surprisingly genuine interest in learning all he could about the colorful and complicated nation of Semites he had conquered. The concept of monotheism was somewhat novel to him, so he and his newfound friend spent many long hours together.

Nebuchadnezzar also gained the unique advantage of seeing the invasion and defeat of a nation through the eyes of one on the losing side who had lost everything. When he heard the story of Daniel's desperate nighttime ride on Regina, and how he had lost the horse, he immediately took him to the royal stables and magnanimously gave him choice of any animal he wished.

Chaldean horses were bred to be the strongest and swiftest in the world, and in the royal stables were the most magnificent animals Daniel had ever seen. The king's eyes glittered with pleasure as he watched his young friend slowly move between the graceful stone arches of the stable corridors, stopping now and then to stroke a soft, flowing mane.

After a time he slowed, then stopped in front of a stall. From behind the ornately carved gate came a friendly whicker as the exquisite Arabian tossed her well-formed head and trotted forward to nudge the newcomer, gently probing for her accustomed treat. Daniel stroked her velvety nose, laughing at her antics as he turned to the king and declared, "This surely must be a replica of my father's mare, Regina. Look—she even seems to know me!"

"Done!" said the king, and he ordered that a special saddle with full regalia be made for Daniel. As they departed for the palace, Daniel did not neglect to give silent thanks to his God for yet another restoration of that which he had considered forever lost.

As their friendship deepened, Daniel could see that there were many things that troubled the king, not the least of which was the very administration of his kingdom. In any court (of any kingdom), jealousy, flattery, and insincerity—all these things hindered rather than helped the efficiency and orderliness essential to the successful rulership of vast territories.

In addition, Nebuchadnezzar was constantly plagued by the vicissi-tudes of the semi-rebellious vassal kings who ruled distant territories and felt the insulating barrier of distance gave them license to form their own alliances and foment rebellion. In short, the pot was always simmering and occasionally foamed over the edge in full boil.

When the time was right, Daniel approached the king, and exercising true God-given wisdom, suggested that his three friends, Mishael, Aza-riah, and Hananiah, be put in charge of governing the provincial affairs of Chaldea, freeing the king to deal with his far-flung territories. Ash-penaz had already been singing the praises of these three young Hebrews, so Nebuchadnezzar readily consented, considering the advice of his two most trusted friends to be unquestionably above reproach.

So it came to pass that the four most powerful men in all the kingdom, except for the king himself, were Hebrew captives: the lowest members of Babylonian society by worldly standards, but extremely valuable in the eyes of the great God who had so carefully placed them in key positions and would use them to change the course of human history according to His sovereign will.

CHAPTER 7

THE VOYAGE

T HE *BUENA SUERTE* had been docked in a small harbor on the Turkish coast by the charming seaside town of Kusadasi since early morning. A small amount of cargo was off-loaded, and the passengers were given a few hours to explore the area. The Mannheims had no sooner set foot on terra firma than an ancient, battered Chevy came roaring around a corner and screeched to a stop.

"You want a taxi? I got taxi; take you anywhere!" grinned the young driver, who could not have been more than seventeen. He glowed with proprietary pride as he patted the hood of his vehicle, painted an impossibly brilliant shade of turquoise.

"My name is Mehmet, and I drive real good," he nodded vigorously, dazzling them with his prowess. Heather, who had accepted Matt's invitation to join the family, and Sarah tried unsuccessfully to stifle a fit of giggles. Jack looked at Ruth, and they both spoke at once, "Why not?" They then found themselves whisked away on a whirlwind tour of the many colorful, aromatic shops of Kusadasi.

Matt found a beautiful leather motorcycle jacket, and Sarah some lovely jewelry. Ruth purchased a good supply of rare spices for her gourmet pantry, and Jack could not resist the carpets. Heather bought some baklava and treated them all to the strong Turkish coffee and sweet pastries at an outdoor cafe.

They began to suspect that Mehmet had an "arrangement" with all of the shopkeepers—who were, coincidentally, also members of Mehmet's family. He always showed a keen interest in how much his passengers were spending and seemed quite pleased with their purchases.

After lunch, they decided to visit the ancient city of Ephesus. It was only a few miles away, so, following a hair-raising taxi ride, they found themselves transported into history. The ruins of Ephesus, where once a thriving city had flourished and gradually died, were truly awesome. Having participated in several important "digs" during his college years, Jack was something of an amateur archeologist, and he was able to accurately describe each area as they walked along.

"The Temple of Artemis, for which the city was famous, has vanished," he said. "Only a fragmented pillar now stands here as a silent sentinel over this large pit, which is filled with water."

"Goodness," Ruth murmured in awe. "And to think this was once one of the seven wonders of the ancient world."

The family passed the harbor baths with their colonnaded atrium, the commercial agora (market place) bordered by a row of richly ornamented columns, gasping in wonder at the carved stone facade of the great library of Celsus. They climbed the hill to the great amphitheater with a capacity to seat twenty-five thousand people.

But the relic of greatest interest to Matt was the main street, the broad thoroughfare of the city that once had led down to the harbor (now filled in with silt to a distance of several miles). The marble paving stones of the street still had the ruts left from thousands of chariot wheels, and underneath the street was a very efficient sewer system.

Much of the city remained covered by the centuries of silt deposits, and as they drove away, Jack was thinking how exciting it must be to discover, layer by layer, the evidence of a lost civilization. *There's a lot in the Bible about this city,* he thought. *I need to read up on it when we get back to the ship.*

The amazing electric blue Chevy pulled up at the dock entrance. The perpetually grinning Mehmet was paid handsomely, and lugging their purchases, the travelers once again boarded the ship. Jack had haggled for a good price on a thick Turkish carpet, so he remained ashore, making arrangements for two of Mehmet's innumerable cousins to carry it on board.

When everything was settled, he decided to use his last hour before departure by making some necessary long distance calls, since it would be cheaper and more private than the ship-to-shore phone. He talked for nearly thirty minutes and, completing his business satisfactorily, headed back toward the dock.

Walking slowly and admiring the panorama of the setting sun over the water, he was totally unaware of the two uniformed men waiting in the shadowed doorway. They took him completely by surprise as they stepped out suddenly, blocking his way. "You will come with us!" ordered the short, stocky one. "We have orders to take you to the police station."

"Hey, hold on," shouted Jack, as they swiftly clapped on handcuffs and nearly dragged him into the doorway. "I'm an American citizen—you can't treat me this way!"

Ignoring his heated protests, they propelled him forward into a semi-darkened, shuttered room where the only perceptible movement was the slow rotation of a ceiling fan overhead. Jack's eyes were dark with anger as he glared at the rather pompous, florid-faced official seated in front of him.

The man said nothing but lifted an eyebrow in contempt as he quite deliberately reached into a drawer and pulled out a greasy, dog-eared newspaper. It was neatly folded and underlined in red ink, and he shoved the top page across the desk toward Jack, who by this time was thoroughly alarmed. Glancing down, he saw his own name under the bold heading, "MANNHEIM SOUGHT FOR QUESTIONING."

Trying to maintain an icy composure, he growled, "Get these handcuffs off me—NOW!" With a curt nod from the official, the two henchmen complied. Remembering his many chess games with his uncle Al and the sage advice, "Son, the best defense is a good offense," Jack now seized the initiative. Rubbing his wrists and ignoring the newspaper, he leaned over the desk until his face was only inches away from the grinning Turk.

"Whatever you have in mind, you had better be very, very careful what you say and what you do. I have certain, ah…friends, who, shall we say, may take violent exception to your foolishness," he breathed menacingly. The Turk, as Jack had hoped, paled considerably at the mention of Jack's "friends" and the grin faded.

With a final attempt at bravado, the official stood and thrust an accusing finger at Jack, shouting shrilly, "You were under surveillance by U.N. authorities when you left United States—I read English real good," he continued triumphantly, "and I could get big reward for turning you in!"

Jack surveyed his antagonist, coolly and correctly assessing him as all bluster. He impaled the Turk with an unblinking, unyielding glare. Finally, with perhaps some trepidation regarding Jack's "friends," the little man's eyes shifted downward, darting nervously from side to side as he sought to regain control.

Better not push it, Jack thought. He pulled out a wad of bills and placed it on the desk. "I have no time to haggle with you—my boat is leaving—but I warn you: we know where you can be found." He turned on his heel and strode angrily from the room. Without a backward look, he forced himself to walk, not run, to the dock where the rest of his family was anxiously awaiting him.

Ruth ran down the ramp, crying, "Oh, Jack, where have you been? We were so worried! The ship was due to leave ten minutes ago, but we begged the captain to wait just a little longer." She chattered nervously as they walked arm in arm up the ramp.

Later in the privacy of their room, Jack's brief explanation did little to assuage Ruth's apprehension. Matt and Sarah were full of questions, but their mother was strangely quiet. Realizing the full import of Jack's brush with a greedy bureaucrat caused her to wonder just how many others they would encounter before the journey would be over.

As if reading her mind, Jack hugged her close, whispering in her ear, "Don't fret, honey—and don't let any frown lines mar that perfect peaches and cream complexion you've been spending thousands of my hard-earned dollars to maintain!"

Ruth gave her husband "that look," and Matt and Sarah beat a hasty retreat, locking the door behind them. The danger already forgotten, they went on deck and stood at the rail. Watching the small island fortress guarding the mouth of Kusadasi harbor slip away into the distance behind them, both Matt and Sarah were suddenly aware of their uncertain status as fugitives.

The ship's wake left a soft pink glow in the dark blue water as the last glowing clouds faded into the western horizon. They were steaming south toward Haifa and, barring any unpleasant surprises, should arrive the following evening at their destination.

"I wonder where we'll live," murmured Sarah dreamily, as she watched the first few stars appear overhead. "We haven't really talked very much about it."

"You know," remarked her brother, "I wonder how those survivors of the Nazi holocaust felt as those boats arrived in Palestine after the war. Did you know that it was illegal for at least the first two postwar years for

Jews to immigrate to Palestine? So many boatloads were turned away."

He shook his head in angry disbelief at the gross injustice. "After all they had endured, that must have been the worst blow of all—to be within sight of home and have to go back. The ships were overcrowded and poorly provisioned, so some of the weaker ones didn't make it."

"I know," agreed Sarah soberly. "It must have been a horrible disappointment. But in 1948, three years after the war, Israel officially became a nation. Would you believe that the very same day—May 14—they were declared an independent nation, the Arab countries invaded Israel?"

She laughed at Matt's obvious astonishment. "Don't be so surprised, little brother; I read up on all this stuff before we came. The encyclopedia program in my computer was a great source of information. The tiny newborn infant nation of Israel, no bigger than the state of New Jersey, repelled those Arab attacks and has never been defeated since. Kind of makes you wonder, doesn't it?"

She glanced at her brother, then resumed. "Thousands of years of neglect had turned much of Israel's soil into wasteland. Long before the State of Israel was established, Zionist pioneers began to reclaim this wasteland. They drained swamps, sank wells, planted forests—and the Israeli government continued the work of reclaiming the land. I seriously doubt if there has ever been a nation in all of history that has worked with such tireless drive and energy to build a modern industrial nation on the ruins of the past—as have our people."

"Our people," echoed Matt, and they fell silent as they each contemplated the new life ahead.

With all the resilient buoyancy of youth, they visualized the journey into a new land as a fresh beginning, an adventure filled with all sorts of possibilities—all successful, of course. These young, hopeful hearts were not yet afflicted with the fearful anxieties that plagued their more experienced elders.

Sarah planned to apply for med school at Jerusalem's prestigious University Hospital. She carried with her several glowing letters of recommendation from her professors at Brandeis in Boston. She also held on to the hope that somehow her Dan could eventually relocate there also, since Israel would always have need of hydroelectric engineers. He had taken her to see one of the massive projects on which he was working, and Sarah's feminine admiration for him grew by leaps and bounds as she observed the high regard in which he was held by his co-workers.

Matt's aspirations for the future were simple: to join the Israeli Air Force and to marry Heather, in that order. He had already obtained his pilot's license after logging the requisite hours of flying time in his father's Cessna. The love of flying was in his blood, and he was never happier than when he was at the controls of an airplane.

Both he and Sarah were blithely unaware of the menacing forces in the cosmic storm of events even now gathering strength to clash in unprecedented fury over their world. To the very young, these gloomy clouds seem far removed from all their hopes and dreams. For the very young, the future is almost always bright.

The Buena Suerte churned relentlessly through the dark waters of the Mediterranean, on course for the port of Haifa. Most of the passengers and crew were asleep in their bunks; the night watch drank their coffee and talked in low murmurs as they planned their itinerary.

The steady throbbing of the diesel engines far below had long since lulled Jack's family to sleep. But he was wide awake. Rummaging through his suitcase for a book to read, he came across a parcel wrapped in brown paper.

"Well, well—if it isn't Randy and Paula's package," he whispered in surprise. "I never really took time to open it." He reached inside, pulling out a box. Lifting the lid, he found several interesting items: three tins of homemade "turtles," peanut brittle, and fudge (which he sampled immediately); a small flashlight with an extra supply of batteries; a couple of paperback books; a map of Israel; two thick envelopes; a black Bible; and a matching concordance.

Jack whistled softly and sat back on his heels; a big grin spread slowly over his face. *Well, well, well—Randy, old buddy, you submarined me, didn't you. Torpedoed right in the midsection,* he thought, inwardly delighted at the thoughtful provision of his scheming friend. Hefting the Bible in one hand and the concordance in the other, the flashlight under his arm, Jack settled into his bunk for a good night's reading, not knowing that out there, somewhere—the angels were laughing.

CHAPTER 8

ENCOUNTERS

IN THE AFTERMATH of the king's dream and Daniel's inspired interpretation, three very significant encounters occurred in quick succession.

After the evening meal, Daniel was walking down by the river when a servant came running down the path with an urgent message. Bowing breathlessly, he explained, "Oh, Your Excellency—pardon this rude interruption, but a most important visitor is here to see you."

"Well, Ahmahl, who is it?" inquired Daniel, amused by the servant's servilitude. He had been raised in a household that had servants, but nothing could have prepared him for the abject humility of these who regarded him with something approaching idol worship.

"Sir, the Rab Mag, Chief of the Magi and Royal Physicians, is even now at the gate, and has requested an audience with Your Excellency."

"Well, show him in, and tell him I'll be there presently," Daniel answered, dismissing the servant. *It would not bode well for me to be too eager for this interview,* he thought as he leaned out over the railing. *Nergal-Sharezer is probably the most influential man in the kingdom. He has seemed unsympathetic toward the Hebrew captives and our worship of the one true God. I wonder what he wants.*

Turning back toward the house, Daniel strode up the path and entered the great hall with its opulent furniture and elegant draperies. His visitor turned to meet him and, to Daniel's utter surprise, bowed low in obeisance, touching his forehead to the floor in the classic Oriental token of submission.

"Please rise, Nergal-Sharezer! You are most welcome in my home," said Daniel cordially, extending a hand to his somewhat elderly caller.

The chief of the magi, Daniel soon discovered, was making a heroic effort to offer his humble apology for the treatment of Daniel and his entire nation. As the two men talked, the older one recounted his trip to Jerusalem with several members of the Babylonian court. Repeatedly he asked forgiveness for the atrocities against the people of the Holy City, which he seemed to hold in high esteem.

"Now, Your Excellency," he continued, lowering his head deferentially, "the members of the Brotherhood of the Magi here in Babylon owe our very lives to you. It is a debt of such magnitude that we could never hope to repay. Our lives, and our families also, were very close to extinction by royal decree. We had, quite frankly, sunk into the blackest despair, for we knew that all our magical charms, chants, and fetishes were useless. No mere human being can know the thoughts and dreams of another man's heart. You, sir, are either a god or have been chosen as a voice for the God you serve. Our king recognizes this; we also recognize and submit to this authority, for it is far greater than ours."

Having delivered this considerable speech, the nocturnal visitor regarded Daniel from under his heavy silk turban. His chest was heaving, his breathing shallow and raspy, so Daniel called for some water. The old physician swallowed something called "foxglove," or "digitalis," his erratic breathing abated somewhat, and Daniel finally responded: "Nergal-Sharezer, I have the utmost respect for you and for your brotherhood of wise men. The great God, whom I serve, has created all that your five senses can appropriate, use, and enjoy here on this earth—the sun, moon, stars, earth, sky, wind, fire, rocks, trees, herbs and medicines, man and beast. But there is another sense, a sixth sense, that dwells in every man, woman, and child. He created us, Nergal-Sharezer—you and I—He created us in His own likeness, that we might enjoy His presence and walk in full fellowship with Him, ruling over this earth with wisdom and understanding all His creatures and the vastness of His creation.

"All this was spoiled when Adam and Eve betrayed their Creator's trust in the garden—yes, you have heard the story, too, haven't you? Then, again, the great flood was recorded in your ancient chronicles also— another terrible judgment against sin, specifically, the sin of rebellion against God's authority.

"And so it goes; any man who honestly seeks the true God will find Him, for the evidence of His handiwork is everywhere—all through creation. He is a God who balances His great love with His majestic justice. *He* saved your life, Nergal-Sharezer, not I."

Daniel rang for his servants to bring the ancient Hebrew scrolls, and the two men talked far into the night. The old man seemed particularly interested in the account of Elijah confronting the priests of Baal at Mount Carmel.

"There was a terrible famine in the land," explained Daniel, "because wicked King Ahab had deserted the one true God, Jehovah, and worshiped Baal instead. Elijah, the prophet of Jehovah, challenged 850 priests of Baal to a showdown at the top of Mount Carmel. They were to call on Baal to send down fire from heaven and consume the sacrifice on their altar. Then Elijah would call on his God, Jehovah, to send fire from heaven to consume his sacrifice. This was to be the final test before the Hebrews: only the true God had the power to send supernatural fire.

"All morning long the 850 priests of Baal leaped about, jumping up on the altar, screaming, gashing themselves with knives as they called on the name of their pagan god to send fire. Along about midday, Elijah mocked them saying, 'Call louder; maybe your god is busy thinking, or on a journey, or maybe he is asleep!' They kept up this frantic, desperate begging all afternoon until sunset, when they finally gave up, realizing that there was no fire, nor would there ever be an answer from their god.

"Elijah then repaired the altar of Jehovah, digging a deep trench all around it, into which he poured twelve barrels of water, soaking the sacrificed bull and the wood. He then called upon the name of Jehovah God; immediately, fire fell from heaven and consumed not only the sacrifice and the wood, but also the stones, the dust, and the water in the trench!"

Nergal-Sharezer sat immobile, his features impassive in the flickering lamplight. Finally, he spoke: "In the same manner, my young friend, your God has again proven Himself to be the true God. Our gods are false."

With such a profound simplicity, the old wise man of Babylon made his declaration of faith. He arose, somewhat stiffly, and with great dignity made his departure.

Several days later, Daniel received another visitor. This time it was Sar-Sechim, the Rab Saris, Chief of the Chamberlains, who requested an audience. Sar-Sechim was a very distinguished gentleman, having been in the service of King Nabopolassar and then his son, Nebuchadnezzar, for many years. He also had been selected by the king to travel to Jerusalem in order to oversee the removal of the temple treasures and establish the vassal rulership over Judea.

Daniel's astounding feat of interpreting the king's dream, and its deep spiritual and moral significance, had not been lost on this Babylonian. Generations of his ancestors had worshiped numerous pagan deities. All his life had been circumscribed by idolatry—Baal, Marduk, Ishtar, and many others. Now he was faced with something entirely new, and he desperately wanted to know the truth.

His primary purpose in coming to see the young Hebrew was to ask Daniel's forgiveness for the destruction of his land, but once again the two men sat talking far into the night. Apparently, he was terrified at the prospect of offending the powerful, omniscient God that Daniel served so openly and fearlessly, and he wanted to make amends as soon as possible.

Sar-Sechim's quick intelligence was intrigued by all he heard, his curiosity piqued, and his innate hunger for something real brought him back repeatedly. Over the next few months the two men became quite good friends. Enlightened by the eternal flame of God's Word, Sar-Sechim finally found contentment and a sense of belonging: the greatest of all earthly treasures.

The third visit came three days later, as Daniel was engrossed in his customary prayer time in the early morning hour just before dawn. The servants knew better than to disturb him, so the visitor waited outside in the courtyard, restlessly pacing back and forth over the colorful mosaic of paving stones.

When Daniel was announced, the man came to attention and bowed deeply in respect. His military bearing and the resplendent uniform marked him unmistakably as Nabuzaradan, the captain of the King's Guard.

"Your Excellency," he began in a deep, rich voice, "I have requested this audience with you at a most inopportune time. Please forgive my inexcusable blunder. Your servants informed me that your early morning prayers to your God take precedence over all else!"

Daniel smiled and nodded. "Yes, General Nabuzaradan, this is quite true. But I am delighted to finally meet you, after hearing so many good reports of you from my friends Ashpenaz and Arioch. Please be seated. I would be honored if you would break the night's fast with me."

The general, visibly relieved, accepted the gracious offer of breakfast on the garden terrace. As the servants prepared the food, the two men strolled slowly through the fragrant garden, admiring the artistic display of rare and exotic specimens.

"This is a special pink jasmine found only in India," Daniel explained, "and this bougainvillea spilling over the gatepost is from my native land, Israel."

Nabuzaradan was covertly assessing his host as they talked and soon decided that he would have the luxury of speaking freely to this unassuming young Hebrew.

"Your Excellency—"

"Please," Daniel waved a hand deprecatingly, "call me Daniel. I possess neither your age nor your experience, sir, and so you have my permission to dispense with unnecessary titles."

Humility in one so young? Nebuchadnezzar chose well, thought the general admiringly as they were seated and served the food. Platters of steaming fish and boiled eggs, freshly baked bread, bowls of fruit soaked in honey, and silver flagons of plum wine were soon dispatched by the hungry men.

Nabuzaradan leaned back in his chair. "It is always easier to talk on a full stomach, is that not right, young Daniel?"

"Well, they say an army marches on its stomach, so, general—what brings you to my home at this early hour?"

"I have brought you something from Jerusalem." The general pulled a long, cylindrical leather pouch from his belt and handed it to Daniel. Inside were several parchment scrolls, and in Daniel's haste to unroll it, one fell to the floor. Out of it fell a smaller, sealed scroll. Breaking the seal, he read it eagerly: a letter to the Jews in captivity in Babylon from the prophet Jeremiah.

Daniel gazed at it in surprise. "How did you come by this? Is he still alive? Did you actually meet him?"

"Yes, my young friend—be assured, Jeremiah lives, and he has not been silenced. A group of Judean princes threw him in a dungeon for his wise and fearless counsel to submit to Nebuchadnezzar's terms. At the king's royal command, we treated your prophet with great kindness. I myself offered him the choice of coming to Babylon to be honored by the king or staying in Judea with the poorest remnant of your country. He chose to stay."

"I am not surprised," Daniel murmured, deep in thought. "Did he say anything about his family here in Babylon? I have heard that some of his relatives were taken with the captives."

Nabuzaradan smiled benignly. "I am glad that you asked. Jeremiah requested that I personally deliver these scrolls to you and that they be read before your people. The smaller scroll is to be read to his family members who were deported to the city of Susa in Persia. I will be glad to send a contingent of my best soldiers to escort you, as it is several days' journey east and south of here. There are bandits, my son," he added, noting Daniel's puzzled expression, "who would easily slit your throat for a bag of copper coins."

The general was quiet for a moment, then said, "There is something else I have not told you." He tried unsuccessfully to maintain a stern countenance, then broke into a sly grin as he extracted another bag from his tunic.

Handing it to Daniel, he explained: "Your relatives Saul and Deborah are safe in Jerusalem. Many of the renegade priests were executed, but he was spared. Having urged the leadership to heed Jeremiah's advice, he was thrust out of the temple by Seriah, the chief priest, whom we later executed at Riblah for treason.

"The cowardly vassal king, Zedekiah—the cause of all this destruction—fled from Jerusalem by escaping through the palace garden by night. But our Chaldean horses are swift, as you well know, young Daniel." As his youthful host nodded vigorously in agreement, Nabuzaradan added, "My men caught up with him in the plain of Jericho.

"There, he was given the prescribed punishment for rebelling against our king: his entire family was executed. The very last sight that he will carry to his grave was that of the headless, bloody corpses of his own children lying in the dust. His eyes were put out, and he was taken away in chains to Babylon. The caravan of prisoners should be arriving in a fortnight."

Daniel absorbed all this gruesome information without flinching, but his face paled in horror as he visualized the dreadful fate of the small royal princes.

Nabuzaradan's deep voice trembled ever so slightly as he resumed. "There was no joy in our camp that night. Many of my men have children of their own, but they are soldiers of the king and must follow his orders. After I returned to Jerusalem, your uncle Saul sought me out and gave me this packet of letters from your family."

Then, for the first time, the general shifted uneasily in his chair. "He was very ill, Daniel; I think it was the plague, which, after three years of famine, nearly wiped out the remaining population of Jerusalem.

"He said to tell you that your aunt Deborah is well, and their home is now being used to care for the sick. I was able to tell him of your great promotion, second only to the king, and how your friends have stayed with you. He shouted for joy! His servants carried him on a litter back home and I could hear him singing; in spite of his weakened state, he could sing."

He shook his head and sighed.

Daniel rose and thanked his benefactor profusely for his help. They talked a little longer, and then Nabuzaradan bowed respectfully to the younger man and left. As soon as he was gone, Daniel retired to the cool privacy of his bed chamber to read the letters from his family. They had arrived in Edom and had blended into the colorful, bustling city of Petra. Having had no word of their own son for several years, they were overjoyed to hear the stories, brought by the caravans, of a young Hebrew captive named Daniel in the court of Nebuchadnezzar himself!

Of Mishael's family there had been no word. Azariah's and Hananiah's families had disappeared without a trace during the confusion of the siege of Jerusalem. Whether they had succumbed to starvation or perished from plague or fire—no one knew. Azariah's younger sister, who had come with him to Babylon, was now a favorite of the queen's court, or so Daniel had heard. Men were not allowed in the women's quarters of the palace.

He read and re-read the letters, the tears coursing freely down his cheeks. Finally he put them away, heavyhearted with the knowledge that he would never again see his mother, his sisters, and his father. The injustice of the forced separation, the death and devastation that had ruined his country—all this began to settle over the young Hebrew like a black cloud. His anger expanded like steam in a kettle, until it threatened to explode.

He called for the servants to saddle his horse, and twenty minutes later, he was riding through the harvested fields of grain between the city walls. Regina was running like an arrow shot from a bow, and Daniel urged her on, faster and faster, until both horse and rider were exhausted and slowed to a walk. His anger spent, he leaned back in the saddle and lifted his face to the warmth of the midday sun.

"O God, forgive me," he whispered, "for taking out my anger on this beautiful animal. You, and You alone, have ordered the events of my life. Please, Lord Jehovah, help me to freely forgive those who were only acting as Your instruments of justice."

Dismounting, he wiped the tears and dust from his face and walked alongside his horse for a while until she had cooled off. Then he rode quietly into the city gate and along the shaded paths behind the palace. Deep in thought, he lost track of his surroundings until Regina came to a full stop, and he was nearly unseated.

There, directly in front of him, was a group of young women, laughing and talking animatedly as they gathered armloads of grapes from the arbor overhead. Belatedly, he realized that these were the queen's quarters, and he bowed in humble apology. As he backed away, however, the girls giggled and fled.

The young woman remaining stepped out of the shadows, and Daniel froze, completely immobile, as he gazed at the most beautiful woman he had ever seen. She stood like a lovely statue come to life, dressed in a simple gown of pale blue unadorned by any jewels. She slowly drew a diaphanous veil up over her shoulder, her glorious black hair, and across the lower half of her face.

Only those extraordinary blue eyes could have the power to render a grown man into a speechless idiot, Daniel thought wildly, as he vainly attempted to regain his senses. *This is a pagan princess, a member of Queen Amytis' court. Nebuchadnezzar will disembowel me and feed me to the buzzards if I am found here!*

The eyes behind the veil crinkled with amusement as Daniel mumbled yet another abject apology, clumsily struggling to turn his horse around. Fleeing down the paths, he was nearly beheaded several times by low-growing branches overhead.

Seal up the Vision

When he had finally reached the safety of his stables, Daniel determined in his heart that he would steadfastly resist any more thoughts of the lovely young enchantress. *Remember,* he reminded himself sternly—*both King David and King Solomon had one fatal weakness: women!*

That very day, he resolutely set himself to the task ahead: to make contact with his people in Babylon, in the outlying areas around the River Chebar, and in the far distant provinces of Persia. His avowed purpose was to strengthen and encourage his people by reading to them the scrolls of Jeremiah and letting them know that their God had not abandoned them.

Preparations were made for a journey to Susa, the capital of Persia. The king was traveling through his western territories, so Azariah, Hananiah, and Mishael were left in charge while Daniel was absent.

Thus, the wheels were set in motion that would initiate a chain of events that would change the lives of Daniel and his three friends forever.

The massive temple of Baal stood silhouetted against the drifting moonlit clouds. Late autumn breezes stirred the leaves of the olive trees in the surrounding groves, sending showers of dead leaves spinning and whirling across the dry ground. It was the last night of the seventh month, and the festival of Baal had been poorly attended. Now the temple was completely empty, except for the night watchman who opened a small door in the base of the edifice to admit a shadowy figure. Several more shadows emerged from the olive grove and disappeared into the temple.

Hurrying down the steps to the subterranean level, they entered a large, torch-lit room. Here, the high priest of Baal had summoned twenty-two others: the former Grand Vizier, the high priest of Marduk, the high priestess of Ishtar, and various disenfranchised satraps and princes. They all had one, and only one, common thread binding them together in this bizarre undertaking: their deep and abiding hatred of the three young Hebrews now governing Chaldea.

Grotesque shadows danced against the four walls of the damp, cold vault as the conspirators silently gathered in a circle around the sacrificial fire pit. Their faces seemed to dissolve into a hideous parody of a demonic inferno as they all, by unspoken signal, began calling on the forces of darkness. This, after all, was no time for a pretty show in honor of a hollow, empty, stone figurehead of a god.

Each one present on this night had always known the evil one who was the real power behind the empty facade of idol worship. The priest of Baal uttered the ancient incantations, and the unearthly noise issuing from twenty-three throats rose to a screeching crescendo. The priestess of Ishtar screamed and fell to the floor, writhing like a snake. There was an abrupt silence in the room as all eyes were fastened on the revolting sight. Then, slowly, she rose unsteadily to her feet, and a deep, menacing growl issued from her throat.

"Fall down and worship me!" The voice was distinct and harsh; it sounded like the rumble of a volcano. Everyone immediately dropped to the floor, and for the next twenty minutes, a plan hatched in the darkest recesses of the evil kingdom was revealed to all those present. Each one was given a specific assignment to carry out, and that night the plan was set in motion.

As they silently hurried through the shadowed streets to their homes, the priestess of Ishtar stayed behind to speak further with the priest of Baal. "Our master has given us the means to destroy the three young Hebrews. That will give me great satisfaction, but we should have asked for more."

"What do you mean?" the old priest snarled, narrowing his glittering black eyes to slits. "Are you questioning the wisdom of our master, Beelzebub? You would do well to watch your tongue, woman," he hissed into her startled face, "as there are spies from below who report on us."

She shuddered, looked around the empty room, and lowered her voice: "I only mean to say that I cannot rest until their friend Daniel is also dead and gone from our midst. I hate him, and I hate his God…" She whirled and left the room.

As she passed through the olive grove, the moon suddenly emerged from the clouds, and she was terrified to see a huge hooded and cloaked creature barring her way.

"You will have your wish, priestess of Ishtar—but it will cost you more than you could ever imagine," he growled; then he was gone.

CHAPTER 9

PERIL

"Is THE ROAD to Jerusalem always this crowded?" The bus driver grinned at Sarah as she leaned forward to ask the question, her pretty brows furrowed in anxiety.

"No, this is really heavy traffic, probably because of the bombing at Haifa." His casual reply did nothing to allay her worry, so he continued, "The port authorities are pretty sure it was an extremist Arab group who planted the bomb in a cargo ship from West Africa. The cargo manifest listed, among other things, a huge shipment of exotic wood. My guess is that its destination was Jerusalem: lumber to be used in the rebuilding of the temple, which the Arabs would stop at nothing to oppose."

Jack stifled a gasp as he digested this information. *Rebuild the temple? How on God's green earth could that be accomplished without provoking all-out war with Israel's extremely hostile neighbors?*

Arriving in Haifa early this morning, Jack and Ruth had been out on deck to catch a glimpse of the beautiful curving harbor before sunrise. The *Buena Suerte* had slowed considerably, and they had watched the lovely, reflected lights slide past, shimmering like jewels in the quiet water of the crescent-shaped bay.

Only as they had drawn closer could they see the pall of smoke drifting over the water and what appeared to be a large amount of debris, mostly logs, floating in the middle of a dark, spreading oil slick. They had watched, fascinated, as a dozen little boats had sprayed a layer of foam around the perimeter of the oil.

"So that's how they do it," Jack had murmured in admiration. "The foam instantly solidifies, floating on the surface around the oil, thereby containing it so they can later pump it out and siphon it off, reclaiming the oil and saving the harbor from certain disaster."

"But, Jack," Ruth had inquired, dismayed as the rays of early dawn further illuminated the disturbing scene, "what do you think happened here?"

"I don't know, but whatever it was, the port authorities seem to have it well in hand by now. Let's go down and awaken the kids. The captain said we would be eating breakfast on board, and we'll need the extra nourishment. From all I can see, it's going to be a long day."

Now six hours later, as they rode in air-conditioned comfort toward Jerusalem, Matt leaned back and closed his eyes, trying to envision the new life awaiting them. Having to say good-bye to Heather had proved to him that the depth of feeling for her ran deep, much more than he could have anticipated. Her family was settling in Tel Aviv, so Matt had promised her that he would travel the distance on his motorcycle as often as he could.

"I have my pilot's license, Heather," he had told her firmly. "If Dad and Mom will agree, I want to join the Israeli Air Force as soon as possible. When I go on leave, I'll spend as much time with you as I can—you'll understand, won't you, Heather?"

She had nodded wordlessly, her lovely blue eyes swimming with tears, and he had held her close for a few moments. "This was more than just a shipboard romance for me, Matt," she had whispered softly into his tear-stained shirt. "Much more."

Ruth had smiled ruefully as she had watched her son, and she had breathed a thought that became a silent prayer: *All the world loves a lover, but—heaven, please smile down on these two; the world has become a harsh crucible for love to flourish, and they need all the help they can get.*

An unusual early November snowfall had nearly obliterated the fence, and snow crunched underfoot as Dan Shepherd got out of his car to check the mailbox. He knocked off the icicles and pried it open. Extracting a gloved hand full of mail, he ducked back into the little red Mustang and headed up his driveway.

Dan was a country boy, born and raised in the little town of Dumas in West Texas. Highly intelligent and well educated, he still could not abide the stifling, closed-in sensation of high-rise, big-city life. His parents had moved east when he was fourteen; times had been hard for a West Texas farmer. Prolonged drought had finally exhausted the underground reservoirs formed by ancient melting glaciers. Now that irrigation had become impossible, entire Western states were turning into a vast dust bowl, far eclipsing the disastrous drought of the early 1900s.

Dan's father had taken a job in a steel mill in Pittsburgh so his family could eat. Eventually they had moved out to the country, where he had bought a small thirty-acre spread and opened up a truck parts business. Dan's high school years were the turning point in his life; six feet four inches tall at the age of fifteen, he still had some growing room to go when the high school coach had selected him for the varsity basketball squad.

Randy Endicott was a tough coach, but he had always earned the respect and undying admiration of his young charges. He had always placed character and sportsmanship ahead of performance, and woe to any athlete who slacked off on his studies. More than once, a game had been lost because the star player was sitting on the bench, glumly surveying the floor as he mentally kicked himself for that F on his math paper.

During his junior and senior years, Dan had been co-captain of the team along with his best friend, Alex Kowalski, and together they had led the team to two successive state championships. Dan and Alex both went on to college on basketball scholarships—Alex to Purdue, where he obtained BS in geology, and Dan to Georgia Tech, where he obtained a degree in hydroelectric engineering.

After graduating, the two friends had met back home and decided to form a business. Eventually, they traveled all over the world working on hydroelectric projects in several different countries. Projects often lasted many months, but Dan was always supremely happy to return to his snug little home in the rolling hills of the Pennsylvania countryside. His parents had died five years before in a collision at a train crossing; his sisters had married and moved to the West Coast.

The farm was a quiet refuge away from the stress of the city life he hated, and a neighbor's young teenaged sons tended his crops and took care of his animals when he was out of the country. There was fresh produce through the growing season, so the boys shared the proceeds from the sales, and his freezer was well stocked for the winter months.

Now, the snow had drifted up against the barn, so he had a time pulling the door open. Once inside, he checked the horses. Greeting Dan with a welcoming whinny, the old quarter horse nuzzled his jacket pocket for a sugar cube.

"I'm glad to see you, too, Boomer. It's been a long flight from Japan, and I'm thrashed, so we'll go on a nice long ride tomorrow, OK?" Dan had a long and affectionate relationship with the old cutting horse since he had, at the age of twelve, broken the young colt to the saddle in his father's West Texas corral.

Trudging up the hill to the house, Dan shook out his snow-encrusted boots, brewed some coffee, pulled a couple of steaks from the freezer, and microwaved some canned beans. With a sigh of pure happiness, he stretched back in the old brown recliner and opened his mail. He eagerly ripped open a long letter from Sarah, reading it slowly and savoring each word.

The last letter bore no return address, but the U.N. insignia was embossed on the back of the envelope. Opening it, Dan sat bolt upright, staring in shocked unbelief at the pages. "Oh, no!" he groaned, dropping his head into his hands. The insistent beep of the microwave went unnoticed as Dan stared, unheeding, at the offending letter on the floor.

The telephone began to ring, and he bounded into the kitchen to answer it. "Shepherd here. Alex? I just got home and found a letter in my— You too? Was it from the U.N.?"

He poured himself some coffee and sat down. "Did you see the postmark? We'll have to call them first thing tomorrow morning. Alex, we are being conscripted like slaves for their hydroelectric project in the Mideast. We're to report immediately to headquarters in New York, then fly out to the Mideast. God only knows when we'll be back—if we even can come back. Things are pretty explosive and unstable out there!"

The conversation with his partner continued for several minutes longer, then, having finalized arrangements with his neighbors for yet another long trip, Dan showered and fell exhausted into bed. Huddled under the old goose down comforter, Dan dreamed of his childhood in the Texas Panhandle—the days when he always had felt so safe and warm and protected. Outside, a fresh blanket of snow was silently altering the landscape he loved so well. And so the man slept, completely unaware that this was to be his last night in his boyhood home.

———⊶⊰⊱⊷———

The November meeting of the High Council of the Trilateral Commission was held in an ancient cloister deep in the Bavarian Alps. Long abandoned by the church, the site was purchased and quietly renovated by a committee of wealthy European bankers. Remote, isolated, and accessible now only by helicopter, it was the perfect place to preserve complete secrecy while at the same time affording a luxurious Renaissance ambience.

A splendid meal had been served, and the members drifted into an adjoining salon for coffee, brandy, and conversation. Promptly at eight o'clock, they entered a third room, convening at the elegant teakwood conference table. Their host, standing in a shadowed alcove, murmured an order, and the lights were dimmed. A lone candle flickered its feeble light onto the faces of the strange assemblage who, for all intents and purposes, held the strings that controlled all the puppet governments of the earth.

The meeting consisted of individual reports from each member, some of which were quite lengthy. Their host remained in the shadows, never uttering a word, but giving a curt nod at the end of each report. The last man rose to speak.

"Sir, Project Babylon is right on schedule. We have assembled the world's finest architects, engineers, and artisans. We expect completion in less than eighteen months!" An involuntary gasp rose from the others as the speaker pressed a button under the table, and, as if by magic, a miniature city rose slowly and majestically, its shining white walls reflecting the spotlight above.

"A perfect replica, if you will, of the original: Nebuchadnezzar's Shangri-la in the Mesopotamian desert—Babylon. Successful negotiations with Turkey, Iran, Iraq, and Syria have paved the way for a massive hydroelectric project to supply electricity. This, of necessity, involves diverting the Euphrates River—yes? You have a question?" He motioned toward a colleague, who rose slowly.

"Did we not discuss the feasibility of nuclear power or solar energy as alternatives?"

"Yes, Mr. Ferelli, we have carefully weighed these options. The hydroelectric project will be eventually supplemented by solar power; nuclear energy has been discarded, however, for environmental concerns raised by Earthprime. In addition," he continued, "the International Monetary Fund refuses to finance any use of nuclear power, and the IMF will be our major source of funds for this massive undertaking."

Mr. Ferelli sat down and nodded in agreement. There was a dramatic pause as the speaker leaned forward and fixed his eyes on the dazzling white miniature city on the table.

"Ladies, gentlemen—the era of separatist nationalism is now as archaic as the feudal fiefdoms of the Dark Ages. Our dreams of worldwide unity under one government will soon be a reality. All the ancient religions will once again thrive within these walls, with two notable exceptions: Christianity and Judaism will be eradicated, a plan that has secured the cooperation of our Islamic friends.

"All roads will lead to this, the greatest of all human achievement. Set high on a hill, the new Babylon will be visible for many miles around—an exquisite alabaster citadel that exemplifies our glorious New Age ideals. As the hub of all the earth's commerce and culture, its massive accumulation of wealth will be funneled into our...ah...shall we say 'projects.'"

Looking around the table with a mirthless smile, he slowly sat down as a ripple of polite applause echoed around the room, then died away into silence. All eyes were upon their enigmatic host, who had yet to utter a word or even to show himself in the light. When he finally spoke, it was in a deep, rumbling, rich baritone with only the slightest detectable accent.

"Ladies and gentlemen, thank you for your diligence in carrying out your assignments. We will be issuing your new orders in the morning— orders directly from the Luciferian council. It is time to retire for the night—sleep well, my friends."

Far below the elegant room, deep in the lowest recesses of the ancient abbey, two men in dirty work clothes sat at a table, huddled over a "satlink," the most highly developed communication device of their day. Removing their headphones, they hid the equipment and turned off the single overhead light bulb. As they carefully threaded their way back up the subterranean passages, one remarked to the other behind him: "My friends? He called them friends? How little they know their role as minor pawns—expendable pawns—in his Machiavellian game of chess. He'll no doubt dispose of them as he did the others when they have served their purpose!"

Seal up the Vision

As the two men rounded a corner and started up a long flight of stairs, they heard a slight scraping noise. The man in front froze; the one behind shrank back into a deep, shadowed alcove. Suddenly his friend was caught in the glare of a flashlight and a deafening staccato of bullets ricocheted off the damp stone walls of the passage.

"Hands in the air! Don't move!" came the harsh command.

Pressed against the wall, hardly daring to breath, the second man heard his friend being dragged, protesting, up the steps. Finally a door slammed shut, and he was alone in the silent passage.

After what seemed like an eternity, he moved carefully to the top of the stairs and laterally through a labyrinth of tunnels until he found the window with their rope ladder still intact. As he gingerly swung one leg over the windowsill, he looked up just in time to see his screaming friend thrown from the parapet above. His head swiveled downward in stunned disbelief as the flailing body of his comrade hit the massive boulders far below and disappeared from sight.

"Oh, no!" he groaned under his breath, struggling against the rising tide of nausea and vertigo. He leaned his head against the ancient stone and cried silently for his murdered friend, then climbed laboriously down the ladder and set off on a steady trot through the forest. He reached his destination nearly two hours later: an abandoned barn in which the two Israeli agents had stashed the battered old Audi sedan. By now, the temperature had dropped well below the freezing point, and a light snowfall was already beginning to cover his tracks.

He pulled open the large barn door, which was sagging on only one hinge. With some difficulty, he managed to start the car, and, backing out of the narrow, twisting drive, he turned and headed for the autobahn. Stopping only once to fill the petrol tank, he drove all night until he reached Geneva.

Nearly fainting with hunger and exhaustion, he spied a small roadside inn with the neon sign: "Zimmer Frei." "Good, they have a vacancy," he muttered. "Good thing, too. I think I could sleep forever." He rented a room and, after eating a hearty breakfast in the cafe, made a phone call from the pay phone in the hall.

"Karl Morgenthal? Lothar Kreisler...*Ich weiss* nicht...we should speak English, sir; the servants won't understand. I have bad news: Reinhardt is dead. But...sir, listen: I also have good news. We taped every session.

I have the tapes in my possession, and Karl—it's much worse than we thought.

"Yes, the Arab nations have a specified condition for their coopera-tion with the NWO: the complete destruction of Judaism! Listen, we need to meet at our prearranged rendezvous. Remember? Right: I have made duplicates. You will be able to pass one on to our contact in the Mossad?"

Later, after a long, hot shower, Lothar sank gratefully into the eider-down bed. As he drifted toward unconsciousness, he wondered idly about the mystery man who had hosted the unholy alliance: *How I wish that we had been able to set up an infrared camera; apparently even his own people don't have a clue as to his identity, but one thing is sure: he seems to have every-one under his control,* he thought bitterly. *Dictator of the world? Could be that's exactly what he has in mind.*

The little commuter jet streaked across the night sky, flying east over the mountains of Ararat. There was no moon, and the land below was a black velvet carpet with only a few sparse lights indicating an occasional tiny desert community. Dan's partner was snoring in the aisle seat next to him, a day's growth of beard darkening his lower face. Dan ran his hand wea-rily over his own stubble and tried to stretch his long legs a little.

The flight to Athens had been uneventful—a long time, though, for an active young man to be confined in such cramped quarters. Transfer-ring immediately from the 747 jumbo jet to the commuter plane, there had been no time to stretch his aching limbs. Dan leaned his head back, closed his eyes, and drifted off into a fitful sleep.

In his dream, he was riding Boomer across a trackless desert. He was bent forward in the saddle, riding like the wild west Texas wind. Looking back, he could see the shadow of a monstrous black bird closing the dis-tance between them, its huge wings beating relentlessly in slow motion as it closed in on horse and rider.

Suddenly, the earth opened up underneath, revealing a deep rocky chasm; as they were falling the shadow engulfed him, and he was grasped by a pair of talons and jerked upward. His last downward glimpse was of his poor horse still falling, falling—and he felt the grief constrict his throat. Tears stung his eyes as he struggled to break free—

"Dan! Hey, old buddy—take it easy." Dan stared, uncomprehending, at the form next to him. Alex was shaking him gently. "Just a bad dream, pardner. Are you OK?"

Dan took a deep breath, scrubbed his bristly face with both hands, and leaned forward, grinning sheepishly. "Yeah, Alex. I'm OK. Just suffering from jet lag and sleep deprivation, I guess. Wow—some kind of weird dream!"

The seat belt light flashed on, and the plane began its long descent, banking to the left as it circled the landing strip far below. It was a rough landing, and as they finally rolled to a full stop, they heard the unearthly noise of the wind outside the sturdy little craft, howling like a pack of wolves.

"Oh, man," groaned Alex as he collected his gear. "A sandstorm! I vote we turn around and go back home!"

"Not likely," muttered Dan tersely. "It looks like we have company; look out the window."

In the glare of the plane's lights, they could see uniformed guards with automatic weapons stationed outside, waiting to escort them—where? There did not appear to be anything resembling the large headquarters they were expecting. Only the silhouette of a small outbuilding, no bigger than a shed, was barely visible through the swirling haze.

Descending from the plane, they shielded their faces from the stinging sand driven by the relentless wind and followed a guard into the shed. Safely inside, they looked around in amazement. The softly lit, completely soundproofed enclosure was lined with padded benches on three sides; the fourth wall was a bank of elevators. The ride down was accompanied by the unmistakable refrain from a Mozart sonata.

"Some elevator music!" murmured Dan, lifting an appreciative eyebrow. "I wonder what other delightful surprises are awaiting us." The guard glanced at him and stepped aside as the doors opened. They entered a large, beautifully furnished anteroom, complete with plush burgundy carpet and sparkling chandeliers.

"Please follow me, gentlemen." The guard smiled amicably as he gestured toward an open doorway. "The hour is late, and the chief left orders that you be made comfortable after your long journey." Following him down a long hallway, they were taken to a large three-room suite.

"Good night, gentlemen. You may sleep as long as you like. Please ring for breakfast whenever you wish." He bowed slightly and was gone.

"Well, well," Alex whistled softly. "Which bedroom do you want? And we've each got our own bathroom with hot tub…and look at this rec room in between; projection TV with a huge library of tapes; pool table; computer banks—"

They looked at each other, the realization dawning on them both at once.

"Well, ol' buddy," Dan lapsed into his soft Texas drawl, "it sure does look like we're going to be here a good long time."

Later, relaxing in his hot tub, he muttered to no one in particular: "An elegant prison; still, all things considered—I'd rather be in Philadelphia!"

By 7:30 a.m. in Geneva, the sidewalk cafe was nearly filled to capacity with the early morning coffee-and-croissant crowd. A van loaded down with ski gear drew alongside the curb, and a lively group of laughing, chattering young people piled out. They crowded around the remaining tables, poring over their maps as they drank their hot chocolate and devoured the platters of pastries. One elderly businessman stopped by a table and, with a courtly bow, asked an attractive blonde girl where they were headed.

"We are going to Alpenstadt, sir," she replied politely.

"You know, the news this morning predicted heavy snows in that region," he told her earnestly. "You may need my newspaper for the latest weather developments."

"Thank you very kindly, sir." She bestowed a dazzling smile on the gentleman as she tucked the paper in her backpack.

"And a very good and safe trip for all of you," he replied, tipping his hat to the group as he left. The girl finished her coffee, looked at her watch, and gasped, "Oh, I nearly forgot to call Greta, our housekeeper. The poodles need to be picked up from the vet—I'll only be a minute."

She picked up her backpack and flew around the corner to a phone booth. Dialing the number, she waited impatiently for an answer as her fingers found the paper; a smile of satisfaction played about her lips as she felt the tiny audio tapes inside.

"Lothar? It's Heidi. Yes, I have it. Listen, I haven't got much time. My cover is a group of students on a skiing holiday. In a couple of days I'll be on my way to Israel with a cast on my left leg, containing the tapes. Yes, we have our reservations on El Al flight 301. I'll be officially visiting my friend Heather. We went to a girl's school together—a very proper, sedate Swiss finishing school. I'll be staying with her parents in Tel Aviv…no, they are unaware that you and I are Israeli Mossad agents. My Austrian citizenship papers are all in order…yes, yes. I'll contact you later. I am so sorry about Reinhardt—take care, Lothar. Good-bye."

"Shalom, dear Lothar," she murmured softly after hanging up the phone. "I can't let myself think too far ahead—to dream of a normal life with you is a luxury neither of us can afford."

The elderly man with the bowler hat and briefcase watched from the doorway across the street. When he was satisfied that the girl was not being watched by anyone else, he stepped into the waiting limousine and sped off to his destination. Karl Morgenthal was very nearly late to the bank.

———— ∞∞ ————

The little Audi raced down the autobahn toward the northern Swiss city of Basel. The poor struggling windshield wipers made little headway against the wind-driven mixture of sleet and snow pelting the highway. Lothar leaned forward and rubbed the glass with his gloved hand, peering through a small circle cleared by the defroster. Visibility was almost zero, but the headlights dimly illuminated the exit sign he was looking for.

His immediate concern was to reach Ingerstrasse No. 18 before the opposition. Reinhardt, his murdered fellow agent, had a wife and infant daughter living in Basel. Lothar knew that as soon as the executioners were able to establish positive identification, his friend's family would be in extreme danger. He drove more slowly now, picking out the street names with difficulty in the storm. Twice he pulled to a stop and consulted a map of the city, which was unfamiliar territory to him. *At least,* he thought grimly, *the vultures will have as hard a time as I am, giving me some advantage.*

Finally, he found it; a charming, somewhat run-down apartment house with tightly closed shutters and sad little empty window boxes dripping with icicles instead of summer flowers. He knocked on the door, and presently it was tentatively opened by a tired-looking young woman in a bathrobe.

"Are you Telvi Reinhardt? Forgive the lateness of the hour, but I am Lothar Kreisler, a friend of your husband. May I come in?"

He tried to avoid the alarmed brown eyes of the girl as she stood aside to let him enter.

"Where is Wilhelm? Has…something has happened to him, no?" Her voice shook with fright, and her hand flew to her throat as Lothar turned painfully to face her. His eyes filled with unbidden tears; no words were spoken, and all he could do was to hold her and wait until the convulsive sobbing subsided.

"I am so sorry…so sorry, Telvi. I will tell you more later, but first I must warn you: you and your baby are in danger. We are prepared to take you immediately to a place of safety. Do you understand, Telvi? We must leave now, this very moment. Let me help you; gather up quickly what you need."

The girl dried her eyes on the sleeve of her robe, took in a deep shuddering breath, and disappeared into the bedroom. In five minutes she reappeared, dressed warmly and carrying a heavy suitcase. The sleeping baby was encased in a down comforter in the infant carrier. Lothar was speechless with astonishment as he took the suitcase and followed her down the stairs.

"Wilhelm always made sure I had a packed suitcase ready for…for such an emergency," she explained dully as he pushed it in the trunk. "I think he knew this would happen some day."

They were silent during the drive to the airport, but Lothar felt the bile rise in his throat as he glanced sideways at the grieving young widow beside him. *Someday,* he vowed silently, *someday I'll have the chance to get even; those filthy devils will pay with their lives before I'm through, and that's a solid gold promise.*

CHAPTER 10

THE OVERCOMERS

O N THE TENTH day of the eighth month, a well fortified retinue of royal envoys, Chaldean soldiers, several scribes, household servants, cooks, and even musicians accompanied the prime minister of Babylonia to his destination. Traveling through the province of Susa, their arrival in the fabled Persian capitol was accompanied by a great deal of pomp and ceremony. Daniel was heralded by a seemingly endless gauntlet of trumpeters, drummers, bugles, and stringed instruments. A group of young maidens ran before them, dancing and throwing flower petals in their path as they rode down the wide avenue to the palace.

"Ahasuerus has truly rolled out the royal carpet," shouted his companion above the din. "Perhaps word of your God's amazing power has also reached the outlying territories. Apparently the king is anxious to impress you." Sar-Sechim, the chief of the chamberlains, when he had heard of Daniel's impending journey, had insisted on coming along on the basis of his vast ambassadorial experience. "Perhaps," he had explained, "I can somehow be of assistance to you in guiding you through the vast maze of Persian politics."

Daniel had gratefully agreed, and the two men had spent many agreeable hours together along the journey. Daniel's eagerness to meet the king and queen had grown by leaps and bounds, as the fascinating account of Queen Esther's rise to the throne of Persia was told. Night by night, by the light of the fire and the soft strumming of mandolins, Sar-Sechim unraveled the captivating tale.

⸻

"Ahasuerus, the young king of Persia, had a very beautiful queen named Vashti. One night he and his friends had been drinking heavily, and the inebriated king impulsively decided to call for the queen to display her beauty before the entire court. Alas, if he had been sober, the thought would never have entered his head. Oriental custom would not allow it, and the king was basically a kind and honorable man who would never bring dishonor on his wife. Her answer? She refused to come.

"How surprised and dismayed he must have been. His proud boasting of the fabled beauty of his queen had led to an act of irreversible folly, and now his authority had been challenged by a mere woman, causing him to lose face.

"Now Vashti possessed, in addition to her rare and exotic beauty, a considerable strength of personality. Morally, she was absolutely within her rights to refuse, but legally, she had committed the unpardonable sin. As a result, she was banished forever from the king's presence, and a new queen had to be chosen.

"Here is where the tale became so intriguing: An edict was sent to all 127 provinces, that the fairest young virgins in all the kingdom would be selected and brought to the king's palace at Shushan. This process took some time to accomplish. First, each girl was given twelve months to prepare, and then, one by one, each was taken in the evening to the king's chambers. In the morning, if the king so decided, she was sent to the concubines' quarters, and so on until he found his new queen.

"A certain Jew named Mordecai, who had been taken captive with King Jehoiachin, had taken in his orphaned cousin, Haddassah, and raised her as his own child. She was now a young maiden of such surpassing grace and beauty that she was taken, along with a large group of Persian maidens, to the palace. Her Persian name was Esther, meaning "star," and under this name she was given over into the custody of Hegai, keeper of the women, with whom she found immediate favor.

"Esther went into the king's chambers on her appointed evening, dressed only in the elegant simplicity suggested by Hegai, who knew with unerring accuracy what would most please the king and what would most effectively showcase her delicate, fragile beauty. Ahasuerus, to put it mildly, was thoroughly smitten. He proclaimed her queen of his entire

101

realm and gave a huge feast for all his people in her honor. His love for her was so great that he sent lavish gifts to all the appointed regents and the people of his kingdom.

"In the course of time, Esther was informed by her cousin, Mordecai, of a hideous plot to utterly annihilate all the Jews in the kingdom. Ahasuerus had promoted an evil man named Haman to the position of Grand Vizier, giving him complete authority—even his own signet ring—over the entire kingdom. Haman was a vain and insolent person who, being insecure, required everyone to bow down to him. All complied except Mordecai, who refused. Haman seethed with fury. Since Mordecai was a Jew, he hated all Jews with an unreasoning hatred and conceived a fiendish plot to eliminate the source of his festering rage.

"He sent out letters, sealed with the king's signet ring, by post to all the provinces of the king. On the thirteenth day of the twelfth month of Adar, everyone in the kingdom was commanded to kill every Jewish man, woman, and child, seizing their possessions. His purpose was now the extermination of the entire Jewish race—virtual genocide.

"Esther was so deeply grieved by this news that she and all her maidens began to fast and pray, seeking guidance. She asked Mordecai to have all the Jews living at Shushan to also fast and pray. She received her guidance. With great faith and courage, she went before the king; dressed in her most resplendent royal robes, she requested an audience, something that is almost never done. Fortunately the king responded favorably, and she invited him, along with her enemy, Haman, to a banquet in her quarters. Haman, of course, was tremendously flattered and boasted openly to all his friends how he had gained the queen's favor. This banquet was held three nights in a row, and by the third night, the king was overcome by curiosity and a renewal of his passion for his queen.

"As the suspense built, at the exact right moment (timing is everything!) the lovely queen exposed the heinous plot to destroy her and her entire nation. The king was exceedingly indignant and asked the obvious question: who was the perpetrator? The queen pointed directly at Haman, naming him as the source of the evil conspiracy. This so astounded her thoroughly confused husband that he had to go outside, pacing back and forth in the garden as he tried to digest this shocking development.

"In the meantime, Haman saw that his only chance of survival was the queen. No one knows exactly what was going through his tortured mind as he attacked Esther, throwing her down on her bed. Her screams brought the king, and running into the room, he saw the demented Grand Vizier blubbering incoherently as he pled for his life. That was the final straw that tipped the balance scale. The enraged king lifted him up and threw him bodily to the floor. Haman was immediately taken out and hanged, he and all his sons, on the same gallows he had himself built for Mordecai!

"A new decree was then issued, sent out on the swiftest horses, that allowed the Jews to assemble and defend themselves. Since the first decree could not be rescinded, the second decree provided for the Jews to rout their enemies, and the entire nation was saved.

"It is said that that no king ever loved his queen as Ahasuerus loved Esther. Their children now run and play happily about the palace, often seen in the company of their grandfather Mordecai, who is now Grand Vizier of all Persia!"

Three days in Susa had given Daniel a strong desire to prolong his stay in this lovely city, perhaps a month or even longer. Having read the scrolls of Jeremiah to Mordecai, Esther, and all his people, there was a feeling of deep repentance, but also there was a general air of rejoicing, of hope for the future.

As the official envoy of His Royal Majesty Nebuchadnezzar, Daniel carried out his official duties as prime minister with all the efficiency and dignity due his position. However, as a young man not yet thirty years of age, he enjoyed the company of King Ahasuerus and his Jewish wife, Queen Esther. The Persian monarch was generous almost to the point of profligacy, lavishing expensive and luxurious gifts on his visitors daily. They traveled to several different areas in the province, so Daniel developed extensive knowledge of the governed territories.

Esther asked Daniel many questions about her homeland. She had been only about three years old when her parents were killed during the initial invasion of Judea, so she could only remember bits and pieces of her history. She listened with rapt attention, eager to hear every detail as Daniel described the beautiful Holy City on Mount Zion.

Mordecai had schooled her carefully in the Scriptures, and she called in her little son, who proudly recited the first psalm of King David. He bowed low, then ran outside to play. "Cyrus is only five years old," she beamed, "but he already knows much about the Hebrew God, Jehovah. My husband has given me his permission to teach my children the ways of their Jewish ancestors."

Daniel was quietly watching every graceful movement as she sat, talked, and moved about. Esther was, indeed, a stunning beauty, even after having borne three children. But everything about her delicate loveliness only served to remind Daniel of the face and form he was trying so hard to forget. Quite uncharacteristically, he decided to abandon all pretense of reserve and tell her of his dilemma. Before he could say anything, however, Esther saved him the trouble.

"Daniel, what is troubling you? Has someone, perhaps someone outside our race, captured your heart?" She spoke softly, yet every word hammered home to its mark. *She misses nothing*, he thought admiringly, and, to cover his embarrassed confusion, turned away to look out the window.

"Your feminine perception truly amazes me, Esther. Yes, you are right." He turned to look beseechingly at her. "I have already determined in my heart, Esther, that I will not marry a heathen woman; it would dishonor the God I serve."

He suddenly realized what he had said, as she dropped her eyes to the folded hands in her lap. She was absently twisting her magnificent wedding ring: a massive Burmese ruby that flashed like liquid fire on her slender hands. Daniel apologized profusely, stumbling over the words.

"Oh, Esther, dear little sister, I did not mean…"

She looked up and dimpled into a mischievous smile. "Of course you didn't mean my marriage to Ahasuerus. God had ordained that from the very beginning, and, Daniel, I couldn't imagine any greater happiness. I am as truly and fully loved as any woman ever could be, and I love my husband more than my own life. He may be a king," she murmured, moving gracefully across the room, "but he's still a man."

And what a fortunate man, thought Daniel, almost envious as she rang the bell for the servants. She returned, found a comfortable cushion to sit, and said in her irresistible, charming manner, "I have sent for some refreshments. Now, dear Daniel, tell me all about her."

And he did.

The activities in Babylon during the absence of the prime minister were taking a decidedly sinister turn. The soft underbelly of the city was alive with rumors of insurrection as the twenty-three conspirators hurried to complete their designated tasks.

On the very day of Daniel's departure, King Nebuchadnezzar returned from an extensive tour of his western provinces. Exhausted from the journey, he remained incommunicado in his quarters for several days, calling only the queen into his chambers. Upon his emergence several days later, the chief goldsmith, the former Grand Vizier, and several other officials of the royal court requested an audience with the king. Rested and refreshed, Nebuchadnezzar granted the request.

Talmez, the former Grand Vizier, approached the throne and prostrated himself in obeisance. "O Highly Exalted One, your servants have formulated a plan to honor our king in such a way as no other ruler in all of history: we wish to demonstrate to Your Majesty our plan."

Mildly curious, the king nodded, and Talmez arose. Clapping his hands, the curtains behind him parted, and musicians marched in slowly, to the beat of a drum. Behind them, on a rolling platform pulled by eight servants was a mysterious obelisk covered by an enormous cloth. The procession came to a halt.

Talmez again clapped his hands, and the cloth was whisked away, revealing a life-sized golden statue of the king standing on top of a large pylon, feet apart and arms folded over his chest. It was a magnificent piece of sculpture, standing about twelve feet high. The brilliant morning sunshine enveloped the entire room in an incandescent, golden glow as the blinding reflections danced and shimmered around the benevolent golden visage of the king's image.

The musical instruments began to play, softly at first—only the melodious sound of tinkling bells, then others joined in until they reached a dramatic crescendo. The cymbals clashed, and, as if on cue, the assembled members of the court fell on their faces before the image. It was a dramatic moment. The king was astounded and began to warm to the flattering vision of such unprecedented adulation.

Talmez, highly observant, lost no time in pressing his advantage. "Your Majesty, be assured that this poor demonstration is only a small token of a much greater plan."

He lifted his voice dramatically in stentorian tones: "Let another golden image of our king, ninety feet high and nine feet wide, be set up outside the city on the plain of Dura, where it will be visible for miles around. When a signal is given, thousands of musicians will play their instruments, and all the people will fall down and worship the golden image that represents the glory of our great king! Whoever refuses to prostrate themselves before the image will be executed immediately, for all who receive the great abundance from the benevolent hand of our great and mighty king must show their allegiance to him."

Ashpenaz watched from a balcony. *The old windbag,* he thought sourly, *never did a thing in his life without an ulterior motive. I wonder what he has up his sleeve this time.*

Talmez had already prepared this edict in writing, so it was immediately brought before the king. Much bedazzled by visions of his own grandeur, Nebuchadnezzar pressed his signet ring into the hot wax, thereby falling neatly into the trap and sealing the fate of a certain group of his subjects.

The priest of Baal gathered his cohorts together one more time, his cold black eyes filled with hate as he revealed to them the remainder of the plan.

"All goes well, my brothers," he gloated, all but ignoring the priestess of Ishtar. "While the cat is away, the mice will play. We have succeeded in a victory far above our wildest schemes. While we were aware that we could not touch his most trusted friend, Daniel, we knew that our master, the lord of darkness, would provide the means to dispose of the three young Hebrews who have supplanted many of you who once held positions of authority.

"Even now, as we speak, the artisans, who have been hard at work since our very first meeting, are putting the final finishing touches on the golden image. The builders tell me the site is now ready for it to be erected, and the princes and governors have made all the arrangements for the dedication ceremony to be held in three days. We must arrange for the three young Hebrews to be in plain view of everyone, so their rebellion will be highly visible."

"Excuse me," interrupted the priest of Marduk, "but how can you be so sure they will jeopardize their very lives in this way? If they do bow down with all the rest, then all of this long and expensive preparation will have been for nothing!"

The priest of Baal only smiled, replying icily, "We have it on good authority: they will not bow." The two officials warily regarded each other in stony silence.

Only the urgent necessity of the present task could have brought together such a divergent group of rivals. Their traditional hatred and mistrust of each other was superseded only by their overwhelming hatred and fear of the Hebrews and their God, who they instinctively knew was the only real threat with the power to overturn their entire idolatrous system.

The hatred of the priestess of Ishtar went much deeper, however. Consumed by jealousy and ambition, she had, quite literally, sold her soul to the prince of darkness in exchange for certain favors. The main gate in Babylon led to her lavish temple, and she herself had eliminated, one by one, all her unfortunate female rivals in her rise to the top.

Her astonishing sexual prowess was also legendary, and the unrelenting pathway to prominence was paved with the bodies of her lovers: influential men who, having obediently fulfilled her wishes, conveniently disappeared, never to be seen again. It was sometimes whispered about the court that when the vultures circled the rock quarry outside the city, the priestess of Ishtar would soon be taking another lover.

When the four handsome young Hebrews came into power, the priestess vowed to use all her considerable powers of seduction in bringing them down. One by one, she set her traps: one by one, they spurned her advances, and with a thoroughness and finality that infuriated her. Stung by the unaccustomed humiliation of rejection, the priestess of Ishtar, seething with rage, withdrew into the secluded chambers of her temple. Days later, she had emerged with the present plan, which she had presented to the priest of Baal.

Now, success was assured, and she savored its sweetness, contemplating the fate awaiting the three she so hated. "Soon," she murmured, "I will be avenged, and your God will be forgotten."

107

SEAL UP THE VISION

⎯⎯⎯∞⎯⎯⎯

The plain of Dura was a flattened hilltop west of the city of Babylon. When the rays of the rising sun hit the golden image of King Nebuchadnezzar, the blinding reflections illuminated the entire area with an almost unearthly brilliance.

The music of thousands of trumpets, harps, flutes, and instruments of all kinds rose in a magnificently orchestrated symphony of praise as sixty thousand people fell to the ground, prostrating themselves before the awesome golden image.

Nebuchadnezzar himself stood proudly, his face uplifted as he beheld the massive golden head of his own image looking benevolently down at him. Although long accustomed to adulation, the exorbitant magnificence of this dedication ceremony impressed even the jaded young ruler.

As the crowd began to chant his name to the rhythmic, pagan throbbing of the great kettle drums, he raised both fists in the air and slowly turned to survey the massive gathering. His subjects were all on their faces—all except three figures who were standing on the edge of the crowd, silhouetted against the rising sun. The king's smile evaporated, and he lowered his arm to point an accusing finger at the three figures. "Bring them to me!" he roared.

Immediately the three were enveloped by a contingent of soldiers who escorted them to the king. The crowd grew silent and parted to let them pass. They drew closer, and the king grew pale with anger as he recognized the three young princes to whom he had entrusted the governorship of Babylonia.

"Shadrach! Meshach! Abed-Nego! How is it that you have betrayed me in this fashion? Do you not know the penalty for disobedience to my royal edict? Fall down now—or you will die by fire!"

Mishael stepped forward, and every ear in that crowd strained to hear his answer.

"King Nebuchadnezzar, we have no desire to dishonor your great and honorable name. You are aware that we serve the God Jehovah, who is well able to deliver us from a fiery death. But be it known to you, O King, that even if He does not deliver us, we will not dishonor our God and disobey His command by bowing down to your image and serving your gods."

Hananiah and Azariah stepped forward and stood by their companion, gazing steadfastly at the king in silent agreement.

Nebuchadnezzar, his senses reeling from the rage that threatened to overtake him, gripped the golden railing for support as he glowered down at the three men before him. Swallowing hard, he muttered hoarsely, "Take them away!" then turned to leave.

Everyone in the stunned crowd saw their sovereign stumble as he left the platform, but only those closest to him knew the truth: the excruciating headaches resulting from unrestrained rages sometimes caused a temporary blindness. The king required assistance in returning to his royal carriage, in which he was returned swiftly to the palace.

Mishael, Hananiah, and Azariah were taken immediately to the palace dungeon, where they were chained together until a furnace could be prepared for their execution. Sitting cross-legged, back-to-back on the damp stone floor, they spent their last hours together in prayer.

Although Mishael and Hananiah had not yet married, Azariah had a young wife, pregnant with their first child. "She is so small, so delicate," he whispered. "I cannot imagine what it would be like—never to see my child born, to watch him grow."

"Jehovah has appointed our times—both to live and to die," replied Hananiah reverently. "If this is not His appointed time for us to die, there is no power in all the universe great enough to kill us."

"Amen," agreed Mishael heartily, and they fell silent with the sure and solemn knowledge that these events were completely out of their hands. A curious peace stole over the three friends, and when their captors took them out, they were amazed to find them relaxed and reminiscing about old times.

Nebuchadnezzar, recovered from his sudden onset of rage-induced pain, was pacing restlessly on the platform as the three young men were brought before him. He whirled to face them. "Hebrews, let it be known that I am a merciful man. I give you one more chance: if you will bow down, your lives will be spared."

He glanced at the blazing inferno, shuddering involuntarily. "You know even a king cannot reverse his own edict, but I am willing to overlook much: all you have to do is bow down this once; all the rest of your fellow Hebrews have done it."

"We cannot do that, O King. It would be in direct disobedience to our

God," replied Azariah decisively. "Do with us as you wish, but we belong to our God, and our lives are ultimately in His hands."

Shaking his head, the king turned away, pointing wordlessly behind him at the furnace. The executioners bound the unresisting young men with heavy ropes that cut into the flesh of their arms and legs. Azariah's wife was weeping uncontrollably, surrounded by her family behind the crossed lances of the Chaldean guard.

Ashpenaz was transfixed with horror, and he stationed himself beside his old friend Arioch, who was also dismayed by the impending death of the three whom he had come to admire. "So young, so noble—this is a terrible waste of men who were surely destined for greatness." Arioch shook his head sadly.

"Their very nobility of soul was, ironically, their undoing," groaned Ashpenaz. "Their refusal to compromise the law of their God came into direct conflict with the law of man, or I should say," he added bitterly, "the cunningly conceived plan of Talmez and his evil cohorts. My sources tell me the conspiracy was carefully plotted; now we see the tragic results."

The drums began to play a slow, steady dirge as the procession wound down the hill to the furnace, which by now had been heated seven times hotter than ever before. The searing white-hot flames leaped hungrily upward, burning every bit of vegetation in the area. The men stoking the fire were throwing in the logs from a distance, and some had already collapsed from the intensity of the heat.

The executioners who were carrying the doomed captives on their shoulders walked more slowly; they glanced back nervously as they approached the blazing inferno. Suddenly, a strong gust of wind drove the leaping flames out in a horizontal firestorm. Those watching from a distance heard only the agonized screams of the executioners as the entire procession disappeared in a massive wall of fire and smoke.

Nebuchadnezzar, throwing royal protocol to the winds, ran down the hill to gain a closer view. Strangely enough, the wind ceased and an unearthly calm enveloped the scene. The smoke cleared away, the roaring flames died down, and the king walked alone down the long ramp. He walked slowly now, his head completely clear, but his heart sickened as he spoke his thoughts aloud:

"I have mortally offended their God, the God of Daniel who…who knew every secret of my soul. These three had the nobility, the strength of character that I lack. They refused to betray Him, and I have put them to death. Have I brought His terrible wrath on myself and my kingdom?" he wondered.

The members of his court watched in numbed astonishment as the king of Babylon now stood at the blazing hot entrance to the superheated furnace. Clenching his fists, he threw back his head and cried out for forgiveness to a God he did not know.

Ashpenaz and Arioch, who had followed some distance behind the king, now came and stood beside him, braving the heat of the furnace to provide support. As the three men stood together gazing into the inferno, they stiffened in surprise. There was movement in the fire, and Nebuchadnezzar instinctively drew closer to the edge.

"Arioch," he shouted hoarsely, "did we not cast three men into the furnace? I see four men in the fire—not three, but four—and…Ashpenaz! They are alive! Do you see them?"

"Yes, Sire. I can see them, but…I cannot believe what my eyes are telling me. Arioch, what do you see?"

Arioch was so numb with shock he could hardly croak. "Your Majesty, the Hebrews are alive and walking about in the fire, but…who is that fourth man with them?"

"That surely can be no mortal man. He must be a son of the God they serve." The king drew dangerously close to the mouth of the furnace and shouted, "Shadrach, Meshach, Abed-Nego—you servants of the most high God: COME FORTH OUT OF THE FURNACE!"

And they did.

THE CHRONICLES OF NEBUCHADNEZZAR

On the seventh day of the ninth month Chislev, the King of Babylon did witness, along with all of his royal court, the deliverance of three Hebrew governors of the province of Babylonia—Meshach, Abed-Nego, and Shadrach—from the midst of a fiery furnace.

These three came forth from the midst of the fire, and the princes, the governors, and captains, and the king's counselors being gathered together, saw these men upon whose bodies the fire had no power, nor was an hair of their head singed, neither were their coats scorched, nor had even the smell of fire passed upon them.

Then Nebuchadnezzar spoke and said, "Blessed be the God of Shadrach, Meshach, and Abed-Nego, who has sent His angel and delivered His servants that trusted in Him. Therefore I make a decree: Every people, nation and language which speak anything amiss against the God of Shadrach, Meshach, and Abed-Nego shall be cut in pieces, and their houses shall be made a dunghill."

Immediately after this, the three Hebrews were promoted to positions of even greater authority. The twenty-four who conspired against them received the fate which they had planned for the Hebrews. They were thrown alive into the fiery furnace, and their gods, alas, did not deliver them.

CHAPTER 11

THE SURVIVORS

THE WINTER OF 1938 in Hanover, Germany, was bitter cold. A stiff north wind was blowing the snow almost horizontally as Abe Lieberman left his office and hurried to his car. The chauffer admitted him and quickly moved around to the front, putting his collar up against the howling wind.

As they drove slowly down the icy street, he glanced over his shoulder; his employer was still shivering from the cold, his frail old body nearly invisible, wrapped in hat, coat, and muffler.

"Sir, the car will be warm soon," he said affectionately, "and we'll be home by the fire before you know it!"

"God bless you, Friedrich," replied the old man. "You must stay and have some good warm brandy with me."

"Thank you, sir. Oh, I almost forgot to tell you. A dark-skinned man from some desert country—Syria, I think—is there waiting to see you. He calls himself an antiquities dealer, although I seriously doubt his credentials. He looks a bit on the shady side, sir, if you know what I mean."

His elderly employer smiled and looked out the ice-encrusted window. He did, indeed, value the intuitive insights of his chauffer, often relying on these little post-workday chats to formulate a difficult decision.

A half-hour later, he was sitting by the fire, sipping his brandy, and listening to the intriguing tale told by his strange visitor. The Syrian's black, hooded eyes reflected little warmth as he politely declined the proffered drink, but he leaned forward and fixed his gaze on a long, narrow, rectangular wooden crate on the floor between them. Abe Lieberman was a collector of rare antiquities and found the suspense irresistible as the story unfolded.

113

Seal up the Vision

"Herr Lieberman, my name is Khamil Assad. I am Syrian by birth, a member of an old and distinguished family in Damascus, and my father was an antiquities dealer, as you are, sir. I attended the university in my city and obtained a degree in archeology."

He drew out a document, written in both Arabic and German, and presented it to his host with the explanation that many of his professors were German with ties to the University of Cologne. *It looks authentic,* thought the elderly man, as he put on his glasses and examined it carefully. He was somewhat surprised and gazed at his visitor appraisingly as he leaned back in his chair.

The Syrian resumed: "Some years ago, I was commissioned by our government to locate the ancient caravan trail that extended from ancient Babylon all the way through Syria and Israel to Egypt. We were assigned several areas along the route that had been camping stops to dig for artifacts.

"This was a massive project that would require several years of hard work. After the first two disappointing years had yielded very little, we achieved some measure of success. As we dug deeper, we began to unearth more than just pottery shards. Hard, tangible evidence of a long-dead civilization is a treasure beyond price, Mr. Lieberman, as you well know."

His eyes were gleaming as he leaned forward.

"On the second month of the fourth year, our digging was interrupted by a howling sandstorm from the west. We abandoned our tools and took refuge in the lee of a sandstone cliff jutting out of the hills nearby. When the storm had ended, everyone went back to camp, but I caught my foot on a stone and tumbled through the tangled undergrowth. I found myself falling and, terrified and confused, slid backward on nearly one hundred feet of smooth stone, until I came to rest in a shallow pool of water.

"I could hear drops of water falling from above, but when my eyes adjusted to the semi-darkness, I was completely surprised. We knew of no caves in this area. And this was an enormous cavern! A small amount of light was being filtered from somewhere above, so I could see my way about.

"Strangely enough, although a little bruised and sore from my fall, I was not alarmed. The cave was spacious and cool, so I began to explore. There appeared to be several tunnels leading off in different directions, but lacking a torch and companions, I resolved to stay within the confines of the central area.

114

"My eyesight improved as it adjusted to the faint light, and eventually I noticed a slight reflection on the far side of the room; on inspection, it proved to be a corroded silver urn that had fallen partially out of a tattered piece of cloth in a crevice. I pulled at it, something gave way, and the entire contents of the rotted linen bag came tumbling forth.

"I was so astounded that I did not notice what was behind it. After inspecting the silver utensils, however, I peered into the opening and could not believe my eyes. There were seven clay jars, something like the Greek amphorae, completely intact, and sealed with a beautifully carved inscription. Dizzy with excitement, I nearly dropped the first one as I carried it over to a beam of light."

The Syrian leaned back and mopped his perspiring brow. "Dr. Lieberman, the engraving on the seal was unmistakably that of King Cyrus of Persia."

Abe Lieberman could contain his curiosity no loner. "Am I to understand, Mr. Assad, that you have in this box a 2,600-year-old vessel that belonged to Cyrus of Persia?"

The white teeth gleamed against his bronzed skin as the Syrian slowly, carefully extracted the prize from its well-cushioned case. Herr Lieberman cast aside all pretense of propriety and dropped to his knees to examine it. The ancient clay jar was beautifully proportioned, about three feet long and perhaps eighteen inches at its greatest diameter. It was circularly inscribed with alternate cuneiform inscriptions and beautifully detailed designs, painted over in muted colors. It was the sealed opening, however, that held his interest.

"You have not opened it?" It was more a statement than a question.

"No, sir. You see, the others were similarly sealed, but when I attempted to open one, the ancient wax just crumbled. I tell you, Herr Lieberman, I just cried like a baby. I decided that the contents were most likely food that had long since disintegrated and the value lies in the seal."

The old man rose slowly to his feet. "Mr. Assad, how much?"

The bargaining began in earnest, and to his surprise, the Syrian soon found himself outclassed by a shrewd and experienced negotiator. However, Herr Lieberman was glad to hand over a satisfactory sum of money, and the Syrian seemed satisfied. As he backed toward the door, bowing deferentially, his host asked one last question: "Are the Syrian authorities aware that you possess these antiquities? What happened to the other six?"

White teeth gleamed as the Syrian replied, "The authorities have four. I, sir, have determined to sell one and to keep one. Unless circumstances intervene, I shall most likely not part with it."

"If you ever change your mind, please let me know." And the elderly gentleman bade his guest good-bye.

———— ✻ ————

The Nazi brown shirts marched through the streets, chanting anti-Semitic slogans as they went. The madness spread like a virus, and former friends and neighbors of the Hanover Jewish population turned out en masse to throw rocks through the windows of Jewish homes and businesses. Children cowered in terror as their parents were dragged into the streets and beaten.

When that awful night was finally over and the insane fury of the mob was spent, Abe Lieberman and his chauffer quietly loaded his car with suitcases and glided silently down the hill and out through the wrought iron gates. When they reached the highway leading west, Friedrich switched the lights on, and the sleek black sedan traveled all night until they reached the city of Muenster.

Here they found Annaliese, Herr Lieberman's daughter, tearful with fright as she heard the reports of violent atrocities against her people. She cried with relief upon seeing her father safe and sound. Together they sat around the kitchen table, drinking tea as the rest of the household slept.

"You must come with me, Annaliese. Soon it will not be safe for any of us anywhere in Germany—even the smallest towns."

"Oh, Papa, I know, but Heinrich is so stubborn. He will not leave the foundry and says that this is just a temporary political cloud and will soon blow over. I cannot leave without him, Papa, and yet…the children. Oh, I am so afraid for my children." She dropped her head on her arms and sobbed convulsively.

"Then you must let the children come with me," he spoke gently. "You can join us later. I will be going to Sweden. I have a business partner in Stockholm, and we have already discussed this possibility. I forwarded most of my money there more than a year ago."

His daughter gazed at him, astonished. Finally she stood, wiping her eyes on her apron.

"I will prepare a good breakfast for you and Friedrich and…and for the children, Papa. They must eat well before they start on this journey."

Two weeks later, the local SS official in Hanover realized that old Abe Lieberman's car had not been seen for some time, so he took the liberty of calling on the elderly Jew. His calling card was a broken front gate as the trucks rolled in to cart out the merchandise. His eyes glittered with greed as he went through the lovely old home, snapping up the most expensive items for himself. The rest were shipped, according to Heinrich Himmler's orders directly from the Fuhrer, to a remote location about three hours from Berlin.

As the last truck was being unloaded, one of the workers noticed a long wooden crate, and when no one was watching, opened the top to look inside.

"An old clay pot!" His nose wrinkled in distaste. "Wonder what the Fuhrer wants with that? I guess that paperhanger is even crazier than I thought."

<hr />

On April 20, 1944, Adolph Hitler celebrated his birthday by viewing the great storerooms of plundered treasure that had been looted from wealthy Jewish families all across Europe. His fevered brain was ignited by Wagneresque visions of glorious Aryan cities to be designed and built by his official architect of the Third Reich, Albert Speer.

Hermann Wilhelm Goering—one of Hitler's most cruel, ruthless, and decadent associates—was truly in his element as he proudly displayed the enormous accumulation of wealth, much of which he planned to spirit away into his own considerable private hoard. People gasped in astonishment as they traversed the narrow passageways between the piles of priceless paintings, tapestries, golden urns, silver candlesticks, and all manner of precious items.

Hitler, after nearly two hours of this, fell silent, brooding as he came to a stop, his hands clasped behind his back, staring at the floor. "Albert, come here," he snapped. "It is too dangerous to keep all of this in one place. We must move it to several different locations, and it must be moved immediately. Albert, I authorize you to take charge of this undertaking. It must be carried out in absolute secrecy. Absolute! Do you understand?"

"Yes, Fuhrer. It will be done as you say." Speer clicked his heels and bowed.

Goering was seething with fury, but he said nothing. Now he would not have the freedom to select the choicest items, which he had hoped to add to his own collection. He sulked and pouted like a bloated, overgrown schoolboy all the way back to the cars, and the effect was certainly not lost on Speer.

I had better move quickly on this assignment, he thought grimly as he sank back into the luxurious velvet interior of the limousine. "Driver," he ordered, "take me to the Chancellory in Berlin. Once we arrive, you may leave; there will be no need to wait." He pulled out a pen and notebook, and during the three hours of his journey, he drew up a set of plans.

Immediately upon arriving at the Chancellory, he called Madame Speer and told her not to wait up for him. Then he called three of his most trusted associates. The four men conferred together until almost two in the morning; when they were finally satisfied with the plans, everyone went home. They were exhausted and did not notice the bulky form lurking in the shadows.

Goering, true to form, could not even trust anyone else to do his spying for him. He had been forced to spend the greater part of the night in a broom closet adjacent to Speer's office, huddled against the wall with a glass to his ear. In spite of all his efforts, however, the conversation was muted— the large room with the thick Persian carpets absorbed most of the sound. He could hear nothing except the unintelligible murmurs of voices.

His sour mood was intensified even further when he walked the dark, cold streets back to his car parked in an alley, only to discover he could not get it started. Nearly three in the morning, it was beginning to pour down rain. He spent the rest of his miserable night huddled in his car, cursing his bad luck, and vowing to track down the hiding places of the Aryan treasure, no matter how long it would take.

Two weeks later, twelve railroad cars were detached from a train at the huge web of rail yards near Munich in southern Germany. Three were diverted to a destination in Spain, where the contents were transferred onto trucks, carried to one of the labyrinth of caves near Gibraltar, and hidden deep inside. The passage was then blocked by a small explosion loosing a considerable fall of rocky debris.

Three cars containing the most fragile and perishable items were diverted to a destination in the northern Italian Alps. An ancient Benedictine abbey had been confiscated by the Germans as an impregnable fortress headquarters. Beneath the fortress were dozens of tunnels and storage rooms, where the temperature and humidity were constant, an important factor for the preservation of tapestries and oil paintings.

Speer's plan to preserve secrecy necessitated a great deal of subterfuge: all the crates were marked with innocuous labels such as "obsolete munitions" and "government documents." Only the most remote underground rooms were used, then sealed off and plastered by Speer's trusted associate after the soldiers had left.

The six remaining cars were diverted to Greece, where their contents were loaded onto barges and shipped across the bay to Izmir, Turkey. This shipment contained the vast bulk of Hitler's purloined fortune, among which was nearly one hundred tons of gold and silver. Much of this had been confiscated from wealthy Belgian Jewish businessmen.

But Speer knew that a great deal of it—a horrifying proportion—had come from the unresisting bodies of Jewish men, women, and children heaped in grotesque piles on the conveyer belts headed toward the ovens of Auschwitz, Dachau, Ravensbruck, Treblinka, and a dozen other death camps. Speer could never forget the sight. It would haunt him to his dying day, so he found neither pleasure nor satisfaction in the completion of his present task.

The barges were unloaded and the trucks ready to travel, so with typical German efficiency, they reached their destination right on schedule. Speer dismissed the German drivers, secured a place to spend the night, and the following morning set about hiring local laborers. During the next two weeks, the great architect built an oversize warehouse out of large clay bricks he had shipped on the barge. When it was completed, he filled the two-story basement to capacity with crates and boxes of all sizes.

After dismissing the workmen, Speer himself cemented over the opening to the basement, rendering it virtually undetectable. The following day, a contingent of SS officials arrived with supplies, and as boatloads of German soldiers followed, it became apparent to the local Turkish population that their neutrality in the war was being ignored.

Speer had deliberately chosen this particular place because he was privy to certain information from the German high command: Hitler had no intention of honoring Turkey's neutrality. He fully intended to extend his base of operations, and Izmir would serve his needs nicely.

His work accomplished, Albert Speer went home to his wife and family in Berlin. On June 6, 1944—one month later—the D-Day invasion of Normandy by the Allies necessitated the withdrawal of German troops to the western front, so the Nazi base in Izmir stood deserted. Outraged by the bare-faced Nazi betrayal of their declared neutrality and emboldened by the Allied invasion, Turkey broke off all dealings with Germany, and the following February Turkey declared war on the Axis powers.

Thus, in the ensuing months, the wild and vain imaginings of a power-mad dictator crumbled into the sooty ashes of his charred body outside the Berlin bunker. Goering and Speer, along with many other war criminals, were tried at Nuremburg. Goering, morbidly afraid of death by hanging, managed to smuggle in a poison capsule and committed suicide, the last cowardly act of a contemptible and cowardly life.

Albert Speer went to prison. Two of his three trusted associates went to their graves without uttering a word about the hidden fortunes. The third told his wife and son as he lay dying; his long years in a cold, dank cell had weakened not only his body but also his resolve. His wife found the story incredible and attributed it to a deranged mind. His son, however, believed the account was truthful and vowed to reclaim the fortune, however long it took.

The postwar refugee camp at Frankfurt was swarming with people, and the tired young American army officer was wearily struggling through a mountain of paperwork.

"Excuse me, sir."

He looked up to see a very old man accompanied by two young boys, about ten or twelve years of age, and a little girl not more than seven. "What can I do for you, sir," he sighed, wondering where these had come from and what horrors they had endured.

"We are searching for my daughter, Annaliese, and her husband, Heinrich Dorfmann. They disappeared from Muenster around 1942. We have had no word for over three years. Could you help us, please?"

The pleading eyes of the children were too much for him. "Please, sir, have a seat; this may take some time."

After nearly two hours of searching files and making many telephone calls, the officer finally stood. He walked around the table and laid his hand on the elderly man's thin, stooped shoulder.

"I'm sorry, sir. It has been confirmed that your daughter and her husband both perished at Dachau. The Germans," he added bitterly, "kept excellent records of their atrocities."

He turned away so they could cling to each other and weep in private. *I'll never get used to it,* he thought. *Six million people robbed of their lives, and for what? A madman's vile dream. May he burn forever in hell!*

CHAPTER 12

REVELATION I

THE CHRONICLES OF NEBUCHADNEZZAR

Nebuchadnezzar the king, unto all peoples, nations, and languages that dwell in all the earth: peace be multiplied unto you.

I, Nebuchadnezzar, was at rest in my house and flourishing in my palace. I saw a dream which greatly troubled me. I called in the soothsayers, the astrologers, the wise men, and the magicians, but they could not decipher the meaning of the visions of my head. Then Daniel, called Belteshazzar, in whom is the spirit of the holy gods, came to me and I told him the dream:

I saw a tree in the midst of the earth and the height thereof was great; the tree grew and became strong, and visible to the ends of the earth. The leaves were beautiful, and it bare much fruit, enough for everyone. The beasts of the field rested in its shadow, and the birds of the air found shelter in its branches.

Then in my vision, I beheld a watcher, a holy one come down from heaven. He cried out, saying: Hew down the tree, cut off its branches, shake off the leaves, and scatter the fruit, but leave the stump in the ground with a band of iron and brass.

Let it dwell in the tender grass, be wet with the dew of heaven; let his portion be with the beasts of the earth. Let his heart be changed from man's and let a beast's heart be given to him—and let seven times pass over him.

This decree is of the holy ones, the watchers, to the intent that the living may know that the Most High rules in the kingdom of men, and gives it to whomever he will.

This was the vision given unto me. Daniel, called Belteshazzar, was astonished and remained silent for one hour, greatly troubled in his thoughts. Then he spoke:

"My lord, would that this dream would fall upon your worst enemies. The tree is you, O King, and this is the decree of the Most High which is come upon my lord the king: they shall drive you from among men, and your dwelling shall be with the beasts of the field; you will eat grass like the oxen and be wet with the dew of heaven for a period of seven years, until you know that the Most High rules in the kingdom of men and gives it to whomever He will. Whereas they left the stump and roots in the ground, your kingdom shall be restored unto you when you have acknowledged the sovereignty of the Most High God.

"Therefore, my king, accept my counsel: break off all unrighteous deeds and show mercy to the poor, if perhaps the years of your tranquility could be lengthened."

At the end of twelve months, I, Nebuchadnezzar, was walking on the terrace of my palace and spoke aloud these words: "Is not this great and glorious Babylon, my kingdom that I have built by the might of my power and for the honor of my majesty?"

Even as I was still speaking, there came a voice from heaven saying, "O King Nebuchadnezzar: to you it has already been spoken; your kingdom is departed from you. You shall live as the beasts of the field for the next seven years until you know that the Most High rules in the kingdom of men and gives it to whomever He will."

The same hour was the word fulfilled upon me; my reason departed from me and I became as a wild beast. I was driven from my palace out into the fields, eating grass like oxen, my body wet with dew, my hair grew long like eagle's feathers and my nails like bird claws.

Queen Amytis was inconsolable. Her maidens did all they could to assuage the pain of their grieving mistress, but they could only stand by her, helpless in the face of her distress.

The shocking events of the previous week haunted her dreams at night and dogged her waking hours with a nightmare sort of reality. Amytis had been with her husband in his palace bedchamber when he spoke the fateful words: "Is not this great Babylon that I have built by my power and for my glory?" She had nearly gone into shock when she saw him collapse to the floor as if dead.

She had rung for the servants, who had called in the royal physicians, but all they could do was to pull him up on his bed and watch; he had seemed completely unresponsive, almost catatonic. Finally, deciding he was under a spell, they had sent for the magicians and the conjurers. The chamber had by now become a chaotic melee of chanting, noisy incantations, and the air was foul with the smoke from the censers burning incense.

Presently, a deathly hush had settled over the vast chamber, as strange sounds issued from the form on the bed. With one ear-splitting, unearthly howl, he had leaped from the bed, landing on all fours, hands and feet moving sideways. Before the eyes of his astonished court, the king of Babylon had lifted his head and howled like a wolf.

Without warning, he had leaped upon a conjurer and had nearly torn the poor man to shreds. With almost superhuman strength, he had fought off all attempts to subdue him. Bodies had flown in all directions, but finally they had managed to throw a blanket over him; it had taken the combined strength of seven men to pin him down with ropes. By now the creature was whimpering piteously, and Amytis had collapsed into the arms of a servant.

The king had been taken outside the outer city walls and released. The last they had seen him, he was loping away through the fields on all fours. The gates of the city had been closed for the night, and Nebuchadnezzar had spent his first night curled up under a banyan tree, sound asleep under the stars and mercifully unaware of his past, present, or future.

One week later, Daniel had a visit from Azariah. "Daniel, I guess you know that my little sister, Hannah, is one of Queen Amytis' attendants—I just received word from her that the queen is urgently requesting your presence in her quarters."

"What?" replied his astonished friend. "Yes, I remember little Hannah, but Azariah—surely she is aware that neither I nor any other man is allowed in the queen's quarters without the king's express permission."

Azariah smiled and nodded. "Yes, I know, but Ashpenaz will accompany you, just for the sake of propriety. I have already spoken to him, and he has agreed to meet you at the palace entrance just after sundown. He knows the back way into the queen's chambers, having gone on errands for the king many times. If we leave now, we should be just in time."

An hour later, Daniel was seated in the antechamber, waiting for the queen. "Ashpenaz," he whispered, "why do you think she wants to see me? I have only seen her on half a dozen occasions and never had an opportunity to speak with her."

"Well, young Daniel, she is a woman of surprising intelligence and discernment. Amytis loves her husband and is nearly grieving herself to death over his insanity. It is said that she goes outside the city walls every day and leaves platters of food in the fields, watching and hoping for a glimpse of him. So far, she has not seen him, but the platters are empty the next day.

"Other wild animals, perhaps? Or just hungry peasants, scavenging for food—who knows? At any rate," Ashpenaz continued with a sigh, "she needs the help and wise counsel of someone she can trust—and she knows instinctively that she can confide in you, Daniel. The king himself taught her that."

Daniel fell silent, heartsick over the terrible fate of his good friend the king. *If only he had listened to my advice,* he thought ruefully, shaking his head.

Ashpenaz rose to go. "I'll wait for you outside in the hall," he explained, "since the queen asked to see you alone."

"But—" the protest died out; Daniel was alone in the room. Presently, the curtains parted, and two young women, their faces covered by veils, motioned him inside.

Amytis was standing on her terrace; the soft night wind stirred her garments slightly, but otherwise there was no movement. As she slowly turned, Daniel was shocked to see her lovely face pale as a ghost; deep, dark circles shadowed her sad green eyes.

"Ah, Daniel—you have come. I am so grateful. Please, sit down. I have much to tell you."

Some semblance of animation enlivened her features as the queen graciously poured a flagon of wine and set it before him. He waited respectfully; she began to speak softly.

"I'll come right to the point. I know you must be curious to know why I requested your presence so urgently. Daniel, I have two reasons for asking you to come. The first reason is that my husband valued your advice far above all others. He respected you, and one of the last things he told me was that, if anything ever happened to him, he knew that his kingdom was in good hands, for Daniel and his three friends were endowed by the gods with a very special wisdom. He told me that he would trust you with his very life!

"Then, not even a week later, he —he —," she could not go on, but fell silent, looking down at her hands in her lap.

She has not taken off her wedding ring, Daniel observed wryly. *Therefore she must have some reason to hope for restoration.*

Her abject misery touched his heart, and he reached across the table. "Amytis, give me your hand. I have something to tell you."

She looked up, startled, and placed her small, thin hand into his. He then told her the whole story of the dream and what it meant. When he came to the part about the kingdom being restored after seven years, she lifted her head and closed her eyes.

Tears of relief poured down her cheeks, and she could only whisper, over and over again, "Oh, thank you, Daniel—thank you, thank you! You have given me hope. My husband will return to me and to his kingdom, as strong and as wonderful as ever."

He rose from his chair and bowed respectfully as she stood and moved away to wipe her eyes.

"Now, dear Daniel—we come to the second reason for this visit. If you will just wait here for a few minutes…"

Before he could say anything, she was gone and he was alone in the room. He picked up the elaborate golden chalice and drained its contents, but his hand froze in midair: there, not ten feet away from him stood the woman of his dreams. Dressed in glowing golden silk, she seemed to shimmer from head to foot as she glided silently toward him. He set the chalice down unsteadily, his head whirling.

"Hello, Daniel." She smiled up at him, and he managed to croak a reply.

"Do you not know who I am?" Her scented black hair gave off a faint, heady aroma of myrrh as she shook her head. "No? Well, perhaps I can fill you in."

She circled him and moved out onto the terrace. He followed her as if he were in a trance, looking down at her soft strands of black hair flowing gracefully back from the circlet of gold filigree around her head.

He wanted to touch her so badly, but all he could do was swallow hard and say, "Yes, I do remember you—that day in the grape arbor—it was unintentional, please believe me…"

She glanced up at him, then continued looking out into the twilight. A soft evening breeze began to stir her garments ever so slightly, and still she remained silent. Finally, she spoke: "In what direction are we facing, Daniel?"

"West."

"That is correct. Do you know how many times I have been out on this terrace at sundown, watching four young men up on that palace balcony?" She leaned over the rail and pointed up to a high tower on the corner of the palace.

Daniel stared at her, amazed. "That is where my friends and I go to look toward Jerusalem, our homeland. Surely you must realize that I am Hebrew, not Chaldean."

Her musical laugh echoed out into the darkening twilight. "Oh, yes, Daniel, I know very well that you are Hebrew."

She turned to look up at him. "Now let me ask you a question: why do you think that I am out here on this balcony every night at about the same time, looking in the same direction as you?" Her features now were earnestly serious, lustrous blue eyes shining with unshed tears as she awaited his answer.

The knowledge finally swept over him like a giant wave, and he grasped her hands. "Hannah? You are…you are Azariah's little sister I used to carry around on my shoulders? I can't believe it!"

She nodded, the tears spilling over now.

"Hannah, little Hannah…" He groaned, and she was in his arms. For a very long time there was no sound on the little balcony except the cooing of pigeons roosting on the roof nearby and the occasional sighing of the night wind intermingling with the whispered declarations of love.

After what seemed like hours, Daniel finally came to his senses when he heard Ashpenaz's voice in the anteroom next door: "Tell His Excellency that I am still waiting, please. The hour is growing late, and we must leave."

With a hurried promise to arrange another meeting, Daniel reluctantly left the chamber, gathered up his disgruntled friend, and left.

"Well," growled the weary Ashpenaz, as they strode through the long tunnel, "what transpired in there that took so long to resolve? Is the queen feeling better?"

"I don't know," replied the younger man with a grin, "but I sure am."

———— ✦ ————

In the following months, Daniel received several more urgent requests from the queen, and Ashpenaz resigned himself to hours of boredom as he awaited his young protégé outside the queen's chamber.

"Just how long is this strange courtship going to last?" he inquired crankily as they trudged down the long stone steps to the tunnel. "I'm beginning to feel like a mole, I've spent so much time underground!"

"Ashpenaz, my dear and faithful friend—there is good news: the wedding will be in one more month, and—no more secret meetings! The queen has graciously consented to release Hannah back to her family so she can prepare for the wedding. And, Ashpenaz, we have decided to name our firstborn son after you!"

Ashpenaz said nothing but looked inordinately pleased. His steps quickened as he considered the possibility of a little godson of his very own!

———— ✦ ————

THE CHRONICLES OF NEBUCHADNEZZAR

True to the word of the Most High God, I, Nebuchadnezzar, king of Babylon, was driven from among men to live as a beast. My reason having departed from me, I ate the grass of the field and was wet with the dew of heaven. Seven times passed over me, and at the end of the days, I, Nebuchadnezzar, lifted up my eyes unto heaven. My understanding returned unto me, and I blessed the Most High, and I praised and honored Him that lives forever, whose dominion is an everlasting dominion, and whose kingdom is from generation to generation.

All the inhabitants of the earth are as nothing before Him; He does according to His will in the armies of heaven and among the inhabitants of the earth. None can stay His hand or question His mighty acts.

At the same time my reason was returned to me, the honor

and splendor of my kingdom was restored to me; I was established in my kingdom, and excellent majesty was added to me.

Now I, Nebuchadnezzar, do praise and honor and extol the King of Heaven, all whose works are truth, and His ways judgment; and those who walk in pride He is able to abase.

The inhabitants of the great city of Babylon and all those in the surrounding provinces were in a perpetual state of rejoicing. Their beloved king had been restored to them; never before in all history had such a remarkable and miraculous event transpired. A time of unprecedented peace and prosperity ensued throughout the entire kingdom and lasted many years.

Daniel and Hannah had three sons and two daughters. Mishael had married and was blessed with six daughters and, finally, one son.

Hananiah had also married, and his wife, unfortunately, died in childbirth. He mourned her death for several years, then married a young widow with two children. He beamed with fatherly pride when she presented him with a third child—a beautiful little daughter he named Miriam.

Azariah's sweet, frail wife died shortly after the birth of their second son. He never remarried, but his sister Hannah mothered his boys, raising them along with her own—a big, noisy, happy family.

The four families stayed close together, woven permanently into the fabric of the large Jewish community in Babylon. They successfully resisted the inroads of the pagan culture surrounding them, retaining their distinctive Hebrew flavor, strengthened in their faith by the awesome knowledge that their God was in absolute control of all the events that shaped their destinies, even in this pagan kingdom so far from their homeland.

Ashpenaz and his old friend Arioch spent many happy hours with their godsons, assimilating much of the culture and faith of their Hebrew friends. Ashpenaz, having been deprived of children of his own, was especially appreciative of the times spent with the children, and he spoiled them outrageously with gifts and sweetmeats.

One day, he failed to show up for his appointed visit, and when they did not hear from him and could not find him, a search party was sent out.

Seal up the Vision

It was Arioch who found him; Ashpenaz was lying propped up against a tree on the bank of the river. He had died with a trace of a smile on his old, wrinkled face.

They buried him there where he had died; under the tree, a simple marble monument stood to honor the life of this great man who had influenced the lives of two monarchs. A mysterious veiled woman was sometimes seen walking there in the cool of the evening, and the next day masses of wilting jasmine would cover the marble tomb.

The years passed, and the friendship between Daniel and the king deepened. Nebuchadnezzar was a radically changed man after his bizarre seven-year departure from reason. The great God had sovereignly chosen to reveal His mighty power to this pagan king.

Daniel described God's revelation to Nebuchadnezzar by saying, "Three times God spoke to him. The first time God showed me both his dream and its interpretation, and he acknowledged Him as *my* God. The second time he saw my friends delivered from the fire and blessed Him as *their* God. But the third time God dealt with him in such a way that Nebuchadnezzar finally recognized Him as *his* God—and worshiped Him as the God of the whole earth."

The first two times Nebuchadnezzar had witnessed God's power, and it had changed his thinking. The third time, however, he had experienced God's power, and it had changed his heart forever. He never abandoned his newfound faith, which became ever stronger as he spent much time listening to the reading of the ancient Hebrew scrolls.

The astrologers, soothsayers, and magicians were never again called into the royal throne room for consultations during the remaining years of his reign. On the other hand, neither did he foolishly attempt to legislate his faith in Daniel's God by issuing threatening decrees to dissenters throughout his realm, as he had done before. Having been thoroughly humbled by the Creator and Sustainer of the universe, Nebuchadnezzar spent the remainder of his years in peace, ruling his empire with mercy as well as justice.

Much of the duties of governorship were delegated to the three Hebrews, whose deliverance from the fiery furnace caused them to be regarded with awe and reverence by the entire populace, sometimes bordering on idolatry. Wherever they went, they were never quite sure if the people prostrate on the ground were offering simple obeisance due their exalted positions or worshiping a divine being.

The worship of Baal, Ishtar, and Marduk nearly ceased altogether, and the temples were deserted, their priests having been executed years before for their part in the murderous conspiracy. The priestess of Ishtar had mysteriously disappeared. There were rumors that she had fled to Persia, but most believed that she had joined her deceased lovers under the rock quarry.

The queen often entertained Hannah and her children at the palace. Nebuchadnezzar also enjoyed their presence and spoiled the children even more than Ashpenaz had. As these little ones grew older, married, and had children of their own, they often brought them to see the kind old man in the palace.

When he was confined to his bed, they brought him wildflowers and told him delightful stories of their adventures outside. He seemed to gain more and more enjoyment of these simple little pleasures, and cared less and less for the extravagant trappings of royalty, as he grew older and feebler.

Eventually, the day came when Daniel was sent an urgent message from the queen. "Come quickly, Daniel. There is not much time, and he is calling for you."

When he arrived, panting from the exertion, he found the hallway lined with weeping servants. In the king's chamber, the queen was sitting by his bed; the king was lying so very still, and Daniel knew with a sinking heart—he was gone.

When she saw him, Amytis smiled wanly. "Daniel. Thank you for coming. He wanted to tell you…to tell you how much he loved and respected you—and not to grieve, for he knew that the Most High God would receive him into His paradise. You know, I think he was actually looking forward to this new adventure."

She rose from the bed, and Daniel held her, speechless with the sorrow that enveloped them both.

Then, he spoke quietly: "Well, he had such a passion for living, and he truly lived life to its fullest. There will never be another like him."

Daniel continued, "The very best thing I could ever say about him: Jehovah God loved him and revealed His glory and greatness to him in a way no other ruler has ever known. He made the life-changing discovery that my God was also his God—and a God of great mercy as well as judgment. This was truly a noble king in every sense of the word, and our lives have been greatly enriched by the privilege of knowing and loving him."

Amytis stifled a sob.

"Dear lady," he murmured, stroking her graying hair, "My Hannah will come and stay with you for a while. She loves you so, and she will be a great comfort to you."

So it came to pass that the entire kingdom of Babylon sat in sackcloth and ashes, mourning the passing of Nebuchadnezzar the great king.

CHAPTER 13

REVELATION II

THE WATCHERS, THE Holy Ones from another sphere, were carefully observant of the frantic activity now escalating, accelerating at a breakneck pace on the planet called Earth. As the forces of darkness, uncloaked from their camouflage, were swirling in hideous array over their assigned targets, they seemed to be congregating in certain areas; the most remarkable area of attack was a semicircle of mideastern desert countries surrounding the tiny state of Israel.

The prince of darkness, knowing that his time was almost gone, exerted every effort to wreak total havoc, destruction, and death on the race of humans he so despised. His prime weapon was (as it always had been) lies and deception. It is supposed that, knowing his doom had for many centuries been foretold, he would have given up to the vastly superior, far stronger forces opposing him. It was not to be so. Being the chief of liars, he ultimately deceived himself, so—believing his own lies, he therefore sealed his own doom.

This malevolent creature, having rebelled and fallen from great heights of glory and privilege, having once known the pure joy of serving his Creator, now sought to sow those same seeds of bitter hatred and rebellion in the human race. Among earth's inhabitants, the ones he targeted most were the ones he feared most: those who were hungry and thirsty for righteousness, those seekers of Truth who would eventually be a threat to his kingdom of darkness.

As a matter of fact, his fears were quite real and well-founded. He had managed for thousands of years to successfully establish countless false religions, most notably—and his proudest achievement to date—the modern apostate "Christians" who brazenly embraced his New Age doctrines, spouting an abominable lukewarm mixture of garbled humanism from their elegant pulpits.

Even more remarkable, he had managed to keep millions of Christians insulated in their "comfort zones," encased in religious traditions while steadfastly resisting any change. They were unwilling to risk the loss of their comfort by reaching out to the lost and dying world around them. Indeed, the "god of this world" had successfully blinded their eyes.

However, an ancient and long-forgotten prophecy in the Book of Joel was being called to remembrance among the forces of Light. "For it shall come to pass in the last days, saith the Lord, that I will pour out My Spirit on all flesh…"

"It is time!" thundered the orders from Headquarters. The mighty Spirit began to move over the vast chaotic sea of teeming millions upon the earth: just a soft, rustling breeze stirring the treetops in the beginning, then a stronger, more forceful wind. This wind became a mighty tempest, blowing through the churches, through the synagogues, even through the mosques. It blew through large corporations, down back alleys and housing projects.

In palaces and tenements, from Siberia to South Africa—no one on earth remained untouched by the finger of God. Hindu women in Calcutta saw visions of Jesus and fell prostrate in worship. Children everywhere were singing praises to God, little songs taught to them by angels. Businessmen in Japan were trying to find someone to explain the gospel of salvation. Churches in Buenos Aires were overflowing with crowds of joyful new believers.

But the most remarkable conversions were happening in the Islamic republics; millions of Muslims, especially the most militant, were turning to the God of Abraham, Isaac, and Jacob—gloriously redeemed by the blood of His Son. This was absolutely the last straw for the prince of Persia, who had to report to his master the loss of so many to the other side.

"The intercessory prayer, those millions of believers who have been systematically tearing down our best strongholds—that is where we should have foreseen this terrible defeat!" he raged. "Why couldn't we just have wiped them out in the beginning—slaughtered them and their entire families? Sought out their weaknesses and destroyed them before they could damage us irreversibly?"

The prince of darkness regarded his irate visitor with dangerous,

134

hooded eyes and said nothing. Finally he spoke: "You are, of course, aware that they belong to HIM, that they are under HIS protection, and we cannot touch them without HIS express permission. Besides, the real damage was done when the walls we had so carefully erected between them—the walls of indifference, suspicion, apathy, mistrust, hatred, and isolation—started to disintegrate because of one little word: LOVE!

"When they began to finally let go of their differing opinions and begin to truly love each other, then they came into unity, and…and then God commanded His blessing. I could do nothing to stop it. Nothing will be impossible to them, unless we can find a way to once again sow the seeds of doubt, fear, and mistrust. Now leave me. I must devise a more effective strategy, and you will be notified."

This last was whispered, or rather growled—and the prince of Persia made a hasty departure. In the next weeks and months, the hellish plans were devised and set into motion. The forces of Light—watchers, warriors, messengers, guardians —those powerful beings who faithfully carried out the orders of the Most High, were already girded for battle, each carrying out his orders in preparation for the final conflict.

The flight from Beersheba to the Golan Heights took only a little more than fifteen minutes. Matt adjusted his mask and transmitted the signal to his companions as their formation turned and headed west into the sun. The immense exhilaration he always felt when he was in the cockpit and streaking through the atmosphere now gave vent to a long, loud war whoop. More than a few times he had incurred the wrath of his instructors by "buzzing the tower."

Now, as he banked left to the south, he could just see the sparkling curve of the Mediterranean below. The city of Tel Aviv was just ahead, and he had to fight the familiar urge to buzz the area where his fiancée dwelled. Heather would be coming home from the university about now, he thought with a rush of tenderness. *She's probably down there now looking up at me.* Matt had never suffered from a lack of self-esteem, and he waggled his wings as he streaked through the heavens.

Since joining the Israeli Air Force the previous year, Matt had received many hours of intensive flight training, but never yet had he seen combat. Something inside him yearned to be in the midst of battle, yet as he drew closer to the day of his wedding, he began to realize that he had chosen an arena of mortal combat as his life's work. Such knowledge had sobered him somewhat, making him just a bit more cautious than the rash, eager young man of only a year ago.

The older, more experienced ones told stories of so many young lives sacrificed in the defense of their tiny nation, and it never failed to move him. Weapons now were infinitely more sophisticated than even those of ten or twenty years ago. In order to use them effectively, skills and judgmental abilities must be finely tuned; one tiny, infinitesimal lapse in judgment could result in lost lives and very expensive equipment.

Additionally, the Israeli Department of Defense was having to make cutbacks in funding because of the lack of support from the United States. Since the third decade of the new millennium, the American policies practically ensured the absorption of the U.S. into the U.N., and traditional American sovereignty had all but collapsed. Their only hope of restoration was the fact that a new Global Coalition was beginning to supplant the old and ineffective U.N., and their objectives were more in the European and Mideast areas.

Matt shuddered in revulsion as he recalled the news reports of gangs traversing the streets of Washington, displaying their lewd conduct in open scorn of onlookers. One young man who, holding up a Bible, stood on the hood of his car to protest was hauled off to jail while the gruesome painted features of two drunken women filled the lens of the CNN news camera, screaming anti-Christian profanities. Anti-Semitism and open persecution of Christians now was in full swing, and the concentration camps built in secret a decade ago were now filled almost to capacity. Many thousands had gone underground; their numbers were growing daily.

Matt shook off the despair that threatened to envelop him and began his descent to the airfield. Far below, a lone figure stood atop a high dune on the Sinai desert, watching the gracefully curving contrails of the Israeli jets above him. Slowly, a satisfied smile split the contours of his deeply tanned, strikingly handsome features.

Prince Hassan Salaameh cut a dashing figure as he stood elegantly slouched with his hands in the pockets of his Savile Row pin-striped suit. His one concession to his Arabic heritage was the kaffiyeh—the traditional headgear shielding him from the glare of the afternoon sun. The clouds above were reflected from the curved Polaray sunglasses atop his slightly hooked nose. He snapped his fingers and turned suddenly, striding purposefully down the dune and back to his air-conditioned BMW, which immediately headed back to the road, enveloped in a cloud of dust.

Before he reached his destination, he had accomplished a great deal, having activated his computer, phone, and fax system. After a lengthy exchange of short, terse messages, he exited the air-conditioned car in favor of an air-conditioned hotel suite, smiling down with considerable satisfaction at the stunning blonde who accompanied him.

The little group huddled around the fire, letting its welcome warmth settle into their weary bones, bringing both relief from the cold and respite from the constant worry of discovery. Ever since they had come to the Cabinet Mountains wilderness of Montana, Randy and Paula Endicott had not even had time to mourn the loss of their home and friends back in Pennsylvania.

Immediately after helping the Mannheim family escape to Israel, they were in great danger of arrest and imprisonment. Two other families from Randy's church had made the decision to move, and then approached the Endicotts. One of the men had a Christian nephew who worked for the Forest Service in northwestern Montana and had helped several other groups relocate there.

There were several areas deep in the back country wilderness that had once been used for hippie communes back in the sixties. One was located near Kalispell, and another about forty miles from Libby, a small logging town near the Idaho and Canadian borders. The Endicotts were already well winterized, so the cold weather was no real hardship, but the reports of grizzly sightings had Paula a little nervous. She kept a close eye on their young charges, as did all the other mothers.

The families were well aware of the constant danger of discovery. Back in the 1990s, the American presidency had quite literally bartered away two hundred years of America's precious, hard-won sovereignty by giving the U.N. certain powers over U.S. lands, especially the national parks and wilderness areas. Without due democratic process or congressional approval, the international alliance had gradually, quietly come in and taken over. Under the guise of ecological diversity, it had set aside nearly 50 percent of all U.S. lands for animal use only, illegal for human habitation.

Seal up the Vision

It had all happened so quietly and quickly that few U.S. citizens were aware until 1997, when a whole group of towns in the Cuyahoga Falls area of Ohio were evacuated and the citizens stripped of their lands. Some Christian groups protested the injustice, but the media remained silent as always. Many years later, detainment camps were built, and the persecution of Christians and Jews was launched on a nationwide scale. The unthinkable had now become reality.

All of the families in these wilderness communes had determined that their number one priority would be intensive intercession for the church in America to rise up and prevail over the darkness that was threatening to extinguish its existence. They were engaged in active evangelism through the Internet, using all technology available to them to spread the true gospel, the power of God for salvation.

From time to time, the Spirit of God would direct them to send some of their men into the cities, where they experienced the divine protection of God as massive crowds of hungry people gathered around them. They preached the gospel of the kingdom, with signs and wonders of all kinds attending the Word of God. Many thousands were healed, saved, and delivered. These, in turn, went about proclaiming the good news. The kingdom of God was growing exponentially, something that had never been seen before in the churches where only a pale, ineffectual shadow of the gospel had been preached for many generations.

So far, the little groups in Montana had escaped detection. The men hunted and fished; their outside provisions were brought in once a week on the nephew's Forest Service truck.

"If Uncle Sam is going to persecute you, we might as well put his equipment to some good use, eh?" He grinned as he unloaded the boxes. God was as good as His Word: they never once went to bed hungry or cold, and they experienced supernatural peace and favor.

Back in Pennsylvania, their children had been excited about traveling west and living like pioneers, their heads no doubt filled with romantic Hollywood-induced visions. But when reality settled in, they also realized that their lives would be permanently changed.

"You need to understand, kids," Randy had gently explained as he neatly fitted the very last of the suitcases into the back of the van, "we can never go back. You do understand that, don't you?"

"Uh-huh." Three little heads had nodded together in unison, but Paula's eyes had filled with tears as her mother-heart broke for them. *They are so young,* she had thought, *to be deprived of a normal, happy existence. Lord, You have protected us so far, and now You have provided a place of refuge. It's so far away, though, and the trip will be charged with danger. Lord—I ask You to get us there safely; I trust in Your provision.* She had dried her eyes, made one last check of the house, then joined her waiting family in the car.

"Ready to go, babe?" Randy had grinned as he backed out of the drive-way. Before backing into the street, however, he had stopped and prayed with his family: "God, go before us as the cloud by day and the fire by night, even as You did for Your people in the wilderness so long ago. What a privilege and an honor it is to suffer even a little for Your name. Amen."

"And take care of my dog Topsy," a little voice had chimed in from the back seat.

"And my cat Jemimah. Don't let her get runned over…" another voice had added with a small sob.

"Amen," the third had declared, and away they had gone, all unaware of their unseen passengers.

The angels guarding the Endicott family felt especially privileged, for it was a well-known fact that the prayers of little children, being pure and unadulter-ated as yet with unbelief, carried great weight in the halls of heaven….

…and the Almighty had very special plans for these little ones.

"A fresh, new beginning. Oh, Jack, I wish we had done this long ago!" Ruth's eyes were sparkling as she energetically cleaned the large bay window in their new living room.

She took one last swipe, inspected it carefully for streaks, then settled with a contented sigh into the soft, tapestried pillows lining the window seat. "What a gorgeous view of the valley, and —*m-m-m*—just smell that orange blossom scented air. A far cry from the foul pollution we used to breathe, right, Jack?"

Her husband glanced up from his drafting table, smiling fondly at his wife's enthusiasm. "Well, this may not exactly be the Garden of Eden—what with the high cost of living, the constant threat of war, and political instability—but, yes, Ruth. I am glad we came to Israel."

He stood up, stretched, and came over to the window, looking out over the valley to the distant skyline of Jerusalem, silhouetted against the glowing sunset. "We've had it so easy. I've met so many who came from Russia, Eastern Europe, Turkey, and so many places where they lived under generations of oppression. They came here with nothing and have worked so hard to make a decent living—yet, when I talk to them, they beam with pride and gratitude. They are so glad just to be here.

"The numbers of those arriving from Western Europe and the U.S. are increasing daily—a pretty good indicator of the level of anti-Semitism in those countries. So many have had to leave everything behind and flee for their lives. They are the ones I feel most sorry for: people used to lives of privilege and abundance, stripped of everything—friends, family, finances."

He paused and shook his head sadly. "We have been greatly blessed to be able to carry on my construction business. Because of the massive influx of immigrants from all over the world, we'll have enough work for many years to provide at least part-time employment for several hundred able-bodied men who desperately need jobs to support their families."

Ruth smiled up at her husband, quietly appreciative of his compassion for others less fortunate than themselves. *My husband, the hard-headed businessman,* she thought fondly, *has a heart of pure marshmallow.*

Their reverie was interrupted by the insistent ringing of the telephone. Jack took the call and Ruth went into the kitchen to start dinner. Sarah came breezing in the back door with her usual load of books, and this time a bouquet of fresh flowers from a street vendor.

"Be back in a little bit, Mom." She brushed a kiss against Ruth's cheek, dropped the flowers on the table, and headed for the stairs. "Big fat letter from Dan!" she grinned over her shoulder as she ran upstairs to her room.

Presently, she came down and set the table for dinner, humming a little tune as she helped Ruth with the food. Jack was still closeted in his study, talking on the phone, so they chatted quietly in the living room as they waited.

Finally Jack appeared. "I'm starving," he announced. "When do we eat?"

"Hi, Toots," he greeted his daughter with the customary bear hug. "What's up? You look like a cat with canary feathers in her mouth."

"Letter from you-know-who," explained Ruth as they sat down to eat. "Jack, dear—speaking of a cat/canary countenance, you could, maybe, let us know where that goofy grin came from?"

"OK, OK—I give. Never could keep anything from you. It seems that

I am needed on a very important project." He paused dramatically. "Very important, indeed,"

"Well," Ruth put down her napkin, leaning forward. "Well, what is it?"

"Do you remember the bus driver telling us the first day we arrived about a project to rebuild the temple in Jerusalem? Believe it or not, almost all the materials for it are already here in Israel, stored in different locations around the country. Since our construction business has done so well this last year, we have been selected, along with several other firms, for the actual construction work."

Sarah looked completely flabbergasted. "But, Dad, that is the greatest storm center of controversy in the entire Mideast! How do they think they're going to displace the Dome of the Rock, Islam's holy shrine? I understood that the Muslims have vowed to fight to the death over their right to the temple area—it will ignite a jihad, a holy war like the world has never seen!"

Ruth's frown reflected her concern. "Jack, this sounds to me like a very perilous undertaking; won't you and your men be in constant danger, even supposing you do somehow secure the site?" She shook her head vehemently. "It's just too dangerous, Jack—this country is a powder keg waiting to explode. I have met many wonderful Palestinians in my volunteer work at the hospital, and I can't imagine being at war with them."

Her husband leaned back in his chair and replied soberly, "All that is very true. To be perfectly honest, I don't have the slightest idea how, or even when, all this will happen. I only know that plans are being made, and when the time comes, I want to be included. Now, let's eat before I collapse from hunger; I'll try to explain in more detail after dinner. Ruth, I think I'll open up that bottle of wine Matt sent us."

Sarah sighed deeply, gazing out the window at the darkening horizon. "I sure do miss my little brother—it seems so strange to think of him out there on those desert training camps, flying those fighters all over creation. Stranger still, Dad," she said with a shudder, "to think of him fighting in a real war, dodging SAM missiles and antiaircraft gunfire—"

"That's ultimately what he is preparing for, Sarah," murmured Jack as he reached for her hand. "Matt knew the risks when he joined the IAF, but he's got what it takes—I guess they call it the 'right stuff' for a pilot, and I'm very proud of my son!"

The family ate their dinner in unaccustomed silence and then retired to the outside terrace for dessert and coffee. By now the stars were making their glittering debut against the dark blue velvet curtain overhead; a slender crescent moon was suspended just over the eastern horizon. The night wind whispered through the bougainvillea hanging above the terrace, and the intoxicating fragrance of night-blooming jasmine drifted up from the garden below.

The low murmur of voices lulled a sleepy Sarah into slumber, and she dreamed that she was drifting over a trackless desert in a hot air balloon, looking for her lost love. The winds took her higher and higher, until she could see nothing but a great expanse of starry heaven all around her. At first she felt engulfed by the loneliness, but then she began to discern the shapes of many other balloons ascending just as hers, and a great peaceful relief washed over her. Somehow, she knew that her Dan would be all right.

Sarah slept on, and her parents did not have the heart to disturb her. They covered her with a blanket and went on to bed.

That very same evening, many miles to the north, the object of her affections was tormented by the now familiar insomnia that seemed to plague him on a nightly basis. Dan finally snapped on the light, sat up in bed, and stared blankly around his room.

"I'll be so glad when this project is finally through," he mumbled to himself, and wandered over to the bookshelf. "I've read and re-read them all," he grumbled aloud, and opened up his suitcase to look for some extra sleeping pills.

What he found, however, was the old brown leather NIV Bible that Randy had given to him at his high school graduation. Dan had never paid much attention to it, but out of respect for his coach and perhaps a little superstitiously, he carried it permanently in his suitcase.

He had been raised in a semi-religious home; his parents had been members of a little run-down Southern Baptist church in West Texas. The dear old countrified pastor was nothing spectacular, but he knew every member of his congregation well and took their spiritual welfare seriously. He used to chide Dan's father good-naturedly about his habit of chewing tobacco and would always compliment "Miz Shepherd" lavishly on her good ol' home cookin'. He and Dan used to sit on the back porch and talk about things like football and horses, baseball and girls.

The pastor was easy to talk to and was genuinely interested in Dan's life, something unusual in adults. "Son," he would drawl as he placed an arm over the boy's shoulder, "you are gonna amount to somethin' when you grow up, and don't forget it! I'll be prayin' for you, son, so —whatever you do—can't run fast enough or far enough to get away from God!"

Dan could still hear the hearty chuckle as he stared at the unopened Bible, so he picked it up, got a caffeine-free Coke from the refrigerator, and settled in for some reading. For lack of any better plan, he started out in Genesis and kept right on reading until sleep finally overtook him nearly three hours later.

He awoke at 6 a.m., curiously refreshed after only four hours of sleep, so decided the following night to repeat the procedure. After several weeks, the hydroelectric project came to a temporary halt while some structural engineers ran their tests and completed the necessary surveys. Dan now had plenty of time on his hands, so, with nowhere else to go, he continued reading through the Bible until he finished it.

By this time, a large package had arrived from the U.S. His house-keeper had forwarded all of Randy's books, which he had left behind for Dan, along with a hasty note explaining their disappearance.

Sorry I can't give you any more information, the note continued, *but I'll try to contact you later. Thought you might enjoy these books —God bless you and keep you —Randy and Paula.*

He did, indeed, devour the books eagerly, for many of them shed much light on Scriptures he had not understood. Many were expounding the End-Time prophecies of Isaiah, Ezekiel, Daniel, Joel, Zechariah, and the New Testament, especially Revelation. The Babylon of Revelation apparently represented the consummate evil of a religious system gone bad, having compromised with the forces of darkness.

Eventually there came a time of reckoning, a confrontation with a very personal God who was calling Dan into a relationship with Himself. He wrestled with this over several nights, then finally—as Jacob had wrestled with his God—he surrendered his will to the One who had paid such an astronomical price to buy back his soul.

Jesus, I'm a sinner—I need you. Be my Lord—be my Savior. I'll serve you as long as I live. And as he arose from his knees, created anew, a hundred thousand angels rejoiced.

CHAPTER 14

THE COUP

BY THE THIRD year of his reign, Bel-Shazzar, co-regent with his father Nabonidus of the kingdom of Babylon, had finally exceeded the acceptable limits of royal protocol: he had become a drunk. As so often happens when young men of low moral character are given too much too soon, his unfortunate reign consisted mainly of a rapid descent into debauchery. Orgies that lasted days, and sometimes weeks, were followed by prolonged bouts of sickness and melancholy.

The strong, stern moral fiber of his grandfather, Nebuchadnezzar, had become considerably diluted by his reign. Nabonidus, the son-in-law of Nebuchadnezzar, had begun to tax the surrounding territories—once so productive and peaceable during Nebuchadnezzar's reign—to the point of revolt. Nabonidus was constantly on the move, always caught off-balance as he frantically traveled from one rebellious province to another. His biggest mistake was entrusting the rulership of Babylon to his profligate son.

Bel-Shazzar and his father had also made one other mistake that eventually would prove to be fatal for them both: they retired Daniel and his friends from royal service, reinstituting the worship of pagan gods in Babylon. The queen mother, Amytis, was extremely grieved by this turn of events. Being only a woman, she had no say in matters of government, so she grieved in silence.

Her loneliness, however, was often assuaged by a visit from Daniel and Hannah or one of their six granddaughters. The queen always marveled that, although Hannah was now in her late fifties, she still retained the same stunning beauty that had hopelessly entrapped her beloved Daniel so many years ago.

Perhaps because of their earlier physical training, perhaps because of the strict nutritious diet they observed—Daniel, Mishael, and Hananiah were still in excellent health for men nearing their seventies. Azariah, however, never completely got over the death of his wife, and several years before, had finally succumbed to a high fever at the age of sixty-two.

After the burial service, the three remaining friends all climbed the long flight of stone steps to the same parapet where they had met as youths so many years ago, gazing sadly toward the setting sun. "We also will be buried here," murmured Daniel with a heavy sigh.

Mishael gripped the stone and looked down, a terrible grief constricting his throat. "Daniel, Hananiah—I can no longer see it. I cannot remember…Jerusalem. After all these years, it is so hard to recall those streets that were our boyhood home…"

"I know, Mishael," replied Hananiah, his voice trembling with emotion. "I can't even remember clearly what my family looked like! My own family!"

With the passing of years, the three men knew that there was no hope of ever returning to their homeland. Each was feeling the absence of Azariah very keenly, and as they turned to descend the stone steps to the palace below, Daniel again reminded them of God's faithfulness through their long and greatly privileged lives.

"We can't keep longing for the past. It is over and done with. But remember the scrolls of Jeremiah? God says that He knows the plans He has for us, plans not for calamity, but for a future and a hope. Azariah would not want us to mourn him, but rather to continue on the journey destined for us by our God. Who knows—perhaps our children or grandchildren will someday return and rebuild the walls of Jerusalem!"

The caravan from Scythia arrived in Babylon at sunset exactly thirty days before the young regent's twenty-fifth birthday. The palace servants were up all night, unloading the camels and storing several thousand wine casks in the vast cool cellars far below the palace. The wine stewards and chamberlains were kept busy for the next several days tasting and labeling the very best for the prince and his friends at the great month-long festival.

The palace was a beehive of activity. All the servants were frantically putting everything into readiness when suddenly, without warning, Bel-Shazzar himself strode into the great hall, followed by his usual train of boasting, swaggering young friends. The servants froze and bowed low in obeisance, but unfortunately, one hapless young boy, who was up on a ladder hanging silken curtains, lost his footing and plunged into the fountain below. Stunned by the fall, he floated face down in the water, and his mother, a seamstress, rushed to pull him out.

"Leave him!" Bellowed the prince, and the poor woman froze in consternation. Bel-Shazzar and his friends encircled the fountain. The prince sat down casually on the edge, glanced up at his giggling friends, and with a sudden, savage thrust—pushed the boy's head down to the bottom of the fountain.

The mother screamed in anguish and threw herself down at his feet, pleading for the life of her son. All the servants watched in shock as the prince of Babylon cocked his head, mocking the woman's pitiful cries. Finally he slowly and deliberately stood up and, still holding her poor dead child by the hair, pulled the still, limp body out of the water and placed it into the mother's arms.

Her soft sobbing was the only sound in the room. He swayed a little, feet apart and hands on his hips, as he spat out the words that would haunt him for the remainder of his life: "His days were numbered, you know. I hereby decree that this is his very last one…"

His words are slurred, thought the chief of the chamberlains sourly. *It is not yet midmorning, and that despicable idiot is already drunk!*

"What are you fools waiting for? Get back to work before I have you all taken out and flogged!" Bel-Shazzar barked out his orders hoarsely and staggered out of the room, followed at a distance by his sickened cohorts.

When they reached the courtyard, he whirled on them, shouting obscenities. "Well, what are all of you looking at? I'm the king—I can do whatever I wish, and right now I wish you gone!"

His uneasy friends disappeared in ten different directions, and Bel-Shazzar stumbled down the garden steps where he threw up, then sprawled on his back in the sun.

The dead little boy was buried, and later that night, Queen Amytis received a visitor. Old Sar-Sechim was carried into her chambers on the litter, requesting to be alone with the queen mother.

"Your Majesty," began the ancient, frail little man, "I am nearly one hundred years old and have seen many strange things in my lifetime, but what happened today is by far the most hideous, obscene act these old eyes have ever witnessed."

"I know. That is why I sent for you." whispered Amytis from behind her veil, and for the first time he took notice that her eyes were puffy and reddened from crying.

"Sar-Sechim, I have come to a decision, and am more than glad for your wise counsel. You see, the seamstress was not only my faithful servant, but she was also a good friend. She would often bring her son with her when he was just a happy, sweet little toddler—" Here her voice broke, and she turned to face the window.

"Many times while she was here working on my gowns, her child would climb up on my lap and ask me to tell him stories or sing a song. That was several years ago, but I loved him as if he were my own. Now, Sar-Sechim, the one who truly is my own grandson—Bel-Shazzar—has finally stepped over the line. He is…he is subhuman, a very devil. I will no longer support his claim to the throne."

The old man blinked in surprise, but she continued with dogged determination. "Sar-Sechim, I need your help. The kingdom that my husband labored so hard to build is now in great jeopardy. My son-in-law Nabonidus is an ineffectual fool. There, I've said it!"

She whirled in anger, facing her elderly caller. "There is now only one course for us to take. We must send a message immediately to Darius in Persia. Someone you trust, Sar-Sechim—you and Daniel choose six expert horsemen and the fastest horses—and it must be done tonight!

"They can transfer to fresh horses at our relay posts, but this fact remains: there is only one hope for our city, for our people, for the entire realm—and that is a strong, honorable, decisive ruler. Darius and his son Cyrus are such men. We must accept the fact that the dynasty of Nebuchadnezzar is over!"

Sar-Sechim was very still, answering her soberly, "You realize, Madame, that your son-in-law and grandson will most likely not abdicate voluntarily?"

Amytis said nothing but knelt impulsively by the old man and took his hand. "Whatever happens, Sar-Sechim, I believe with all my heart those things taught to us by Daniel: that the affairs of this kingdom rest ultimately in the hands of his great God."

———∞———

The spring rains had come early to the Valley of the Chaldees. Hostilities had ceased between the two armies facing each other across the rain-drenched plain as the horse-drawn carts carrying the military supplies were helplessly mired in mud. The messenger from Susa came riding into the Persian camp just before dawn and, dismounting on the run, brought the urgent message to the pavilion of Cyrus.

Bowing low before the Persian prince, the winded man remained on one knee as the message was read. Cyrus was still a little groggy from sleep and ran his fingers absently through his thick dark, unruly curls as he read the scroll. When he had finished reading, he sat absolutely still for a moment, staring at the deep carpet. His handsome features were a study in concentration, and he appeared to have forgotten the courier's presence in his tent.

Suddenly he stood and strode to the entrance. "Sergeant, take this man to the cook and give him something to eat, then let him sleep for a few hours. I will send my answer back with another courier."

The man gratefully bowed and left; the answering message was quickly composed and sent, then the prince called for his generals, Gadatas and Gobrias. These two young brothers from a noble Persian family had been Cyrus's loyal boyhood friends. The three had grown up together under the tutelage of Cyrus's mother, Queen Esther, and her uncle Mordecai in the royal palace at Shushan, so they had the sublime advantages of wise counsel, strict discipline, and a great deal of affectionate nurturing.

Gobrias and Gadatas had four younger sisters, all of whom came often to the palace and were accorded a great deal of freedom, considering their female gender. The oldest daughter, Natassi, was renowned for her beauty, and young Cyrus had found himself making plans to claim her as his queen. *Someday, when I am king,* he had mused dreamily, *Natassi will come to me as my mother, Esther, came to my father—and I will step down from my throne and throw my royal cloak down for her dainty feet to walk on…*

His fantasies had grown ever more elaborate as Natassi blossomed into the full-blown beauty of young womanhood, and the day finally came when she sweetly accepted Cyrus' proposal of marriage. The joyous occasion of their betrothal just happened to coincide with a visit Nabonidus, the newly crowned king of Babylon, and Bel-Shazzar, his teenaged son, made to the Persian capital. The days of mourning for Nebuchadnezzar had been completed, and the new monarch wished to survey his kingdom, traveling from province to province.

During the festivities at Shushan, Bel-Shazzar cast his eye upon the lovely Natassi and decided to pursue her. She adroitly repulsed his unwelcome attentions, which enraged him. He sulked for days while he plotted his revenge. On the last night before his departure, Natassi mysteriously vanished from her quarters.

The next morning she was found, wounded, bleeding, and disheveled on the bank of the Tigris River, far downstream from the palace. Her lustrous dark eyes were large with fright, and she could not speak. Her family took her home and kept her in quiet seclusion for several weeks. Cyrus was nearly out of his mind with worry, and her brothers tried to comfort him with news of her gradual, steady healing, but they were truly as bewildered as he was.

Finally, the day came when she spoke her first words since the tragedy; all she could whisper was "Bel-Shazzar." That was enough. Gadatas and Gobrias told Cyrus, and the three enraged friends made a solemn vow of revenge. From that time, Bel-Shazzar's days were truly numbered.

As Natassi gradually regained her strength and vitality, Queen Esther spent much time with her future daughter-in-law. Love has a way of healing the deepest wounds, and Cyrus watched with quiet admiration as the wise counsel of his mother brought the sparkle back to the eyes of his beloved. They were married that autumn and entered into a union that, birthed in adversity, was to last a lifetime.

From that time, a deep-seated enmity existed between the two nations. Darius the Mede, also called Ahasuerus, ruled his far-flung Persian empire with the gracious ease of a true monarch. He had wisely chosen Mordecai the Jew—Esther's cousin—to be his prime minister and thus operated under the full blessing and favor of Jehovah God.

On the other hand, Nabonidus had foolishly chosen to disregard the God of his father-in-law Nebuchadnezzar. This had created a massive void, an empty vacuum in both his character and his kingdom. Into this void were sucked all manner of bizarre ideas, destructive behavior patterns, and pseudo-religious systems. Chaos reigned supreme in Babylon.

Seal up the Vision

Nabonidus' latest folly had been to declare war on Darius, who was occupied in a distant province. Cyrus, as commander of the Persian army, took a good-sized, well-equipped contingent to meet Nabonidus on the field of battle. Several skirmishes had ensued, but no real fighting due to the inclement weather.

Nabonidus, however, faced an even more worrisome enemy than Cyrus' well-trained and far better equipped troops: his own Babylonian army was tired and poorly equipped, and his generals were on the verge of revolt. The constant rain and mud had further dampened their spirits, and a sort of malaise hung like a thick, gray fog bank over the Babylonian camp.

Cyrus leaned against the doorpost of his pavilion, peering out into the fog-enshrouded valley below. Far across on the other side, there was no perceptible movement in the enemy camp, which was almost invisible except for the faint glow of the sentinel fires around the perimeter. He shivered in the early morning chill, drawing the heavy camel hair blanket around his broad shoulders. He closed his eyes and thought longingly how good it would feel to be safe and warm at home in the vast feather bed with his wife.

He shook his head impatiently and turned back inside the tent, followed by Gadatas and Gobrias, who had suddenly appeared out of the fog. He motioned them to sit down as he picked up the parchments.

"My friends," he began grimly, holding up one of the letters. "This is a desperate cry for help from Queen Amytis of Babylon—Nebuchadnezzar's widow—and this..." holding up the other letter, "is a directive from my father to drop this silly skirmish, proceed immediately to Babylon, and take the city!"

His two friends, their faces frozen masks of astonishment, gazed up at him. Gobrias leaned forward, his eyes glittering in the firelight. "Take the city? But how? Babylon is an impregnable fortress with walls eight hundred feet high—double walls! How does your father propose that we do this?"

Gadatas jumped up and paced the floor, his words tumbling out, his fists clenched. "This is our chance, Gobrias. I just know it—there must be a way. Remember our vow to repay Bel-Shazzar for his vile treachery against our sister!"

Cyrus leveled his gaze somewhere over their heads and spoke softly through clenched teeth: "Yes, Bel-Shazzar will pay. Indeed, he will forfeit his worthless life for the evil he has done."

He lowered his eyes and smiled slowly as he took their hands. "But…this goes far beyond a personal vendetta. The great God Jehovah has surely delivered him, as well as the kingdom of Babylon, into our hands. We have a golden opportunity to bring order back to the kingdom and rule jointly, my father and I, over all of Persia and Babylon—a vast empire. We must proceed with all haste, but also with great caution. Now, here is the plan."

He quickly spread out the maps, and for the next three hours, they carefully formulated and recorded the details for the invasion of Babylon—the regal queen mother of all cities, the sovereign ruler of a far-flung empire, the glittering jewel and golden prize secure and serenely indestructible behind her massive walls.

On the fourteenth day of the great feast, Bel-Shazzar was busily occupied with his only talent: a seemingly inexhaustible ability to consume vast quantities of alcohol while he remained in a semi-coherent state. At least he was able to keep a running commentary on the immense treasures of his inheritance. Indeed, he showed a remarkable ability to remember from the long inventory lists the most dazzling and impressive of Nebuchadnezzar's exotic collection.

Taking his nearly one thousand guests on a guided tour of the treasure houses, he eventually happened upon the most impressive of all: the vast hall packed with all of the golden vessels from Solomon's fabled temple in Jerusalem, stored for more than sixty years in the temple of Baal. An unaccustomed hush fell over the crowd as the late afternoon sun shot its rays through the parting clouds and the arched windows of the temple and slowly lit the entire room into a vast fiery golden conflagration.

Bel-Shazzar threw his arm over his eyes and stumbled backward; the crowd gasped in awe. Without a word, Bel-Shazzar turned and fled down the marble stairs as if the very hounds of hell were pursuing him. Reluctantly, the guests turned and followed, as royal protocol demanded.

Later that evening, the feast began as the prince swaggered into the hall, dressed in his most resplendent clothes. He mounted the steps to his throne and, turning to the crowd, held up his scepter. Bel-Shazzar was embarrassed. The sense of humiliation from his behavior this afternoon lingered like a foul taste in his mouth, and he had been casting about for a way to redeem himself.

"Chamberlain of the feast," he roared dramatically, "go and fetch me the golden vessels of Solomon, that I and my guests may take our wine from them this night!"

The chamberlain bowed low and hurried from the room, his features pinched and pale with fright. For over six decades, no one had ever touched the temple treasure—not even the superstitious priest of Baal—for it was widely believed among the people that it was guarded by powerful beings from another place. Years before, Nebuchadnezzar had issued an edict that whoever dared to trifle with the golden vessels of the Most High God would be executed.

It took nearly two hours before the servants began carrying great wooden chests filled with the temple treasure into the banquet hall. The vessels were distributed among the guests, and Bel-Shazzar's drunken laughter echoed through the hall as he stood. Swaying unsteadily, he raised a large golden chalice filled with wine.

The hall grew quiet as he spoke: "A toast, my friends—here is to wise old King Solomon, who lost all his gold; and here…" he croaked, somewhat emboldened by his success, "is to his God, who seems to have lost all His people…"

Convulsed by a fit of giggling, he sat down abruptly and raised the elaborate golden chalice to drink. Wine flowed copiously over both sides of his scanty beard and stained his robes, but he drank steadily until he drained the chalice. A low rumbling ovation went around the room as he once again laboriously heaved his somewhat obese body to his full height and raised the vessel in triumph.

As he leered at the crowd, however, the lamps flickered and the room began to darken. A curious glowing light appeared to slowly illuminate the north wall. The chalice fell from the nerveless fingers of the prince and clanged against the table, clattering down the onyx steps and rolling to rest at the feet of the chamberlain.

Two thousand terrified eyes watched as a man's hand appeared and began writing on the wall in characters that were unfamiliar to all who were present from all parts of the civilized world. Bel-Shazzar was seized

152

by a violent fit of trembling. His knees gave way and he sat down suddenly, overturning the table.

"What is it? Someone tell me—what is it? What does it mean?" He blubbered, and his voice rose to a shrill scream.

"Call the conjurers, the shamans, the magicians!" His face was white, his knuckles too, as he desperately gripped the arms of his chair. No one moved, mesmerized by the strange apparition. "Go!" he screamed, and the servants fled.

Soon the magicians arrived, then the others, but no one could decipher the words. The atmosphere in the room was electrified; the prince on his royal dais was very near collapse, and still no one moved.

Presently, the doors opened again, and a slight, veiled feminine figure was ushered into the hall. She spoke to the prince directly, simply: "Bel-Shazzar, have you so soon forgotten that there is a man who faithfully served your grandfather, a man in whom the Spirit of the great God resides, and who is able to interpret visions and dreams? Have you forgotten Daniel?"

Bel-Shazzar lifted his glazed, bloodshot stare to his grandmother and, surprisingly, reached out to take her hand. Amytis was the one and only person Bel-Shazzar loved, feared, and respected. As a child, she alone had given him the only love and discipline he ever experienced.

"Grandmother," he whispered hoarsely, "please send for him. If he can translate these words on the wall, I will make him the third highest ruler in the kingdom, next to my father and myself."

Amytis turned away, her eyes filled with tears. *Oh, my poor child,* she thought, *you have no idea of just how short your reign will be.*

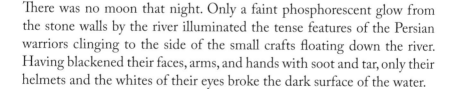

There was no moon that night. Only a faint phosphorescent glow from the stone walls by the river illuminated the tense features of the Persian warriors clinging to the side of the small crafts floating down the river. Having blackened their faces, arms, and hands with soot and tar, only their helmets and the whites of their eyes broke the dark surface of the water.

The only perceptible sound was the rippling of the gentle waves against the stone and the soft, rhythmic lapping of the long, slender oars in the water. Far upstream, the Euphrates River had been dammed by a contingent of Cyrus's soldiers, so the water level had dropped. Thus the

Persian army had been enabled to enter Babylon by actually walking under the massive gates over the river, which was now reduced to only a shallow stream.

Occasionally, someone with a torch would come down the steps to fill a water jar from one of the many little stone reservoirs along the course of the river, but there was very little activity on the Euphrates. As it flowed quietly through the heart of that great city, it carried the Persian strike force unerringly toward its destination: the royal palace. Silently the boats edged toward shore and discharged their deadly cargo. Quickly and effortlessly they dispersed into the darkness, awaiting their final command.

"MENE, MENE, TEKEL, UPHARSIN.

"The Most High God has given you this message, Bel-Shazzar: you have been weighed in the balances and found wanting; this very night your kingdom will be taken from you and given to another!"

Daniel's rich, resonant voice reverberated through the hall. The stern reprimand hung like a Damascene scimitar over the entire room. Not a breath of air stirred the heavy tapestried draperies; for a long time the great hall waited in shocked silence for the prince's reply.

Bel-Shazzar sat in abject misery as his overloaded mind processed this information. Finally, after what seemed like an eternity, he stirred, sighed, and stood up.

"Daniel, O man of great wisdom and understanding, my grandmother spoke truly. Bring the golden chain," he gestured feebly, "and put it on his neck. He is to be the third ruler in the kingdom of Babylon, by decree of Bel-Shazzar, regent of Babylon."

Having discharged his promise, the unhappy regent sat down again; apparently he had no will left in him to resist his declared fate. He was still there, staring vacantly into space, when the great doors burst open and the Persians swarmed through the hall like locusts. The palace guard had already been eliminated, and the few who remained offered little resistance.

Bel-Shazzar was immediately shackled, and Gobrias and Gadatas took him from the hall to the river, where they threw him in to drown. "We heard about your infamous drowning of the little slave boy," they spat at him from the shore, "and we felt this to be just punishment for all your crimes, including the rape of our little sister!"

They watched with revulsion and contempt as the terror-stricken, bloated features sank beneath the water and disappeared. They returned to the hall.

"Well, gentlemen," murmured Cyrus, as he stood looking up at the strange handwriting, "Bel-Shazzar has finally reaped what he sowed—a fitting end for such a cowardly and despicable life."

He glanced at them, then strode to the doors. "Well, we have business to attend to. My couriers tell me there are still a few pockets of resistance. We must secure the city before sunrise. My father is on his way and should arrive in less than a week. I want his entry to be peaceful, victorious, and, as I suspect, welcomed by the general populace.

"This has been a relatively bloodless coup, because Amytis arranged for our secret entry. Did you know that? She will be a valuable ally in this transition—she and the man so beloved by my parents, the Hebrew Daniel."

CHAPTER 15

THE GIANT-SLAYER

THE SIXTEENTH FLOOR penthouse apartment of the swank new Osiris Suites in Cairo was dark and silent. All the members of the United Arab Pact had met in a tense, noisy meeting that lasted until nearly 3 a.m. Finally, their business settled, they left, and Prince Hassan retired for the evening.

He glanced in at the shining blonde hair spread out on the pink satin pillow in the guest bedroom, then backed out quietly and closed the door. *She is so young and innocent,* he thought wearily as he fell into bed. *It is safer for her that she does not speak my language right now; she can learn it after we are married and settled in my father's palace.* Hassan's thoughts drifted off aimlessly into a deep, dreamless sleep.

Presently the shaft of moonlight illuminating the thick gray carpet was broken by a shadow. The girl watched him from the door for several long minutes and then, satisfied that he was asleep, stole softly to the front door and let herself out.

Taking the service elevator to the thirteenth floor, she quickly found a telephone alcove and dialed the number. Speaking fast in low, breathless tones, she passed on the necessary information and hung up quickly.

She had just pressed the elevator button when she heard voices. She ducked into the elevator, but as the door was closing she heard words in Arabic that chilled her to the bone: "She was just here! Spread out—we'll find her...." And the closing doors shut out the rest.

Her heart pounding, her hand shook uncontrollably as she inserted the front door key. Back in her room, Heidi flew soundlessly to the elaborate closet and drew out a black leather jacket, black wig, boots, and a curious leather case. Setting to work in front of the dresser mirror, the transformation quickly took place.

When she finally stood up and surveyed the results in the full-length mirrored closet door, her terror dissipated enough to think clearly. *Surely,* she thought, *they would never connect this shabby, somewhat pudgy young man with the slender, classy blonde from the penthouse!*

Taking a pad of notepaper, she wadded two pieces into balls and stuffed them into her cheeks, already partially obliterated by a large black mustache. Pulling the cap down over her ears, she took out another piece of paper and wrote a short note, propping it up on the mirror.

"Dearest Hassan—I am meeting a girl friend from Villanueva School for breakfast and shopping. See you this afternoon. I miss you already. Love forever, Heidi."

A nice touch, she thought grimly as she propped it up on the dresser. *I may yet be able to bluff my way through this.*

Grabbing the leather case, she stuffed it and as many towels as she could into the pink satin pillowcase and threw the bulging bag over her shoulder. *If I am seen,* she thought, *they may dismiss me as just another hotel burglar. But still…if I am seen,* she shuddered, *I will most definitely run!*

Lothar groaned and turned to peer at the luminous dial of his bedside clock, then groped for his beeper. "Five-thirty in the morning! Who could be paging me at this hour?"

Leaning on one elbow he switched on the light; the prearranged Israeli Mossad code numbers came into focus and instantly galvanized him into action. In less than a minute he was dressed and pulling on his jacket as he galloped out the front door.

Once inside the car, he gunned the accelerator while punching out the number of his Mossad contact. "That you, Shkedi? Yeah, it's Kreisler. She's on the run, so I'll make the pickup. All the eggs in the basket? Good—let's hope none of them are rotten! I'll get in touch with you later."

In less than ten minutes he was parked across the street from the mosque near the hotel district. The streets were empty, so he turned off the engine and waited. Suddenly a man's face appeared, rapping on the window, and the startled Lothar shrank back from the apparition. With one swift movement the door opened and the stranger was inside before Lothar could even start the ignition.

"Hi." It was a soft little voice that spoke, followed by that unmistakable giggle he knew so well.

"Heidi! You gave me quite a scare, you little vixen." He grinned, and the car roared to life, pulling out into the street. Heidi remained in her disguise, crouched down in the seat as they cruised slowly past the Osiris Suites.

"Look, Lothar," she exclaimed, pointing upward, "the penthouse suite is still completely dark. They haven't awakened him—that's good! He'll probably sleep until long past noon, and that'll give us more time. I'll get in touch with Heather and stay with her a few days longer. Don't worry, it's safe," she added with a sidelong glance at Lothar's face. "They have absolutely nothing to connect me with her family in Tel Aviv, and the family has no idea that I'm an Israeli agent."

They made the long trip from Cairo to Tel Aviv, stopping only twice, for breakfast and for gas. Heidi changed clothes at the first stop, but as a precaution she kept on the black wig and wore sunglasses like a proper tourist. As they drove, Lothar's craggy features creased with worry as Heidi began to unfold the gruesome details of the plot.

"Lothar, there is so much I do not know, but of this I am certain: the secret experiments back in the 1990s are now a factual reality. They have the funding, the technology, and the burning zeal for a jihad, for a holy war. To make matters worse, they now have the official blessing of the New World Order. The Soviets and the U.N. are openly antagonistic to the Jews, but as you well know, the NWO has only one manifest agenda toward Israel: total annihilation!

"We don't know when it will happen; I couldn't get that information. Up until now the Arabs have lacked only one thing: a strong leader unifying all the Arabic factions." She fell silent, and Lothar glanced sideways, cocking one eyebrow.

"Up until now?" He prodded gently.

"Now," she replied softly, turning her head away, "there is Hassan."

Lothar's hands gripped the steering wheel, and his jaw muscles betrayed the rising anger. The unbidden picture of his lovely Heidi with the dark prince clouded his vision for a few moments. *We are never to allow our personal feelings to interfere,* he thought savagely. *How does a man—any man—keep his honor without protecting the one he loves?*

"Far be it from me," he muttered in bitter undertones, "to question the wisdom of our superiors."

Heidi soon fell asleep to the strains of "Liebestraum" on the CD player. Lothar drove on, wrestling with the growing certainty that the problems surrounding them were too overwhelming, too fearfully, catastrophically massive for any human agency to solve. Enveloped in the blackest despair, a deep longing for release arose from the very depths of his being, crying out, *God of Abraham, Isaac, and Jacob—HELP US!*

The chopper pilot banked to the right, circling the gleaming white city below, and came to rest on the helicopter pad atop the tallest of the buildings. The three passengers exited and took the roof elevator down to the third floor where they were joined by eight well-dressed men and three very elegant women. They proceeded to the adjacent conference room, the doors were closed, and two guards were posted outside.

"Ladies and gentlemen of the Illustrious Triad, I have called you here to apprise you of the latest developments."

Startled, everyone looked around for the source of the voice, which seemed to emanate from every direction but remained invisible.

"As you can see, the city of Babylon is very nearly completed. The hydroelectric project will be finished, I have been assured, within the next ten days. On the twenty-seventh day of this month, the power will be turned on, and the entire city will be ablaze with lights. A worldwide celebration has been planned with delegates from all over the globe, a celebration of world unity and peace unlike any other in all of history.

"Two of the largest airports in the world—one for commercial flights and the other for freight—have been constructed near the city. Babylon will soon be the primary hub of all world commerce, as well as being the undisputed center of all the world's religions, dwelling together under the New World Order banner of tolerance and unity.

"As you know, we have secured this site in return for our guarantee of Arab supremacy in the Middle East and victory over their ancient adversary, the State of Israel. This will soon be an accomplished fact; everything is in readiness. The United Arab Pact is even now making the final arrangements for the computer-controlled attacks.

"Your job, ladies and gentlemen, is twofold: first, to concentrate the world's attention on the Coalition for World Peace here in Babylon and contrast it with the Israeli's dangerous, aggressive, and intolerant stance. Then, after the attack, make certain the world media is fed reports of Israel's atrocities against her neighbors. A packet of preprinted press releases is on the table in front of you. Thank you for coming. You will be notified of the place and time of our next meeting."

The distinguished-looking group dispersed, and two of the delegates rode in air-conditioned comfort to the underground engineering head-quarters bunker where they went immediately to the U.N. commandant's quarters. Since he was using the library's computer, they met with him there, and for the next hour discussed the imminent events.

"So he's absolutely certain the Israelis have received no intelligence reports—they will be taken by surprise in this attack?" The U.N. commandant, a high-ranking German named Rudy Weiss, paced the floor and nervously smoked a cigarette as he absorbed the information.

"Of course, sir, there is always that remote possibility of a leak some-where, but…even if they knew, how could they prevent it?" answered the delegate with an eloquent shrug. "The whole nation will be exterminated in only a matter of minutes.

"The first wave of missiles will be conventional weapons directed at strategic defense emplacements throughout Israel. The second wave, to follow immediately, will be chemical bombs released on the most heav-ily populated cities. The third wave will be armored troop transports—a massive force from the north, Egypt and Libya in the south, and the remaining Arab Pact countries from the east—sent to occupy the entire territory.

"This will effectively wipe out not only the six million inhabitants of Israel, but also any opposition the Islamic nations may have to our plans for world domination."

"Fiendish plan. Absolutely diabolic," mumbled Commandant Weiss as he stubbed out his cigarette, collected his briefcase, and turned to go. The three men went their separate ways, leaving the library in darkness.

Presently a figure detached itself from the shadowed book stacks in the rear of the room and emerged into the hall. Looking around carefully, Dan Shepherd returned quickly and quietly to his room.

Alex was still at the dam site, so Dan, frantic with anxiety, paced the floor, trying desperately to think. *Dear God, what can I do? Six million people in another… another holocaust. Sarah and her entire family!*

He sank into the leather chair, taking deep breaths to clear his whirling thoughts and dispel the cloud of despair threatening to engulf him. During the next hour he traversed the entire gamut of emotions as a prayer of desperation took him from panic to peace.

I must leave as soon as the compound reopens in the morning, unless… unless… The thought exploded like a charge of dynamite. *Alex flew Apache helicopters in the Iraqi war! Of course—why not!* He quickly packed two small briefcases, made some entries into the computer, and was gone.

Three hours later he and Alex were heading south over the Syrian desert. The late afternoon sun cast long purple shadows on the rocky terrain below, and the chopper, buffeted by the high winds, rocked uneasily back and forth.

"Airsick, pal?" Alex, at the controls, grinned, glancing sideways at his friend. "I must admit, it's been a while since I flew one of these babies, but I've been paying close attention during all of those daily shuttle flights back and forth to the dam site. Doin' OK, ol' buddy? Quite frankly, you don't look so hot."

Dan managed a sickly grin as he looked down at the undulating landscape. "Yeah, I'm a little queasy. I still feel bad that we had to tie up that poor pilot, gag him, and put him in a closet. I know he'll be found in the morning, but, well—I really liked that kid and hated to betray his trust. Know what I mean?

"What really worries me, though, is—what kind of twist are they going to put on our escaping this way? Will they be able to change the timing of the attack? Maybe we shouldn't have jumped the gun and waited it out—we only had one more week to go."

"Dan, you and I both know that Israel doesn't even have a week," Alex rejoined soberly. "Let's face it—possession of intelligence this vital really leaves us no choice. We had to act quickly."

Dan shuddered involuntarily. "I hate to think of what would have happened if I had not been in the library at that precise time…you know, Alex, I really believe that God engineered it."

Alex shifted uneasily. "Now, Dan—don't start with that religious stuff again. It was just lucky coincidence, nothing more. But, yes—I'm glad you were there. Y'know, I've never thought of myself as much of a hero. If we get out of this alive, though, we might just qualify."

The sky above began to darken as the sun slipped beyond the horizon. Alex flipped on the overhead light to study his charts. "We should be over the Golan Heights in about fifteen minutes," he said. "That's a sort of buffer area between Syria and Israel."

"That brings up another problem," he added with a worried frown. "This is a Syrian copter in Israeli territory; we may get some antiaircraft fire. Something tells me they may very well shoot first and ask questions later."

Dan ran his hand wearily through his hair and tried unsuccessfully to stretch his legs. "We've been flying for quite a while, Alex. Do you have a pretty good idea of how far this bird will go on a full tank?"

Alex grinned ruefully. "More or less—but I have a sinking feeling that it may be a bit close," indicating that the fuel gauge was now directly on empty.

Dan leaned over to look and gasped in dismay. "Are we flying on fumes? It's already down to the red—"

"No need to worry—not just yet, that is. These newer choppers have a small reserve auxiliary tank. The problem is that I don't know if we're already using it!"

They flew in tense silence for the next few minutes, then their question was answered. A slight cough in the engine galvanized Alex into an immediate descent.

"Hang on—things may get a bit dicey; these things don't glide like airplanes. A helicopter will drop like a rock when the engine stops!"

It seemed to Dan that the descent was accelerating at a steeper and steeper angle. *This is no time to offer up a nice, civil little prayer,* he thought.

"Lord, help us! Bring us down in one piece…" he shouted with his eyes shut. He was gripping the ceiling handholds for dear life as he continued praying, reminding the Almighty that He had gotten them into this mess and they fully expected Him to get them out.

"…or we're sunk," he ended the prayer somewhat lamely. He opened his eyes, quite sure that his untutored prayer had hit the ceiling and bounced off. Surprisingly enough, however, the craft had leveled out and was rumbling along about forty or fifty feet above the ground. Looking down, he could see the startled faces of people below as they watched their passage.

"Is this Syria or Israel?" queried Dan somewhat hoarsely.

"Don't know," muttered Alex tersely, and Dan noticed his white knuckles gripping the steering column. Just ahead was a massive row of hills, and as they rounded the top, their hearts sank. About three hundred yards ahead was a semicircle of tanks with all their guns pointed at the copter, loudspeakers blaring as the searchlights converged on the hapless pair.

"This is it. Let's hope they're friendly," muttered Alex darkly, and they hovered for a few anxious moments as he gingerly set it down. The engine shut down, and they stepped out into the blinding searchlights, hands in the air.

"We're Americans," shouted Dan as several soldiers moved forward, pointing their weapons at the two. "Does anyone here speak English?"

There was a long silence, then suppressed laughter as a deep voice came from the darkness. "We all speak English, sir. What are you doing flying a Syrian helicopter over Israeli territory?"

"It's a long story," Dan answered with a relieved grin. "Do you think you could get those searchlights off us? We need to talk to someone in command—it's pretty urgent."

No one moved.

"Come on, guys. We risked our necks to get here—we're a couple of engineers from the Euphrates dam project. We have some information that is vital to Israeli security."

The searchlights flicked off and headlights came on. A soldier stepped forward and saluted smartly, then offered his hand with a smile. "Charlie Benjamin from Milwaukee. Glad to meet you!"

He took Alex and Dan to see the company commander, about half a mile from the group of tanks. After the debriefing, he seemed convinced that Dan's account was truthful and politely excused himself to make some phone calls. Returning after about fifteen minutes, his face white and tense, the commander informed them that a plane had been dispatched to take them to Tel Aviv.

Immediately they were driven to an airfield and unceremoniously whisked away. Forty-five minutes later, there was another debriefing, rather more intense and much more thorough. This was accomplished in the Mossad headquarters, interrupted only once by a woman who brought in hamburgers, french fries, and chocolate shakes.

"We thought you might enjoy American food for a change." explained the very polite, very patient middle-aged man who was doing most of the interrogating. "It is the least we can do for two such courageous young men. This is not your fight, you know. We are used to being under constant threat by our neighbors and vilified by the world press. Even your own country—once our only staunch ally—has taken an official stance against Israel. This may end up bringing you into disfavor back home."

Dan and Alex glanced at each other guiltily.

"Well," Dan drawled with a grin, "I didn't mention this, but…well, I'm engaged to an Israeli girl who moved here with her family about three years ago.

"Also, the very last thing I did at Babylon was to transfer all my funds to the Nations Bank in Jerusalem. Alex already had his in a Swiss bank account. You see, we had already talked this over, and each of us had independently made a decision not to return to America, at least not yet."

The official nodded impassively. "Well, young men, Israel is no Garden of Eden, but we do welcome you both here. It is getting late; we will put you up in a hotel for the night. I'm sure you, Mr. Shepherd, would like to let your fiancée know that you are here."

He sighed again, and closed his eyes. "We knew most of the details of this operation—" Dan looked at Alex and dropped his head ruefully, "—but what we did NOT know was the time of the attack. Please understand, gentlemen: we needed this information desperately. I'm sure you realize that this is now highly classified material. Our people will take it from here."

The meeting was over. The men rose and shook hands, and an aide took them to a charming inn called the Carmody Arms, run by, of all people, a retired English butler and his wife. Dan showered and sank gratefully into the soft, lavender-scented sheets.

He called Sarah, who was away for the weekend at a medical seminar, but her delighted parents, both talking excitedly at once, promised to tell her the minute she returned. They urged him to come the following day, so he finally hung up the phone and, tired but happy, sank immediately into blissful oblivion—his first night in Israel, his new home.

The streets of Bethlehem were teeming with tourists celebrating an early Easter. Young David Shkedi threaded his way through the crowded street, running up the outside steps to his family's home above their little bookstore, gift shop, and souvenir stand. His older brothers were all in the Israeli army, so David spent a great deal of time alone at home, doing household chores.

He was nearly fifteen, a brilliant but very lonely boy. Most of his neighbors were Palestinians, and he never quite felt completely accepted; so while the other boys were out playing soccer or riding bikes, he immersed himself in books and computers.

David's parents were blithely unaware of the true extent of his genius in the alien world of cyberspace. However, David was quite well aware of his father's deep cover activities as an agent of the Mossad—the Israeli equivalent of the American CIA. Sometimes late at night he would hear the meetings at the kitchen table, the muffled phone conversations at all hours, and the mysterious disappearance of one or both parents for hours, sometimes days.

On this particular spring day he was feeling the elation that overflows from being noticed by a pretty young girl for the first time. Rachel Dayan lived on the other side of town in a nice big home with a terraced garden. David had nursed a secret crush on this charming red-haired creature since third grade, when her parents had moved to town.

During the last year, he had taken up weight lifting to bulk up his lanky five-foot-ten-inch frame, but it was only last month that she had noticed him enough to give him a faint ray of hope. Then, today after gym class, she had waited for him and walked him back to class.

David was on cloud nine as he bolted into the kitchen and rummaged in the refrigerator. Fortified with milk and cookies, he wandered into the spare bedroom that was used for an office and checked the computer.

"Dad, there's some e-mail for you. Dad?" There was no answer, so David sat down and copied off the message.

"Very urgent—repeat—urgent priority. Project Goliad imminent. Report immediately."

For the next few hours David did some serious hacking, and he was astounded by what he found. When his father came home and David gave him the message, his face turned white. He sat down heavily on the kitchen chair, staring into space. David said nothing more but went to his bedroom to pore over some charts and maps he kept under his bed.

Presently he heard his father knocking on his door. "David, I'll have to leave for a while. Tell your mother I've left a message for her on the bedroom mirror. OK?"

"OK, Dad," echoed David miserably. He buried his head in the pillow and sobbed, wondering if his dad would ever come back. *It's not fair—it's just not fair!* he thought. *We all have to die, and my life is just now beginning!*

The tension in the conference room was almost tangible. Fifty-six of Israel's finest leaders were carefully listening to every word from the prime minister. "And so, we all know the grave danger of our situation. Now the Minister of Defense will address this issue."

The distinguished gray-haired gentleman rose slowly with great effort. As he stood at the dais, it was obvious that he had not slept for a very long time. He looked around the assemblage, cleared his throat, and began.

"Thank you, Mr. Prime Minister. First on the agenda will be to look back several years. One of my predecessors, Yitzhak Mordecai, disclosed to the *Jerusalem Post* in November of 1996 that the Russians were helping Syria develop lethal nerve gases. These included VX, one of the most toxic nerve agents; only a minute quantity on the skin can kill within seconds. Unlike other nerve gases, VX can persist as a deadly agent for days or weeks.

"At that time, the Syrians also had several hundred Scud missiles with the capability of reaching every part of Israel that could easily carry the nerve gas in specially adapted warheads to centers of Israel's population. Defense sources say the Syrian Scud Bs are capable of carrying a 1000-kilo warhead up to 300 kilometers—188 miles—and the Scud Cs a 770 kilo warhead up to 500 kilometers—313 miles—thus putting virtually all of Israel under Syrian missile threat.

"In the case that Israel chose the option of a preemptive nuclear strike, Egypt let it be known that they would stand by their Arab allies. The U.N. would not tolerate all-out war from Israel, no matter how grave the threat from her Arab neighbors, even to the point of annihilation.

"We know that decades ago Arafat had used funds sent for humanitarian aid to the Palestinian refugees to build himself a bunker in Gaza, four stories deep. His aim had always been jihad: to rid the Middle East of Israel, then set himself up as president of an independent Palestinian state."

With a deep sigh, he put down the papers. "So you see, ladies and gentlemen, Syria has been planning war for a long, long time. The Israeli military is now monitoring changes in the positions of Syria's surface-to-surface missiles, as well as the many Syrian military movements along the Golan Heights border.

"There have been attempts in the past to launch an attack: In November of 1996 Prime Minister Netanyahu decided to keep the incident under wraps, but he informed a closed Knesset committee meeting that Syrian President Assad had already attempted to strike at Israel by sending Syrian troop-carrying helicopters. They were turned back by Israeli warplanes already on high alert to prevent a surprise attack.

"The next attempt was in May 2013, and this time was narrowly averted by a—shall we say—miraculous intervention by a higher power. They planned to send their nerve gas canisters plummeting down on our cities. They very nearly succeeded, but in the last few minutes before the launch code was sent out, a strong south wind blew out of the desert and accelerated upwards of 80 miles per hour. When it hit 100 mph, the launch was called off by a very red-faced Assad. His panic-stricken scientists informed him that the nerve gas would be carried throughout all Syria, annihilating its entire population along with a portion of Israel's.

"Now, however, after consulting the weather charts, they feel it is perfectly safe to attack again. The new president has no such compunctions about any 'miracles' to defend us and is ready and eager for our extermination. Our intelligence reports had given us all the information we needed—how, where, and from whom the attacks will come—but we did not know *when* until two days ago.

"Two brave young American engineers working on the Babylon project risked their lives to bring that information to us by hijacking a Syrian helicopter. Our intelligence teams were sent out immediately to do damage control. The Syrian helicopter pilot was spirited away from the broom closet at the dam office. The Syrian officials found the charred remains of a helicopter with three burned bodies on the desert floor the next morning, so it will be assumed that our Americans perished in an accident. One of our female operatives will be sent in to pose as the grieving American sister come to claim the body. She will confirm the identity and make sure the cover story is secure. We cannot afford any leaks.

"Gentlemen, ladies—we have three days left: three days to find a solution. Let's get to work."

⸺⸻⸺

Alex, Dan, and Jack sat at the breakfast table sipping their coffee and talking long after the women had left. Sarah and her mother had gone to shop for the wedding gown, leaving Jack and Dan in a delightful cloud of perfumed hugs and kisses as they drifted out the door. The men had agreed that it would be prudent to keep the distressing news from their women as long as possible.

"Well, Alex, how did it feel to be behind the controls, flying again?" Jack asked his guest.

"It may be a few more years before the next flight!" Alex laughed good-naturedly. "That was some experience for us both, and we've been in some pretty tight situations."

"The Knesset committee is meeting in closed session today, discussing our options," replied Jack tersely. "Somehow I don't think that evacuating the entire population is a valid option."

The discussion continued for another hour; then Jack announced that it was time to go on a tour of Jerusalem. Alex and Dan readily agreed; after all this was going to be their home.

As they descended the stone steps to the garage, Dan was somehow convinced that God had not brought him all this way just to destroy them in three days. *What was the title of that old Frank Peretti Christmas story that Randy used to play for us?* he thought. *"All Is Well."*

⸺⸻⸺

Two days later a pall of gloom had settled over the members of the Israeli Knesset. The military was holding out for a preemptive strike, to take place immediately. Matt's orders were to stay on permanent alert, and he and his fellow pilots were flying three times as many sorties, sleeping in shifts. Everyone was on edge, and their sleeping hours were ravaged by nightmares of carnage and devastation from Dan to Beersheba. Matt worried constantly about Heather and his family, but high alert meant staying incommunicado, so he stayed glumly in his quarters, awaiting his next turn to fly.

The deeply religious Orthodox members of the military were in constant prayer to the God of their fathers. The majority of Israelis, though, were fairly agnostic and took the brash, fatalistic approach: *If it comes, it comes. So, we face it—that's all.*

At that time several groups of Messianic Jews existed in Israel. One of these groups was an organization called MAOZ, meaning "strength." These Christian Jewish believers held Jesus to be their Messiah, and thus were considered by their fellow Jews to be a detestable minority. They were constantly maligned by the Jewish press and given little freedom to be heard. They had grown from a tiny band of believers in the 1970s to nearly 50,000. Neither wealthy nor influential, their members were still shunned as misguided deviants from the "norm." Many of their numbers came from the CIS—the Russian Jews.

It was one of these, the commander of the military unit that met Dan and Alex at the border, who transmitted the request for intercessory prayer. Without divulging details, he asked for three days of prayer and fasting by all 50,000 members. The Spirit of the Lord came through the gift of prophecy to all the separate groups, confirming the imminent danger. Never before had there been such intense intercession within the borders of the State of Israel.

There was much activity outside the borders as well. The Holy Spirit sped the message all over the globe through dreams, visions, and prophecy. Randy and Paula, already vitally interested in the affairs of Israel, both received revelation from the Holy Spirit that God's people were in danger of annihilation. They called together the whole Montana community, indeed, the entire U.S. community, to fasting and prayer. A heavy early spring snowfall had blanketed the whole area, so they kept the log fires roaring in the fireplace of the lodge they had built for winter shelter. As they earnestly prayed, the invisible warfare in the skies above Jerusalem increased, escalating to immense proportions.

A few miles from Jerusalem, the little town of Bethlehem—the ancient city of King David, the giant slayer—slept peacefully under the starlit sky. All except one, that is: David Shkedi had kept a watchful eye on his mother all day. Since she had received the note from her husband, who had still not returned, she had stayed in her room, weeping inconsolably. Now the hour was late, and she had finally fallen into a sleep of exhaustion.

David remained at the computer all evening, hacking his way determinedly through the same trail he had followed the previous evening.

Tonight, what he found at the end of the trail was truly alarming.

He looked down at his watch. "Oh, no! They've jumped the gun. They're armed, and the countdown has already begun!"

Quickly he pulled the list of computations from his pocket, double checking them carefully against his chart. Satisfied, he made his deletions, then entered the new set of numbers. "Launch THAT, you creeps," he muttered darkly, shaking a clenched fist at the screen.

Faintly ashamed of his uncharacteristic outburst, David went to the refrigerator, grabbed a sandwich, a Coke, and some chips and went up the steps to the flat roof where he crouched down and waited. His home was at the top of a hill, and from the roof he could easily see the skyline of Jerusalem, five miles away to the north.

There was a full moon, and the Dome of the Rock reflected its silvery glow, serenely awaiting its fate, which came in exactly twenty-eight seconds. The screaming arc of the Scud missile streaking in from the north descended in a graceful arc, demolishing its target with unerring accuracy.

"All RIGHT!" roared the young victor on the roof, doing a little dance all by himself. He watched fascinated, as the smoke billowed heavenward, then ran downstairs to turn on the TV.

There were days and weeks of national rejoicing as all the details were broadcast to the incredulous Israeli populace. It seemed that the Syrians had planned to take out Israel's defenses first with conventional weapons, then launch the nerve gas missiles against the heavily populated centers.

Somehow—no one knew exactly how—their plans had gone terribly awry. The attack coordinates had somehow been revised, and the only missile to get through the border defenses was directed into Jerusalem and hit the Holy Shrine of Islam—the Dome of the Rock. All the other missiles had been redirected into Iraq, Iran, and Egypt. Egypt's missiles had been redirected into Syria. All had wreaked considerable damage, and tempers were hot. Also, the nerve gas—the second phase of the attack—was never launched. One could easily guess why.

Hassan and his cohorts were hunted down and beheaded publicly in Baghdad.

As for David, well, that's another story. Jehovah God had plans for the irrepressible young man—plans for a hopeful future. His father returned home the following day to celebrate the victory with his family. David kept his secret.

Those believers who had fasted and prayed were jubilant, offering thanks all over the world for the mighty hand of God, who had been faithful to His Word.

CHAPTER 16

THE PIT

Brilliant shafts of early morning sunlight sliced through the shadows, soft buttery yellow beams gliding across the vast expanse of Persian carpet and coming to rest gently on the fragile frame of the elderly man in the bed. He shivered slightly as the chilly spring breeze riffled the bedclothes.

A servant immediately sprang up to close the curtains, but the old man waved him away and with great effort managed to pull himself up on one elbow. As his watery gaze slowly focused on the almond blossoms dancing merrily on the breeze outside his window, Mordecai the Jew, Grand Vizier of all Persia, whispered his last request: "Bring my family to me."

Mordecai was dying. Nearly eighty-seven years old, the great prime minister had finally reached the end of his journey. His adopted homeland of Persia—all 127 provinces extending from India to Ethiopia—had learned to respect this great man who wielded his massive powers with such godly wisdom, justice, and dignity.

Darius had chosen well, and so, during these years under the tutelage of Mordecai, his kingdom had grown and prospered, experiencing an unprecedented period of peace.

Now, in these early morning hours, the king was awakened by his weeping servants with the distressing news. Hastily throwing on his garments, he rushed to the bedchamber of his trusted old friend, where he found the entire palace staff assembled.

Queen Esther stood alone by the bed, her soft cheeks pale and streaked with tears. Her magnificent mane of raven-black hair, now liberally streaked with gray, tumbled in sleepy disarray about the silken shoulders of her scarlet robe, and Darius' heart melted with tender concern.

She looks so young, so vulnerable and helpless, like a little wounded bird, he thought as he wrapped his arms around her in protective embrace. Darius glanced down at the form on the bed and his heart constricted painfully.

"How can I ever replace him?" he murmured into her hair. "He's a national treasure."

Together they knelt by the bed, and Mordecai once again struggled to rise. The servants raised him somewhat with pillows into a sitting position, and Mordecai sighed heavily and closed his eyes. After a long, alarming silence, he spoke.

"Esther, my child, my own—how I hate to leave you, but it is with such gratitude to the God who blessed me so through you. You are, like your name, a "shining star" who will be held in great esteem by all generations to come, as long as the earth exists."

He closed his eyes again for a long moment, then held out his hand. "Darius, come closer, my son." The king meekly obeyed, and the frail old hand descended upon his head. The voice continued, weak and quavering at first, growing stronger and stronger.

"I bless you, my son, as generations of our people have passed the blessing of Jehovah God on to their children. You and your son, Cyrus, have been destined for greatness, far greater than you know. From the first year of your reign, Darius, a very special, very powerful angel was dispatched from the council halls of heaven to be a strengthener and a protector to you.

"Your reign has been blessed by Jehovah God as none other ever has been. Although your son, Cyrus, is not here, this paternal blessing will be passed onto him by you, and he will ultimately be instrumental in bring-ing about the will of God for our people."

Exhausted, the old man collapsed back against the pillows. At that moment, the sounds of small children, laughing and playing in the gar-den below, drifted into the room. With a contented smile, the creased old face relaxed and Mordecai the Jew was carried by the waiting angels to the bosom of his father Abraham. Gathered to his people on the four-teenth day of the twelfth month of Adar, Mordecai celebrated the Feast of Purim in the heavenlies—the anniversary of the deliverance of God's chosen race from certain annihilation.

Seal up the Vision

⊸∞⊶

The caravan from Babylon arrived on the twelfth day of the ninth month Chisleu. Shushan the palace had been in feverish preparation many months for the arrival of the great potentate from Babylon, the legendary man of God named Daniel. The prime minister who had ruled Nebuchadnezzar's vast empire now had been summoned by Darius to rule as second in command over the Persian empire, which, by virtue of Cyrus' military victory over Bel-Shazzar, now included all the lands of former Babylonian rule from India to Africa.

Daniel's caravan included all of his servants, his children, grandchildren, great-grandchildren, horses, family treasures, and a vast array of material possessions. They were accompanied by a large contingent of Cyrus' palace guard, sent for an extra measure of protection against the nomadic bandits who roamed the desert region.

Since the days of mourning for Mordecai had been accomplished, a great feast was held in Daniel's honor, and all 127 yielded up their tribute, sending thousands of royal representatives to the capital city of Susa.

Daniel, Esther, and Ashasuerus the king (also known to his subjects as Darius the Mede) spent many long hours together during the next few weeks. The reunion of the three friends, who had not seen each other for nearly forty years, was both joyful and sad. Esther had lost her cousin Mordecai, and Daniel had lost his beloved wife, Hannah, the previous year.

Hannah had taken a large basket of food and medicines to a Hebrew woman down by the canal. The poor woman had no husband, and three of her five children were sick with the fever. Living in a rat-infested canal barge, making a living as a prostitute, the woman was destitute, shunned as an outcast by her own people. Hannah was determined to help her.

Nearly a week later, Hannah developed a fever and a sore throat. The physicians and magi all came to Daniel's home with various herbal remedies, but the fever continued to rage out of control. Daniel fasted and prayed the following four days and four nights, never sleeping, never leaving her side. On the fifth day, she breathed her last, slipping away peacefully.

Her husband withdrew to grieve alone for several weeks, then the gentle ministrations of his children brought him back to normal. Eventually Daniel realized that his home no longer held any enchantment for him, because with Hannah's departure all the light, warmth, and gaiety had gone with her. He therefore welcomed the summons to a new life in Persia.

The festivities at Shushan Palace lasted nearly a month. During this time, adulation of the man Daniel bordered on idolatry. Tales of his bravery and supernatural powers were told and retold among the people, and all this attention was not lost on one particular person who dwelled in the ancient, abandoned stone hut near a rock quarry outside the city walls.

Hunters sat around their campfires at night and told hair-raising tales of bewitched sheep and cattle who wandered too near the stone structure and were never seen again. It was said to be inhabited by an ugly old crone, a witch who danced naked in the moonlight with an assortment of demons, howling at the moon. The whole area seemed haunted and was carefully avoided by the local peasants. No one knew how long she had lived there; the older folks vaguely remembered a mysterious, beautiful woman appearing about forty years before, but she never ventured out, and many years later the legend began to take its sinister shape.

Indeed, the old crone was out and about, this being a moonless night. She hurried through the backstreets of the city, climbed some steps, and rapped at a door. "Let me in!" she croaked, "I have news!"

The door opened, and she disappeared inside. The satraps and governors, the magicians, sorcerers and occult prognosticators—formerly the elite of all Persian society preceding the reign of Darius—were gathered together in one crowded, dimly lit room. These elderly men, having been displaced by Darius, had long nurtured their bitterness in wounded silence. This night, they were gathered in the home of Kameel, the deputy chief of the present governor, along with 120 other younger (and much angrier) men.

"Friends, we have gathered here for only one purpose: I cannot, you cannot, we cannot abide the intrusion of this detestable foreigner—the Hebrew captive Daniel—into our midst. Lording it over us, he will eventually bring in his despicable Hebrew friends to displace us, just as he did so successfully in Nebuchadnezzar's court. Therefore I have summoned one who knows the final solution to our problem: gentlemen, meet—the priestess of Ishtar!"

A low murmur went through the room as the curtains parted and the malevolent features of an old witch peered at them from the darkness.

Seal up the Vision

"The priestess of Ishtar died in Babylon many years ago—my grandfather told me so!" whispered one shocked young satrap to his friend.

The room crackled with fear as the old woman sprang into their midst, her shrill laughter piercing their ears. "Ha! Who told you that?"

She spat contemptuously at the hapless speaker. "I cannot die! The goddess Ishtar has promised me eternal life if I would continue to serve her, and I have done so all these years!"

Lowering her voice, she approached the young man and grasped his collar. "Your grandfather was wrong," she rasped, her fetid breath in his face.

Wincing, he tried to pull away, but she was strong. "How would you like to know my secrets?" she continued coquettishly. "I have powers you can only dream about!" And she flung him to the floor, turning away. "The handsome young Hebrew who scorned me more than forty years ago will pay dearly. Daniel will die; I can guarantee his death. This plan was revealed to me by the lord of darkness himself, and it cannot fail."

Her black eyes glistened in the flickering lamplight, as she drew back her lips in a mirthless grin. "I have waited many years for this."

The oil lamps burned far into the night as the plan was revealed. Finally the guests departed, and the house was dark and quiet. The creatures of darkness winged their way to report to their master; the old crone returned to her stone hut and drugged herself into a stuporous, dreamless sleep.

The angels of light encircling the household of Daniel kept watch and patiently, quietly awaited their instructions.

———❧———

> *Give ear to my prayer, O God; hear my supplications. Because of the voice of the enemy, the oppression of the wicked, they charge me in their iniquity and in their wrath they hate me...for wickedness is among them in their dwellings. As for me, I will call upon God and my Lord shall save me. Evening, and morning, and at noon will I pray and cry aloud, and he shall hear my voice. He has delivered my soul in peace from the battle that was against me.*

Daniel prayed aloud, repeating the ancient words of the warrior-king David's psalm. Kneeling on the soft carpet of his balcony and facing west toward the city of Jerusalem, he prayed according to the Holy Scripture: during the time of the morning sacrifice, the evening sacrifice, and half-way between—at noon. This was now a familiar discipline that somehow had always brought great comfort and strength to him in his lifetime of exile, far from his own land.

Presently, his prayer finished, Daniel arose and went inside. The sun was just rising in the east, and the two men in the shadows below the balcony slipped quietly away.

Later that morning, Darius called Daniel to the palace, where he out-lined his plan: Daniel had been called to the highest position of authority in Persia. Two other Persian presidents, as well as 120 princes, would be under his rulership, accountable only to him. Since Darius' son, Cyrus, was now the reigning monarch in Babylon—and Mordecai was gone—Darius had need of a wise and experienced counselor to oversee his mas-sive kingdom. Daniel gallantly and humbly accepted the challenge.

Unfortunately, neither he nor the king could possibly have known how this would affect the court. Highly agitated, deeply incensed, affronted and jealous, these men soon found their disappointment whipped into an unreasonable, almost insane fury. Their resentment drew them together in secret meeting places, uniting this diverse group of rulers as nothing else ever had.

Actually, there was no real reason for their revolt. Each one of these men had retained their original positions of authority. The only difference was that they were now subservient not only to one who was a despised minority, but also to his God.

Having rejected the authority of the one supreme God, their rebellion rendered them wide open to the demonic forces under the control of the demon prince of Persia. These dark beings lost no time; they immediately moved in and set the evil plan into motion. They worked in the invis-ible realm, pulling the strings and moving the foolish, arrogant men like pawns on a chessboard.

Finally, the day came when the presidents and princes all assembled together at court in the king's presence. Kameel, the appointed spokes-man, stepped forth and bowed low in obeisance.

"O King Darius, may you live forever. All the presidents of the king-dom, the governors, princes, counselors, and captains have consulted together to establish a royal statute. Any person who shall ask a petition of any god or man for thirty days, except of you, O King, shall be cast into the den of lions. Now we ask you, mighty Darius, to sign this document so that we may bring honor to our great king who so graciously grants our petitions. Your royal signature will make this an unalterable decree according to the ancient law of the Medes and Persians."

Darius, who had been somewhat uneasy concerning the allegiance of his subject rulers during the recent change, was greatly relieved by this apparently spontaneous outpouring of loyalty. He signed the decree, and the rebels went to their homes rejoicing.

Daniel received word almost immediately. A breathless grandson, who had heard the decree spoken and had watched the unsuspecting king sign it, ran all the way from the palace to bring the devastating news. Daniel's finely chiseled features clouded only for a moment, then he gently raised his grandson to his feet.

Face to face, Daniel placed a hand on the young man's shoulder. "Thank you for telling me, Joshua. This explains the uneasiness I have felt whenever I speak with these men."

"Ah, well," he smiled wanly, "this is only a little bump in the road, Joshua. It may upset my cart, or I may go on. That is up to our God, in whose mercy I have always trusted."

"I understand, Grandfather. You will not…compromise."

"No," replied the elder man severely. "No, I will not compromise. Now you must go and tell the family to intercede for me, but only in their secret chambers. I will pray openly as I always have, as the head of this family.

"Do not fear, Joshua," he continued, "but remember that our God IS God—the only true God! Whether we live or whether we die—we are His, and His alone."

Turning away, Daniel opened the doors to his balcony and, kneeling for his accustomed midday prayer, he murmured, "Lord, where have I heard those words before…?

"Oh, now I remember: when I was a boy and the invasion was coming, all of us there in the courtyard standing in the shadows and I holding onto my mother, so desperately afraid—Then Hananiah's uncle Elihu said to all of us that night so long ago, 'We may never meet again, but *whether we live or whether we die, we are His and His alone.'*"

There on his balcony, in the warmth of the sun, the man so beloved by God made his petitions known. The deep, rich voice raised in prayer and praise was heard with great delight and satisfaction by the One on the throne, who immediately dispatched legions of angels on his behalf. Daniel, greatly strengthened and comforted, arose, washed, and joined his family for the midday meal.

The angels took their places and waited.

The Egyptian was a nervous wreck. He had known bad nights before, but this was the worst. Sitting on the edge of his bed, he held his throbbing head and dreaded the rising of the sun. Another sleepless night, another endless day, he thought dully, as he arose stiffly to go about his duties.

As the official keeper of the animals in the royal zoo at Susa, Asafa had enough to worry about. The hunters were kept busy day and night, working to bring in enough meat to feed the leopard, the beautiful white tiger, the pair of wolves with their cubs, and most of all—an entire pride of lions trapped and brought from Ethiopia. These last were kept in a deep pit dug for the purpose of displaying them (or so the Egyptian was told).

Actually, the lions had developed a very unhealthy taste for human flesh, having been used for some time as executioners against enemies of the royal family. Asafa suspected that this could be the only viable reason for keeping such a large group of flesh-eating animals.

Asafa hated the executions. The terrified screams of the victims as they fell…the unearthly snarling and cracking of breaking bones as the voracious lions fed…was too much for his sensibilities. He was required to withhold food from his lions for three days previous to an execution, and this was the third day. The ceaseless roaring of the hungry prowling beasts unnerved him, and if he approached too closely, the snarling creatures would leap up the walls of the pit, sometimes nearly reaching the top.

Today's execution was scheduled at sundown. As he went about his duties, feeding the elephants, ostriches, and monkeys, Asafa wondered idly who the next victim would be. "At least he'll die quickly—if not mercifully," he muttered wearily, "and I'll sleep quietly tonight."

Darius was desperate. For three days following the accusation against Daniel, the king and his assembled scribes and historians had vainly attempted to find some legal loophole. Working day and night, poring over rooms full of parchment scrolls and clay tablets, the ancient chronicles were unyieldingly consistent. There was no precedent for setting aside any edict signed and sealed by a Persian king. Time was quickly running out, and Darius glanced out the window at the late afternoon sun as he paced the floor of his chamber.

"I'm the king!" he muttered angrily. "But king of what? I was a fool to listen to their flattering tongues; now I'm a prisoner of my own arrogant pride. I've consigned the great man of God to death and perhaps destroyed my kingdom as well."

At that moment, the curtains parted and an elderly servant entered, bowing low. "It is time, sire. Daniel has been taken to the entrance. Everyone is assembled and awaiting your orders."

With a weary sigh, Darius nodded his assent and departed his chambers. The silent group gathered at the mouth of the den parted respectfully, and the king approached. Daniel was standing quietly, and as he raised his head to meet the king's gaze, Darius was astounded by the peace that seemed to radiate from this man.

It was very difficult for the words to come, but after a long silence, the king finally spoke: "Please forgive me, Daniel. My counselors and I have labored long and hard to try to find a way out of this, but to no avail."

The king took a deep breath, then continued. "Your God, whom you have faithfully served all your life, is fully able to preserve and defend you, for you have done no wrong. I commend you to His mercy."

The executioners closed in on Daniel and approached the mouth of the pit. Deep inside the cavern, the starving lions sensed the movement and began to roar. The sound was deafening; the air seemed electrified as the terrifying snarling of the beasts drew closer. For one anguished moment, Daniel seemed to hang in midair, then disappeared from sight.

Quickly and efficiently, the executioners moved the stone cover over the pit and applied the hot wax seal. Darius pressed his signet ring into the wax, then returned immediately to the palace. Sending everyone away, he spent a sleepless night in agony of soul, refusing food, entertainment, and even the comfort of his wife.

Esther and her maids had been fasting and praying the last three days, having sent word to all the Jews in the kingdom to do the same. Thus, ironically, the very edict that forbade any supplications to God only served to trigger an unprecedented outpouring of fervent intercession.

The kingdom of Persia slept little that night; the king slept not at all. Apparently, the only citizen of that great city who slept undisturbed was the victim himself. Daniel spent the night with his head pillowed in the rough yellow fur of a large male lion. The animals lay perfectly still, unwilling to disturb the slumber of the exhausted man.

The massive angel guarding him moved slowly among the pride, touching each animal until all were sleeping. The glowing luminescence of his robes illuminated the eerie scene; he watched and waited all through that long night until dawn, when he heard running footsteps.

"Push harder!" grunted the king, as he and his four servants tugged at the stone far above the floor of the pit.

The angel touched Daniel lightly on the shoulder.

He stirred, then yawned and stretched. For a moment, his sleep-drugged eyes stared uncomprehendingly at his unusual bedfellows, still sleeping peacefully, stretched out in a jumble of dull yellow bodies across the rocky floor of the cavern.

Daniel gingerly stepped over and around the lions, carefully avoiding stepping on an occasional paw or tail. When he looked up, however, his heart nearly stopped. He was face-to-face with the biggest, most powerful being he had ever seen.

"God has sent me to shut the mouths of the lions." The deep voice seemed to come from everywhere, echoing through the cave; the bright light surrounding him was nearly blinding.

Daniel managed to stay on his feet, but when he opened his eyes again the angel was gone; instead, light was pouring out from the opening above, and a voice was insistently calling his name. "Daniel! Daniel—are you there? Are you still alive? Has your God delivered you?"

As Daniel approached the entrance, he saw the astonished face of the king peering down at him from above. "Yes, Your Majesty, you are correct.

My God has sent His angel and shut the mouth of the lions."

The faces disappeared, and Daniel could not be heard any longer over the tumult of shouting and rejoicing above. A rope chair was immediately lowered into the pit, and when he emerged on top and stepped out onto the platform, he was immediately enveloped in a bear hug.

The jubilant king, alternately shouting orders to his men and roaring with relieved laughter, could not contain his delight. "Your God delivered you! Ha! I knew He would! I knew it! What did the angel look like, Daniel? Did you talk to him—ask him questions?"

The king of Persia was delirious with joy. "My servants will see to your needs—you must break the night's fast with me in the palace this morning. We will have a great feast—all your family is invited."

Later that morning, at the king's command, the conspirators and their families were all brought to the lions' den. When they were thrown down, the ravenous beasts below leaped upward and caught them in midair, crushing them and breaking their bones before they ever hit the bottom. The lions ate their fill that day, gorging themselves on those whose pride, ambition, and jealousy had made them pawns of the devil.

His plan once again foiled, the territorial ruler of darkness known as the prince of Persia withdrew to recoup his forces. Angry and frustrated at his defeat, he sent the destroyer to the little stone hut outside of the city. The tormented old witch was driven by the dark winged creatures who formerly were subservient to her will to the brink of the quarry where she fell headlong, screaming curses all the way down. In the end she died, alone and unmourned, a pathetic heap of broken flesh and bone.

"God is a God of mercy, Joshua," Daniel explained to his grandson later, "but He is also a God of justice. Our ancient King Solomon wrote that no human or demonic plan or counsel formed against God will ever succeed. Don't ever forget, young Joshua: Ultimately, OUR God always, always has the last word."

CHAPTER 17

THE TREASURE

T HE SLEEK LITTLE cutter *Ladyfair* rode gently at anchor in the waters of Skiros Bay. The deck seemed deserted, the only sound that of waves softly lapping at the sides of the boat, punctuated by the cry of seagulls wheeling over the fishnets drying on the shore.

The tranquil scene was suddenly shattered as two divers simultaneously broke the surface. "Race you for the boat!" gasped the man, but the woman was already halfway there.

"You'll never make the Olympic team that way!" laughed the woman as she pulled herself up the ladder.

"Need a hand up, old man?" She wriggled out of her scuba gear and leaned down to pull up her struggling companion, only to find herself launched in a flying arc back into the sea.

"Serves you right, young lady," laughed the man, now on deck. "I didn't know I'd married such a tease. I'll just have to teach you a lesson."

Dropping his equipment onto the polished teakwood deck, he turned and executed a perfect jackknife dive into the water. Screaming with laughter, the two splashed, played, and dunked each other until they were exhausted. Finally, they clambered back up the ladder and disappeared into the galley below to prepare the evening meal. Soon the enticing aroma of frying fish drifted across the deck, and once again the picturesque little bay was serenely quiet, all pink and coral in the light of the setting sun.

For the three weeks following their wedding, Dan and Sarah had been sailing the Greek islands. This was a honeymoon that most lovers could only dream about: lazy days and nights afloat on a luxurious single-masted cutter. The sailing vessel had been purchased on the island of Rhodes for a fraction of its value from a Swedish businessman (whose love of the sea had been thwarted by an unfortunate business reversal back home). Dan couldn't believe his good fortune. Marrying Sarah and acquiring a boat all in the space of one week were the fulfillment of long-cherished dreams.

They had set out on their delightful adventure, charting a clockwise course through the islands of Karpathos, Crete, Kithira, and Milos. They had meandered through the delightful group of Cyclades, then north to Skiros, where they had remained the last two days.

On this night, a little rain squall blew in, and the boat pitched about in the choppy waters. Sarah looked over at Dan, who was sleeping soundly; she sighed and switched on the light. Since the only book above her was Dan's Bible, she settled in for a good night's reading. The book fell open at Paul's Epistle to the Thessalonians, which she had never read. Immediately, her heart was warmed by the blessing of the great man of God to the believers at Thessalonica:

> Grace to you, and peace…We thank God for unwavering hope in the return of our Lord Jesus Christ the Messiah…for you welcomed our message, in spite of much persecution, with the joy of the Holy Spirit.
>
> Everywhere people are hearing of your great faith, how you turned from idolatry to serve a God who is alive and true and genuine, and how eagerly you await the coming of His Son from heaven, whom He raised from the dead…Jesus, who personally rescues us, and delivers us from the wrath coming upon those unrepentant ones, AND DRAWS US TO HIMSELF.

Sarah could go no further. She leaned back against the pillows. Breathless with the wonder of what she had read, Sarah knew with an astounding certainty that this same Jesus was even now drawing her to Himself.

The Spirit of God had long been preparing her heart, quietly and systematically removing all stony obstacles, plowing up the precious soil and softening it with the little rain showers of the Spirit, and then quietly planting the seed of truth. Now Sarah received from God and immediately responded. She gave her heart to Him completely, yielding up all her life, hopes, and dreams to the One who had called her to Himself.

The wind finally died down, and Dan stirred in his sleep. She touched his tousled hair tenderly, then switched off the light and snuggled up to her husband. *Tomorrow*, she thought drowsily, *I'll tell Dan. I know he's been praying fervently for me, never pushing or shoving or making me feel inferior—what a man!*

Overwhelmed by the sheer joy of belonging to the Eternal One, Sarah finally drifted off to sleep, charting in her mind a course due northwest to Thessalonica.

———

The fleet of empty army trucks rattled along the road by the ravine. The hard Montana winter, with record snow levels, was beginning to soften into spring. The melting snows trickling down from the high country had swollen the Clark Fork River to a dangerous torrent that carried along rocks and trees, and in places undercutting the river bank. There was always the imminent danger of flooding, so the lead truck driver kept a careful eye out for debris on the road.

The uniformed official next to him sat impassively, his craggy features an unreadable mask of stoicism. The truck driver stole a furtive glance at his unperturbed passenger now and then, wondering why the venerated council member of the Blackfoot tribe would ever venture into the jungle of the white man's government bureaucracy.

Jim Greywolf was the liaison officer between the army and the National Guard. It was his assignment to ferret out nests of Jews or Christians in hiding, round them up, and transport them to the concentration camp near Billings. Aided by a natural-born instinct, Jim was the perfect man for the job. He was fueled by a generations-long hatred of the white "Christians" who had long ago massacred his people and herded the remnants onto a reservation, consigning them to a life of emptiness and alcoholism.

During the last few months, persistent rumors—reports of a group hiding somewhere in the Cabinet Mountains wilderness—had surfaced. Jim Greywolf was, like his name, a hungry predator on the scent of his prey. For days, he had crisscrossed the mountains in an army helicopter, scanning the landscape and taking serial shots with a telephoto lens over gridded areas. In the end, his patient persistence had paid off. One of the telephoto images had yielded some suspicious geometric areas, which, upon computer enhancement, turned out to be buildings.

Seal up the Vision

Now, in hot pursuit and nearing his quarry, Jim felt the old familiar bile of hatred rise in his throat. *Liars and hypocrites*, he thought sourly, *sitting in their fancy churches on Sunday, then treating us just like they used to treat the blacks in the south: so very patronizing in their disdain.*

He turned to look out the window. Down below, the twisting torrent raced through the ravine, raging against its confinement. Just ahead was a sharp S-curve, shadowed by an overhanging rock ledge. The four empty trucks thundered along, closing the distance between them as they negotiated the turn.

Suddenly, without warning the entire stretch of road buckled, then dropped four or five feet, angling down from the cliffs on the left. All four trucks careened crazily for a few seconds, then rolled over down the embankment into the swollen river below. The last three trucks sank immediately, but the lead truck stayed afloat just long enough for its stunned occupants to drag themselves through the windows and onto the roof.

The driver sprang out onto a floating log as the truck sank beneath the water. Jim Greywolf was carried along by the current, kicking desperately to stay afloat. His waterproof nylon jacket had trapped just enough air to buoy him up in the water.

Bruised and battered, nearly unconscious and choking in the icy water, he finally succumbed to hypothermia. About half a mile downriver, three children gathering firewood nearly stumbled over his inert body lodged against a fallen tree on the river's bank. With great effort, they managed to pull him up the slippery bank and onto dry ground.

The oldest boy felt for a pulse. "I think he may still be alive! Kevin, you run back to camp and get Dad. Lisa and I will stay here. Hurry!"

The six-year-old boy, who had been staring in mesmerized horror at the grayish face of the poor drowned man, turned and ran into the thick stand of lodgepole pines. The other two crouched by the man, and Lisa reached out a tentative finger to touch his face.

"O-ooh, Tommy—he's cold as ice!" Lisa shook her long dark curls in shuddering protest. "Do you think he's already dead?"

"I don't know, but Dad should be here any minute," replied her brother.

Lisa didn't answer; she stood up. "I hear someone coming. Dad!" she shouted through cupped hands. "Dad, we're over here!"

Crashing through the underbrush, Randy Endicott broke into the clearing, followed closely by two other men and little Kevin. Kneeling by the body, Randy started CPR.

The other two men knelt down, and one quickly extracted a stethoscope. "We have a faint heartbeat, but he's still not breathing."

The men continued CPR for several long minutes until the man finally took one shuddering gasp, then coughed up a great deal of river water. The children were wide-eyed with wonder, but the cautious men, having turned him on his side to prevent aspiration (for by now the poor man was projectile vomiting even more river water!) made another discovery.

The flesh under his shredded jacket, indeed, the entire back, sides, and front of his body were a mangled mass of torn and bruised flesh. Apparently the damage was severe, and in addition to multiple fractures, there had been a massive loss of blood

"He'll be in shock. We'll need to get an I.V. going pretty quick."

The third man dashed for the campsite, calling over his shoulder, "I'll be back with the Medikit and blankets for a stretcher!"

By the time the shafts of late afternoon sunlight were slanting through the pines, the weary group had arrived back in camp. The men carried their moaning patient out of the chilly wind and into the tent where they carefully stripped off his wet clothing and wrapped him in blankets warmed by the fire pit.

After a lengthy and animated consultation, it was decided to stay the night in camp and then start out early in the morning for the compound, four or five hours away. They agreed to watch their unstable patient closely through the night, Randy taking the first shift. After a hastily prepared meal of smoked rainbow trout and cornbread, they gathered around the fire pit for a short time of prayer and thanksgiving for the life rescued from certain death.

The last comment that night was a small voice coming from the corner of the tent: "Dad, I wonder if this is what Jesus meant when He said we would be 'fishers of men'?"

Three weeks later Jim Greywolf finally awoke. The women were setting the long tables for breakfast, and the enticing aroma of bacon and coffee wafted through the main hall and drifted invitingly through to the infirmary. The "nurse" on duty, an eleven-year-old girl named

Jessica, stared in amazement as the big Indian struggled up on one elbow.

"Mom! Come and see—he's awake!" She called through the doorway. Several women came running, wiping their hands on their aprons.

The patient collapsed back against his pillow, looking around in evident confusion. "How did…what happened?" he managed to croak.

Paula Endicott beamed down at him, explaining softly, "Sir, you were in an accident at the river and nearly drowned. Some of our children found you, and you were brought here."

"What…where is this place?" Again, he struggled to sit up; Paula gently but firmly settled him back on his pillow.

"Sir, you need to be as quiet as possible, at least for now. You have several fractured ribs, a broken arm, and possibly a skull fracture—there was bleeding from both ears. As a matter of fact, you lost a great deal of blood in your ordeal on the river. There is some severe soft tissue damage to both legs, which will take quite some time to heal, so it would be best if you did not try to get up just yet."

She cocked her head at him and smiled. "You know, not too many men would have survived the beating you took in that river. God must have gifted you with some enormous inner strength. You rest now, and we'll bring you some food."

He managed a semblance of a smile, grimacing at the pain of a swollen, bruised face. "Yes, I'd like that. I'm hungry."

The women all filed by his bed, murmuring their motherly satisfaction with his sudden improvement. As the door closed, he called out weakly, "Thanks. Thank you all."

During the next few days and weeks he gradually gained strength from the nutritious diet. The only medical professional in the compound, an EMT named Chuck, was quite worried about the severe bruising to the kidneys. Gradually, however, the blood cleared from the urine, and he concentrated on some low-impact physical therapy to strengthen the muscles, increase circulation, and speed healing.

The constant topic of conversation among the adults was speculative: who is he, and why was he wearing a high-ranking officer's uniform under his jacket? The answer finally came when their benefactor, the forest ranger, came with his monthly delivery, three weeks late.

"Sorry, folks," he apologized as he let down the tailgate of the truck, "but the roads have been impassable—flooded out in some places, blocked by rock slides in other places."

The men greeted him warmly and, after unloading the provisions, sat him down to a meal of deer sausage, sourdough biscuits, and gooseberry pie. While the hungry ranger wolfed down his food, they filled him in on their strange visitor.

"How long did you say he's been here?" he inquired as he finished his second piece of pie.

"I think it's been almost six weeks," ventured Chuck. "His fractures are pretty well healed, and he's able to hobble around a little on makeshift crutches. I'll take off the casts in three more days."

The young ranger kept looking at his empty plate, then slowly met Randy's eyes. "I think I know who he is. Bad news if I'm right." He took a deep breath and looked around the table. "The latest scuttlebutt around Forest Service headquarters is that old Jim Greywolf had supposedly located a large group of fugitives hiding out in the mountains somewhere. He bragged to the general that it was no different than cleaning out a nest of wasps, and he would get the job done right this time.

"The reason I remember this so well is that I realized he was using a direct quote from General Custer, who talked about massacring an entire tribe of Indians as being no different than 'cleaning out a nest of wasps.' This tribal bitterness goes 'way back, folks, and the shabby way our government has treated them ever since hasn't helped any, either. Jim Greywolf has a real big burr under his saddle."

Shaking his head, he continued. "You see, every time—every single time he's closed in on one of these groups during the last two years—they're gone. They just simply relocate. No one seems to know how they are alerted. Ol' Greywolf must have somehow located your position and was...sort of, well...waylaid."

He finished with a grin. "He disappeared with four army trucks just about six weeks ago.

No one moved. The room went silent for several minutes, then Randy rose to his feet. "Want to meet him? On the other hand, maybe it's better if you don't. He won't be going anywhere for quite a while.

"In the meantime," Randy looked around at his fellow fugitives, a distinct twinkle in his eye, "We'll just wait and see what the Lord is up to this time."

———— ∞∞∞ ————

"Priority message for you, Mr. Mannheim."

Jack turned from the drafting table, slightly irritated at the interruption by his foreman. "What is it, Ghatti? I'm just finishing these revisions, and the men need to get started on them this morning."

"Begging your pardon, sir, but the caller is most insistent." The man bowed respectfully and handed over the phone.

Jack took it into the construction office and closed the door. "This is Jack Mannheim. Hello?"

"Mr. Mannheim, how good to hear your voice again. This is Karl Morgenthal." There was a momentary silence, then the smartly accented, clipped voice continued. "Do you remember, sir, the Jewish banker who helped you escape in Geneva?"

"Oh, of course, of course! It's been a few years, but my family and I are eternally grateful to you, Mr. Morgenthal. Did you receive our letter of invitation to come and visit us in Israel?"

"Yes, Jack, I did, and I fully intend to take advantage of your kind invitation. However, another matter of great urgency has arisen, and we need your help. This is a matter of utmost importance to the Israeli government, and to come right to the point, I need for you to bring six of your most trusted construction workers and meet me in Athens by tomorrow night. We will arrange your flight and accommodations."

Jack was thunderstruck. "Mr. Morgenthal, I absolutely cannot leave now," he explained. "The work on the temple here in Jerusalem is only two-thirds done, and we are working against a deadline. Surely you must realize that if I were to leave, all work on our section would come to a stop!"

"Then I will tell you this much: perhaps you are unaware, Jack, that the Israeli gold reserves are in danger of drying up very soon. The NWO has been systematically imposing sanctions on all trade with Israel, requiring payment in gold; supposedly the idea is that if they cannot exterminate us physically, they can choke the life out of us economically. The temple project will be the first casualty, I'm sorry to say, since it is not considered essential for the survival of the nation."

The banker paused, then spoke more slowly, enunciating each word clearly. "You may have heard of the International Commission for Jewish Restitution. Back in the late 1900s the Swiss Bankers Association was pressured to return millions of confiscated Nazi accounts, long dormant and unclaimed, to the rightful Jewish heirs of those slaughtered in the Holocaust. Of course, it was only a tiny fraction of the vast fortunes stolen.

"A great deal of gold was hidden away in various places. We have successfully located two of the three main stashes, but the largest one still remains elusively beyond our reach. Some information came to light just last week, and we are moving fast. Our intelligence reports indicate a leak of this information to the ODESSA, a powerful group of fanatic Nazi descendants. We believe they intend to find this vast treasure before we do, so you can see that it has become a dangerous race against time."

Jack's rising excitement was tempered by some bewilderment. "But, sir, how in the world could you possibly think I would be of any use to you? I would think a job like this could only be entrusted to highly trained professionals."

"That is precisely where you would be invaluable," the voice replied with a throaty chuckle. "Our enemies would recognize any of our trained agents on sight, but a tourist such as yourself…"

"A tourist?" queried a startled Jack, rising to pace the floor. "Just what do you have in mind?"

"We know that your daughter and son-in-law are now anchored off one of the Greek islands close to our target area. We can have you there in twenty-four hours to make contact with them. The three of you will be a harmless, innocent little group of travelers gawking at the sights with your—ah—shall we say 'cameras.'"

"That does it, Morgenthal. I won't have my daughter exposed to danger. I'm more than willing to help, but not at her expense. You'll just have to come up with some other scenario," Jack replied coolly.

"I understand how you feel; I would do the same, Jack. But—please understand our urgency and hear me out—we have already contacted the young honeymooners and secured their eager and willing cooperation. They are looking forward to your arrival with great anticipation."

Jack sat down heavily, his office chair creaking its protest. "I guess you have all the bases covered. All right, I'll do it."

Again, a hearty chuckle came from the other end. "You know, Jack, I suspected all along that you were a seat-of-the-pants flier with a taste for high adventure. Glad to have you aboard, son. You'll receive your tickets and instructions within the hour. Any questions?"

"Oh, I'm sure by the time we arrive in Athens I'll think of plenty!"

Jack spent the next hour making arrangements to cover his absence, selecting six of the strongest and most trustworthy workers to go with him. Without going into detail, he told Ruth he was needed in Athens for a "project," but he faced an unforeseen obstacle.

Somehow, Ruth knew from years of experience that her husband was off on another of his dangerous adventures, and this time she refused to be shut out. "I'm going, too," she announced.

"You're not going."

"I'm going." Her chin raised defiantly, Ruth knew she had won, and she turned away to pack.

"OK, you're going," sighed Jack resignedly.

O God, he thought, *this wasn't part of the deal, but You just keep her safe and … and I'll serve You the rest of my life.*

Even as a little boy on his father's farm near Heilbronn, Rudy Weiss had known he was different from other boys. His father had been born in Cologne after the war to wealthy parents who had lost all their estates during the intense Allied bombing of Germany. Rudy's grandfather, a fanatically dedicated Nazi, had been a close associate of Albert Speer and had shared his fate as a war criminal during the Nuremburg trials. He had been sentenced to a prison term at Spandau and had emerged from his incarceration embittered, terminally ill, and vowing revenge against his enemies.

On his deathbed, Rudy's grandfather had transmitted certain information to his son. Gerhardt Weiss, being the only living soul privy to this information, had chosen to keep it to himself. When he was recruited into the ODESSA organization, Gerhardt had considered it his sacred duty to pass on the baton of Nazi/Aryan ideals—racial superiority and hatred of Jews—to his son Rudy.

The child was inoculated early in his life with a deadly viral mix of embittered pride. He soon developed a disdain for others and a highly inflated ego, which served to propel him into carefully calculated positions of influence. The ODESSA had done its work well, with characteristic Teutonic efficiency.

By the time he reached the age of forty-two, Rudy Weiss was the most feared man in Germany. Master of all the occult practices that had energized and empowered his hero, Adolph Hitler, Rudy now knew that he could have whatever he wished. He was not satisfied to be commandant of the European NWO forces, but he considered this only a stepping stone to bigger and better things. The majority of German government officials regarded him as a dangerous loose cannon and opposed him vigorously, having long since recognized the danger signals. Rudy knew he would never succeed in the political arena of his own country.

An opportunist par deluxe, Rudy Weiss cared little for politics. In fact, he did not care at all for anyone or anything. The only person in his entire life that he had loved was his father, and after his death the grieving son became hard as steel. The sudden and unexpected aneurysm bursting in the brain took the life of Gerhardt Weiss when his son was only thirteen.

Unfortunately for Rudy, his father had never written down any of the vital information he received from the dying grandfather. All Rudy knew was that a massive treasure in gold bullion was hidden in three different places. Gerhardt had used up all of his inheritance in a futile search for it, so his widow was left with very little. She secured funds from ODESSA to send Rudy off to military school, then she married a wealthy Canadian and moved away. Rudy never saw her again.

The seeds of hatred his father had planted grew quickly in the boy's embittered soul, which had been so mercilessly plowed and furrowed by the pain of his mother's abandonment. He withdrew from all friendships, carefully cultivating only those that could advance his career.

Eventually, inevitably, his personality fragmented into two personas. He was the outgoing, polished, successful, expansive pillar of society—suave and silver-tongued to the utmost degree. And then he was the private, hidden Rudy: the cold, hard, calculating, manipulative sociopath whose colossal lust for power, yoked together with and fed by his newly acquired occultic powers, propelled him rapidly from one pinnacle of success to another.

His ascent to worldwide prominence was dizzying, to say the least, and certainly would have turned less secure heads than his own. Having used, then discarded, the subversive neo-Nazi ODESSA organization to achieve his high position as chief commandant of the NWO military forces, he then secured a membership in the exclusive Trilateral Commission for World Peace. When the members of ODESSA began to disappear under mysterious circumstances, the panicked leadership concluded that Rudy had sold them out in exchange for his appointment. In this assumption they were entirely correct.

Inflamed by the gross ingratitude of the young Aryan they had so carefully prepared and groomed for prominence, they hastily convened a meeting. One by one, they arrived at the lavish country estate once owned by an infamous S.S. officer and were escorted quickly to an underground bunker. The discussion was short, grim, and the vote unanimous: young Herr Weiss was to be immediately targeted for assassination.

However, Rudy had obtained knowledge of this meeting, and his men had already surrounded the building. Well hidden in the thick forest, they closed in and quietly dropped cyanide canisters into the ventilation system. The escape routes were all sealed, and within minutes the entire ODESSA organization vanished. A short time later, after the hit team left the bunker, there was no trace that this neo-Nazi group had ever existed.

Like shooting ducks in a barrel, he thought with perverse satisfaction. Easing back into the leather-cushioned comfort of his silver Rolls-Royce, Rudy signaled the driver to take him to the Flughaven at Frankfurt.

I'll just have time to make my flight to Athens, he mused as he poured himself a brandy. *If my sources are correct, this time all I have to do is—"follow the yellow brick road." Yes—follow the yellow brick road!* And he roared with laughter. *That fool Morgenthal will lead me right to it, and he has no idea I'm onto him. A fortune in gold just waiting for me all these years, somewhere hidden away in the darkness.*

God, it's good to be rich and powerful! Startled somewhat by his own reference to the Deity he disregarded as a nonentity, he cursed himself as he turned up the Bartok CD.

The moon hung over the Aegean Sea like a huge, yellow Japanese lantern. The sighing of the wind in the cypress trees on the hillside murmured its comforting lullaby, singing a gentle duet with the slow, measured cadence of wavelets lapping softly on the glistening sand

"Some enchanted evening," murmured Sarah as she laid her head on her husband's shoulder. "Makes me feel like breaking out into song.

"Some enchanted evening…" she warbled, throwing her arms out dramatically toward her imaginary audience.

Unfortunately, the impromptu concert was abruptly ended by her husband's hand clapped over her mouth. "Sarah, Sarah, my darling: I married you for your looks, your brains, and—uh—uh—oh I forget…but surely there must be something else!" he added rather lamely.

"Oh, yes, now I remember: you promised never to sing to me in the moonlight, like those corny old musicals. You know, where the orchestra music swells up out of nowhere, and—"

"Oh, Dan, you killjoy! I loved 'South Pacific'! I adored 'Seven Brides for Seven Brothers'!"

She laughed gaily, pulling her husband behind her. "C'mon—let's call Mom and Dad. They gave me the name of their hotel in Athens, and they should have arrived just hours ago!"

Dan and Sarah trudged up the beach and out on the dock to their boat, where they placed the call to Athens. Several hours later, Dan lay awake, his arms stretched behind his head. *Wish I knew,* he thought uneasily, *exactly what this Mr. Morgenthal is up to. I'd sure feel a lot easier about it if I knew Sarah wasn't in any danger.*

He glanced at his sleeping wife, then at the luminous dial of the cabin clock. *Nearly 2 a.m. I can't shake this uneasiness, so there's only one sure remedy: prayer.*

Dan Shepherd slipped noiselessly from his bed and, climbing to the deck, inhaled great, deep lungfuls of sea air. He dropped quietly to the dock and walked slowly along the shore, gripped by the gradually growing, very distinct awareness of a Presence.

Dan stopped. *Lord, is that You?* he breathed

Suddenly, all the night sounds receded, and he was enveloped in that Presence. Wave after wave of liquid love poured over, around, and through him, and Dan found himself on his knees in the sand.

Heedless of the waves lapping at his feet and ankles, he was thus introduced to the Helper, the Comforter, the Teacher. Dan knew all about the Father God and his Savior, the Lord Jesus Christ. But now he was experiencing something more: the manifest Presence of God, the "promise of the Father" that he had read about in Acts.

For some time now, Dan had been longing to personally experience the same miracle-working power he had read about in the Bible and had heard was happening in other parts of the world. He also had a deep hunger to know his God more intimately and had just recently discovered the words of Jesus in the seventh chapter of John.

> If any man thirst, let him come unto Me and drink. He that believes on Me, as the Scripture has said, out of his innermost being shall flow rivers of living water.

That night, long after the moon had disappeared over the far western shore, the man was still pacing the beach, lost in the awesome wonder of sweet fellowship with his Creator.

The little band of tourists clambered aboard the ancient bus, their gap-toothed tour guide beaming down the aisle at them like a beneficent genie. Strapping himself into the driver's seat, he announced proudly that his was the oldest and most thorough tour leaders of the environs of Izmir, "also known as the ancient city of Smyrna in your Book of Revelation," he added.

"Izmir is the oldest continuously occupied city in this part of Asia Minor. Most of the others—with the notable exception of Ephesus—are in ruins. Some were destroyed by earthquakes. The city of Philadelphia no longer exists, for it was built right over a major fault in the earth's crust."

His voice droned on, describing the devastating earthquake of 1939 that killed 50,000 people in Anatolia to the east, and the deadly quake of 1999 with its epicenter in Izmir itself. "There has been," he explained soberly, "ever-increasing seismic activity in recent years, and the authorities expect a massive outbreak of earthquakes and volcanic eruptions sometime soon along the Mediterranean fault as well as the infamous 'ring of fire' in the Pacific."

Sarah nudged Dan, who had dozed off during the long dissertation. "Wake up, husband; did you not sleep at all last night?"

"Nope. Not a wink." Dan half-opened one eye, grinning sheepishly at his wife. "Important meeting with the Chief," he whispered.

"Oh," she nodded sagely. "Go back to sleep then. You'll need it."

Sarah knew that ever since her Dan had read the works and biography of Peter Marshall, he had adopted his somewhat quaint reference to the Lord as "the Chief." She reached across the aisle and took her father's hand.

"Mom OK? Are you two—ah—enjoying this?" she inquired, cocking her head inquisitively.

Jack glanced at Ruth's lovely, classic profile and murmured, "Yeah, Toots—we're OK. I just wish we actually could make this a real vacation instead of a whirlwind tour."

Ruth turned her luminous smile on her daughter. "Sarah, your father and I had talked for years of buying a sailboat and going on an extended vacation. I'm just so pleased you and Dan have done this while you're young. In the meantime, I'm enjoying just being here with my family. I only wish Matt…"

Her smile faded, and she looked out the window. Jack squeezed her hand, explaining to his daughter, "Sarah, we didn't want to burden you with this, but Matt has not reported home for almost six weeks now. We've tried to get some information, but apparently he's on some super-secret mission. That seems to be all we could learn—not much, I'm afraid."

Sarah was silent. "Dad, Dan and I have so much to tell you. Just be assured that we have felt an urgency to pray for Matt many times. We pray until the urgency leaves us. We know that somehow he's been in danger, but God is protecting him."

Jack stared in open-mouthed astonishment at his daughter. *Has marriage changed her this much*, he wondered, *or… or is it something else?*

Sarah was looking demurely down at her lap, her lips curved in that age-old Mona Lisa smile that leaves men somewhere between exasperation and total bewilderment. "Tell you later, Dad. We're coming to our first stop."

Jack's senses were immediately on alert. *The Nazi installation that Morgenthal told us about,* he thought. *Careful…just wander around and take pictures like any ordinary tourist. The Mossad are all around us—he absolutely promised. Hope he's right.* With a sigh, Jack followed his family out of the bus to view the beautifully proportioned, massive structures, so distinctively emblazoned with the proud eagle of the Third Reich.

The men on deck were restless. The sleek gunboat Italia, lying at anchor several miles off the Turkish coast near Izmir, had not moved perceptibly for several hours. Having requisitioned it from the NWO's Mediterranean fleet of patrol boats, Rudy Weiss had stationed himself like a spider waiting for an unsuspecting fly, and, like the proverbial spider, his patience was eventually rewarded

"There's the bus now, sir!" exclaimed his aide, handing him the binoculars.

"Get me in closer. I want a better look at these tourists. Pietro!" he barked. "Get that GPS imager on them and download everything onto my laptop! I want detailed close-ups of each one of them. Now we'll see what kind of a crew we're dealing with!"

His power binoculars focused in on a motley crew, indeed: a few Arab women in black, several elderly pensioners on holiday—*probably Austrian or Swiss*, he guessed—a pair of honeymooners with a middle-aged couple, what looked to be three Russian Orthodox (maybe Greek) priests with long beards, an awkward adolescent and his exasperated mother, and finally a very heavy, florid American wearing shorts, a Texas Rangers T-shirt, and baseball cap. He could not recognize even one face among them.

He swore under his breath, and turning on his heel, he went below. "Call me immediately, Pietro, when anyone else comes into view!"

Rudy was in a foul mood and beginning to wonder if his sources were wrong. "If I miss out on this one, heads will roll!" he growled.

Pietro, however, visibly relaxed with the exit of his sour-faced superior. "Let him rot," he growled to no one in particular. "I'm not his little galley slave! I'm getting out of this broiling sun," and he headed to the crew's lounge for a cold beer.

So it happened that, sullenly ensconced in his cabin below, Rudy and his entire crew missed entirely the remarkable events going on ashore. At that very moment, an earthquake 6.9 on the Richter scale rocked the entire western Turkish coast, toppling office buildings in Izmir, rolling southward until it hit the German installation. The imposing edifice constructed in 1945 by Albert Speer swayed back and forth like a hula dancer, then fell in slow motion until it was an unrecognizable pile of bricks and mortar.

The shocked tourists, who had already piled back into the bus and headed on down the gravel road, could not have imagined such a scenario. As the little vehicle valiantly struggled to stay upright, they screamed and clung to each other, the Russian Orthodox priests as terrified as all the others. The driver, apparently intent on outrunning the earthquake, had gunned the accelerator in a spasm of terror. Now he suddenly braked to a stop. The road ahead was completely impassable, covered by a rock slide.

The little bus sat and shuddered as the earth shook beneath them, but it stayed upright. Presently the terrifying roaring sound ceased, and people began to move, getting out of the bus to survey the damage. Sarah and Ruth, more than a little shaken, sat down on a rock. Dan and Jack climbed the hill for a better vantage point.

In the distance, the city to the north was spotted here and there with fires from exploded gas mains. To the south the arid landscape was littered with debris. Not a single tree was left standing. To the east there was not much damage, and Dan thought he saw a small town through his binoculars.

Swinging back to the north, he focused in on the ruined Nazi headquarters. By now, the sun was lowering in the west, and Dan gasped involuntarily. He waited until he was quite sure, then handed the binoculars to Jack, saying quietly, "Take a look, Jack. Tell me what you see."

Taking the binoculars, Jack scanned the landscape for a few seconds, then stiffened to attention.

All that was left of Albert Speer's careful building project was a huge, jumbled pile of bricks that were taking on a distinct, golden, incandescent glow, shimmering like a thousand candles in the light of the setting sun.

"Great balls of fire! Will you look at that!" He breathed reverentially, lowering the glasses. "So that's how he did it. That sly Nazi fox: encasing the gold bullion inside the clay bricks of the building itself. Who would ever have guessed?"

"I guess that solves our mystery, Jack. But now, the problem is—if we can see it, they can too!" Dan took over the binoculars, scanning their surroundings while Jack fished out his cell phone.

After several attempts, he finally got through to Athens. "Karl—this is Jack. So you've heard. Yes, we're at the site now. No, everyone here is quite safe—a little shaken, maybe. Listen, Karl, we have had the answer to the problem literally dropped in our lap, but we're going to have to move quickly—tonight. Yes, tonight."

Jack continued his explanation as Dan surveyed the western horizon. "They're out there, all right!" he muttered tersely, "just like vultures waiting to move in on the kill. I don't see anyone on deck though. Maybe they got careless."

The two men went back to the bus, where they found the anxious driver trying to settle his charges. "We'll go to a little inn about four or five miles east," he explained. "All will be well—do not worry!"

The faithful little vehicle rattled along the road to the village. The passengers were given their rooms, and, after rather sketchy explanations, Sarah and Ruth decided to spend the night in the same room.

Under cover of darkness, Dan and Jack hiked the nearly five miles back to the ruined building, their flashlights piercing the darkness ahead of them. Storm clouds were coming in from the north, obscuring the moon.

Hurrying down the hill, both men were startled when an armed sentry stepped out in front of them, shining his penlight briefly in their faces. "Sorry, guys," he apologized over his shoulder. "Follow me. Things are already in full swing. We've already on-loaded nearly a third of the cargo. We want you to take a look at something peculiar, though."

Stepping gingerly over the debris, Dan was amazed at the quiet speed and efficiency with which the Israelis were working. All the bricks were now piled in neat stacks, being transported onto the darkened profile of a steamer anchored just a few hundred yards offshore. Working without lights, they had already accomplished a great deal.

"Jack—over here!" Some men were in a semi-circle, bending over something on the ground. Jack very nearly did not recognize the elderly Mr. Morgenthal, now dressed in black sweats from head to toe.

Stepping forward to shake Jack's hand, he explained in hushed tones, "The foundation looks different in this corner, as if someone hand-plastered it. And—look here at this L-shaped crack."

Jack leaned over for a closer look. "I'd bet my bottom dollar there's a sub-basement under this foundation."

A jack hammer was produced and they drilled, carefully following the projected lines of the crack. Suddenly, the entire corner caved in with a resounding crash. The men jumped back, but when the choking dust had subsided, crowded around for a better view. The powerful beams of their flashlights slowly crisscrossed the room below. Untouched for over eighty years, the richness of the treasures below them reduced the men to an awed silence.

"These, my friends, are all that remain of our people slain in the Holocaust." Karl Morgenthal's voice broke as he sank to one knee.

"And I will give you the treasures of darkness, and secret riches in hidden places…'" Dan murmured absently. "Something I read in Isaiah 45:3."

They stood quietly for a moment, then galvanized into action by the lateness of the hour, ten men were assigned the monumental task of carrying out the treasure.

"I don't need to caution you, gentlemen: some of those paintings and tapestries are extremely old and fragile."

Dan and Jack pitched in to help wherever they could, until the Israeli foreman, Shimon, called them up and pointed to the lightening sky in the east. "We're nearly through," he said. "We've brought in trucks to take out the rest. The boat is leaving before dawn, running along the coast without lights, a risky business indeed. I will take you both back to your hotel now, just in case anyone gets suspicious when you don't show up for breakfast."

Twenty minutes later, overcome with great weariness, the exhausted men fell into their beds for a few hours' sleep.

Just about the time that the first pale pink streaks of dawn appeared over the eastern horizon Rudy Weiss was carefully scrutinizing the downloaded images taken the day before, trying to find a computer match with any in his file of known Mossad agents. Having attempted to assuage his anger the previous night by downing a full bottle of vodka, he had awakened with a searing headache and found it hard to concentrate. Even computer enlargements and enhancing failed to turn up anything positive.

He was almost ready to give up, when his eye caught something vaguely familiar. "Henri! Enlarge and enhance this," he said, pointing to a photo of the honeymooning couple. In a few moments, he found himself staring at the face of a tall young man in khaki shorts and shirt. Well tanned and wearing sunglasses, he was laughing down at the pretty redhead looking up at him.

"Blow up all the other photos you can find of him. Make it snappy!" His computer technician soon had the images ready, and Rudy, his heart hammering like a hound on the scent of his prey, bent over them carefully.

A few tense moments passed, then the frown relaxed into a satisfied smile. "Of course. Now I remember. The American hydroelectric engineer who disappeared with his friend. But, wait—their bodies were found in the helicopter wreckage."

His eyes narrowed, and he continued slowly, speculatively. "Their bodies were identified by a…sister? Now, isn't that convenient."

He stood to his feet, his face distorted with rage as he gripped the edge of the table. "Of course—the Mossad. And we wondered why our plans for Israel's extermination were foiled. The leak came right from our headquarters!"

He whirled and raced up the companionway, shouting orders to his men. Soon they were underway, cruising toward shore. The sun was just rising over the eastern hills, and its rays temporarily blinded those on deck.

As they drew closer, Rudy was confused. Nothing was as it had been the night before. "Pietro, did we drift from our position last night?"

"No, sir. We only pulled anchor a few minutes ago."

"Well, then, where is the old German installation? Send out the launch immediately with a shore party. I want to know where we are."

The crew obeyed, returning in about thirty minutes with their report. "Sir, there has been a major earthquake. There is only a large hole where the building used to be."

Rudy stared at the young seaman, uncomprehending. "A hole, you say. And where are the bricks…the bricks…oh…the bricks!"

Gradually, as the truth dawned on him, Rudy actually found the knowledge overwhelming. Dizzy, he sat down heavily. *All this time,* he thought despairingly, *all these years, it has been right out in the open for every schoolboy, every tourist, every fisherman to see. The gold was actually encased in the bricks used for the building. Now I remember reading that he brought all the building materials with him on a barge and hired local builders…and there's no telling what else they found in that hole that was a basement.*

As Rudy sat, lost in despair, he remembered that his contacts had received intelligence reports that the Israelis were hot on the trail of the treasure and had been moving fast the last several days. *Now,* he thought bitterly, *they jumped the gun, and I've been rooked.*

After a few moments, his hard, disciplined mind took control. He jumped to his feet, ordering a course set for the south coast of Turkey. They proceeded at full speed, giving chase to a ponderous steamer loaded with heavy cargo.

It's got to be some old, innocuous tramp steamer that would never attract any attention, he thought, and Rudy's eyes gleamed with the anticipation of triumph as he made his calculations, plotting his possible point of interception.

His plan, of course, was to take everything for himself and share it with no one. Every megalomaniac always considers himself an undefeatable superhero, and Rudy was no exception. After using the crew of the *Italia* to board and defeat the Mossad guarding the gold, he planned to keep only a skeleton crew, scuttle the *Italia*, dispose of the remainder of the crew, and divert the Israeli ship to his own destination. It all seemed so simple now, reduced to a few nautical coordinates on a chart.

In point of fact, he might certainly have succeeded. It was actually only three and one-half hours until they spotted the steamer ahead.

"Sir, are you sure this is the one we're looking for?" asked the captain, as Rudy restlessly paced the deck, chain-smoking nervously.

Tossing his cigarette over the rail, Rudy smiled confidently. "Have all the deck guns manned and a boarding crew ready. If it is, they'll not give up without a fight."

He made his way to the stern and, well hidden behind a large tarp, studied the approaching vessel through his binoculars. Written on the side near the bow in faded red lettering, he could barely make out the name *Odyssey*. So far there was no sign of resistance. The crew appeared to be the usual scruffy lot and apparently unarmed.

As the *Italia* pulled alongside, the captain shouted through his bullhorn, "This is International Shore Patrol…captain of the *Odyssey*—you must shut down your engines and prepare for boarding!"

Crouched in his position, Rudy watched while the boarding was accomplished without much fanfare. His men stationed themselves with automatic weapons ready, while the captain made what appeared to be his routine inspection. Only when he approached the cargo hold did the gunfight break out. Powerful deck guns appeared from under camouflaged tarps, booming away at the *Italia*, whose deck guns responded in kind.

Determined to put a quick end to the Israelis without sending the gold to the bottom of the Mediterranean, Rudy inserted the can of deadly nerve gas into the launcher. Signaling his crew, they all pulled out and donned gas masks.

For one long, sanguine moment, Rudy Weiss allowed himself the luxury of savoring his victory. "They have no way out of this…" he muttered triumphantly as he aligned the target in his sights. "All that Adolph Hitler ever wanted is now mine! Let them pray their stupid prayers—Nobody's listening…"

As the sound of gunfire broke out again, his finger tightened on the trigger, but the smile faded quickly as he realized the bullets were coming from above and behind him. He whirled around, but it was already too late.

The Israeli gunship overhead was firing down on his men, and he found himself staring into a face he knew only too well. "Kreisler!" His lips formed the snarl of protest even as he pulled a long, gleaming dirk from his boot, crouching to meet his assailant.

With deadly precision, the two opponents warily circled each other, seeking for the advantageous position. Lothar's intense gaze never wavered from the eyes of his enemy as he deftly evaded each lightning quick knife thrust. Rudy grew more and more infuriated, slashing so recklessly that he lost his balance and fell.

Springing up, he tried to dive behind a barrel lashed to the deck, but it came loose. He gave it a vicious kick toward his opponent, hoping to pin him against the cabin wall, then grabbed a crowbar.

Turning slowly, he glimpsed him moving out of the cabin's shadow and, like an enraged bull, rushed headlong for the kill. "You're a dead man, Kreisler," he shrieked hoarsely.

But Lothar was younger and faster. Dispatching his opponent with a single thrust that Rudy never saw, he stood impassively over the body, coldly detached as he watched the life ebbing from his mortal enemy. "This is for Telvi Reinhardt, you murdering swine, and a thousand other women you have widowed."

With only a sigh of protest, the immortal soul of the man lying on the deck was claimed by the dark tormentors awaiting him. To his utter surprise, he, like so many millions of others, made the belated discovery that, alas, life does not end. Not ever. Rudy Weiss had tragically consigned himself to an eternity of the most exquisite, wretched torment, forever separated from the God who had always loved him.

CHAPTER 18

THE DEPARTURE

T HE ENTIRE KINGDOM of Persia was in mourning. King Darius' body lay in state at the royal palace, having been brought back from the battlefield five days before. He had been mortally wounded during his campaign against the Scythians, and his grieving men had brought their sovereign home to die at Susa.

Esther had remained by her husband until long after he had breathed his last breath, then her son had gently led her away. "He's gone, Mother. He was a wonderful father and a great king…"

His voice had broken, and they had clung to each other, weeping silently. "I will take you to the household of Daniel, Mother—he'll be a great comfort to you now. I must make arrangements for the funeral."

Thousands of people filed by the casket to say their final farewell to a king who had ruled his kingdom so wisely. The large Jewish community at Susa paid him great homage for his part in rescuing their nation from Haman's evil conspiracy many years ago.

Even Queen Amytis, King Nebuchadnezzar's widow, made the journey from Babylon to pay tribute to the man who had sent his son to rescue her husband's kingdom from the foolish, destructive Bel-Shazzar. Although she was frail and thin from a long illness, Amytis arranged to meet with Cyrus at the house of Daniel.

"I wanted to thank you again, young man, for all you have done." She spoke softly and still moved with queenly grace as she rose to take his hand. He bowed respectfully to her, and the three sat together, talking for several hours.

Many days later, after the funeral, Cyrus approached his mother as she walked in the palace gardens, again needing her wise counsel. "Amytis has offered me the palace at Babylon for me to use as my headquarters."

His mother looked at him quizzically, and Cyrus grinned, running his hand through his hair as she had seen him do so many times when, as a child, he was embarrassed.

"Of course, I know that as the conqueror I have the right to use any place or title I want in Babylon. But out of respect to the queen—and gratitude for her help to us—I have chosen to keep a low profile, staying with my men at the fortification across the river.

"Amytis now suggests—wisely, I think—that my presence at the palace during various times of the year would stifle any undercurrents of rebellion. Babylon is still a very rich prize, and there are those who might, given the opportunity, attempt to pluck it as a ripe plum. You, as the queen mother, and Daniel as the prime minister, wield considerable power here at Susa; Persia is safe in your hands. When I am not here to rule, Daniel will carry my full authority. What do you think?"

Esther sat quietly. Her abundant mane of silver hair was pulled back and caught with an elaborate jeweled comb that sparkled in the morning sun. Dressed regally in deep blue and scarlet, she looked every inch a queen. *No wonder*, thought Cyrus as he dropped to one knee beside her, *no wonder my father loved her so.*

Her hand reached out to touch his dark, unruly curls. "Having lost my husband, will I also lose you, my son? At least, you'll be here with me for part of the year."

She sighed, the dark, puffy shadows beneath her eyes betraying her grief. "Yes, it is a good plan, Cyrus. Do it."

THE CHRONICLES OF EZRA

Now in the first year of Cyrus, king of Persia—seventy years after the first Jewish captives were taken to Babylon—that the word of the Lord by the mouth of Jeremiah the prophet might begin to be accomplished, the Lord stirred up the spirit of Cyrus, king of Persia, so that he made a proclamation throughout all of his kingdom and put it also in writing:

"Thus says Cyrus, king of Persia: The Lord God of Heaven has given me all the kingdoms of the earth, and He has charged me to build Him a house at Jerusalem, in Judah. Whoever is among you of all His people, his God be with him, and let him go up to Jerusalem in Judah and rebuild the house of the Lord, the God of Israel, in Jerusalem. He is God.

"And in any place where a survivor of the Babylonian captivity sojourns, let the men of that place assist him with silver and gold, with goods and beasts, besides freewill offerings for the house of God in Jerusalem."

Then rose up the heads of the father's houses of Judah and Benjamin, and the priests and the Levites, with all those whose spirit God had stirred up, to go up to rebuild the house of the Lord in Jerusalem.

And all those who were around them aided them with vessels of silver, with gold, goods, beasts, and precious things, besides all that was willingly and freely offered.

Also, Cyrus the king brought out the vessels of the house of the Lord, which Nebuchadnezzar had brought from Jerusalem and had put them in the temple of his gods. These Cyrus king of Persia directed Mithredath the royal treasurer to bring forth and count out to Zerubbabel, the prince of Judah who is the legitimate heir to the throne of David.

All the vessels of gold and silver were five thousand, four hundred. All of these Zerubbabel brought with the people of the captivity back to Jerusalem.

Nearly fifty thousand men, women, and children followed Zerubbabel out of Babylon, returning to their homeland with great rejoicing. Many Jewish families, such as Daniel's, elected to stay with their elderly parents, fearing that they would not survive the arduous journey.

During all the excitement, word reached Daniel that Mishael was very ill and had asked to see his old friend one more time. Of Daniel's three friends, only Mishael was yet alive. Azariah had never recovered from the shock of his wife's death and had died at the age of sixty-two. Just last year, a greatly aged Hananiah had journeyed to Susa to visit Daniel one last time. They both knew they would not meet on earth again. Soon after his return to Babylon, Hananiah simply died in his sleep, a great man, old and full of years.

When Esther heard of Mishael's request, she insisted that the king's own royal carriage be used for Daniel to travel in comfort to Babylon. And so he found himself on a road crowded with Jewish families who were traveling from Persia to Babylon, where they would join the second caravan to Jerusalem.

An atmosphere of festive merry-making pervaded the entire journey. Daniel's grandson Joshua especially enjoyed the games, music, dancing, and storytelling around the campfires at night. After the camp was set up and the animals fed and tethered, the boys stripped to the waist and had wrestling matches, ran races, and competed in the rope pull and various games involving a small leather ball. All this activity, of course, was intended to impress the pretty young girls who watched from a discreet distance in the shadows.

Following the evening meal, the instruments were brought out, and they sang the lively folk songs of their homeland. Then someone said, "Where's Rachel? I want to hear her sing."

Presently, a young girl stepped out of the shadows, carrying a small harp. She moved carefully through the crowd and, seated near the fire, picked up her harp and began to sing a plaintive ballad of the captivity.

Joshua was mesmerized; never in all his young life had he ever seen or heard anything quite so exquisite. Her soft red curls beneath the veil shadowed her face as she bent forward to skillfully strum her instrument. From her lips poured forth the rich, haunting strains of a psalm.

> By the rivers of Babylon…
> We wept bitter tears…
> Torn from our homeland…
> The beautiful city of Zion, our homeland…
> Our hearts too heavy to sing the Lord's song…
> By the rivers of Babylon…
> We hang our harps on the willow trees…
> Until our return…

The night was utterly still as the music died away. For a few moments, no one moved or made a sound; then Rachel looked up, and Joshua saw that her wide-set green eyes were swimming with tears. He felt a lump rise up in his throat, and his heart beat a little faster as she arose and left the way she had come. He glanced sideways at his grandfather, who was staring into the distance, his large brown eyes also filled with tears.

Then, to his utter surprise, Daniel began to speak. "I am remembering a night long ago—the last night I spent with my family as we tried to escape Nebuchadnezzar's advancing armies. Would you like to hear it?"

There was a unanimous chorus of assent, mostly from the younger ones who never tired of hearing tales of adventure, so Daniel launched into his story of the wild ride on Regina, his father's prize mare.

Joshua was amazed, for he had never heard this account before. Now, as he listened, he could finally understand his grandfather's great affection for Mishael, for they had gone through so much together. *No wonder*, he thought, *he is willing to make this trip to Babylon.*

Later, in the tent, Joshua plied his grandfather with questions. "What happened to the captain of the cavalry unit who took you and Mishael captive? Did you ever see him again in Babylon?"

"No, son, I never saw him again. General Nabuzaradan told me that he did return to Babylon, but his wife and son had fallen ill with a fever and died just a month before his return. I heard that he was later killed during the siege of Tyre."

"Oh," Joshua's face fell. "Well, what happened to you four boys when you got to Babylon? Were you separated?"

"No," Daniel's face creased in a smile. "We were put immediately under the care of the king's chief eunuch; we lived and were educated at the great palace library. We were taught the Chaldean language and customs and had to wear Chaldean clothes.

"They even changed our names, but we were determined to never forget our Hebrew heritage, and so we always called each other by our Hebrew names. You see, Joshua, my name—Daniel—means 'God is my Judge' in Hebrew. I abhorred the Chaldean name they gave to me—'Belteshazzar'—for it contained the name of their vile false god Bel.

"Every night for many years, Joshua, we would climb the steps to the western parapet of the castle and look out over the far horizon to the setting sun. We liked to pretend that we could actually see the city of Jerusalem in the far distance. As the years passed, though, it became harder and harder to remember."

Joshua was silent for a long time. "Grandfather," he ventured, "how is it that you have never spoken about going back to your home?"

"My home and my destiny are here, Joshua. Jehovah God has made it very clear to me that He had a purpose for my being here during this time in our history."

He sighed heavily. "It was here I met the great love of my life—your grandmother, Hannah. It was here that I served under three great kings, helping to bring forth the will of our Sovereign God in their kingdoms. Most importantly, it was here that revelation concerning the future of our people was brought to me by heavenly messengers.

"No, young Joshua. My life is nearly over, and I feel no need to return to Jerusalem. However, young man, yours is just beginning, and that is another matter entirely. We will speak of this later; now, it is late and we must sleep."

As Joshua drifted off to sleep, his dreams were punctuated by insistent, fleeting visions of red curls and wide green eyes.

Mishael was truly glad to see his old friend, and the visitor from Susa seemed to rally his spirits somewhat. But Daniel was quite alarmed at his friend's deathly pallor. Indeed, Mishael was dying; Daniel resolved to spend their last days together, so he settled into the household for an indefinite stay.

Joshua was glad to have the free time to explore the city and lost no time in locating the caravan for Jerusalem. He was unsuccessful, however, in finding the mysterious young Rachel of his dreams.

On the very last day, just as the caravan was about to depart, he heard the unmistakable sound of someone singing, and his heart nearly stopped. Following the lilting strains of the music, he found her under the pavilion of a gaily colored wagon.

He waited until the singing ceased, then stepped up and into the tent. "Hello, Rachel," he ventured tentatively. "I'm Joshua, the grandson of Daniel from Susa. Do you remember me?"

She looked up and regarded him gravely, her green eyes quietly assessing the tall, gangly youth whose head touched the top of the tent. Joshua bit his lip nervously, awaiting her reply.

Then she smiled, offering him her hand. "Yes, of course I remember you, Joshua. You do, by the way, bear a marked resemblance to your famous grandfather. I watched you run the foot races and play in the tug-of-war many times during our trip here to Babylon. Are you going with your family to Jerusalem?"

He looked at his feet and grimaced, "No, Rachel, my family is here for another reason; we will not be traveling to Jerusalem in your caravan."

Just then, the shofar—the ram's horn—sounded for the travelers to move. Joshua talked fast as he backed out toward the tent opening. "Where will you be going, and what is your father's name, Rachel?"

"We are of the tribe of Benjamin. My father's name is Eliezar, and our home is in a little village called Anathoth, near Bethel."

As Joshua jumped from the moving cart, he shouted back, "I'll see you again, Rachel. Someday soon, I hope. God keep you!"

"And you, Joshua."

He watched her face disappear in the swirl of dust surrounding the caravan, then he turned to go. He mounted his horse, vaulting into the saddle in the hope she was still watching, and rode away, whistling a little tune. *I'll find you someday*, he vowed silently. *I am quite sure of that.*

The end came quickly for Mishael, who died quietly in his sleep. A part of Daniel died with him, for now all his friends had departed this life for a far greater adventure. Suddenly he felt so very alone. After Mishael's funeral, upon returning home to Susa, he felt his ties to this earth less and less with each passing day.

CHAPTER 19

THE RESCUE

THE ODYSSEY STEAMED into the harbor at Haifa, the cargo quickly and efficiently off-loaded onto a fleet of trucks. The gold bullion was whisked away to a super-secret underground vault, the site of which was known only to the highest echelons of government. The antiquities were transported to the National Museum, where they were painstakingly examined and cataloged by a large team of very excited experts. Dr. Herschel Levinson, the museum director, was quite concerned that as much as possible be identified and returned to the heirs of its legal owners.

"We must face the fact, ladies and gentlemen," he addressed his crew soberly, "that many of the owners have simply disappeared in the Holocaust. Finding their descendants will certainly require some very clever detective work on our part. The Wiesenthal Foundation has offered us unlimited access to their quite considerable computerized archives. So...let's roll up our sleeves and get to work!"

Seemingly undaunted by the monumental task ahead, the crew began the long, arduous process of patiently examining each object. Eventually, as an owner was located, the entire crew would celebrate.

In Jerusalem, Jack and Ruth rested from their ordeal. Occasionally they stopped by the museum to admire the vast storehouse of priceless treasure and chat with the director, who introduced them to his crew.

"Ladies—gentlemen—I have the immense pleasure and privilege of introducing to you the man primarily responsible for all of this: our newest national hero, Jack Mannheim and his lovely wife, Ruth."

Applause broke out as everyone crowded around, wanting to shake Jack's hand. Ruth beamed, but Jack ducked out at the first opportunity.

"Low key, Ruth. You know I like to keep it low key. We spies have to stay out of the limelight, you know."

"But of course, Jack. I'll keep that in mind," she answered demurely.

He steered her through the crowd to a little outdoor restaurant where they had a leisurely lunch. Ruth wanted to see the new temple, so Jack took her on a tour.

"Come on in, Ruth—look around, and tell me what you think." Jack proudly showed her the magnificent structure as they walked from one end to the other, sometimes stopping to chat with the workers.

"You've made some wonderful progress, Jack, since the last time I saw it!" Her eyes were wide with amazement.

"Well, you know I've been telling you I have a great crew, and they have really been working hard the whole time we were gone."

They lingered for a while, then reluctantly left and drove home.

"Jack, do you ever…do you ever—in spite of the modern architecture— ever feel the…the ancientness of the place?"

He was quiet for a long time.

"Ruth, I have—many times—felt that I was intruding into a centuries-old holy place. This was the ancient place of Abraham, Isaac, Jacob, David, Solomon, and then later Zerubbabel, who rebuilt the second temple. This is the third Jewish temple to be built in this holy place. Yes, I feel it—my workers feel it, too. Sometimes it is overwhelming."

After the long, hard Montana winter, then a short, hot summer, September's cool autumn breeze was a welcome relief. The aspens, sumac, and birches, already kissed by an early frost, were blushing coral, crimson, and golden all up the valley. In the little compound hidden away in the Cabinet Mountains wilderness, sounds of merriment issued from the central lodge.

"Sing 'Rocky Mountain High' one more time!" begged the children as they crowded around Jim Greywolf.

He strummed his guitar, laughing. "Oh, that's an old John Denver song. He was into all that New Age stuff, you know."

"I know," chimed in Kevin, "but God gave him the gift of music, and I love his songs. Play 'Grandma's Feather Bed.'"

Jim launched into the song, tapping his toe to the lively rhythm as the children danced and sang.

Paula leaned her head on Randy's shoulder. "Just look at them, Randy. We're going to miss him so dreadfully when he goes back again to the reservation. I really look forward to his visits."

"I know. This is important to him, though, to come back here for teaching and fellowship. This man, Paula, has already led nearly his entire tribe into the kingdom of God. When he left here last year, he could hardly walk because of the severity of his injuries from the beating he took in that river, but he was truly a 'new man' on the inside. Since then, the Lord has healed his physical body as well as his soul."

By then, several other instruments had joined in, and they were playing and singing, "We will dance on the streets that are golden," an old Vineyard tune from the 1990s.

"Come, dance with me, my love," Randy whispered romantically into his wife's ear as he drew her out onto the wooden floor. "When the Lord returns, I want Him to find me dancing with my wife."

Wish granted, son.

A long contrail of dust marked the passage of the Land Rover as it careened along the embankment of the Blue Nile River in central Sudan. The 130-mile trip from Khartoum took Alex and Dan south along the steppe region, the high plateau marked by miles of coarse grass and scrub that extended to the El Obeid in the south. The vehicle slowed and came to a stop, and the two men climbed out to stretch their legs. The driver waited at the wheel, glancing uneasily at his passengers.

"Didn't Mr. Khalil say he would meet us at the dam site, Dan? It looks like we're the only humans for miles around." Alex glanced anxiously at the crumbled remains of the Sennar Dam ahead. "Wow—would you look at that. What a disaster!"

Dan shook his head sadly. "This one was built to replace the old Sennar Dam of 1925, but it sure didn't withstand the latest earthquake. What a mess!"

"You know," Alex scratched his head quizzically, "I could have sworn from all the geological surveys of this area that there are no known fault lines in the underlying strata here in Sudan."

"I noticed that, too," replied Dan quietly, "but in the last few years earthquakes have been occurring in unexpected places with increasing frequency and intensity. Ever since we completed our work in Japan, I've worried about the twenty-seven million people in Tokyo. An earthquake higher than 8.0 on the Richter scale, or a major tsunami, could wipe out almost that entire nation."

"Perhaps all these earthquakes are just an evolutional cycle in the earth's development," remarked Alex smugly, glancing at his partner.

Alex loved to bait Dan into a theological argument, and the two often engaged in good-natured banter. However, now Dan's face was grim as he gazed up at the remains of the once massive concrete structure.

"I don't think you could possibly understand the significance of these disasters, Alex, outside of understanding the clear warning of Jesus: one of the major events He predicted as a sure sign of His return was a marked increase in the number and intensity of earthquakes around the world. He said it would be like labor pains, increasing in number and intensity until the time of birth."

"Aw, c'mon—lighten up, Dan," Alex retorted sharply.

"It's true. 'Matthew 24 is Knockin' at the Door'—an old Johnny Cash song, Alex—look it up sometime!"

The two men spent the better part of the next hour inspecting the damage and making their assessments. Finally they were interrupted by the arrival of the Inspector General, Colonel Azir Khalil, and his retinue. They spent the rest of the afternoon walking the site, avoiding the more dangerous areas, and dictating copious notes into their recorder as they went.

Later that evening, back in the hotel dining room, the two partners ate a long, leisurely dinner as they discussed the pros and cons of the daunting task ahead of them. Wearied from the long day's travel, they retired to their rooms early.

Dan had just fallen into an exhausted sleep when something startled him back into consciousness. He sat bolt upright, but the room was dark and silent. Then, there it was again—a tentative knock at his door. Dan wearily pulled himself out of bed and padded across the floor.

Opening the door, he saw a small figure in the shadows; all he could make out in the semi-darkness were two terrified eyes gazing up at him.

"Please, sir, may I come in?"

Dan stepped aside, and the boy darted inside, looking behind him as if all the demons in hell were pursuing. "Well, young man—I see you speak

English. That's good. Would you like to have a seat and tell me what is so important it can't wait until morning?"

Dan collapsed into a chair and surveyed his small, obviously nervous visitor. He was a young black Sudanese, about twelve or thirteen, Dan guessed, and dressed from head to toe in a black cotton garment. He was slowly looking about the elegant hotel room, wide-eyed with wonder. *Probably never been anywhere but mud huts*, mused Dan.

Again he inquired, more gently this time, "Son, if you could just tell me what it is you want, I'll see what I can do to help you."

The head swiveled suddenly, the large eyes fixed on him. "You…you will help us, sir?" The words tumbled out as the astonished Dan watched the boy fall to his knees, clasping his hands in supplication.

"Oh, sir, we are Christians. It is now illegal to be a Christian in the Sudan since the fundamental Islamic government took over. Just in this last year alone, hundreds, thousands of us have been tortured and killed, thrown into prisons, our homes and possessions taken from us.

"My own parents were dragged from our home in Berber and beaten to death by the government police, and my little sisters were taken away. I escaped to my uncle's home in this city, and he said…he said…" He bowed his head, squeezing shut his eyes in pain as the tears began to flow. "He said that my little sisters were taken to a slave compound where they will be sold! Oh, sir, please help us!"

The poor boy was now prostrate on the floor, his shoulders shaking uncontrollably. Dan leaned forward, elbows on his knees, head in his hands. *O God*, he thought despairingly, *how could I ever help these people?*

He was acutely aware of the boy's sobbing as all the possibilities raced through his head. *Money? The Bank of England hasn't enough money to buy back thousands of slaves. Terror and intimidation? Me? Don't think so. Influence? I have no influence on their corrupt government.*

Suddenly a thought exploded, clear as crystal. *Then why are you dealing with a corrupt government?*

Dan's eyes widened in surprise at the insistent thought. *Is that You, Lord?* he breathed.

I will make a way; it is time. Read Isaiah 61.

By now the tears had ceased, and the boy was sitting cross-legged on the carpet, looking abjectly downhearted. Dan crossed the room, offered him a tissue, and patted him somewhat awkwardly on the shoulder.

"I have some cold Cokes in the ice bucket. Would you like one?"

A few minutes later the boy was seated at the table, devouring a bag of chips and sipping his Coke carefully. His name was Amahl, and he came from the little village of Berber, near the fifth cataract of the Nile.

After consulting a map, Dan was astounded. "How did you manage to come so far? It's a long way from Khartoum!"

"We hitched a ride on a truck carrying wheat and rice from Egypt, sir."

"We?"

"My cousin and I came to Khartoum to look for my uncle. We have been living with him for almost a month."

I wonder if he ever gets a decent meal? Dan thought compassionately, as he watched the boy wolf down two oranges, a banana. and another bag of chips.

"Is…is your uncle in Khartoum a Christian, Amahl?"

The boy froze, his eyes wide with fear, and nodded his head slowly. "Please, sir—you won't turn him in, will you? He will lose his job at the government office if it is known to the authorities, and he has six children plus the two of us to feed and care for."

Dan stared at his young visitor thoughtfully. "No, I would never betray another Christian. But tell me, Amahl—they sent you to me because you were the only one who speaks English: isn't that right? How did you find me?"

The boy stopped eating and wiped his mouth with a napkin. After a short pause, he spoke.

"Sir, my uncle drove you to the Sennar dam today. He speaks a little English, and he overheard you speaking of our Jesus coming back to earth. You are the first white Christian he has ever seen. Many others have come to help our people, bringing us Bibles and helping to rebuild our burnt-out churches, but in our little village no one has ever come. I learned English from my father, who wanted me to attend university some day."

At the mention of his dead father, Amahl's eyes again filled with tears. "It would be too dangerous if my uncle, an employee of the Inspector General's office, were seen coming to your room."

Dan felt a wave of weariness, mixed with pity, sweep over him as he regarded the boy who watched him so eagerly. *He's only a child,* Dan thought, *who has seen too much tragedy for one little broken heart to cope with. How can I turn him down? God help me, I can't.*

With a sigh, Dan reached for a pen and wrote a long note. Sealing it in an envelope, he leaned over, handed it to his young visitor, and warned him soberly, "Amahl, you must see that this gets to your uncle immediately. Do not allow anyone else to see it. OK?"

"OK! Thank you, sir!" And with a wide grin the boy started out the door.

Suddenly he turned, ran back in the room, and impulsively threw his skinny little arms around Dan; then he disappeared into the darkness.

Later, as Dan was again drifting off to sleep, something kept nagging elusively at his consciousness. He switched on the light one more time.

I almost forgot; Isaiah 61—let's see, it says in verse 1...

> The Spirit of the Sovereign Lord is upon me
> For He has anointed me to preach good news to the poor
> Bind up the brokenhearted, proclaim liberty to the captives
> And the opening of the prison to those who are bound...

Dear Sarah,

It's been over a week since we talked on the phone, and so much has happened during that week. Remember Amahl, the boy I told you about? He arranged for me to meet with his uncle and some Christian leaders from the area surrounding Khartoum. The meeting was carried on in the utmost secrecy; we met in an old abandoned warehouse near the railroad yards.

Oh, Sarah, darling, how could I ever convey to you the incredible load of pain and suffering these people have had to endure the last thirty years? The fiery persecution launched against Sudanese Christians has once again erupted in genocidal fury.

You have no idea how many thousands of young children have been torn from their families, sent to "re-education camps" where they are tortured into submission to Islam, and then sold as slaves. They are forced to recant their Christian beliefs and convert to Islam.

The adults who survive the persecution—beatings, floggings, imprisonments—emerge to find they have no jobs, no homes, no possessions, and, too often, no children. They feel betrayed, isolated, all but forgotten by the rest of the world.

We talked far into the night; I shared with them my impression from the Chief that it was time to take action, but first we must pray for guidance.

Two days later we met again, and, Sarah, I learned to my astonishment that it was Khalil himself—the Inspector General who contracted with us for the rebuilding of the Sennar Dam—who has benefited the most from the very lucrative slave trade. I had seen his home and knew that he lived in unusual luxury for a government official, but when I realized that he had achieved all this at the expense of thousands, perhaps millions, of broken lives—my blood began to boil.

We made our plans: the leaders had located five slave compounds in various areas of Sudan. Our part was easy—just organize five groups of armed men to raid the compounds, immobilize the guards, evacuate the children into ten waiting trucks, and get them out of the country. We figured that the most logical way would be to head for the Ethiopian and Egyptian borders.

But the Lord had another plan. All ten trucks were to converge on Khartoum—the last place the authorities would look—and keep the children (nearly a thousand of them) hidden right there in the empty warehouse where we were meeting. Then their parents or relatives would be located and the children returned.

Can you imagine, Sarah, the logistics of just food, water, and bedding for nearly one thousand children? It was overwhelming, but we spent some more time in prayer, felt greatly strengthened, and went ahead with the plan.

I contacted Lothar Kreisler—remember the former Mossad agent we met at your dad's home not long after the "Nazi treasure" episode? He was the one man Rudy Weiss could never get by—actually, he should be a national hero right along with your dad, but he never wanted his part in it to become public knowledge. I don't really know him too well and didn't know what to expect.

But when I told him the whole story of the children in the slave compounds, he got real quiet; then he said something I'll never forget: "While there's breath in my body, no child will be tortured and enslaved if I can do anything about it! Yes, Dan, I'll use every ounce of influence I have; the men, the body armor, the ammunition, and the trucks will be there in one week. I give you my word."

Well, Sarah, to make a long story short, everything went like clockwork right up until the time for the raids. We had coordinated our efforts by staying in radio contact so they would take place simultaneously.

Oh, yes—I almost forgot the most important part. I had contacted a friend at CNN News headquarters and located their Middle East correspondent, who just happened to be in Addis Ababa, Ethiopia on a news assignment. He flew up with his camera crew and, intrigued with the possibilities of a major expose of human rights violations, agreed to come along on the raid.

Now don't get the idea, sweetheart, that your Texas-sized hero of a husband just barged right through this operation totally fearless and self-confident. Not on your life! By the time we got within ten miles of our target, believe me, I was plenty scared.

By the way, I forgot to mention that in the very beginning, when I talked this over with Alex, he was dead set against it. Said I was a crazy fool for jeopardizing our contract for the dam. I agreed, and we didn't speak of it for several days, but then one night at dinner he said his conscience had been keeping him up nights, and he wanted to help. Said we'd already been through other escapades together, and if we died in this one, at least we'd be together. I told him he couldn't die, he wasn't saved yet.

Like I said, I was really scared, and the closer we got, the worse I felt. We were a pretty quiet bunch in the back of that truck, all dressed out in body armor, carrying our semi-automatic weapons and faces blackened with shoe polish—all you could see were the whites of our eyes. All of a sudden it struck me funny; I tried to stifle the laughter, but I just couldn't, and pretty soon everyone was laughing and pretty much relaxed.

The trucks stopped in a clearing not far from the compound, and we walked, then crawled to the edge of a large clearing. In the middle was a low, long, rambling mud building; there were two boarded up windows at each end and the door was slightly ajar, spilling light onto the ground outside. Our sources informed me that there were usually two, never more than three guards on duty during the night. One of them was leaning against the doorframe and smoking a cigarette.

"Piece of cake," whispered our leader, as he motioned his men forward. I could hear the click as the news camera behind me started whirring. Just at that very moment—I can't explain it, Sarah, but—my senses were extremely alerted. Something was wrong; I knew it, and so did the company commander. He motioned his men down, and as he did, the clouds parted.

In the moonlight we saw the ground sixty or seventy yards in front of us literally come alive with moving shadows. Too many to count, the shadows began to fire ceaseless rounds of ammunition in our direction. We hugged the ground and prayed. There were only seven of us, including the CNN guy and his cameraman; there must have been twenty or thirty of them! It was obvious that we had been betrayed.

We waited for what seemed like an eternity; I listened carefully between rounds of gunfire for any groans that would indicate that one of our men had been hit; I heard nothing. One of the things I had prayed for was that there would be no loss of life on either side.

Then, right in front of our eyes, we saw it happen: the entire compound was lit up by the strangest light—it seemed to come from the trees just ahead of us. We watched the whole scene with astonishing, unforgettable clarity. The entire group of Islamic extremist terrorists threw their weapons down, their faces contorted with terror. Most fainted dead away. The light continued to glow steadily as we finally stood up and tentatively moved forward.

We moved slowly, as if in a dream, until we reached the door and looked inside. Nearly two hundred terrified children were crammed into one end of the filthy barracks; the stench was intolerable. Their pitiful faces galvanized us into action; the interpreter we had brought with us explained everything carefully to them. We inspected their living quarters, the CNN news camera whirring away, and the CNN correspondent dictating rapid-fire notes, mixed liberally with expletives, into his handheld recorder.

"This ought to silence those supercilious braggarts," he muttered in his clipped accent, "who keep insisting that there is no such thing as slavery in the twenty-first century. Lord God Almighty—how could such a thing be countenanced by the authorities, even in a third world country such as this?"

I replied matter-of-factly, "The Lord God Almighty, as you say, is the very One into whose nostrils this stench has arisen. Enough is enough, and He's the One who has arranged for it to stop."

The man glanced out the door uneasily; the unearthly light had not diminished. "Quite frankly, I don't know how I'm going to find an acceptable explanation for what happened here tonight," he admitted with unusual candor. "Do you have any ideas, Dan?"

"Not one that's 'politically correct,'" I smiled. "We'll talk of this later. Right now we need to get these kids out of here and into the trucks."

As we left, I noticed that the four terrorists who were still conscious had been handcuffed to a tree, and the interpreter was leaning over to speak with one. When the last of the children had disappeared into the dark woods, we looked back. The strange glowing light was fading away as we were leaving.

Later, as we were passing out granola bars and oranges to the children in the truck, I asked the interpreter what the terrorist had told him.

He replied, "I asked the man why they were so afraid, since there were only seven of us. He said to me, 'Didn't you see them?'

"I answered, 'Who? What did you see?'

"He shuddered and replied, 'Those giant men standing all around you—they were just standing there with those huge, fiery swords drawn…I think—I think, sir, that we have been serving the wrong god!'"

Six months later, four young couples arranged to meet in Tel Aviv at a pizza parlor not far from the university. Dan and Sarah drove in from Lebanon, where they had been visiting some Christian Palestinian friends. Alex brought his current girlfriend, a nurse he had met while he was recuperating from his gunshot wounds at a hospital in Jerusalem. Matt was on weekend leave from the Air Force base, so Lothar picked up Heidi and Heather to meet him. Still driving his battered old Audi, he parked across the street, and they walked into the restaurant, to find Dan and Sarah already there.

"Sarah! You look wonderful—pregnancy agrees with you; you're positively glowing!" exclaimed Heather as she embraced her friend.

"It's a girl!" beamed Sarah. "We got the sonogram last week."

Lothar introduced Heidi to Dan, and they settled in to wait for the others, munching on a platter of fried cheese and antipasto while they chatted. Alex and Mitze soon arrived. As Dan rose to shake hands, he thought, *The poor guy really looks smitten this time, and ain't it about time.*

After a good half-hour had elapsed, Matt finally drove up on his motorcycle. Heather ran out to meet him, and after a few minutes they sauntered in. Patting his sister's tummy with brotherly solicitude for her condition, he plunged into the steaming hot pizza.

"Man, I'm so hungry I could eat a horse!" he exclaimed between mouthfuls.

"The pizza here is genuine, 100 percent American style; the owner, Moishe Steuben, is from Chicago!" quipped Dan. The exuberant diners immediately launched into a chorus of "Chicago, Chicago, That Toddlin' Town," breaking up in raucous laughter. The talk soon turned to all the wonderful U.S. restaurants they remembered so fondly.

"But the last four or five years we lived there," Matt reminded them, "only the very wealthy could afford to eat out. Whoever would have dreamed that in the United States, land of overflowing abundance, there would have been such severe food rationing?"

"Let's talk about something more cheerful," Heather interposed softly. "Did you know—is it OK, Heidi? Did you know that Lothar and Heidi are getting married next week?"

There were exclamations and congratulations all around, then Lothar stood up and, beaming proudly with his shoulders erect, lifted his glass.

"A toast to my future wife. Yes we will be married right here in Tel Aviv in a little Messianic Jewish church—actually, it's just a storefront building doubling as a church and coffeehouse ministry. You're all invited."

"Yes, Matt," Heather explained a little nervously as she twisted the napkin in her lap, "we three have been going there ever since Lothar came back from the Sudan. It's so wonderful—I wish you would come with us."

"Lothar came back from the Sudan a changed man." Heidi's eyes were shining as she turned from her fiancé to Matt. "Dan and Alex can probably fill you in on the details."

Alex looked around the table and held up his hand. "Wait a minute; Lothar's not the only one who came back a changed man!"

SEAL UP THE VISION

"You can say that again!" Dan drawled, lifting one eyebrow as he leaned back in his chair. "You, Alex—you just caved right in!"

Alex leaned forward eagerly, a torrent of words spilling out from the newly filled abundance of his heart. Matt was strangely silent, toying morosely with his glass while he covertly watched Heather. Her eyes glowed as she listened once again to the story of the heavenly visitors, warriors from another sphere sent on an assignment of protection and deliverance. The unusual part of this story, Alex explained, was that although there had been many similar incidents since the beginning of time, this was the first time it had ever happened simultaneously in five different places.

"Whatever happened to Khalil?" inquired Heather.

"Oh, he was stripped of his office and property, having been the cause of a very embarrassing international investigation into Sudan's long-standing genocidal policies. Last I heard he was holed up somewhere in the Sahara Desert. A fitting end for a heartless tyrant."

"As for Amahl, the little boy who first approached me—he and many other of the orphaned children have been assimilated into the new Christian villages springing up all over the land. A few of us guys decided to keep in contact with them, and Amahl has been offered a full scholarship in a Ugandan Christian university when he is ready," said Dan.

There was a long thoughtful silence, then Matt abruptly spoke out.

"Well, Heather, maybe I should check this place out—you were telling me about a Messianic coffee house right here in Tel Aviv—right?" Then, smothered in fragrant hugs, he managed to add, "And I'd sure be honored to come to your wedding, Lothar and Heidi, if I can get leave."

"Wait a minute; I'll take a picture of us—we don't get together that often." Heather rummaged in her purse. "Oh, bother! I left the camera in Lothar's car—I'll be right back."

She was headed out the door and across the street when Lothar, staring out the window, saw the shadowy figure dart from behind his car and around the corner. Instinctively, his heart racing, he vaulted over the bench and out the door. "Heather!" He screamed as he raced toward her, "NO! NO! No, don't—" His cries were obliterated by a muffled explosion, followed by a much larger one, and a fireball filled his field of vision.

As Matt watched through the window, horrified, his last glimpse of his beloved was her surprised face as she half turned to look back, her hand already pulling the car door open. Dan and Alex had to physically restrain him from plunging into the fire, his agonized cries echoing far down the street.

Finally, hours later, he awoke in a hospital, Alex's girlfriend sitting quietly by his bed. "We had to give you a sedative, Matt," she explained gently. "Go back to sleep now. We're all here."

Matt was dimly aware of his family and friends close by; a grim Lothar, his hair and eyebrows badly singed by the blast, was sitting on the bed next to him as the nursing staff treated his burns. Sarah, Dan, his weeping parents—they all receded into nothingness, and a little seed of bitterness was dropped into the seething cauldron of his tortured soul.

Slipping into oblivion, his aching heart cried out, *O God, if there is a God—why did You let my Heather die? I swear that as long as I live, I'll never forgive You for this…I'll never forgive…*

CHAPTER 20

THE RETURN

THE WEARY LITTLE group of riders crested the hilltop, the first rays of dawn shooting out past them to illuminate the golden gates of Babylon, far to the west. They stopped for a few moments, stricken with awe as all travelers were, at the sight of the magnificent gleaming citadel in the distance. Partially shrouded in early morning fog, the city appeared to be floating in air, taking on a great glowing incandescence as the sun rose higher.

Reluctantly, they descended single file through a rocky ravine, dismounting to let the horses rest and drink from the brook.

"Joshua, when we finally reach the city, I'm going to sleep until the next sunrise!" The young man drank greedily from the clear stream, then threw himself down on the grass. "Your grandfather Daniel sent us on this mission, and you know I am honored to be a part, but you never did explain the urgency."

Joshua brushed the dust from his clothes, sat down on a boulder, and trailed his fingers absently in the water as he spoke. "Eliel, there wasn't time for an explanation, and to be perfectly truthful, I'm not sure I completely understand what happened myself. My grandfather had been reading the scrolls of Jeremiah, the prophet of God at Jerusalem. As he read these prophecies, he became aware that God had determined that the land of Israel would remain desolate—a 'Sabbath rest'—for a period of seventy years, and that our people would be in captivity during those seventy years."

He paused to drink from his water flask, glancing down at his young friend. Then he stood up, stretching to his full height, and mounted his horse.

"Come on, fellows. We're nearly there, and I don't want to lose any more time. Eliel, come ride by me, and I'll try to put this all together. My grandfather was brought from Judea with the first group of captives when he was about the same age as I am—fifteen.

"Several years ago, at the age of eighty-two, he began to realize the full impact of the terrible sin we as a nation had committed against our God: even after sixty-seven years of exile and chastening, we *still* had failed to admit our guilt. It literally sickened him. He became quite ill and set his face toward God in fasting and prayer.

"Our family was quite worried about him, a man of his advanced years going without food, but he was determined. Grandfather explained it to me this way: as the people of God, we had gradually lost our uniqueness, taking on the coloration of the prevailing culture around us just as the desert chameleon takes on the coloration of its surroundings.

"Our people had become so ensnared and seduced by compromise that they had no desire to return to their homeland! We had come right up to the crucial time of our deliverance, and our people were dangerously unaware of possibly losing their freedom forever!"

The boys rode in silence for a while, considering the full impact of this sobering information.

"But Joshua," ventured Eliel, his brows knotted in consternation, "your grandfather certainly has never compromised. Why did he have to be the one to repent in sackcloth and ashes, going without food, crying out for forgiveness—why him, of all our people?"

"Because he was willing to stand in the place of intercession. Repentance is a gift, granted by God, and he prayed for God to grant it to our nation. Grandfather believes that is one reason that God spared his life from the lions—to intercede for our nation.

"Actually," continued Joshua, "we knew that several years ago, during the first year of the reign of King Darius, my grandfather sought God in repentance and fasting, and…and…" Joshua glanced sideways at his companion, swallowed hard, and continued in a lower voice. "And, Eliel, he was visited by an angel sent from heaven to give him a revelation of the future…of the coming Messiah!"

Eliel's deep brown eyes widened in shock as he digested this information. Joshua took a deep breath and continued.

"It was then that my grandfather knew it would not be long before our time of exile would be over and our people would be free to return. He showed the prophecies to King Darius, who passed them on to his son, Cyrus. Three years later when his father died, one of the first things Cyrus accomplished as king was to free our people. As you know, Eliel, over forty-two thousand left at that time, taking all the temple treasure back with them to rebuild the temple in Jerusalem. Our parents decided to stay in Persia because our grandparents are too old to make the trip, and we cannot leave them behind."

"I'm aware of all this, Joshua, but why are we making this trip now, and why the urgency?"

"Be patient, Eliel, and I'll explain: four weeks ago, my grandfather once again undertook a fast and continued night and day in prayers of repentance. On the twenty-fourth day of the month, the third week of the fast, he was standing on the bank of the Tigris River. I was there with him, along with several cousins, uncles, and about a dozen servants. We were so worried about him, you see. We thought he might collapse and die from weakness—you'll never guess who turned out to be the 'weak' ones!"

Eliel waited expectantly. Their horses negotiated a very narrow turn through a ravine and down a steep slope before Joshua continued.

"He was looking up, and I watched his face suddenly drain of all color. He was white as a sheet, and that's all I remember, because—because all the rest of us ran away!"

"You, Joshua? Whatever could have made you run?" Eliel registered his shock, swiveling around in the saddle to stare at his friend.

"It's hard to explain, Eliel, but I'll try. You can imagine how ashamed we all felt afterward, but it truly was the most terrifying experience of my life, and I didn't even SEE the vision! I felt my body quaking like a giant hand was shaking me—all my bones turned to jelly and such a terrible dread came over me; all I could think of was to escape into a grove of trees nearby.

"Later, my grandfather told me some of what he saw. Eliel, he looked up and saw a being so immensely powerful, so magnificent, so overwhelmingly beautiful—his eyes were pure flashing fire, his body glowed like gemstones, clad in white linen with gold, and his legs were like polished brass. His voice echoed and reverberated like the thunderous sound of a great multitude. Grandfather fainted dead away—who wouldn't?

"But an angel came and touched him, strengthening him greatly, and interpreted the words he had heard. This angel's name was Gabriel, and he helped Grandfather to his feet. He told me that he was still trembling so badly that the angel told him not to be afraid. Actually, the angel addressed him like this:

> "'O Daniel, man greatly beloved, understand what I am saying to you, for I was sent to you in answer to your prayer. Don't be afraid, Daniel, for from the very first day you set your face toward heaven in fasting and repentance, your words were heard, and I was dispatched to come to you. However, the demon prince over Persia fought against me for these twenty-one days, trying to prevent my arrival, so Michael—your national guardian angel, and one of the most powerful chief princes—was sent to help me.
>
> "'Daniel, I have come to give you understanding, for the vision is for the far future; you are to know what shall befall your people in the latter days.'"

Joshua drank again from his water flask, and they rode in companionable silence for a while.

Eliel finally spoke, his voice almost a whisper. "Joshua—what does happen? To our people, I mean?"

"It's a long story, Eliel. The angel spoke of many future kingdoms, perhaps far, far into the future. He spoke of the coming of the Messiah and of a wicked, evil king who brings terrible tribulation to our people, opposing our great God!" Joshua's countenance was grim as he looked ahead of him with unseeing eyes.

"Eliel, there is so much I do not understand about the visions; there was much that my grandfather could not fathom, but one thing was crystal clear: our God will eventually triumph over the evil one. That is sure and certain—an unalterable truth. More than this, Eliel, I could not begin to explain. When my grandfather asked the meaning, the angel explained that it was for a far future time, and for now, to 'seal up the vision.'

"Now, we are approaching the city gates, so we'll talk later. First, we must find the house of Ezra and give him time to prepare for the journey back to Susa."

Joshua glanced sideways at his friend and smiled. "This, Eliel—in answer to your question—is the reason for our journey. My grandfather feels a great urgency to commit the visions to a scribe he can trust, and Ezra is the chief of all the Hebrew scribes in Babylon. He can prepare for the journey, then we will deliver some letters to King Cyrus at the palace, and perhaps even have a few hour's sleep before our departure."

The sun was fully up, the fog had disappeared, and the immense bronze gates of the city had been opened. Joshua and his friends rode slowly, awe-stricken by the magnificent architectural details.

"See those stone lions on each side? These same lions watched our ancestors enter into their captivity through this same gate of Ishtar. Over seventy years ago, they walked these same pavement stones, displayed to the pagan crowd as the trophies of Nebuchadnezzar the king. See, there is the palace up ahead. The flags are flying, so King Cyrus is in residence there now."

The next few hours were spent in a dizzying melee of sights, sounds, and activity. They located the house of Ezra, the great scribe who was the president of the Hebrew synagogue in Babylon. Having delivered Daniel's message, they carried a large packet of documents and letters to the palace, then returned to the house of Ezra where they were given a sumptuous meal and a comfortable place to rest.

"I wish we could have caught a glimpse of the great Cyrus himself," murmured Eliel as he drifted off to sleep.

Joshua did not reply. He lay awake, staring at the ceiling. Somewhere down deep inside he knew that his grandfather was dying. *O Lord Jehovah*, he breathed, *please, please let us get back home in time.*

On the eve of his ninety-seventh birthday, Daniel lay awake long after the household was silent in sleep. The stars shone with exceptional brilliance, and the thin crescent of a new moon hung over the horizon, stirring the dormant memory of a night long ago on a Judean hillside. Four little boys—no older than five or six—lay encamped on the hill behind Mishael's house, staring sleepily up at the stars. The last dying embers of their campfire crackled, and the wind sighed through the trees, bringing the pungent scents of juniper, cypress, and wood smoke from below. The boys whispered tales of bravado and derring-do, tales that reflected a wistful longing to be like the great heroes of old.

Daniel's wrinkled old face creased into a smile, his heart strangely warmed by the memory. He arose somewhat stiffly, stretched and yawned, then went outside to sit on the terrace. The huge yellow ball of fur uncoiled from the folds of the bedcover and followed Daniel outside. Jumping onto his lap and purring extravagantly, Yasmin the cat—who had never suffered from a lack of self-esteem—allowed her master the privilege of stroking her long, silky fur, then jumped down and stalked with elegant dignity out into the darkness.

"Ah, well," sighed Daniel, "anyone who has ever loved a cat can never hope to be loved for himself alone, isn't that right, Yasmin? You and I are growing old together, my friend; indeed, I think that you shall outlive me. Ninety-seven years! Where have they gone?"

A little twinge of loneliness gripped his heart as he gazed unseeing into the darkness. *All gone*, he thought wistfully. *All my beloved boyhood friends, my parents and sisters, gone. Nebuchadnezzar, Amytis, Ashpenaz, Arioch, my beloved Hannah, Esther, and Darius—all gone.*

Cyrus has proven to be faithful to God's calling on his young life. Esther and Mordecai trained him well—he will be a great ruler all his life. I wonder...I wonder how Cyrus must have felt when he discovered the amazing fact that God had called him by name two hundred years before his birth! How humbling it is to read those ancient scrolls of Isaiah and know that our great God made such an amazing provision for this time in our history.

Daniel leaned back and breathed deeply of the cool night air, listening to the alluring sounds of the rustling willows by the river, interwoven with the distant, melancholy calls of night birds and the insistent, friendly chirping of the tree frogs. Once again he sighed wearily, closing his eyes tightly as a little spasm of pain gripped his heart. He rang a small silver bell by the table, and immediately three servants came running to help him back into bed.

"Only a few hours until dawn, great one. We will awaken you when your grandson returns. Sleep well, sire."

The demon prince of Persia was furious. Still stinging from his humiliating defeat at the hands of the great prince Michael, he desperately cast about for some way to redeem himself in the eyes of his master. Satan himself was in a towering rage, and sent out scouts throughout the entire kingdom to report any new developments directly to him.

"We cannot allow this to continue!" he growled. "It is intolerable that Gabriel was allowed passage to reach the man Daniel with the visions. Each time God's people gain more understanding of His plans and purposes, HIS power grows stronger on the earth—and MY power declines. Daily, daily, my power grows weaker as Daniel records the visions and offers prayers of thanksgiving and praise to his God.

"It is intolerable that after thousands of years of uninterrupted rulership of this world, I must give way to first Nebuchadnezzar, then Darius acknowledging Daniel's God—and now Cyrus! Because they acknowledged His sovereignty over their lives and their kingdoms, God has bestowed on all three rulers His blessing, His strength, and His wisdom, and worst of all—HIS PROTECTION!

"Bring the prince of Persia to me," he snarled. "I will have some answers to this dilemma, or he will pay dearly."

No sooner were the words out of his mouth than the offending angel of darkness appeared before him. Satan rose to his full height, indeed a terrifying and intimidating presence.

"Kneel before me!"

The demon prince obeyed with unusual alacrity. After a short, tense silence he spoke. "I have news for you, my master. Good news."

"What news could you possibly bring me, except defeat!"

The terrified prince rose to his knees and spread his hands wide in supplication. "Please hear me, sire. We have found a point of entry whereby we can prevent the precious scrolls from reaching their destination."

"Tell me more." A malevolent gleam appeared in the glowing eyes of the evil one.

"Your satanic majesty, my scouts tell me that the old man is dying. His youngest grandson has been dispatched with a small group of riders to bring the Jewish scribe Ezra from Babylon to Susa. Daniel will then commit to him the visions of the future for all generations of his people—far into the future—to gain insight and wisdom into God's plan for his people. If the people of God really found a source of untarnished, undiluted truth—I shudder to think of the devastation to our side, great master. We cannot allow it.

"Our plan, sire, is ridiculously easy: we will bring together several hundred roving bandits who roam that desert region. We will assign many of our demons of rage and murder into their midst, stirring them into a frenzy at just the crucial time when the grandson and Ezra are returning to Susa. We will, however, leave one lone survivor: Joshua's best friend, Eliel. He will ride wounded into Susa, and when the news is related to Daniel, it will finish the old man off. He is extraordinarily fond of his youngest grandson. The visions will die with him."

The hooded, glowering eyes watched silently from the darkness, then the archangel of consummate evil spoke softly.

"You will, I trust, oversee this operation personally. You are aware, of course, that there must be no slips this time. My kingdom will suffer untold defeats for many centuries if those documents are not destroyed. Eyes that I have carefully blinded will be opened. Understanding that I have painstakingly darkened will be enlightened. My spies tell me that these scrolls may even carry in them the revelation of…of…the coming MESSIAH —and of His triumph over ME! It cannot be!"

The astounded Persian lord of darkness drew back, watching his master pace the floor, agitated beyond belief. Finally the evil one whirled to face the wall, growling only one word.

"Begone!"

Hasib drew in his breath sharply as he waited with his men in the cool darkness of the desert hillside. A small torchlight gleamed from the rocky outcropping on the other side of the ravine below.

"They have been spotted," he whispered hoarsely. "Pass the word, and wait for my signal."

Hasib could not explain the excitement surging through his breast. A seasoned desert raider for most of his life, he had plundered many hundreds of unwary travelers of their belongings. Sometimes he had been forced to kill those who resisted, but for the most part he had always disliked the killing, dulling himself insensible with fermented wild kumquat wine for days afterward.

Now, he glanced uneasily at his companions, wondering if they felt the same wild anticipation. Fingering his long, sharp dagger, he licked his dry lips, then with a shrill cry, issued the command. Down the rocky incline they descended like locusts into the darkened depths below toward the hapless little band of riders, their shrill cries echoing off of the nearly vertical cliff.

Reaching the bottom, Hasib drew his dagger and, his eyes adjusted to the darkness, headed for the nearest rider who, unaccountably, was sitting perfectly still on the back of his mount. An unreasoning rage to kill burst upon him, and Hasib leaped upward toward the rider. In that last split second, he glimpsed the eyes of the enemy, and to his utter surprise, found himself impaled on the end of the Persian's lance. As he lay dying, acutely aware of the screams and groans of his dying henchmen all around him, Hasib had one short moment to regret his life, then was gone.

The Persian soldier dismounted, retrieved his bloody lance, and wiped it on the grass. Kicking the limp body to the side of the road, he called out, "Good work, men. Check our passengers to make sure everyone is accounted for. We will camp at the oasis ahead, then resume our journey in the morning."

As the contingent of Cyrus' elite palace guard rode out of the dark ravine into the moonlit desert landscape, the little group of riders in the center was silent, each giving thanks to God for their escape from certain death.

Later, as they warmed their shivering bodies around the campfires, Ezra learned the truth: King Cyrus, Joshua explained, had called him urgently to the palace the morning after their arrival in Babylon. God had warned him in a dream of their impending danger, he explained, so he was sending two hundred of his royal guards—highly trained Persian horsemen—to escort them back to Susa.

"I have great respect for your grandfather, young Joshua," he explained. "God has shown me that the visions are prophecies of the times to come, and it is extremely important that they be protected and preserved. My men have instructions to await Ezra in Susa and accompany him back to Babylon with the precious scrolls in his possession. Go now, and God be with you."

Cyrus was true to his word. His men did indeed wait patiently the six weeks during which Ezra recorded every detail of the final vision, and the young scribes he had brought with him faithfully transcribed all the copies of Daniels's work of an entire lifetime. When it was time for the caravan to leave for Babylon, however, their departure was unexpectedly delayed.

They must also carry back in their midst a royal carriage, resplendent in gold, silver, and jewels. Drawn by four plumed Arabian horses, the carriage contained the frail body of Daniel, the man greatly beloved by his God.

At the very moment he had breathed his last breath, the Watchers who had faithfully stood guard by him all during his long, adventurous life on this earth were accorded the distinct honor of escorting this man to his heavenly reward. As he was gathered to his people, he finally heard the words he had been waiting to hear all his life.

"Yes, Daniel: those who know their God are indeed strong and do great exploits. Well done, good and faithful servant!"

———◦◦◦———

Joshua stood before the plain marble sarcophagus, tracing the names: "Hannah" and "Daniel." Under the willow tree on a hill overlooking the river Euphrates was the final resting place of the great prime minister of three kingdoms. Daniel's last request was that he be buried beside his beloved Hannah behind their family home in Babylon.

"No grand memorials, Joshua," he had instructed severely. "Remember that when I am gathered to my people. I want nothing remaining behind me to tempt people to idolatrous worship of one who was just a man."

Just a man, Joshua thought despairingly. *What will become of us, my grandfather, without your wise and godly counsel?*

As he turned to go, something caught his eye, and he looked upward. Fluttering gaily in the wind, a brilliant blue and scarlet flag streamed out from the western parapet of the palace.

"Let's go!" he called to Eliel, and set off at a run.

Puffing from the exertion, the two boys ran the distance, climbed the marble steps to the palace library and emerged, breathless, on the parapet above. The setting sun outlined a ribbon of molten gold winding its way through the darkening valley below.

"Look at the river, Eliel. My grandfather told me so many times how he and his friends used to climb up here at evening to talk, to watch the sunset, and…and always longing for home."

The boys fell silent, overcome with shadows of the past, an intense, wordless longing. Then, an infinitesimally small thought began to grow, eclipsing the despair lingering from the youths gathered here so long ago.

"Joshua, are you thinking what I'm thinking?"

"Yes, Eliel. We have the opportunity they wanted so desperately and never had. We can go home."

Home. That ancient longing for the mother city they had never seen began to grip the boys with an intense fervor. They stayed there a long time, speaking in hushed tones of their future.

———⁂———

The searing heat of midsummer beat down oppressively on the long caravan queuing its way through the Syrian Desert. The camels plodded impassively onward; having been born to a life of servitude, they were oblivious to the heady sense of freedom, the heightened exhilaration that possessed their riders. Nearly three hundred Jewish families were headed back to their ancestral home, loaded to the hilt with seventy years' accumulation of possessions, and something else: more materials sent by King Cyrus himself for the rebuilding of the temple.

The caravan was halted at a large oasis, the camels unloaded, and camp set up. The cool of the desert night brought sweet relief to the tired, thirsty travelers. The abundance of water and dates from the palms brought refreshing and a renewal of energy.

The caravan chieftain, a tall, burly Syrian tanned by the sun to the color of cordovan leather, shook his head in amusement at the wild, abandoned music of these strange Hebrews.

"They dance around their fires every night," he muttered to an aide, "as if they had just inherited a fortune in jewels. What a God-forsaken, desolate land they call home! When they see Jerusalem with its broken walls and burned gates, I guarantee you that will sober them up quickly enough."

He glanced up at the scudding clouds racing across the moon and, holding a wet finger to the wind, remarked to his friend as he bent to enter his tent, "Hassan, wake me early. I didn't like the looks of that red sky at sunset tonight. We might be in for a hard day's journey tomorrow."

The following morning, dawn appeared as a faint red haze on the horizon. The sky had turned a strange coppery hue, and the wind was picking up. Orders were passed to load the camels and evacuate the camp as quickly as possible.

"No one has ever yet outrun a desert sandstorm," shouted the chieftain. "We will turn south and head for the safety of those hills. Perhaps they will afford us some measure of protection. Now, move!"

Those on horses galloped on ahead, the camels running behind at a lumbering gait. They too sensed disaster and were spurred onward by the stinging, burning sand driving against their haunches.

Ezra leaned over to check the clay jars, one of which contained his priceless scrolls. Securing them tightly in the wagon, he waved the driver on, then mounted his horse and sped toward the safety of the hills.

Lord God, protect the scrolls! He breathed the desperate prayer through the choking dust that now filled his nostrils, finally pulling his horse to a halt in the lee of some rocks. He stood throughout the storm, holding a cloth over his horse's nose and mouth, his face pressed into its mane.

The driver of Ezra's wagon was only a stone's throw from safety when the storm hit with full fury. The horses screamed in pain and confusion, backing the cart into a ditch where it tipped over. Then they broke loose and bolted for safety.

"Stop! Wait!" yelled the driver, then cursed loudly and proficiently as he watched them disappear. He crouched on the lee side of the wagon, then suddenly the ground gave way beneath his feet, and he found himself falling.

Down through the underbrush and into the dark, smooth stone of a tunnel he shot like an arrow, accompanied by the contents of the wagon. His terrified senses fought for control as he clawed the air in the darkness that enveloped him. Finally he came to a sudden, violent stop and slumped over, battered and unconscious, surrounded by an assortment of clay jars, boxes, and rope-covered trunks.

Meanwhile, far above the cavernous depths below, the storm had long since abated, and the caravan once again emerged, relatively unscathed, to resume its journey. Ezra rode slowly along its length, searching anxiously for his wagon. When he finally found it, devoid of its contents and driver, he nearly fainted with consternation. A thorough search was launched, which eventually proved fruitless, and the journey was resumed.

Ezra, of course, was heartsick. His faith was very nearly shattered. For a few days, at least, he could not pray because he was in such deep depression. *Didn't I pray?* his dazed brain thought over and over again—*didn't I entrust those priceless manuscripts into the hands of my God?*

When they finally arrived at Jerusalem, Ezra went into seclusion at the home of a relative, refusing to see anyone. The double burden of losing

Daniel's lifework and then seeing Jerusalem, the holy city, trampled down like so much burned-out stubble from last year's harvest was too much for the brokenhearted man.

At the end of the seventh day, the bell for visitors once more sounded at the outer gate. The elderly servant wearily trudged out to turn away yet another visitor, but he soon returned to knock tentatively on the guest room door.

"Go away," growled the hoarse voice within. "I told you—no visitors."

"But sir," the servant called out in a tremulous voice, "it is Joshua, the grandson of Daniel. He must see you, sir. It is urgent."

A long silence ensued, then the door opened. A bleary-eyed Ezra followed the servant through the long, cool hall to the anteroom by the inner courtyard. When Joshua saw the shockingly altered face of the great scribe, he ran forward and embraced him warmly, then led him to a seat in the warm sunshine.

"Ezra, please hear me," he spoke gently. "I was in a little village near Bethel, visiting the family of my friend Rachel, when I heard the news. You must mourn no longer. I have the scrolls. Yes, all of them. I brought them with me to Jerusalem on last year's caravan from Susa. Ezra, my grandfather had copies made of each one and gave them to me before he died. See, here they are!"

Joshua pulled a large, leather packet from his bulging tunic and pressed it into Ezra's trembling hands. Healing, cleansing tears poured forth, dropping onto the leather as Ezra clutched it to his chest. Raising his bloodshot eyes toward heaven, Ezra the scribe poured forth his thanksgiving and praise to the God whose faithfulness he had doubted, and ten thousand angels responded to Michael's shout of triumph. The powers of darkness, however, withdrew for a season, having been considerably weakened by Ezra's prayer.

The grandson of Daniel remembered the testimony his grandfather had given after God delivered him from the pit of starving lions. Daniel had been right: God always has the last word.

With great difficulty, the wagon driver opened his eyes and struggled to his feet. The cold, wet floor, slippery underfoot, impeded his progress as he attempted to move about. As his eyes adjusted to the darkness, however, he realized that dim, filtered light from somewhere overhead was illuminating the contents of the room.

His foot hit something on the floor, clattering a circle around him. Bending to pick it up, he peered through the semi-darkness at the golden gleam of a jeweled chalice. Consumed by greed, he dropped to all fours and searched for more. There was much more than he could have ever imagined. Removing his tunic, he filled it with treasure, then, as an afterthought, he crammed all the clay vessels into crevices in the rocky walls of the cavern, intending to return for more.

He could see quite well by now and, pulling the heavy sack behind, laboriously made his way up to the light source and out into the open. Marking the spot with crossed tree branches, he set off down the road and back to the oasis. That night as he slumbered alone beneath the stars, the desert raiders found him and slit his throat, disappearing into the night with his heavily laden tunic.

In the cool, dark cavern beneath the Syrian desert, the precious scrolls remained hidden, sealed in their clay vault, patiently awaiting their appointed time.

Jerusalem was rebuilt; the Persian empire faded and the Grecian arose; then came the Romans, and the earth shook with the sound of their marching. But only a faint film of dust marked the changing of the centuries in the little cave.

CHAPTER 21

THE UNSEALING

For two thousand years, the church of Jesus Christ had worked and waited, praying and longing for His promised return. The imminence of that event was marked by the increasingly fervent desire of millions of believers to purify their hearts, as a bride preparing for that glorious encounter with her bridegroom. As the last few grains of sand trickled through the hourglass, an unprecedented move of the Spirit's grace and the love of God inundated the globe, sweeping away the long established barriers of ignorance and unbelief.

In the same way that persecution in the first century had scattered the newly birthed church to all parts of the world, the fiery persecution unleashed on millions of twenty-first-century Christians now only served to intensify the spreading of the good news of salvation. In a relatively short period of time, the entire population of the earth—which now far exceeded the sum total of all previous generations combined—was hearing the true, undiluted gospel.

For the last several years, many missionary organizations and evangelical ministries around the world, formerly separated by rivalries, minor doctrinal differences, and strife—now had been networking together, formulating effective strategies to reach the lost. United, energized, fully equipped. and empowered by the Spirit, the church was now a formidable foe. Indeed, this mighty army threatened the demolition of the very gates of hell, which had for so long afforded the demonic hordes unchallenged access to Planet Earth.

To make matters worse for the prince of darkness, a vast army of prayer warriors—millions of fervent believers all over the world—had released the massive power of the heavenly host. While the Spirit of God was being poured out on every living soul on earth, war was declared in the heavens.

The powers of darkness were marshaled by ranks, countless demonic hordes encircling the planet in fearful array. As they waited, nervously watching the skies overhead for the threatened invasion, the agitation mounted to a fever pitch, and many fights broke out in the ranks. Suddenly, mass confusion set in as millions of snarling demons turned on each other like mad dogs.

At that very moment, the blinding lights from above descended; like bolts of white-hot lightning, the angels of light cut down the swarming mass of evil, and, like so much volcanic rock, they all fell, wounded and disarmed, to the earth. Their humiliating defeat sent their commander in chief into a towering rage, and he flew immediately to his mountain headquarters to regroup his forces and formulate a new strategy.

Having summoned all his generals, Satan remained in seclusion for a very long time. One of those dark angels was heard to mutter, "But it was just like it was before: we were outnumbered two to one…" Unfortunately for him, those were his last words.

The good news of salvation was being taken to every living human being. Interestingly enough, however, the very last person on earth to hear and understand this gospel was not from some remote jungle or desert tribe; actually, it was a little deaf boy who lived with his grandfather in a small brick hut just a stone's throw away from the ancient site of Antioch in Syria, where the believers were first called "Christians."

Someone had set up a projector and screen in the village square and was showing the *Jesus* film, so little Fuad left his goats on the hillside and came down to watch. Overcome by curiosity, he watched the story unfold about the kind man in the white robe who went about doing good, then was whipped, beaten, and died on a wooden cross. Although little Fuad could not hear, he watched through his tears, jumping with joy as he saw the man alive again. Fuad's heart was transformed there on that rocky hillside, and the angels immediately received their orders from the Spirit.

"The last one has heard; it is time. Satan's armies have been defeated. He is

no longer the prince of the power of the air but has been cast down to earth. The skies have been cleared for the passage of My people."

During the cataclysmic events of the next instant, little Fuad's ears were opened, and he heard with astonishing clarity what every other believer—dead or alive—on the face of the earth was hearing: the unmistakable triumphant sound of a trumpet, and a voice saying:

"COME UP HERE!"

And in the twinkling of an eye they were gone.

———❈———

Jack Mannheim sat on the porch swing, absolutely motionless, staring out over the valley. Thunderclouds hung over the horizon, and as the midmorning rainstorm moved closer, he sighed heavily and moved back under the porch awning. Ruth sat inside on the window seat with her knees drawn up like a child, watching the approaching storm through weary, bloodshot eyes. Matt, home on leave for the weekend, was pacing the floor in his room, trying desperately to sort out the strange events of the previous day. He had no answers.

Sarah, Dan, and their new little baby girl had disappeared. They had been many hours overdue for a lunch at the Mannheim's, so after repeated unanswered phone calls and pages, Jack finally drove to their little home on the hillside near Jerusalem. He found their silver gray BMW two blocks from their home, off the side of the road in some bushes.

The doors were closed and the engine was still running, but the car was empty. Sarah's purse, the diaper bag, and baby carrier were still inside, but his daughter and her family were gone. Checking the house, Jack found it locked and empty. Panicked, he broke in, called Ruth, then attempted to call the police, but unfortunately, all the lines were busy, so he drove to the station.

His insides knotted with a gnawing fear, Jack turned the corner to the police department and braked suddenly to avoid the crowds of people milling about. He finally found a parking place and made his way through the crowd to the station. With a growing apprehension, Jack swallowed hard and tried to push his way inside, but found the door barred by two policemen standing guard at the door.

"Please, sir," he inquired desperately, "my daughter is missing, and I need help. Is there anyone who can help me?"

The officer shook his head grimly "Sorry, sir, this seems to be the day for disappearances. Every one you see here has reported someone missing. My advice is to go home and stay tuned to the news. We have heard—" he bit his lip nervously and glanced at his fellow officer, "—we have heard that this is happening all over the world. I'm sorry, but there is nothing we can do."

Jack nodded his thanks and turned to go. He blindly worked his way back through the crowd and, fighting back the tears that threatened to overwhelm him, drove home. Ruth met him at the door, and they clung together for a moment. They were startled to hear the news reporter announce: "Ladies and gentlemen, we have a late breaking story on the disappearances. Please stay tuned."

During the next few hours, they stayed glued to the TV, hoping desperately for a logical explanation. All through that long, tortuous evening, one recurrent theme seemed to be repeated over and over again by certain politicians, government officials, and even several well-known religious leaders: UFOs. Since there had been an apparent increase in UFO activity during recent decades, it was postulated by the "experts in paranormal phenomena" that a sudden invasion of these "aliens" could indeed have spirited away a certain portion of the world's population.

Jack and Ruth looked at each other in stunned disbelief the first time it was mentioned, appalled by the idea that so many otherwise sane, civilized, well-educated intellectuals could seriously contemplate such a bizarre explanation. As the night wore on, however, their battered, bewildered minds were numbed into insensitivity. *Maybe it's true*, Jack found himself thinking, and with a growl of disgust he suddenly, savagely switched off the TV.

Ruth had long since cried herself to sleep, curled up on the sofa. Jack covered her with a soft afghan, then settled into his recliner for a fitful, intermittent night's sleep.

Early the next morning, Jack, being a man of action, set off to Tel Aviv to track down Alex, Lothar, and Heidi, a trip that proved to be unsuccessful. They had also disappeared. Frustrated, he circled back, stopping once again at Sarah's deserted home. He wandered from room to room, finally settling at the old teakwood desk he had given them for a wedding present.

Sifting through papers, looking for clues, he had almost given up when he spotted a thick envelope marked "Mom and Dad." Tearing it open, he pulled out the contents: a long letter from Sarah, another one from Dan, and a photograph of the proud parents with their baby.

"Dearest Dad and Mom," her letter began, "I know that some day we will be gone, and you will be left with a broken heart, not understanding what has happened. Do you remember the many times we talked about the possibility of something called the 'rapture of the saints'...

Jack's hands were shaking uncontrollably as he read the rest of Sarah's letter, and then Dan's. Afterward, he sat for a long time, staring at the photograph.

"It won't be long," she had said, "only a short time, and we'll all be together again, IF ONLY YOU WILL BELIEVE..."

For many long hours, the young man lay unconscious, half buried in the burning sands of the Syrian desert. As the setting sun cast long violet shadows against the barren dunes, a slight breeze stirred the dusty terrain, and he began to stir. Squinting upward into the azure sky, he saw the buzzards circling relentlessly far overhead, desert scavengers patiently awaiting their leisurely meal.

Fully aware of his perilous situation, he struggled to free himself from his sandy prison but was hampered by his flight suit. Pulling off his oxygen mask in frustration, he tried again, and with a massive effort, managed to free himself. As he attempted to stand, however, a stabbing pain in his left ankle brought him groaning to the earth.

Matt had been shot down. His plane fatally crippled by antiaircraft fire, he had bailed out just in time to see it smash into a rocky hillside. He had no time to mourn the fiery loss of his aircraft, however. He had been flying in low over enemy territory, so his parachute only opened seconds before he hit the ground, and he hit hard, shattering his ankle.

The sun dipped low and was gone; the azure turned to dusky blue, then the total darkness of the moonless night engulfed him, settling over his body and soul like a shroud. Matt shuddered, for the sudden drop in temperature had brought about a late-autumn chill. Groping about in the darkness for his parachute, he finally located it and wrapped himself up in it for the night. Sleepless, he gazed up at the vast expanse of the starry universe. Gradually, inexorably, a little hole opened up in the hardened crust over his soul, and some of the anger and bitterness began to leak out.

During the long months following Heather's death and the confusing weeks following the disappearance of Dan, Sarah, and their baby girl, of Lothar, Heidi, and Alex—Matt had retreated into a numbing despair. His wounds were seemingly incurable; no one could reach him, not even his mother. At the base, he withdrew from all his friends and was always the first to volunteer for the most dangerous missions. It was whispered about that he had lost all fear of death, and his superior officer worried that he might have even become suicidal.

Now, as Matt had time to think about all this, he began to realize how his anger might have actually jeopardized their missions, and he felt the first sharp pangs of remorse.

"I didn't do it on purpose," he whispered. "honestly, I didn't do it on purpose." Something deep inside him broke loose, and he turned face down, burying his head in his arms. His shoulders shook as deep, heaving sobs racked his body.

"God, forgive me," he cried over and over again. "God, please forgive me. I've tried to blame You for everything…for Heather…for everything. Please God, forgive me! Jesus, forgive me!"

Matt sobbed out his pain for a long, long time that night, crying himself to sleep for the first time since he was a little boy. Indeed, during that night he slept well for the first time in years—cleansed, refreshed, and relaxed as an innocent child.

Some time during the night, he dreamed that a man in glowing garments came down out of the sky. Standing over him, the man said, *"Matt, get up."* As he arose to his feet, the man pulled out something from his pocket and held it up for Matt to see: it fit neatly into the palm of his hand, and as he drew closer, he pressed it into Matt's forehead.

"There. Now you are sealed with the seal of the Living God. Matt, you are one of the 144,000 young Jewish men called by our God to be the special envoys of Jesus, your Messiah, during the coming time of tribulation for your people. You are of the tribe of Judah, Matt. You will be operating under His authority and will be under His protection.

"I am the angel called Rafael; I have been assigned as your personal guardian. Sometimes you will see me, sometimes not, but I will always be there until the day when you and your fellow travelers are caught up to His throne. Do you have any questions?"

Even in his dream, Matt was speechless. Suddenly he remembered his broken ankle and that he was standing, so he involuntarily looked down. When he looked up again, the angel was gone, and Matt called out, "Wait, wait—please come back!"

He awoke to find himself in a half sitting position, reaching toward the sky. With an ache in his throat, he fell back against the sand. *Only a dream*, he thought despairingly, and rolled over onto his side. Extricating himself from the parachute, the first faint rays of dawn illuminating the landscape, he looked down at his feet. The pain and swelling in his left ankle were gone. Having seen it bent at a grotesque angle the night before, he was now amazed to see it completely straight. Suddenly a thought occurred to him, and he jumped to his feet.

The rays of the early morning sun slanted across the desert floor, casting into perfect relief the huge, unmistakable footprints of the angel.

"The Eastern Gate."

Ruth looked up from her book. "Did you say something?

"The Eastern Gate," Jack repeated slowly. "He'll come back through the Eastern Gate. Read it just the other day in the book of Ezekiel, forty-third chapter, I think."

Ruth gazed at him in speechless wonder as he continued.

"You see, all the prophecies of the Messiah coming back to Israel seem to point to certain unalterable facts: He will return as the victorious sovereign ruler, as King. He will return at a time when the world is poised for self-destruction and all armies are gathered against Jerusalem.

"His enemies (who have persecuted and martyred millions of Christians and Jews) will be completely and suddenly destroyed. He will return to a *specified* geographical site (prophesied both in the Old Testament Book of Zechariah and the New Testament Book of Acts), namely the Mount of Olives, east of Jerusalem."

Jack, who had begun somewhat self-consciously, now leaned forward as he warmed eagerly to his subject. "Ruth...do you realize that almost all the ancient prophecies regarding the regathering to Israel have already been fulfilled—all, that is, except one: the rebuilding of the temple. Now, with that project being completed, surely His return must be very near!"

Ruth looked pained, as she turned away. "Oh, Jack—He has already come. Or so you say. Anyway, it's too late for us. Why do you persist in bringing up all of this 'prophecy' stuff?"

"Ruth, please listen to me," Jack replied softly. "The church was taken away, yes—but that was just the first stage of the end."

Jack tried to explain how God's ancient covenant with the nation of Israel had never been revoked or forgotten. The conversation continued far into the night until Ruth, exasperated, threw down her book and went to bed.

It seemed that Randy's parting gift of a Bible had triggered in Jack an intensive interest in biblical study, fueled by a newfound hunger for the solid foundational truth of his ancestral heritage. Night after night during the months since Dan and Sarah's disappearance, he had pored over the ancient books, devouring their contents like a starving man.

Ruth tossed and turned in the bed, feeling the familiar loneliness beginning to engulf her. She had watched this new turn of events with her usual unruffled aplomb. She was long accustomed to tolerating her husband's many passionate obsessions: hot air balloons, collecting antique cars, photography safaris, bow hunting in Canada, sky diving, prospecting for gold, and more.

Many years ago he had joined a humanitarian group called TTR ("To the Rescue"), in which he and several other men piloted their Cessnas into inaccessible, strife-torn regions in Central America. They ferried provisions and medical personnel in and out of dangerous areas, and for several years managed to bring a great deal of relief to destitute villagers. This was really the only long-term project Jack had ever involved himself in, and it is more than an even guess that Ruth was never aware of his many narrow escapes.

Lately, however, she had sensed a change in Jack; he seemed to be so much more introspective, quietly withdrawing into an area unfamiliar to her. Ruth had no spiritual resources to cope with the disappearance of her daughter. The explanations of God's "catching away" or "rapture" of His Christian believers only increased her bitterness. Already confused, bewildered, and frightened, she slowly withdrew to grieve alone.

Jack, however, had been so wrapped up in the thrill of discovery that he failed to notice his wife's disinclination to accompany him on his odyssey. As time passed, he awoke somewhat belatedly to the slight, but unmistakable rift growing between them. Not completely understanding the cause, he made an extra effort to be sensitive and loving, relying on the solid foundation and closeness of their relationship to bring healing. It wasn't working. Outwardly, there was no apparent change, but still—things were definitely different. Their relationship had shifted, because Jack's whole focus had shifted.

Somewhere on this past year's journey, Jack had encountered, in the pages of this astonishing Book, the Author Himself. It didn't come all at once—a blinding revelation to knock him flat—but instead a gradual realization of the timeless truth overtook his consciousness like the unrelenting light of dawn, which grew brighter and brighter until the full light of day. It was so incredibly satisfying, so cleansing.

He found passages that thundered majestically like a Beethoven symphony; others shimmered quietly like the light of a scented candle. The one, however, that he devoured over and over again was the first chapter of John; he would take it out like a prized jewel from its velvet box and hold it up to the light, admiring its facets as they flashed their dazzling fire.

> In the beginning was the Word, and the Word was with God, and the Word was *God* Himself...All things were made by Him...in Him was Life, and the Life was the Light of men, and the Light shines on in the darkness, for the darkness cannot overcome it.

The more he read, the more his faith grew. There were some changes in his lifelong habits, too: the habitual bourbon on the rocks no longer accompanied his Bible study times, simply because he found that a clear head greatly accelerated comprehension. Finally one night Jack went to the balcony where, kneeling before his Creator, he freely confessed his sinful nature and his need of a Savior. He arose forgiven, clean—a new man.

During this time Ruth grew more and more restless and finally decided to spend her days at the museum. Although she had obtained a degree in music history, she had developed a keen interest in art history as well, having visited many of the world's great museums while traveling with Jack. The current work at the museum in Jerusalem was irresistibly intriguing, so she volunteered her help and was immediately put to work in the ancient Semitic culture section.

As she worked side by side with these dedicated young Israelis, Ruth's admiration for them grew more and more each day. Having worked tirelessly during the past year, painstakingly identifying and catalog-ing each item of the Nazi treasure hoard, having used every means at their disposal (especially the Internet) to locate the rightful owners, they could be justifiably proud of a job well done.

Many times they would gather at cafes and clubs during their off-hours, chatting and exchanging information, drinking wine and dancing until the wee hours of the morning. It was a heady and exhilarating atmo-sphere, fraught with the excitement of new, imminent daily discoveries. Ruth soon found herself caught up in it and welcomed the work as a much-needed diversion from her problems. Even the eminent museum curator, Dr. Levinson, recognized her quick intelligence and growing proficiency and assigned her to more and more important tasks.

And so it happened that on one rainy night in midwinter, Ruth stayed late, working on an old crate in the corner of the vast underground stor-age room. Having brewed a cup of tea, she pulled down the ceiling spot-light and knelt down on the floor. Sipping her tea, she ran her fingers over the smooth clay vessel nestled in crushed, yellowed, old newspaper. She set her tea down and pulled out some of the papers, smoothing them on the floor.

German! Ruth wrinkled her nose in dismay. *Wish I could read it—wait: here's something—Hanover Zeitung, 16 April 1939! The owner is from Hanover!* Unaccountably, her heart began to pound as she carefully pulled out more papers, carefully smoothing out each one. Somewhere near the top of the crate, just sticking out from under the jar, was a paper of a different color; a yellowish white envelope with spidery, illegible handwriting. Ruth sat back and forced herself to take a deep breath and drink her tea.

I'll go get Dr. Levinson, she breathed, *but first…* Ruth carefully pulled the long, slender clay jar from its resting place and turned the light on the seal. The ancient inscription was perfectly intact, engraved permanently into the wax; Ruth stared at it for several long minutes, then carefully lowered it back down. She ran to the research library and, locating the books she wanted, went immediately to Dr. Levinson's office. The office was dark and empty, but as she turned to go, she ran into Dr. Elie Dorf-mann, his research assistant.

"Elie—do you read or speak German?" The words tumbled out, and Ruth blushed as the young man replied, "Yes, of course—I am German—

but what's happened to you, Ruth? You look like you've seen a ghost!"

"Maybe I have; come with me!" She grabbed his arm and pulled him down the hall. Bounding down the stairs at an alarming pace, she outdistanced him to the dusty old corner of the basement. The ceiling light was still swinging, creating eerie moving shadows everywhere.

"What are you doing down here at this hour, Ruth?" gasped a breathless Elie. "You should be home by the fire with your husband, sipping brandy or something."

She ignored his protests; pulling down the ceiling light and opening the book, she knelt by the dusty old crate. "Come and look, Elie."

He knelt beside her. Carefully examining the clay vessel, its seal, and the reference book, he sat back on his heels. With a low whistle, he mopped his brow and collapsed onto the floor.

"What a find," he whispered. "What an incredible find! We are looking at the seal of Cyrus the Great himself, perfectly preserved exactly as it was imprinted in that wax over 2500 years ago! I wonder what's inside…and how it came to be here."

Ruth then handed him the envelope. "Read this. It was in the crate."

Reverently, Elie pulled out the contents: a long, handwritten letter on fragile yellowed vellum and what looked to be an official receipt or bill of sale. The typed numbers were faded but readable.

He began to read it aloud. His voice echoing eerily off the stone walls of the vast underground storehouse seemed to come from another time, another place far, far away.

> To whom it may concern:
> Let it be known to all that this vessel and its contents are the property of Abraham Lieberman, who bequeaths it to his rightful heirs and descendants upon the event of his death. Here is the story of the vessel., and how it was acquired: A certain Syrian, an antiquities trader named Kamil Assad, came to my home…

———⦿———

The streets of Tel Aviv were nearly deserted. The sad little bar on the corner was brightly lit and the inevitable rock music throbbed from its interior, but the false gaiety failed to inspire Elie. Sitting in a darkened corner, he stared morosely out the little window while his bored date toyed with her drink, smoking incessantly. Finally, after repeated attempts to engage him in conversation, she stubbed out her cigarette, tossed back the remains of her drink, and left in disgust. He hardly noticed.

Dr. Elie Dorfmann had made so many discoveries in such a short time. He was completely overwhelmed. This brilliant young Israeli had all at once discovered the fate of his own great-great-grandfather, Abraham Lieberman. His great-grandparents, Annaliese and Heinrich Dorfmann, had disappeared along with millions of others into the hideous crematoriums at Dachau. He stared unseeing in the darkness as he thought of his grandfather, only a little boy when he lost both parents in the Holocaust.

Almost eclipsing his grief, however, was the unsettling discovery of the contents of the clay vessel. Having read the letter from his own great-great-grandfather and understanding that the priceless ancient artifact had been bequeathed to him, Elie had been consumed with excitement and curiosity concerning its contents.

He had devised a fool-proof plan to laser the seal out, painstakingly and patiently working it out intact. The moment of discovery was far more intense than he could ever have anticipated. The world's most famous expert on Babylonian and Persian hieroglyphics had flown to Jerusalem from London and had corroborated Dr. Levinson's assessment of the inscription along the bottom of the jar; it definitely contained parchment scrolls.

They had been carefully extracted, but they could not be read until they had gone through a series of treatments that would soften and preserve the parchment, allowing it to be unrolled without disintegrating. During the days and weeks, then months of careful examination, the growing suspicion had become a stunning certainty: these were the original scrolls written by the prophet Daniel twenty-six hundred years earlier in the city called Susa, the capital of the Persian empire.

Confirmed by the newest carbon-dating methods, which boasted an accuracy rate of plus or minus thirty years, the scientific world had been stunned into silence, and it was that very silence that now spoke volumes to Elie's questing heart. The scrolls were virtually identical in form and content to the modern translations of the Book of Daniel in the Bible, available in every language for anyone who cared to read it.

For the countless thousands of scientists, theologians, and philosophers who had for many decades systematically and ruthlessly disdained the Bible as a book of "myths" and "old wives' tales," it had been a massive rebuke. They had no answer, so they had remained silent.

Characteristically, the secular press had also been silent. There had been no press conferences, no media blitzes, nothing at all. That is, nothing until a young reporter unearthed the news, and, sniffing a big story, wrote a brilliant piece of journalism. Surprisingly, his editor had agreed with him, and the *Jerusalem Post* had finally carried a four-page spread on the major discovery, complete with pictures and Bible references.

The news had spread like wildfire; the Associated Press had picked it up, and soon it had encircled the globe.

VOICE FROM THE PAST VERIFIES
BIBLICAL ACCOUNT

Elie had always been so sure of his atheism. After all, it was the only rational, logical, intellectual approach for a young mind saturated from early childhood with the all-pervasive religion called "humanism." *And besides,* his whirling brain inquired, *how could so many great scientific minds agree on a flawed consensus: that man is the center of his own universe?*

Disgusted, he flung down a bill on the table and exited the bar. Outside in the cool, fresh air, his head cleared a bit, and he walked slowly, savoring the silence as the jarring musical rhythms faded behind him. *I have to know,* he thought desperately. *I've read and re-read the Book of Daniel until I've almost memorized it. Where did he get his strength?*

I have never felt such overwhelming admiration as I do for this man who lived in a society every bit as pagan as ours, and yet who refused to be swayed or influenced by the tremendous pressure to conform. Instead, he was the one who changed the society, influencing the lives of kings, changing the course of three kingdoms. He rose to unprecedented power, and yet NEVER ONCE DID HE EVER SURRENDER HIS INTEGRITY TO COMPROMISE. NEVER.

Elie shook his head, then looked up into the night sky.

God, if You're there…

———— ⌀₪⌀ ————

The big gray limousine moved steadily through the snow-covered Swiss countryside, its headlights reflected back inside from the heavy snowdrifts alongside the road. Karl Morgenthal sat huddled in the back seat, glancing nervously out the back window, more afraid than he had ever been in his life.

The frail little banker had lived through far more danger, indeed, as a very small child in the concentration camps—but there he had been completely alone, surviving only by his wits. Now, although widowed for nearly fifty years, he had the responsibility of his two sons and four daughters and their families. All together, counting his grandchildren, great-grandchildren, and remaining great-great-grandchildren, the family now numbered fifty-two. *Fifty-two precious lives*, he thought despairingly, *and they are all dependent on me.*

For the last few months, the Jewish community in Geneva had been harassed and hounded unmercifully, and their movements were increasingly restricted. Anti-Semitism was approaching a fever pitch all over the world, far greater than ever before. This alarming trend seemed to have erupted in earnest not long after the "disappearances" of millions of Christians from the earth, an event which still lacked any satisfactory explanation.

Thirteen of Karl's great-great-grandchildren had disappeared on that terrible day, and the entire family was left torn and bleeding. Numb with grief, they had given passive agreement to Karl's urgent warnings: leave now, or we will all be swallowed up in another Holocaust.

As the limousine turned to enter the airfield, Karl peered anxiously out the window. The private jet he had chartered was fueled and ready in the hangar, but the field outside looked deserted. His heart began to pound erratically, and he grimly popped a nitroglycerin pill under his tongue.

"They should have been here by now," he called hoarsely to his driver. "Herman, do you see anything yet?"

His chauffeur got out, peered into the darkness, then ducked back in. "Sir, it's hard to see through all that heavy snowfall, but I thought I saw a light blinking on and off across the field. I'll drive across to the other side."

Karl nervously pulled on his gloves, increasingly alarmed at the height of the snowdrifts outside. He seemed to be encased in a world of white, from which there was no escape.

Suddenly the old horror enveloped him, and once again Karl Morgenthal was a terrified child in a white room. Masked men and women in white were standing in a circle around him; the bright white lights overhead blinded him, and the piercing cries issuing from the writhing little body on the table seemed to come from someone else. Again and again the scalpel blade probed relentlessly, over and over and over until the terrified shrieks subsided into agonized groans. Little Karl was only one of many such children subjected to those unspeakable Nazi atrocities they called "medical experiments." Karl was one of the lucky few who survived.

Staring unseeing into the swirling whiteness, he was jolted back to consciousness by voices outside the car. "Hurry, Papa. We must hurry. We are all here, and the plane is waiting."

And so it was that the Morgenthal family, like Moses and the children of Israel escaping Egypt, finally returned to their ancient homeland.

The insistent ringing of the telephone jarred Ruth and Jack from a deep sleep. He groped for the phone in the semi-darkness of the Madrid hotel room, cleared his throat several times, then croaked out a "Hello!"

"Dad, it's Matt. I only have a few minutes—I'm calling from a pay phone. Sorry to wake you both, but this is important. Can you hear me OK?"

"Yes, Matt. What's up?" Jack switched on the light and sat on the edge of the bed, running his hands through his rumpled thatch of graying hair. "It's 4 a.m., son. This must be pretty urgent."

"It is," Matt replied tersely. "I don't have a lot of time to explain, but we just came from a meeting, and—"

"We? Who is 'we'?"

"Sorry, Dad—no time for lengthy explanations—gotta keep this short. Do you remember Lothar telling us about a super-secret mountain hideout in the Bavarian Alps where he heard a group of elite world leaders making their plans? Remember he said they discovered and murdered his friend, then later tried to murder his widow?"

After a short silence, Jack answered tentatively, "Yes, I do remember, Matt, but what —"

"Dad, their leader, the enigmatic, shadowy figure behind that conspiracy, has finally come out into the open, emerging from his camouflage to take total control of the New World Order. Haven't you been watching the news lately, Dad? It's happened so swiftly, so subtly, that maybe being on an extended vacation you didn't know.

"But Dad, listen—you and Mom are in great danger. You remember how three years ago he negotiated that permanent peace treaty—backed up by the NWO forces—with all the Arab nations? The Knesset has, to a man, practically deified him. But there is something they don't yet know. Get this, Dad: he is running a massive scam on our nation. He is even now making preparations to move his capitol to Jerusalem, and—Dad, he has specifically asked for you to build him a mansion on the Mount of Olives.

"You see, he has read the prophecies of the Savior's return to the Mount of Olives, so he plans to take control of the area by building on it and stationing armed guards to protect it from invasion! Isn't that just the craziest thing you have ever heard? The man must be stark raving mad if he thinks that anything made by man could prevent God from accomplishing His plan!"

There was dead silence. "A mansion? The Mount of Olives! Wherever did he get my name? Son, how did you come by this information?"

"Wait, Dad—listen, that's not the worst of it. We believe—we know— that eventually he plans to take over the Temple, abolishing Jewish sacrifices and setting himself up as—as a god, demanding worship!"

Jack was stunned, but even before he could open his mouth to protest, he knew. *It's true*, he thought, his head throbbing dully. *It's all true.*

"Dad? Dad—are you there?"

"Yes, Matt. Listen son: your mother and I will be on the next flight to Tel Aviv from Madrid. We'll be flying El Al, so try to meet us there, OK?"

"OK, Dad, but—"

"It's all right, son. You see, Matt, I've been reading Dan's and Randy's books and reading the Bible a lot lately, especially the Book of Daniel. All of this is shocking, but not surprising. I just thought we might have a little more time, that's all. Good-bye, son, and thanks."

After he hung up the phone, Jack immediately made another call to the reservation desk of El Al airlines. Ruth was already up, resignedly pulling out the suitcases to repack, and wondering if Matt was in any danger. Her husband and son seemed so unbearably unreachable to her now, and try as she might, she simply could not bridge the ever-widening gap.

Since Matt's miraculous return from the Syrian desert, he had been a totally changed young man. Gone were the deep depressions, the unpredictable outbursts of irrational anger; now he seemed to walk in another dimension altogether. He was unfailingly cheerful, and his little acts of kindness were now interspersed with times of deep, intense meditation as he devoted himself more and more to prayer and Bible study.

He had been on an extended leave from the IAF following the accident, so he spent much of his time in mysterious meetings that resulted in all sorts of nocturnal phone calls and sudden, unexplained absences. His new crop of friends were all exceptionally fine, clean-cut young Israelis who exhibited none of the arrogant, agnostic fatalism that seemed so pervasive in their present culture.

Indeed, Ruth should have been wildly enthusiastic, but instead she felt a growing dread surprisingly common to a great many mothers. *He doesn't need me any more*, she thought despairingly. *My darling son is a grown man with a life and destiny all his own.*

Matt's attempts to explain his newfound faith to his mother, though he was ever so gentle, fell on deaf ears; she seemed to be receding. A strange, insulating cocoon was being relentlessly spun around her heart; a spirit of rejection was weaving its deceptive web of lies around her mind, so that she became more and more resistant to the truth.

Now, as Jack and Ruth took off from the Madrid airport, Jack knew that it was now or never.

Jack's heart was pounding like a schoolboy, and as he took her hand he shot up a quick silent prayer: *Lord, help me; reach her heart Lord—I can't do it. I'm going to have to ask her once again to flee our home, give up my job and all our friends, and—do what, Lord? Live in a cave out somewhere in the wilderness for a while until You come? So many decisions, so many sudden changes; it'll be hard for her, but somehow in my heart I know I can trust You. You have always made provision for Your people.*

And at that time shall Michael stand up, the great prince which standeth for thy people, and there shall be a time of trouble, such as never was since there was a nation even to that same time, and at that time thy people shall be delivered, every one that shall be found written in the Book.

And there was war in heaven: Michael and his angels fought against the dragon…and the dragon was cast out, that old serpent called the Devil, and Satan, which deceiveth the whole world. And when the dragon saw that he was cast unto the earth, he persecuted the woman that brought forth the man child. And to the woman were given two wings of a great eagle, that she might fly into the wilderness, into her place, where she is nourished for a time, and times, and half a time, from the face of the serpent.

True to His Word and His character, God had indeed made abundant provision for His people. Hidden away in the wilderness of Edom, He had prepared several places of refuge for the Jews who would soon be undergoing the fiery persecution unleashed by their enemy.

The ancient city of Petra was one of those refuges, and it was to this particular ancient rocky fortress that the Mannheims were directed. In fact, they were among the very first families to arrive. Jack felt a strong sense of urgency that he should bring truckloads of building materials, household necessities, and electrical and electronic equipment. One of the first things he and his men did was to clear an airstrip on a level area several miles from the city and to construct a large hangar under the camouflage of a rocky overhang.

Ruth at first was a little apprehensive, but to her utter surprise, she found the interior of the ancient buildings carved from stone to be refreshingly cool—a welcome respite from the desert heat. Another surprise was in store for the intrepid settlers: they found an abundant supply of water, boxes stacked ten feet high full of canned food, and generators for electricity! No one knew how all this got there, but everyone who arrived exhibited first fear, then surprise, then jubilation.

Ruth, the quintessential homemaker, set about making her new quarters as comfortable and attractive as possible. She too had become a new person, and that transformation had come almost overnight. Actually, it had come over her like a tidal wave—as Jack had talked to her on the plane from Madrid, speaking of the plan of salvation. The eyes of her heart were opened and she saw the blackened, hopelessly lost condition of her own soul, and immediately she cried out to the Lord for forgiveness.

Jack continued speaking from his heart with a simple directness and earnestness that tugged irresistibly on the strings that bound her heart. All at once it opened, and she was free. Like a dove released from the snare of the fowler, she soared immediately to the heights. Leaning her head back against the seat, she shook with uncontrollable laughter.

Jack was alarmed, thinking perhaps he had pushed her a little too far, but she finally found her tongue and gasped, "Oh, Jack, darling, I believe. I do—I believe! Why have I been so blind? You and Matt have possessed this enormous treasure and have been trying all this time to share it with me, and yet I was so resentful and stubborn, and —oh, Jack, it's wonderful! He's real—He's really real, and…and He loves me!"

This last was said in an awe-stricken whisper, and Ruth laid her head happily on her husband's shoulder, her flushed cheeks streaked by tears of pure joy.

The Watchers who had been assigned the guardianship of the Mannheim family, flanking the plane that carried them home, were now joined by legions of angels—innumerable, powerful beings of light dispatched by their Creator to do the most delightful task in all the universe: to rejoice exceedingly, for one more had been born into the kingdom and now belonged forever to the King!

Six months later, the little band of Israeli believers had grown to more than a thousand. With more refugees straggling into Petra every few days, the leaders began to worry about water and supplies, but strangely enough— just like manna in the Sinai wilderness—there was always enough.

Out of respect for the Orthodox rabbis who had joined them, every- one had begun to observe the ancient Shabbat, the Saturday Sabbath that began at sundown each Friday. By sundown Saturday, however, the quiet times of prayer and meditation gave way to an exuberant celebration of thanksgiving and praise, for many of these people had been literally deliv- ered from the jaws of death. Young and old alike rejoiced together in the dance; musicians led the way into higher and higher levels of Spirit-anointed praise. Prophecy began to flow, and as the Word was taught with great authority, understanding grew steadily like the light of dawn, brighter and brighter.

On rare occasions, Matt and a few of his friends would fly the Cessna into Petra for a short visit. These young men always carried with them a powerful, quiet authority that everyone recognized immediately. When they spoke, people listened carefully, for they spoke the oracles of God.

On this particular Sunday morning Matt and his father arose early and, stepping quietly through the sleeping compound, climbed the rocky hillside to the summit where they sat and watched the sunrise. They waited, shivering in the early morning chill, and watched the miraculous unfolding of yet another day, the blue black darkness fleeing before the relentless rays of the glowing golden sphere. Soon they were enveloped in the shimmering light and warmth all around them.

Matt sighed deeply. "Read it again, Dad. I'd like to hear it one more time before I leave."

Jack nodded wordlessly and picked up his well-worn Bible.

This is the road map God has given us to follow through to safety during these perilous times, he thought with a sudden clarity. *Our omnipotent God made provision for us twenty-six hundred years ago through my kinsman Daniel, so that my son Matthew may know with certainty that his ways were set in a perfect order long ago. The same God who cared so tenderly for the prophet Daniel and his people cares for us now.*

"The Book of Daniel, chapter twelve," he began.

> …And at that time of the end, Michael shall arise, the great angelic prince who defends your people, Daniel. There shall be a time of distress as never before; but at that time your people shall be delivered, every one whose name shall be found written in the Book. And many of those who sleep in the dust of the earth shall awake, some to everlasting life and some to shame. Those who are wise shall shine as the heavens, and those who turn many to righteousness as the stars forever and ever. But you, O Daniel…shut the book and seal up the vision, for it belongs to the distant future…

To Contact
the Author

jenniehassett@yahoo.com